# THE
# LAST
# APARTMENT
## IN
# ISTANBUL

ALSO BY DEFNE SUMAN

*The Silence of Scheherazade*
*At the Breakfast Table*
*Summer Heat*

# THE
# LAST
# APARTMENT
## IN
# ISTANBUL

## DEFNE SUMAN

## Translated by Betsy Göksel

HEAD
of ZEUS

*An Apollo Book*

First published as *Çember Apartmanı* in Turkey in 2022 by Doğan Kitap

First published in the United Kingdom in 2025 by Head of Zeus Ltd,
part of Bloomsbury Publishing Plc

This is a work of fiction. All characters, organizations, and events
portrayed in this novel are either products of the author's
imagination or are used fictitiously.

9 7 5 3 1 2 4 6 8

A catalogue record for this book is available from the British Library.

ISBN (HB): 9781035902385
ISBN (E): 9781035902378

Cover design: Simon Michele

Typeset by Siliconchips Services Ltd UK

Printed and bound in Great Britain by
CPI Group (UK) Ltd, Croydon, CR0 4YY

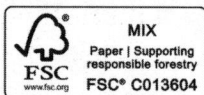

MIX
Paper | Supporting
responsible forestry
FSC
www.fsc.org
FSC® C013604

Bloomsbury Publishing Plc
50 Bedford Square, London, WC1B 3DP, UK
Bloomsbury Publishing Ireland Limited,
29 Earlsfort Terrace, Dublin 2, D02 AY28, Ireland

**HEAD OF ZEUS LTD**
5–8 Hardwick Street
London, EC1R 4RG

To find out more about our authors and books
visit www.headofzeus.com
For product safety related questions contact productsafety@bloomsbury.com

# The Ground Floor

I gave up on love the year my wife died. The same year that Ulker vanished into thin air, as a matter of fact. There were those who thought that it was because of Ulker that my wife died, and there were those who wondered whether it was because my wife had died that Ulker left. It may be that both theories are true. But many years, many long years had passed since all that. So many that time had come to a standstill for me. I had understood nothing of this new century, the first quarter of which had almost gone. Whatever life held for me had remained in the past. I'd been able to bring neither love nor spirit into the present, only grief and longing. Thus was I bemoaning my circumstances to my friend and neighbour, Berin, as we sat together in her top-floor flat with its magnificent view of Topkapi Palace, she drinking tea, me coffee.

Then I saw Leyla.

It was January 2020. I was seventy-five years old. I remember the month because the cursed virus that went on to terrorize the entire world had not yet entered our lives. We were still shaking hands with new acquaintances and hugging old ones, and we were not yet regarding with suspicion anyone breathing the same air as us. Two months later, everyone of my age was imprisoned in their homes. 'We will not see the end of this pandemic, Pericles,' Berin said. She was the same age as me and in excellent health, which she put down to her eating just the one meal a day, at twelve noon precisely. So when she said that, I didn't take her seriously. I didn't take the virus seriously either. During my many years as a pharmacist I'd dispensed medications for three or four Asian flu epidemics, and I assumed that this one would be no different.

I had been on my way out. I was going into Beyoglu, as I did every midday. Where Berin attributed her good health to her ascetic diet, for me it was walking. Despite my age, I could walk a long way without needing to rest. I had faith in my lungs and my bones. In the spring months and on winter days, when the weather was cool but sunny, I would walk from the Tarlabasi neighbourhood to Galatasaray, from there to Tunel, and then, if I was in good spirits, on down to Karakoy. I'd have soup at the fish restaurant there and then drink tea in the courtyard of the old building next door. Over the years, I'd made friends with the old master blacksmiths and joiners, with their apprentices, and also with the young men and women who worked in the modern architectural firms on the upper floors.

The day I first set eyes on Leyla was cool, bright and sunny. As the cage lift reached the ground floor, shafts of purple, yellow and blue light streamed through the stained-glass fanlight above the heavy-duty front door and cast colourful shadows across the mosaic floor. When I was a child, this play of light had enchanted me. But now The Circle was in a miserable state. No matter how frequently we had it cleaned, how often Samiha mopped the stairs with soapy water, within two days you couldn't even see the floor for all the dirt. Berin and I were the only ones left who knew that the floor was covered in Italian mosaics of dark red, blue and white. Edip would probably have known that too, back when his memory was sharp, but now he was no longer in his right mind. He lived in the first-floor apartment, cramming it with whatever he found in Istanbul's garbage bins.

Back when the basement was occupied by Fortune Nightclub, we thought they were bringing in all the dirt and grime, so we cursed Nejat and his men. Veli, who owned the coffeeshop on the corner, wouldn't allow his sister Samiha to clean our building in that time. Even at seven in the morning, you could smell raki fumes and cigarette smoke coming from the nightclub, and sometimes it rose all the way up to our apartments. It was no easy job to clean up the filth left by its customers, who vomited and urinated right outside the door and crashed out on the marble steps. The Fortune Nightclub did have its own entrance, separate from ours, on Temrin Hill Street. The club's owner, Nejat, only used the main entrance for special guests. The VIPs used to make a lot of noise when they left the club. A fight broke out beside the lift once, and blood was spilled. It seeped into the mosaics and we couldn't get it out. Veli was right to forbid his sister from cleaning our building back then.

But Fortune Nightclub shut down a long time ago, and the basement has been empty ever since. Nejat had the stairs down to the club laid with red carpet, and the bannisters and walls upholstered in thickly padded velvet, presumably so that the VIP guests wouldn't injure themselves on their way up or down and cause him any headaches. When Nejat disappeared, the velvet curtains, vomit-stained carpets and padded bannisters remained. The Circle still stands in a world of dust and dirt. Outside, there is non-stop construction work. Not a day goes by without a building on a backstreet or on the other side of the road being demolished.

As I went down in the lift, I heard Ferit, the estate agent, talking to someone from behind the half-opened door of the apartment that was for sale on the ground floor. He was once again singing its praises. Yes, he could not deny that it was in a dilapidated state, but it was a marvellous investment opportunity. He'd been repeating that same line for two months and I'd not yet seen anyone fall for it. It had once been a hairdressing salon, filled with cigarette smoke and hair clippings of various colours. Mirrors still hung on the walls. Cross-dressers used to get hair extensions there, which I learnt about from going in and out of the building. Neither the hairdresser, Barbaros, nor his customers were ever anything but polite to me. When I went past his open door, they never failed to say good morning, have a nice day.

'You know, girls, Monsieur Pericles is the building's most senior resident. Isn't that right, sir? How many years is it that you've lived here?' Barbaros would say.

When I said that I'd been born there, the women would exclaim in surprise and invite me in. I would give them a tip of my hat and continue on my way.

One day the previous November, when I exited the lift as usual at noon, I saw that Barbaros's salon was completely empty. It had been abandoned overnight. They had taken away the seats, the hair-washing armchairs and the sink. Only the mirrors remained in place. I was sorry. Barbaros's salon had been there for more than twenty years and I'd become accustomed to it. I'd even planned to accept their invitation to tea one day. But I was too late.

That same day, Ferit began bringing round potential

buyers. He replaced the fancy red lettering on the window with a huge sign announcing 'FOR SALE BY OWNER' and attached a slip of paper underneath it with a phone number underlined.

Some time later, I collared Ferit in front of his office, which was in The Circle's old coal cellar.

'Are you the owner of this apartment?'

'No, Uncle Pericles. How could I own an apartment?'

He was lying, of course. Ferit owned condominiums in a thirty-storey tower in some neighbourhood that I didn't know the name of. I had heard this from Berin's adopted daughter, Tulin. But laid-back Ferit was not overly concerned with the truth.

'I get more calls when the ad says "By the owner". They come to see it. I show them around.'

'And what if they don't give your realter commission?'

'Then we will handle it, Uncle Pericles. Just let them like it and let us agree on a price. The rest is minor detail.'

I first set eyes on Leyla in one of Hairdresser Barbaros's mirrors, the one that could be seen through the crack in the door. Ferit had been talking to her, and she was looking up at the water stain that had ruined the paintwork on the ceiling. A couple of years earlier a pipe had burst on the floor above, but Edip wouldn't let anyone inside his apartment – including repairmen – so Barbaros had to shut off the main valve in the basement. This resolved the problem, but it also turned off Edip's water supply. Edip's electricity had already been cut off by then, because he hadn't paid his bill. I don't know how he managed with his water cut off as well.

Through the crack in the door a mirror could be seen, and in the mirror was Leyla. She was wearing a long, light-blue knitted jacket and a beret of the same colour. The hair curling out from beneath the beret was red, and even in the cold fluorescent light of Barbaros's salon, it shone. For some unexplainable reason I wanted to stand there and gaze at her. However, with that sixth sense that people have when they know they're being watched, she turned towards the door and saw me. Ferit, aware that his client's attention had been distracted, also turned round. Seeing me, he opened the door wide with a flourish.

'Oh, Monsieur Pericles, won't you come in? God willing, Leyla Hanim will be your new neighbour.'

Leyla smiled politely which, I immediately understood, meant that she had absolutely no intention of buying the ground-floor flat. She wanted to get rid of the estate agent and leave. Of course, Ferit understood that as well as I did. He was trying to use me to make the building seem more respectable. It had not escaped my attention that Ferit always brought his clients to the building at midday, just as I was leaving for my walk. He was trying to show them that, though the ground floor was shabby, the residents of the upper floors were distinguished gentlemen who still wore hats when they went out and about in Beyoglu. It was an attempt to distract his clients from the reality of residents like Edip, with his boxes and bags of rubbish; from the stains left by the nightclub; from the floor so filthy that you couldn't see its mosaics; from the strands of hair that littered the linoleum.

'Monsieur Pericles lives on the third floor. He and Berin Hanim, who is on the fifth floor, have been here the longest. How many years have you lived here for, Monsieur Pericles?'

I did not reply. In fact, by the time Berin and her late husband, Mansur Bey, had moved into The Circle, I was already married and in my forties (though for someone of my advanced years, that might as well have been yesterday). But

I didn't correct Ferit. I was preoccupied with looking at Leyla, looking awkward and lovely.

Getting no reply from me, Ferit said, 'Leyla Hanim is moving to Istanbul from Bodrum.'

Leyla opened her mouth to say something, but by then Ferit had gone into the corridor, so she simply shrugged and then smiled at me, her eyes like a cat's. I followed them both.

Ferit was showing Leyla the middle room, behind the kitchen. Its floors were sticky and the wallpaper was peeling off. Ayten, who worked for Barbaros, used to use that room for hair-removal treatments. Once, when I was walking up the hill, a breeze blew the net curtain aside and I accidentally caught sight of a woman lying on a massage table. It was Zishan, one of the singers from the nightclub. Her legs were covered from top to bottom in green wax. It reminded me of how, at the beginning of summer, before they decamped to the islands, Aunt Ismene and Mama used to cook up their own hair-removal mixture in our kitchen. The whole apartment would smell of burnt sugar, like caramel. They would dip a wooden stick into the mixture and give that to me so that I wouldn't bother them, and then they'd shut themselves up in the little room. Stick in hand, I would press my eye to the keyhole and try to fathom the mysteries of that forbidden, sugar-scented world.

If Ayten hadn't come to the window that day, I would never have realized that I was absentmindedly watching them from the pavement. Reaching for the wooden shutters, Ayten shouted at me, 'Pericles, you are just too much!' I didn't even have time to apologize before she clattered the shutters closed in my face.

'You see this room, Leyla Hanim? It's the most beautiful room in the apartment. You will never tire of its view in the evening light. This room is a library in Monsieur Pericles's apartment.'

Hearing this, Leyla raised her head and looked over at me. I smiled, one booklover greeting another. She reciprocated, a dimple at the corner of her mouth.

'The previous tenant didn't take such good care of it, but that's easily rectified. A lick of paint should do it, and once the linoleum's been taken up, the wooden floor will creak just as it did on its first day. I presume you'll be renting it out for holiday lets, yes? Tourists love this district. It's close to Taksim and Sultanahmet, and they like the atmosphere of its traditional streets. The building's at least a century old. It was designed by an Italian architect – his name is carved into the front. Did you see the bas-reliefs on the side and the wrought-iron flowers on the door? European tourists love those sorts of details. Am I wrong, Monsieur Pericles? You used to rent to tourists at one point.'

'I'm looking for a flat for myself,' said Leyla. 'To live in.'

Her voice was a little rough, nasal, a contrast to her slight figure. She walked back out into the corridor and, without even sticking her head into the kitchen, where it looked like an atomic bomb had exploded, she returned to the living room.

'There are two more rooms in the back,' Ferit called out behind her. 'One is a bedroom. The other's a bit dark, but...'

Leyla was not interested in the back rooms, the pantry, the bathroom which had supposedly been renovated. She had stopped in front of the living-room window, beret in hand, and was watching a bulldozer repeatedly striking the building opposite, which was stubbornly resisting its blows.

I left them there and went out. Paying no heed to the din of the construction work, which I had long since gotten used to,

I turned right and took a couple of steps towards the church that marked the end of Kaymakcalan Street and its junction with a bigger road. Kaymakcalan Street was a sorry sight, its two- and three-storey stone buildings having either fallen into extreme disrepair or already been demolished. I turned and looked back at The Circle. Despite its faded shutters and discoloured marble steps, it stood solid and intact on the corner of Kaymakcalan Street and Temrin Hill Street. Its sides as well as its frontage were decorated with elegant circular bas-reliefs of snakes swallowing their own tails. I felt a familiar stab of pain as I remembered their plan to apply for a demolition order. Gentrification had been advancing on us from all sides. Like a fire that had raged out of control, it was devouring every one of the old buildings that stood in its way. The new city born from the ashes would in no way compare to the old city – not even close.

To distract myself from these painful thoughts, I glanced up at Barbaros's former salon. Leyla was still at the window. She was standing right behind the 'FOR SALE BY OWNER' sign. I imagined her watching the destruction of the building opposite with sadness. When she waved to me and smiled, I was momentarily confused. I raised my hand, but my fingers were indecisive. Eventually, I touched the brim of my hat in greeting. Her smile was infectious. As I passed the church, out of habit I almost imperceptibly made the sign of the cross and pressed my hand to my heart.

Walking through the fish market on my way to Beyoglu, everything looked so colourful – the red trays that shone under the lightbulbs, the silver-backed anchovies that the fishmongers were dousing with water, the heads of lettuce, the rocket leaves, lemons and turnips. The young lad who was unloading stuffed mussels smiled at me. A tortoiseshell cat slipped out from under the fish trays and rubbed herself against my trouser leg. I petted her head, her white neck. She was pregnant. When I got to Galatasaray High School, I stopped as if compelled to do so. The clouds were thinning into cotton wisps, scattering across the light-blue sky. The smell of coal came to my nose from far away. I realized that it was imperative that Leyla move into The Circle. She was the injection of life the building and its residents needed. I heard this like a command in my brain. A clear signal. With abrupt decisiveness, I turned back, pushing my way through the Beyoglu crowds, retracing my steps at speed as I raced down the streets that I'd strolled along just minutes earlier. It had been a very long time since I'd wanted anything so much.

# Apartment Building Meeting

This wasn't the first time that The Circle had come under threat. When the Istanbul Municipality began planning the construction of an eight-lane boulevard through the Tarlabasi neighbourhood in 1986, our building had been one of those earmarked for clearance. The end of the boulevard was going to encompass both Kaymakcalan Street (which was a dead end and comprised mostly dilapidated houses), and Temrin Hill Street, and would give access to neighbourhoods lower down, like Dolapdere. To achieve this, it was essential that The Circle, which was on the corner of Kaymakcalan Street and Temrin Hill Street, be razed. They offered us a pitiful amount of money for our homes, far below market value. We resisted. Berin's husband, Mansur Bey – in his capacity as building manager – sat down to negotiate with the city officials. I got Nejat involved.

Then suddenly the Istanbul Municipality changed its plans. The boulevard would no longer go through Kaymakcalan Street, so there was no need to knock down The Circle. Mansur Bey was angry. He'd reached an advantageous agreement with the authorities, an agreement that would have offered enough compensation money for each of us to buy an apartment in one of the modern districts like Atakoy or Levent. It was clear Mansur Bey would jump at the next available opportunity to have our building torn down.

And so, when a crack appeared in the tiled floor outside the bathroom in Barbaros's salon, Mansur Bey called all the property owners to a meeting. It was Ayten who had first noticed the crack. She worked at the salon and swore that the crack had appeared after the earthquake in 1999. It cut right across the corridor and extended from the bathroom door all the way to the kitchen.

The meeting was held in Fortune Nightclub. Mansur Bey and Berin attended, as did Edip, who lived on the first floor, and I. Nejat, who held the title deeds to all the other apartments, was also there, as was Barbaros, the tenant of the damaged apartment. We sat together on a plush red velvet sofa, beneath a silvery disco ball. As we sipped the tea that Galip and Zulfu, two young men in Nejat's employ, had offered us, we surreptitiously inspected the nightclub that we'd all been so curious about. Although I'd been to the club before – Nejat was my business partner and we often met in his office at the back (outside club hours, of course) – this was the first time I had sat down at a table in the main room.

A skinny boy was mopping the floor on the other side of the bar. A truck driver was unloading crates, and Galip and Zulfu hurried over, picking up the crates and carrying them to the kitchen. No food was ever cooked in Fortune Nightclub's kitchen. All that was prepared in there was thinly sliced past-their-best cucumbers and dried-up carrots, and decanted nuts which had lost their flavour in the humidity as they passed from one plate to another. I knew this because, whenever

I sat down with Nejat, I was presented with the same pitiful offerings.

Mansur Bey started the meeting. He believed, he said, that it was necessary to demolish The Circle immediately. We were not surprised to hear this. Apparently an earthquake expert he knew had determined that the crack in Barbaros's salon was a screw-type fracture, whatever that meant, and that the building's foundations had been damaged in the quake. For all of our safety, we should have a modern building constructed as soon as possible, with two apartments on each floor. The day would come, Mansur Bey declared, when our neighbourhood – indeed the whole of the Tarlabasi district – would be cleansed of its mongrels. Our wretched nest would regain its former glory. As he said this, he waved his cigarette in Nejat's direction. Without uttering a word, Nejat swivelled his wheelchair around and turned his back on the table. Galip and Zulfu rushed to his side and the two of them wheeled Nejat behind the bar.

Ignoring Nejat, Mansur Bey continued. Once Tarlabasi had been liberated from the swamp, we would be able to rent out our apartments to foreigners working at the consulates, he said, gesturing in my direction with the tip of his lighted cigarette. He clearly assumed that I worked for a consulate. Reinforced from top to bottom against an earthquake, the new Circle, with its views that extended not only to Maiden's Tower but also to the Golden Horn, would earn us a fortune, with two apartments apiece. Since the earthquake, everyone was on the hunt for buildings with strong foundations. We should capitalize on this great opportunity.

I looked at Berin. Rather than slouch on the red sofa with us, she was sitting ramrod straight in a chair across from us. She was a slender, refined woman. Her black hair was gathered in a bun on top of her head, her white skin was very slightly wrinkled and her cheeks were fresh. When her eyes met mine, a mischievous smile passed briefly across her face. The only apartment with a view that extended from Maiden's Tower to the Golden Horn was theirs. The rest of us could glimpse only a bit of blue water between buildings and rooftops. Berin had noted this egocentric error of her husband's, but said nothing. Years later, when the two of us were friends, Berin told me that when he talked about the 'foreigners working at the consulates', Mansur Bey had been referring to spies.

It was my turn to speak. I talked about how The Circle had been built by a famous Italian architect in 1922, how it was an important feature of Istanbul's urban landscape, widely praised for its beauty. Its foundations were set in stone, I said, and extremely sound. My grandfather had watched it being built and had so much confidence in it that he'd bought one of its apartments for his daughter, who'd been born that year. Mansur Bey muttered something – I think he said 'Get on with it' – but I pretended not to have heard him. I didn't believe a word of his 'earthquake expert' story. I suggested that we ask another engineer to look at the building and present us with a plan and a budget to strengthen it against future quakes.

Edip was moved by my speech. He too had lived in The Circle since he was a child. He nodded enthusiastically. Mansur Bey looked at both of us with disdain. 'It's not even clear who owns your apartment, Edip,' he said. Edip flushed. After all, he was a fifty-five-year-old man. He opened his mouth, then closed it.

As children, back when we used to slide down the hill with cardboard under our bottoms, Edip had stuttered.

I didn't go to the same school as him, but Ali, the baker's son, did, and he used to mimic the way Edip talked to the whole neighbourhood. I saw the adult Edip's face flush in the same way it used to back then, as if resenting his tongue for preventing him from speaking.

'To tell the truth, I'm not certain that the crack appeared after the earthquake,' Barbaros said suddenly. 'It may have happened in the spring, while we were retiling the corridor.'

'Then why did you create such a fuss and make us all so anxious?' It was Berin who asked this. We all turned to look at her, which prompted her to sit up even straighter. She believed that Barbaros didn't like her because she never had her hair done at his salon. In the years that followed, I did notice that whenever Berin and I went out together, to a film festival or an exhibition opening, Barbaros never once greeted Berin. On this occasion too, Barbaros, who was sitting next to me, ignored her question.

'Let's put it to a vote,' I said. 'Nejat Bey should also take part.'

Nejat was over by the double doors leading into the kitchen, inspecting the bottles coming out of the crate. When he saw me looking at him, he gestured to the boys. Galip and Zulfu grabbed hold of the wheelchair, one on each side, and brought Nejat to our table. The sleeves of his black shirt were rolled up, and in the light of the disco ball his gold Rolex glittered against the black hair on his wrist. Nejat was not afraid of clichés. Using a wheelchair had given him extra kudos, for he told everybody, even the boys who worked for him, that he'd been shot in a duel while defending someone's honour. He made sure that this story was spread far and wide. Only I knew the truth about why he was confined to a wheelchair.

'Let whoever holds the title deed to the first-floor apartment vote,' said Mansur Bey. 'We all know it doesn't belong to Edip.'

'Monsieur Panayiotis left that apartment to Edip's father, Tahsin,' I said.

Nejat looked at me pityingly, as if I didn't know that his safe was stuffed full with dozens of title deeds left from the Greeks. It had been part of an unofficial state policy since the beginning of the republic. By force or by law, local Greeks were expelled from Istanbul, and their properties remained abandoned for many years – until people like Nejat obtained the deeds through their shady connections and complicity with state officials. 'From now on,' he said, 'the apartment Edip lives in will be in Galip's name. I'm transferrin' the title deed to him.'

A tiny muscle twitched on Galip's otherwise poker face. This appeared to be news to him. Nejat was about to take off for Canada, to try and cure his illness by volunteering in a medical experiment, and it seemed he was in the process of distributing his possessions to his boys.

'The ground floor,' Nejat continued, 'is also Galip's now. He will collect the rent from Barbaros.'

I looked at Nejat's other boy, Zulfu, who was holding the wheelchair's other handle. We all knew Zulfu was a gambler. Nejat knew that too. But if he didn't give them equal shares, those two idiot heavies would have it out with each other. They might even use weapons.

'The fourth floor will be Zulfu's.'

My eyes were on Galip. His face showed no emotion. It wasn't a bad deal for him.

'I am keepin' my rights of usufruct. Durin' my lifetime, the apartments can't get sold without my permission.'

Just then, a young man with a thin moustache turned up. Zulfu's friend, apparently. He pretended to be surprised to see us. Nejat was not appeased by his flattering smirk, nor by his attempt to kiss Nejat's hand in the middle of the meeting.

'Off you go now, son. Can't you see I'm in a meeting?'

Zulfu cleared his throat. 'Sir, Ferit is my friend from middle school. You remember there was the question of his renting the coal cellar... We were going to go into the property business. While everyone is here, shall we—'

Nejat threw Zulfu a filthy look, but Mansur Bey took his chance.

'What was your name, son? Ferit, right? Searching in the sky, we found it on the ground, as they say. Since you are in the property business, you can help us. If we pull down this building and construct a chic, modern apartment block in its place, approximately how much would each square metre sell for?'

I looked at Ferit's smoothly shaved face. He was probably only about twenty-five back then, give or take, but he immediately understood the situation and what was required of him. He pretended to be calculating a price and threw out the first number that came into his head. It didn't work. None of us, except for Edip and maybe Zulfu, trusted Ferit. We had the vote.

'Technically, Nejat Bey cannot vote,' said Berin. Galip had not yet raised his hand. I did not know then that Berin had studied law at university. I was surprised.

'Nejat Bey may have cobbled together some sort of title deed for this basement, but both this room and the old coal cellar, which the young man is intending to rent as his office, are areas of common usage.'

Mansur Bey nodded smugly. All eyes turned towards Galip, who had not yet raised his hand. He was standing behind Nejat, across from us. He was about the same age as Ferit, short, dark-skinned, and wearing a gold necklace; a younger version of Nejat. He even smelled the same, as they used the same brand of oil to slick back their hair.

Galip's eyes were darting between me and Mansur Bey, and Nejat was getting impatient. He turned and looked at his employee, who was gripping the wheelchair with sweaty hands.

'Come on, son, we don't have all day. The musicians need to go over their set.'

I felt like laughing at that. Did Fortune Nightclub's musicians really rehearse?

'I vote against a new building,' Galip said.

Mansur Bey stared at him with hatred. Then his eyes slid to me. He looked at me as if I had personally wrested from his hands the vast amount of money he'd been due to make. I'd been subjected to looks of that sort my whole life. If I had known then that in a few years Galip and I would be heaving Mansur Bey's naked body out of his bathtub, I would have paid no heed to his derisive look, his belittling of my Rum identity, my Greekness. But one often forgets that life is like being on a train with a handful of passengers, speeding towards death. One takes small struggles too seriously, giving too much importance to victories and losses.

As I left Fortune Nightclub, I remembered what Berin had said to Nejat. Technically, he was not the owner of the basement floor. So what about his other apartments; was Nejat really the owner of the title deeds which he had so wilfully distributed to his shady underworld princes? Had he bought those apartments with the sweat of his brow? Was it he who paid the taxes? For years, Nejat had stockpiled property. But that property had previously belonged to my relatives, classmates and neighbours, those who had been thrown out of their homes on one fateful night. And I called this man my partner? In that moment I despised myself. I couldn't even find pleasure in the fact that The Circle had been saved.

A celebration of our reprieve would have been premature, as it turned out. Not twenty years later, vultures were now once again circling above the beautiful building in which I'd been born and raised. This time, though, it was the construction mafia who were demolishing almost all of Istanbul in the name of gentrification.

# The Apartment on
# the Second Floor

It was only once I'd got back to Kaymakcalan Street from Galatasaray that I stopped to wonder what I would do if Ferit wasn't in his office. I didn't have his phone number. Although I had no reason for thinking like this, it was eating me up inside that Ferit might sell Leyla a different apartment in another building. When I turned the corner into Temrin Hill Street and saw Ferit smoking a cigarette in front of his office, I relaxed. That meant he hadn't shown Leyla a different apartment. This prompted a new wave of anxiety. Maybe she had given up on our neighbourhood entirely? I feared for my blood pressure: I was not used to this much excitement.

I was out of breath when I got to his office, which spurred Ferit into action. He took me inside, gave me some water, ordered tea, placed a cushion behind my back. He was clearly concerned.

'Uncle Pericles, you aren't having a heart attack, are you?' he twice asked.

'No, don't worry, Ferit,' I said. 'This happens to me every now and then. My heart beats too fast.'

'That means you have tachycardia. You need to be careful!'

I nodded. What could I say? Should I tell him that I wanted to ensure that the lady he'd just shown around came to live in The Circle? That it seemed I had fallen for her, which was why I was acting so hastily? Ferit was a man of the world; he would have understood straight away.

'Ferit,' I said, as if the idea had just occurred to me while I was sitting there, 'you know my second-floor apartment?'

'I am listening, Monsieur Pericles.'

'I want to sell it.'

Ferit, standing in the doorway, was suddenly serious. He threw his cigarette onto the pavement, came inside, circled his desk and sat down across from me. There was surprise written all over his face, but he did not miss a beat.

'We will sell it, Monsieur Pericles. No problem. The second floor will go in a flash. You have looked after it well and I doubt the tourists have caused any damage. The floor is still in its original condition, am I right? The ornamental plasterwork on the ceiling is intact. I understand. You've had enough of the short-term rental business. But... what will your son say?'

What a memory Ferit had! He was, of course, referring to ten, maybe twelve years earlier, when I had asked him to look over the place and value it. There could not have been a single estate agent, seller or buyer in the area that he didn't bring to see it. Finally, in order to get rid of him, I had been forced to tell a lie: 'This is my son's apartment. He will live there when he returns from overseas.' And so I extracted myself from the situation.

This time, I said, 'My son won't be coming back, Ferit. He's setting up a business overseas, so I want to be of some financial assistance to him.'

How easily the lies came. I frowned to hide the foolish grin that was spreading across my face.

'Let's contact the lady you were just showing around Barbaros's old hair salon.'

'Oh,' said Ferit. 'Her budget won't stretch that far. She couldn't afford even a quarter of the price of your apartment. Three bedrooms, one living room, a dining room, pantry, kitchen… You've refurbished the bathroom. High ceilings. Original features. We'll get dollars or euros for your apartment, Monsieur Pericles. What should we do about the furniture?'

His eyes were shining, but I couldn't keep on with the charade. I was in the latter stages of my life, and couldn't afford to jeopardize my plan by worrying about what someone else might think of me.

'Ferit, listen. Either I sell that apartment to Leyla Hanim or I don't sell it at all. She can have the furniture as well, if she'd like it. If not, she can sell it. I'll pay your commission in euros, don't you worry about that.' With that, I set down my empty tea glass on its metal saucer, put on my hat and stood up.

Before I had even finished speaking, Ferit was already on with the business, his phone pressed to his ear. I couldn't bear to wait there. I walked up the three steps to the street, turned the corner, leant against the wall and caught my breath. The digger across the street was on manoeuvres, beeping as it reversed. Pushing open the building's heavy front door, I went in.

Vera was not expecting me back so early. She was startled. She'd carried the ironing board into the living room and was watching a soap opera on television. When I walked in, she switched the channel to the news. It was being reported that a new SARS virus had been identified in China.

'I do beg your pardon, Monsieur Pericles. I thought you'd be out walking for longer. I'll tidy everything up straight away. Your evening meal is prepared. I baked a chicken. With potatoes. It's in the oven.'

She picked up my white shirt, shook it out and placed it on a wooden hanger, doing up the top button, just as I'd taught her.

'Thank you, Vera. It's fine. You may carry on with your work. I'm going down to the second-floor apartment.'

My faithful helper's blue eyes sparkled. 'Will guests be coming? If so, I must clean it up. It's been empty for a long time now, as you know.'

I used to rent the second-floor apartment out to tourists. It was Berin's idea, and she dealt with the bookings and communicated with the guests. Berin had attended the American Girls' School in Uskudar, and she liked to read novels in English, so it made sense for her to handle the correspondence. Tulin let the tourists in, showing them the bathroom, the kitchen, the flagon of drinking water, and she gave them a card with the address of the apartment, the wi-fi password and Berin's mobile number on it. It was Vera's job to clean the apartment and change the sheets and towels after the guests had left. We had continued this arrangement for ten years and, for better or worse, all made money out of it. Ferit was right. Tourists loved our poor neighbourhood, loved to marvel at the washing lines full of colourful clothes that were strung between apartment buildings.

Recently, though, I'd become reluctant to bring tourists to the neighbourhood. The construction mafia signposted young lads high on paint thinner to our entrance. Since the rumours of imminent gentrification had begun circulating, the prostitution and drug-dealing had moved right outside our building – potentially the work of the contractors, who wanted to get us out. At the beginning of the year a white van had started parking up nearby, completely blocking the entrance. Two dodgy-looking young men sat inside it, blasting Arabic music on the sound system, morning and night, loud enough that the whole neighbourhood heard it.

All of this, combined with the mountain of permits we had to beg the municipality for, made us decide to give up on the short-term rental business. Of all of us, Vera missed this arrangement the most. She used to get generous tips from the tourists.

I had to let her down now. 'No, Vera, there are no new guests on the horizon. I'm going down there to see to something else.'

Knowing how private I was, Vera asked no further questions. She had been working for me for twenty years and we knew each other well, warts and all.

Taking the key from the nail beside my front door, I went downstairs. The door creaked open. The apartment hadn't been aired in a long time. I drew back the curtains and opened the window, then walked around the apartment, fluffing up cushions and giving the etagere shelves a quick dust; I wanted Leyla to be impressed.

Returning to the living room, I surveyed it with a buyer's eye. I had to agree with Ferit. It was a beautiful apartment. High ceilings. Some of the furniture had been left by Aunt Ismene, the apartment's first owner. Aunt Ismene was my father's first cousin and my mother's closest friend. During my childhood and high-school years, we lived above her. Aunt Ismene's copper pot and sieve were still there in the kitchen; her dresser was still in the dining room.

When my wife died and Mama came over from Athens, she stayed there. She bought the dining table, the chairs and the fridge. When we started renting the apartment to tourists, Berin and I renovated the whole place. We had the walls painted, the floors polished, the kitchen cupboards fixed, the window frames repaired and painted. Both the sink and the bathtub leaked badly, so Tulin searched the web and found modern replacements. To my eye they seemed like bad imitations, but they functioned properly and many of our online reviews praised the lion-footed bathtub and the brass taps.

I looked down from the window on the Temrin Hill Street side. Where was Ferit? My hand reached for the phone in my back pocket. I restrained myself. I shouldn't act so keen. But I could hardly contain myself. It was as if Leyla's buying this apartment, living there in my downstairs flat, being near me in this last quarter of my life, was a matter of life and death. Of course, it was ridiculous that I should be thinking that way about a woman I didn't know. But, in fact, love is exactly that. A person always falls in love with a stranger.

Now that the building on the corner opposite the second-floor apartment had been knocked down, the view had opened up. In between the rooftops, satellite dishes and chimneys spouting smoke, a sliver of sea could be glimpsed. For a few seconds, the ferry shuttling between Uskudar and Eyup would come into view in this aperture. This patch of blue filled us Istanbulites with longing, having once been able to see the sea from every window.

While I was gazing down at Ferit's office, I saw the white van drive in again, blocking off access to Kaymakcalan Street. This was upsetting. If Leyla saw that, she would decide not to live here. I hoped they wouldn't turn their music up too loud. I closed the window and removed the white dustsheet from the armchair. I sat down. It was a large armchair, with floral motifs carved into its wooden arms. When Aunt Ismene had been thrown out of this apartment with no warning, she wasn't allowed to take it with her. 'It wouldn't fit anyway, my son,' she had said. 'The apartment I've rented in Samatya is very small. Let the chair remain here. It is not needed. Let it be theirs.'

Aunt Ismene's husband, Uncle Stelio, had been kicked out of the country with whatever he could fit into one twenty-kilo suitcase. She was not going to worry about an armchair.

My parents had also been forcibly expelled from Turkey, along with Uncle Stelio. I had seen them off from Sirkeci Train Station, both of them carrying a single suitcase in their hands, a couple of kurus in their pockets. Then the three of us – Aunt Ismene, her daughter Elena, and I – returned to The Circle, carrying with us the shame of those who stayed behind.

The morning's excitement had tired me out. I leant my head against the back of Aunt Ismene's abandoned armchair and closed my eyes. Ferit would call me when he found Leyla. As I listened to the perpetual roar of the city, the car horns honking on Tarlabasi Boulevard, the thuds of the bulldozers, I ran my fingers over the floral carvings on the chair. When I was a child, they had always made me think of the chocolates at Baylan, the patisserie. The chocolates were shaped like flowers and came in purple, blue and green velvet boxes; half of them were dark chocolate, half were milk. Whenever Mama and I went down to Aunt Ismene's, it was all I could do to stop myself from licking the chair arm.

Mama and Aunt Ismene were as thick as thieves when I was young. Uncle Stelio had a toyshop in the inner courtyard of Hazzopulo Arcade, in the corner. I could never get enough of his shop window. He was a bad-tempered man. He would scold children for touching the toys even when they were with their mothers. Aunt Ismene and Mama would run up and down between their two apartments from morning till night – until they drifted apart, that is. They exchanged letters but never regained the close relationship of their youth. My mother had followed my exiled father to Athens, but Aunt Ismene didn't follow, and that broke Mama's heart. Perhaps deep down she was jealous of her dearest friend.

Aunt Ismene was passionately attached to Istanbul. She could give up her husband, her friends, even her daughter when she reached university age, but she could not tear herself away from the city she loved. My mother, on the other hand, had never in her life been passionately attached to anything, except to her husband of course. Maybe she resented my aunt.

Papa was a very handsome man. He had his suits made with fabric bought from Paris. He was tall and whatever he wore looked good on him. His light auburn hair was combed back with lemon pomade, his moustache artfully twirled. Women went crazy over the soulful expression in his dark-blue eyes. He and I would leave the apartment together in the mornings, he to go to his pharmacy, me to go to school. As we walked from Tarlabasi to Beyoglu, women would steal sideways glances at Papa. They seemed to me to be competing with each other for a smile from him. He was faithful to Mama, whom he had fallen in love with as a very young man, and he didn't even notice the flirtatious neighbourhood women who greeted him, who stopped us to stroke my chin.

But Mama was insanely jealous of Papa. When a fit of jealousy came over her, she would drop whatever she was doing, hurl herself out onto the street and run to the pharmacy where he worked. Aunt Ismene would hurry along in her wake. These frenzies mostly happened on the days when Despina, the daughter of the draper Yorgo who lived on the fifth floor, came to our apartment for a dress fitting. Despina was young, fifteen or sixteen years old. She was very skilled, an expert at making up French fashions from the fabric her father sold in his shop. While she was tacking up the hem of Mama's skirt or making pleats on the shoulders, she would gossip about what she had seen and heard in the other homes she went to in Beyoglu, Sisli, Harbiye. If something Despina said upset Mama, she would seem suddenly possessed by an evil spirit. Standing there in front of the big mirror, she would abruptly push Despina aside and tear off the dress she was trying on.

In the years before I went to elementary school, I was in love with Despina. During the fittings, I would go into Mama and Papa's dimly lit bedroom, lie down on the satin coverlet and watch Despina's reflection in the mirror. Her long, black, wavy hair reached down to her waist and her big black eyes sparkled. She used to wear short-sleeved white shirts over long skirts that spread out like a carousel when she sat down. Her long, thin fingers were so assured as they held the scissors and cut the fabric. With a mouthful of pins, Despina would smile at me in the mirror. This filled me with such uncontainable happiness that I would hop up and down on the big bed, knowing full well that Mama would hit the roof.

When the fits of jealousy came over Mama, her eyes would bulge, her cheeks would hollow and her cheekbones would become more prominent. Hearing the tap of Mama's high-heeled shoes echoing on the marble stairs from her own apartment, Aunt Ismene would immediately prepare herself and catch up with Mama and me at The Circle's front door.

Because there was no one to leave me with, Mama would take me with her on her raids to the pharmacy. I wanted to stay home with Despina. But the minute that Despina noticed the change in Mama's breathing, she would quickly gather up the scattered lengths of cloth, the bits of lace, the buttons. Then she would tie up her bag and be gone, before Mama had even got her shoes on. Elena was a baby at that time, so Aunt Ismene would have to push her pram up the hills between Kaymakcalan Street and Beyoglu. Leaving the apartment in such a hurry, I was always afraid I would trip over my hastily tied shoelaces. Halfway there, Mama would remember that she was hatless.

Papa's pharmacy was on the corner where Asmali Mescit Street entered Beyoglu, a fifteen-minute walk from The Circle. All the way there, Aunt Ismene would be calling out to Mama, trying to calm her down.

'Alexandra *mou*, my darling, slow down. The man has done nothing wrong. You are imagining things. For the love of God, do not make me run.'

Aunt Ismene was not an athletic woman like Mama. The hills used to leave her breathless, poor thing.

Although Mama would call back to her, '*Endaksi*, Ismene. Okay, I am calm. I am not going to cause a scene,' when she got to the pharmacy, she would pull open the door with such force that the glass would rattle in its wooden frame. If she found not Papa but his diminutive assistant, Aristidis, behind the counter lined with brown pill bottles, syrups and perfume from Europe, she would dive straight into the back of the shop, separated off by a screen, paying no heed to the apprentice's objections.

In the dim coolness, with the smell of cologne rising from the stone floor, I would close my eyes. Most often Mama would find Papa at the tiled counter next to the sink, consulting a book in French while mixing up some paste, or injecting the flaccid arm of a toothless old woman. Aunt Ismene would hurry behind the screen, place her hand on Mama's thin shoulder and without saying a word, propel her outside. I would take over pushing Elena's pram and we would walk along the avenue filled with fashionably dressed women and men. It was always Aunt Ismene who bought me a profiterole at a patisserie so that I would forget what had happened.

Mama's frenzy would continue even as we made our way back to The Circle from the pastry shop. But in the evening, when Papa came home, the subject would not be raised. After one of her fits of jealousy, Mama would shut herself up in the kitchen and prepare Papa's favourite cabbage dolma, with lemon sauce on the side.

The doorbell rang. I sprang out of my chair. It was Ferit. Without even having seen inside it, Leyla had agreed to buy my apartment. She wanted the furniture as well. My heart began to beat as if it were jumping out of my body. I compromised by leaning my back lightly against the wall.

Ferit was shaking his head in the doorway. 'What have you done, Uncle Pericles? You have thrown away your beautiful apartment.'

This time I couldn't hide from Ferit the foolish grin that was spreading across my face. He was preoccupied, so I don't know whether he noticed.

# Teatime

On the day of the sale, Leyla and I met at the Beyoglu municipal offices. The weather had become rather cold and she was wearing her blue beret and a long coat the colour of camel hair. Her face was pale, and she had slight shadows under her eyes. She was in a hurry. She signed the documents at speed and gave me part of the fee we'd agreed on in cash; the rest she paid by bank transfer over the phone, right there in the land-registry department. I had planned to invite her to a small celebratory luncheon in the Istanbul Restaurant, a clean, calm place on a backstreet near Tunel Square, where the waiters were respectful. I often ate my lunch there, for it reminded me of days gone by. But she raced off without even shaking my hand. I was very upset.

Ferit, on the other hand, was in high spirits. I'd paid him a higher commission than he'd anticipated and so it was he who wanted to take me to lunch. He knew of a restaurant that served Circassian food. I got out of it by saying I needed to go home and take my medicine, which was a lie. When it began to rain, I turned up the collar of my coat. Even at my age, I still never thought to take an umbrella with me.

From Galatasaray I walked down to Tarlabasi Boulevard. As I strode through the underpass that stank of vomit, my depression began to lift. So what if I hadn't been able to take her to lunch today? Leyla was my neighbour now. Our paths would cross for sure, and we would certainly eat together one day.

Earlier that morning, on our way to the municipal offices, Ferit had told me that Leyla had looked after her sick father for a long time. When he died, all his property went to Leyla. She sold the house and all its furniture and came to Istanbul. An acquaintance of Ferit's in Bodrum arranged the sale. When Leyla said she wanted to live in a building that still carried traces of old Istanbul, the estate agent in Bodrum immediately sent her to Ferit. As far as Ferit knew, the girl had nowhere to stay in Istanbul, so it suited her very well that my house had its own furniture. With the title deed in her hand, she could settle in right away and begin her new life.

When I got home, I sat in the orange bergère armchair in front of the window overlooking Temrin Hill Street and watched for her arrival. From time to time I would get up to check the Kaymakcalan Street side from the French balcony. Kaymakcalan Street is a dead end, but there's a corkscrew hill right across from Veli's coffeehouse that leads to Tarlabasi Boulevard. It was raining more steadily by then, and the sky had darkened. A couple of windows in the apartment across the way had been flung open and the laundry that had been suffocating the street was being taken in.

Vera brought my coffee and placed it on the side table. She was going to the market. She said something about chicken. *Chicken again?* I withdrew two hundred-lira bills from my wallet and handed them to her. 'Buy fresh anchovies and make anchovy rice with salad and turnips on the side. And pickles.'

Treading down the backs of her shoes, she headed off. When Vera went to the Beyoglu fish market, she was always gone for at least an hour. The cold wouldn't bother her; she was a tough woman. That was good. I also had work to do.

A pedlar of used goods was pushing his cart along the street, paying no heed to the rain. Edip opened his window and shouted down something I didn't catch. I could only see the top of his head, the bald scalp obvious beneath the dyed hair of his comb-over. Leyla... Soon she would appear at the top of Kaymakcalan Street with a suitcase in her hand, wearing her camel-hair coat and blue beret. When she got to the front of the building site, she would raise her head to look at the corner of her new home, The Circle, and she would see me there. I took the empty coffee cup to the kitchen, left it on the counter and returned to my place in front of the window, to my orange bergère. I dozed off.

Contrary to expectations, I did not see Leyla for weeks. Several times a day, I knocked on the door of the second-floor apartment. There was no answer. I had not thought to get her phone number the day we met at the Beyoglu municipal offices and I was too embarrassed to ask Ferit for it. I had not appreciated the smirk on his face when I went to his office to sound him out.

Other men had suddenly become my rivals. I knew that feeling from my youth; it must have been passed down from my mother. When I first met Markela, I drove myself crazy thinking she seemed to be as close to the doctors at the hospital as she was to me. At the end of the day, I was a pharmacist and they were doctors. But Markela was a patient and not the type of woman to have the sorts of sexual encounters I was imagining. In the end, though, Markela did catch me unawares. As a jealous husband, I'd searched in the wrong places for evidence of cheating – Dr Lefteris, the men she met on Imbros Island, her childhood friends from Buyukada... It seemed I should have looked closer to home, right under my nose. That's the mistake jealous men make. They're so suspicious of so many things that they lose their perspective.

The situation with Ulker had been more complicated. For one thing she was not my wife. Secondly, I was a married man. She didn't want to be tied to me. I would wake up at midnight, run out onto the streets and reach her place in Tunel Square in no time flat, just so I could catch her in bed with another man. She even gave me her keys to try and cure me of my jealousy, but still I did not trust her. She had left me once when we were young, so I always felt she could do it again. In the end, that is what she did.

During the loveless years that had followed, I forgot that side of myself, but in essence that was still the kind of man I was. I hadn't changed into a mature, self-confident, sympathetic person, it was only that my feelings had been numbed. But they were still there, where I had left them – jealousy right alongside love, desire alongside fear. Leyla had revived them. She had released that poison called jealousy into my bloodstream once more. And for some reason she hadn't moved into the apartment.

There was one possible explanation that I didn't even want to contemplate: Leyla was staying with a lover. Why not? She was beautiful. She had looked after her father for years, frittering away her life at his side. Now that she had at last gained her freedom, might she have fallen in love? I wondered where her mother was. And there was worse.

Never mind what she'd said in her rough, deep voice – 'I'm looking for a flat for myself' – from time to time she might stay at her lover's house, or even bring the scoundrel here. I could not endure that! No, that would be intolerable.

Berin laughed at the state I was in, then said, 'Tulin, bring Pericles his coffee, then take a look at my emails on the computer and reply to them as necessary,' sending her adopted daughter away to the middle room. She did this very rarely. Years ago, when Tulin was a little girl, Berin had brought her from her village to Istanbul to do her housework. She was like her actual daughter. When I stopped by in the late afternoon for tea, she would sit with us and give us news from the outside world. Tulin must have been at least forty, but had never married, instead staying with Berin. For this reason, perhaps, she still seemed like a child to me. She was an excellent sleuth and knew everything that what went on in the neighbourhood. Yet she was still innocent enough to take Berin's jokes seriously, even after so many years of living with her as her daughter.

When the two of us were alone in the living room, I opened up to Berin. I did not mince my words. 'I wanted Leyla to have the apartment. She fascinated me from the moment I saw her, Berin,' I said. 'So I sold it to her for a very low price. But now she hasn't even moved in.'

Neither then nor since did Berin ask what kind of fascination this was. Nor was she concerned at my having sold the second-floor apartment, our goose that laid the golden eggs, without consulting her. My neighbour was cool-headed, and I was expecting her to calm me down by proposing various logical explanations. However, she clearly felt I was not in need of consolation, for she burst into laughter, prompting her cat Shadow to emerge from behind the gilded mirror beside the piano and rub herself against Berin's silk-stockinged ankles. 'What are you even hoping for from this Leyla girl? Careful, or we'll accuse you of being a Humbert Humbert, Monsieur Pericles!'

I was offended. My situation was a source of amusement for my neighbour. She bent down and took Shadow onto her lap, scratched her under her chin.

'Leyla is almost thirty years old,' I objected, as if this would save me. 'She is not an adolescent.'

When we were completing our business at the land-registry office, I had looked at Leyla's ID card several times. I say 'several times' because it was the first time I had met an adult with the birthdate of 1990. Also, I'd assumed Leyla was older than that; if not forty, then perhaps in her late thirties. Maybe the long years spent nursing a patient had weighed heavily upon her. It was as if she were a child who'd spent a lot of time with old people rather than her own age group.

Berin and I had similar tastes in literature. This was reason enough for us to be friends. Both of us believed that the essence of friendship lay in liking either the same novels, the same music. This was the quickest way to get to know someone's inner world. When I heard that Berin was also a Nabokov fan, I knew that we would become close friends.

Berin and Mansur Bey bought the fifth-floor apartment in the early 1980s when the neighbourhood had fallen out of favour. They had done extensive renovations. Speaking of those days, Berin would say, 'Mansur bought this place for nothing. When I saw the owner, poor lady, counting her two kurush, I was ashamed, but he didn't even blush. Yes, the apartment was falling apart and we went on to spend a lot of money on it, but we had a home in this beautiful building.

Just look at the view! Mansur believed that property values in this neighbourhood would increase – as you know. He was a very forward-thinking man. Unfortunately, he left us before he could see it.'

After Mansur Bey's sudden death, Berin and I became closer. We went to the Istanbul Film Festival, to exhibitions and to church concerts together. At the Beyoglu cafés which we frequented, people assumed we were husband and wife. We did not correct them. We could have had a romantic relationship, but we did not. Berin had made it perfectly clear after the death of her husband that she did not want the stress of having another man in her life. As for me, after losing Markela and Ulker, the two most important women in my world, I preferred short-term relationships. Both Berin and I knew that, at our age, continuing our friendship would be more beneficial in the long run. In the evenings I would have tea or coffee at her apartment and we would discuss films, books and music.

'Let's say she falls for you. It's possible – why not? Some women like mature men. And you are in great shape, God be praised. Your hair may be white, but it's still all there. Your posture is good. To tell the truth, you are a handsome man. You won't divulge your real age, so as not to frighten her away.'

She was right. At every stage of my life I had paid attention to my appearance, and this had ensured that I remained popular with women. Women liked my face and my eyes, but also my well-ironed shirts, my trousers cut from high-quality cloth, my polished shoes. I danced well. I had an ear for music and a talent for rhythm. I was never shy when dancing. At high school and in my student days, I used to throw girls in the air and catch them. At weddings, women of all ages would look into my eyes in the hope that I would ask them for a waltz. Berin knew all that. From time to time I would dance with her.

'But you know… What can you really offer her?'

I did not answer Berin. In truth I didn't really know myself. All I knew was that when I saw Leyla, I had felt excited about life for the first time in a very long time. There wasn't much left for me at this stage. It was nice to feel something.

Berin must have sensed my melancholy, for she changed the subject. She said, just as I had wanted her to, that Leyla would move in soon, that a woman who had gone to all the effort of buying a place would be in a hurry to settle into her new home. I should not worry my sweet soul. She would have continued, but stopped when Tulin came into the living room.

'One person in France has died of this coronavirus. I just saw it online. The number of cases in Europe is rising.'

She stood directly in front of us and looked us full in the face. When neither of us said anything, she dropped her stout body into the velvet armchair next to me like a sack. She reached out to the coffee table and stuffed one of the salty crackers Berin had put out for me into her mouth. She spoke with her mouth full.

'I'm scared, I tell you.'

I turned towards Berin. I cannot bear it when people speak with their mouths full.

'Do not be frightened, Tulin,' I said. 'If you remember, back in 2004 a SARS virus from Asia spread around the world. It infected several people with weak immune systems. Those same people might well have died even if they'd just caught a particular strain of flu. This is the same kind of virus. You are, thanks be to God, a strong woman. Nothing will happen to you.'

'I hope it will be as you say, Monsieur Pericles.'

'I am reminded of the film *Twelve Monkeys*,' Berin said. 'Do you remember it? With Bruce Willis and Brad Pitt. In the film a virus that has the potential to finish off the human race is transmitted through airports. Could this virus spread in that way?'

Tulin had not seen the film. For a while we discussed *Twelve Monkeys* and other films and novels about viruses. I thought I had humiliated myself by telling Berin about Leyla, but later, as I watched night descend over the neighbourhood from my own apartment, accompanied by a glass of Metaxa and with the construction noise finally silenced, I felt good about having a friend who knew.

# New Year's Eve

Thirty-five years ago, I was in love with Ulker. Now it feels like the stars had completed their circuit and were back in their same positions in the sky, and I was once again ready for love. Whether Leyla reciprocated or not was unimportant – the scales of love are never equally balanced anyway. What interested me was what was happening inside me, my newly awakened feelings. Even if Leyla didn't give me so much as a second glance, knowing that she was in the downstairs flat would be enough to keep me vital. Just her moving in would be sufficient.

Ulker and I crossed paths again for the first time in many years at a New Year's Eve party celebrating the arrival of 1986. It was hosted by Kemal, an old university friend. It had been twenty-two years since Ulker had left me and gone to Germany. My wife Markela was not with me that night; she was in the care of Aunt Ismene. Markela no longer set foot outside our apartment – she had moved into the dimly lit back room of our flat. She spent all her days and nights in there. The room had a single window, which looked out onto the gloomy backs of the apartment buildings and allowed only pale grey light to filter through its dark, frosted glass. My melancholic wife, who had been in many psychiatric wards and received all sorts of treatments, was happy in that cell of a room and nowhere else. While bright winter sunlight filled the rest of the apartment, Markela sat on her single bed and watched non-stop American soap operas on her tiny black-and-white TV.

I was determined to look after my wife without hiring professional help. Her family was wealthy and we could have employed a nurse, but the only person Markela would tolerate in the apartment was Aunt Ismene. She was also okay with Nejat, who used to come up and see us on Sunday mornings after he'd closed up at the Fortune Nightclub. But that was it. She even stopped wanting Rayiha to come in once a week to clean. In the early years of our marriage my wife had loved that young woman, who lived in the next-door building with her husband and two daughters. While Rayiha was cleaning the floor-to-ceiling windows of the French balcony, Markela used to chat to her, holding the ladder steady for her with her foot. Then all of a sudden Rayiha disappeared. I assumed that Markela had told her not to come any more. Maybe they moved away from the neighbourhood. I don't know.

Aunt Ismene stayed with my wife during the day, keeping the apartment tidy and cooking for us. She had retired from her hospital job right after the military coup of 1980. When I got home in the evening, she and I, plus occasionally Markela (if she came out of her room), would eat our supper sitting at the dining-room table, watching television. After supper I would call a taxi from the stand and send my elderly aunt back to her home in Samatya. Aunt Ismene much preferred buses – she liked to take them to random destinations and get lost – so she always tried to tell me not to call a taxi. I made sure the taxi driver, whom we knew, waited at the other end to see that she got safely through the door of her house in Samatya.

That 1986 New Year's Eve, Markela had once again refused to go out. We'd promised her parents that we would join them for dinner at their home in Yenikoy. We'd even bought presents. Markela's sisters and their husbands and children would be there. They were one of the rare Greek families whose members had all managed to stay in Istanbul. At Christmas, New Year's Eve, Easter and on name days, the children would fill the Yenikoy apartment and we would eat together with a joyousness that reminded me of my very distant past.

Given that she'd grown up in such a happy family, I couldn't understand why my wife was so melancholic. Back then, psychiatric diagnosis was not common, and we didn't have the medicines to regulate the brain's chemistry that we have today. We all handled Markela in the wrong way. It's only now, at my advanced age, that I've come to realize that. What a shame.

When Markela reneged on her promise and refused to go to the New Year's Eve party back then, though, something broke inside me. I knew it was not her fault. She wanted to change. She wanted to get better, to eat dinner at her family's table, to laugh. More to convince herself than me, in the weeks leading up to New Year's Eve, she had vowed that she would attend. I encouraged her. She was going to leave the apartment for the first and only time that year. She would not be going to a strange place but to Yenikoy, where she'd been born and brought up. She would be safe in her parents' home, among her sisters. On New Year's Eve she would wear one of her beautiful old dresses. She would wash and brush her long black hair, put blusher on her cheeks. We talked about it every day, as a sort of therapy, repeating the same sentences over and over in a murmur, as if we were praying. 'You'll pin your hair up with your diamond-studded combs. You'll wear your purple dress with the lace. Your patent leather shoes will see the street for the first time.' We'd laugh about it together.

Because Markela didn't want to take a taxi for fear of breathing the same air as a stranger, I'd borrowed Kemal's car for the evening. The previous week's snow had transformed into black ice, blocking the already labyrinthian streets of Tarlabasi. Getting down to Kaymakcalan Street was a real headache, but eventually I found a gap and parked in front of our building. So when I went upstairs to find Markela still in bed, wrapped in her blanket and watching the thousandth episode of *Dynasty*, I lost it. There was a thermostat inside me which regulated my tolerance, but right then it went haywire. My temples and ears burnt red hot. It was pointless picking a fight with her – you couldn't argue with Markela – but this time I just couldn't bear it. I stormed over to the VCR and stabbed the 'off' button.

'Come on, Markela, get dressed. We're going to be late.'

She raised her head. Her big black eyes had purple circles around them. She stared at me like a child who didn't understand the language I was speaking.

'Come now, my love. Markela, *agapi mou*. Your dress is on the bed. There's no time now to wash your hair, but you can give it a good brush. The diamond-studded combs...'

I was about to repeat our prayer of intent when Markela stood up, placed her blanket on the bed and went out into the hall. I followed her to the kitchen in hope. She took a piece of cheese from the fridge, added a biscuit from the jar and began nibbling. She had her back to me, and the collar of her sweater had slipped down, exposing her shoulder blades, the vertebrae sticking out from her hunched back. She'd lost so much weight. Just half a kilo was keeping her faded blue jeans from slipping off her hips. Her hair had grown very long, its scraggy ends reaching below her waist. Because she wasn't using a plate, biscuit crumbs were spilling onto the counter and the floor. I went into the bathroom to cool down, and, one by one, closed all the cupboard doors that Markela had left open as she'd wandered around. I crossed to the living room and phoned Aunt Ismene. She was watching television with her neighbour, Ani Hanim.

'What New Year's celebration, Pericles *mou*, my son? Ani and I will be asleep before the clock strikes ten thirty. Of course I will come. My daughter Markela and I will sit together and eat nuts. At midnight, there will be belly dancing on the television and we will watch that. You go out, have fun. Get some air. It will do you good.'

After hanging up, I did not wait for Aunt Ismene to arrive. Markela was using the old carpet sweeper (which we'd named 'Girgir' because of the sound it made) to clean up the crumbs on the floor. Without even saying goodbye, I opened the door and left. I got into Kemal's silver-grey Renault 12 and drove through Dolapdere to Taksim with the window down. As the cold air blasted my face, my temper cooled. I didn't get angry with Markela any more. I didn't curse my fate. It was I who had wanted to marry her. Aunt Ismene and Mama had been against it; they'd objected again and again. Two days before the wedding, Aunt Ismene had come to The Circle – a big deal, since she never used to set foot in our building back then – and practically begged me to give up on this marriage business. I didn't listen to them. I wanted to be a hero. I was going to rescue the unhappy princess shut up in her tower. And now I was facing the consequences.

At the red light, I glanced around at the happy families inside the cars alongside me. They were chic, their hair elegantly styled, and their children were hopping about in the back seats. They were clearly going to dinner with friends and family, carrying presents, boxes of chocolates and containers of grapevine dolma on their laps. I loosened my tie. If only I could keep on driving, leave Markela behind, The Circle, my city – which was with every passing day becoming a more dangerous, more rootless town – and head off into the distance. If only I could cross the bridge, put my foot down, speed down the road and wake up in a cold room in a small hotel. Maybe in Ayvalik, or in Ankara, or in some other corner of the world.

I parked the car in front of Kemal's apartment on Cihangir's Altin Bilezik Street. The front door was unlocked. I pushed it open and, without even thinking about it, went upstairs. The clatter of knives and forks and the hum of conversation and laughter from Kemal's apartment filled the stairwell. I rang his doorbell. I would return his car keys and leave.

Kemal was both surprised and pleased to see me there. 'Ooh, welcome! Come in, my friend,' he said, pulling me by my arm.

Kemal and I had opened our first pharmacy together. If Nejat hadn't begun harassing me, mine and Kemal's partnership would have lasted at least ten years longer. But I had not wanted to expose my friend to the danger posed by Nejat and his men, so I suggested that we go our separate ways. My friend was not the type who could cope with Nejat's dirty work. He went back to university after our partnership ended, received his doctorate, and joined the faculty as an assistant professor.

It was warm inside. The flat smelled of roast turkey, cinnamon and perfume. I tried to explain the situation to my friend on the doorstep, but my eye was caught by the crowded dining table, visible through a crack in the living room's double doors. A colourfully decorated plastic Christmas tree had been placed on top of the yellow enamel stove. There were shiny glass baubles and cotton-wool snow on its branches. That was Kemal's wife Betul's doing, I thought. A picture came to my mind of the two of them hanging baubles and stars on the tree. I felt a lump in my throat, a pain in my chest. When had I become so cold inside? How did I end up so alone? My loneliness was hollowing me out.

I didn't say anything when Kemal took my coat. Then suddenly I was in the living room, at the head of the dining table. I realized how hungry I was when I saw the turkey, the rice with currants, the potato salad. The chatter and laughter of the people sitting across from me in groups of two and three came to my ears as a howl, rising and falling, and the smell of cigarettes mixed with perfume was making me dizzy. Kemal must have seen me sway, for he grabbed my arm.

'Hey, friends, can you squeeze up? We'll put a chair here and a plate. Here in the back. Betul, honey, would you bring him a glass of wine? Great. Does anyone not know my old friend Pericles? Let me introduce you...'

Ulker and I caught each other's eye just at that moment. She was sitting at the far end of the crowded table, smoking a cigarette. Later she confessed that she'd paid no attention when I first came into the room. The drunk man across from her had ensnared her, going on and on about politics without taking a breath, and Kemal had added several new people to the table throughout the evening. It was only when she heard my name that she took notice. How could I be angry? I'd not immediately picked her out among Kemal and Betul's guests either.

As Kemal began to introduce me to everyone, Ulker stubbed out her cigarette and stood up. From the moment our eyes met, I could look only at her. Smiling, she came to my side. I had forgotten how much I missed her.

'Ulker! Is it really you?'

We embraced. She was so petite! Her hair smelled of rosemary. I wanted to rest my cheek against her head and stay there. The pain in my chest evaporated, my loneliness eased. I had found Ulker again. After twenty-two years. I wanted to take her hand and leave, walk arm in arm on the snowy Cihangir streets until dawn, sit in a soup kitchen with her and watch the sky lighten. I would tell her how I had searched for her in courtyards, down alleyways, in coffeehouses and outside cinemas after she left me. How, like a madman, I had followed her trail around Beyoglu for years. I would speak of my stupidity, my regret.

Kemal was shocked. 'How can you two know each other? Pericles is my friend from university, and Ulker has just got back from Germany.'

We laughed at the same time. We were looking not at Kemal but at each other. She no longer wore glasses, and her beautiful hazel eyes were striking. She used to have a fringe but now her hair was cut short. Her freckles had faded and a deep crease had appeared between her eyebrows.

Later on, whenever I ran my finger over that crease, she would joke and say it was the mark of a philosopher, that it came from thinking too much.

'About me?' I would ask. 'Was it me you were thinking about?'

To which she would reply, 'You're crazy! What was there to think about? You were just a boy. And you rejected me.'

'And you left me.'

Then we would kiss. For a long, long time. Deeply. I came to understand that the body is a many-stringed instrument, able to play all of love's arpeggios. As a man in his forties, I had, of course, heard that sex was even better when you were in love, but in truth I had not experienced that. I had been in love with Markela at the beginning – or at least I thought I was. But the pleasure I got from making love to her was not so different from what I'd felt with women with whom I'd had brief flings. But that winter, making love to Ulker in her book-filled apartment in Tunel Square, I discovered that love could be experienced as a physical sensation in every square centimetre of the body. Love turned into something I could feel on my skin, like my pulse, my heart. I did not want to separate my skin from Ulker's even for a moment. I couldn't get enough of her.

Ulker's bedroom window looked down onto a small courtyard with a grapefruit tree. In its branches, which reached up to the third floor, doves cooed and sparrows chattered, but no one picked the fruit, which fell and rotted on the ground below. We could see the sky from where we lay, and as we made love the evening sun would fill the room for a short while, slipping through the net curtains and making stripes on the wooden floor.

Ulker and I made love every afternoon of the ten months we spent together that year. We were never in a hurry, never considered going anywhere else. If our stomachs growled in the middle of our lovemaking, we would go to the kitchen, make ham and salami sandwiches and bring them back to bed. We'd fill a thermos with tea or open a bottle of wine and have a picnic on top of the blue satin quilt, wrinkled sheets and orange- and green-flowered pillows. When spring came, we were going to go for picnics outdoors. Maybe on the island? On Camlica Hill? Or in Polonezkoy? Ulker objected to the latter. There were little guest houses in Polonezkoy where men took their mistresses. Her silence after I suggested this spot reminded us that we were a man and his mistress. Then we laughed.

I'm relating all this in the generic past tense because, like a pair of naughty children or a couple that could never agree, we always talked about the same thing. And then we'd go back to making love.

Ulker's shoulders and breasts were still as freckly as they had been in her youth, but the plump and clumsy eighteen-year-old who somehow couldn't shake off her adolescence had gone, replaced by a slender woman. She too was over forty. I would say, 'Praise God forty-one times for you, Ulker!' And she would laugh and climb on top of me. She had the most stupendous bottom. Although it was slimmer than it had been, its roundness remained. I would cup it in my palms. I owed her, as she loved to remind me. I owed her dozens if not hundreds of bouts of lovemaking because of all the pleasure I'd withheld from her in our youth, when I'd been too afraid. Such were the demands my beautiful lover made of me on those evenings.

It was as if we had a lifetime to spend together. As if I didn't have to return to my apartment, to Markela. Putting my apprentice, Aydin, in charge, I would leave the pharmacy two hours early and return home one hour late. Aunt Ismene never said a word, although she was aware of everything. Those brief, stolen moments were worth an eternity. During those interludes there was no past, no future, no world outside Ulker's apartment in Tunel Square. I finally tasted undiluted pleasure.

Almost thirty-five years had passed since then. The stars had returned to their original positions. I was ready for a new beginning.

# Under the Bed

Night descended. In the view that had opened up behind the ruins of a neighbouring building, I could see that seagulls were settling down to sleep. In the middle room, which was piled high with books, I wrote until the joints of my fingers became too painful for me to hold a pen. I had taken Berin's advice and begun writing my memoirs, which I had promised to Istos publishers. The noise of squabbling children filtered in through the living-room windows. Every evening at this hour on Kaymakcalan Street the neighbourhood boys pushed and shoved each other.

I poured three fingers of Metaxa into a fat glass and turned on the television to watch the evening news. Italy was falling to pieces. They'd identified 1,694 cases of coronavirus so far. Eighty people had died. Hospitals were overwhelmed, and the elderly were dying one after the other in isolation units while their children waited desperately outside. I couldn't bear it. I turned off the television, finished my Metaxa in one gulp. Not even the world's most developed countries, with the most advanced healthcare systems, could prevent the spread of the virus. As for Turkey, not a single coronavirus case had yet been reported. We had no access to information on the danger that was stalking the rest of the world. I now understood that when Berin had said, 'We will not see the end of this epidemic, Pericles,' she'd not been anticipating that she and I would catch the virus and die from it, but rather that it would take a very long time for the world to get rid of it.

As I walked to my bedroom, my eye was caught by the horse-head walking stick hanging on the edge of the console table. On the day I first saw Leyla, I'd tripped over it in the downstairs apartment while I was waiting for Ferit. I'd brought it upstairs and Vera must have found it and hung it on the console. I grasped it, raised it high, wrapped my painful fingers around it. It was made from the branch of a Cornelian cherry tree and in the dark corridor the beady eye of the horse shone like an emerald. Someone was shouting on the street. Maybe it was those children fighting. My ears were ringing.

'First your possessions, then your lives!'

I shut the bedroom door, lay down and closed my eyes. The horse-head cane was beside me. My memory was playing tricks on me again. But it was still wise to take precautions.

I was ten years old the year of the Events of September 1955. On the afternoon of that cursed day, Aunt Ismene and Elena were at our house. They had returned to Istanbul from the island of Imbros two days earlier. We'd been away for the summer too, on the island of Buyukada, in a house we rented on the same street as my grandfather's house. Summer was over now. The days of island freedom, of swimming and riding my bicycle, had ended.

Mama and Aunt Ismene were sitting in armchairs in front of the window on the Temrin Hill Street side, drinking coffee and catching up on everything that had happened in the months they'd been apart. Aunt Ismene's family on her father's side was from Imbros, and she spent the summers there so that Elena could get to know her *yaya* and her *papou* better.

Elena and I were playing at the suntanned feet of the two women. I had set up railway tracks on the rug, having been happily reunited with my trainset on our return from the island. I was making puff-puff noises while I pushed the locomotive and its wagons along the track. Little Elena was laughing. She was six years old at the time.

All of us were surprised when Papa came home early. His spirits were low. Aunt Ismene stood up, shook out the skirt of her flowered dress, took Elena by the hand and pulled her up. Elena objected softly.

Papa looked at the trainset on the floor and in a thoughtful voice said to Mama, 'Alexandra *mou*, Ismene and Elena should eat with us this evening. Let us stay here together until Stelio comes home. Don't go downstairs, Ismene.'

Uncle Stelio kept his toyshop in the Hazzopulo Arcade open until late.

'What's happened, Papa?'

'Nothing, son. Nothing.'

Papa went to the back room to change his clothes. He'd forgotten to take off his shoes and Mama was about to say something, but decided against it. Aunt Ismene and Elena remained on their feet. Suddenly the bells of the big church on Kaymakcalan Street began to toll.

Mama stood up and opened the balcony door. 'Is there a funeral at this time or what?'

I joined her and together we went out onto the balcony, leaning over the railings and looking up and down Kaymakcalan Street. A breeze gusted in through the back room, lifted the net curtains and made them swell. My nostrils filled with the smell of musty netting. The apartment had not yet been thoroughly cleaned since we'd got back from the island. I hung over the railings and tried to see the church – I was tall for my age. Instead, I saw a gang of twenty men at the top of Temrin Hill Street. They had clubs in their hands.

'Alexandra, my dear, don't go out onto the balcony.' Papa came running from the corridor. 'Get back! Pericles, come here!'

'It's nothing,' said Mama, closing the balcony door and drawing the curtain. 'There was a demonstration about Cyprus today, that's why they're there. Do not be so anxious, I beg—'

Before she could finish her sentence, there was a loud crash, and some of the men in the group at the top of the hill yelled 'Infidels! Death to infidels!'

Aunt Ismene was still on her feet and Elena was still holding her hand. Mama grabbed me and pulled us both face down onto the floor. She was shouting, more out of bewilderment than fear.

'They're throwing rocks! Themis! They're throwing rocks at the houses.'

My trainset was squashed underneath us and one of the wagons was sticking into my stomach. The crashing noises got louder and more frequent and the church bell began tolling more insistently. Sounds were coming from all four directions now. A rock smashed into our balcony door and the floor-to-ceiling glass fell out of its frame and splintered everywhere. Shards of glass scattered all over the living-room floor. Mama wrapped her arms around me to protect my head. My face was pressed against her stomach. She was wearing a summer dress and I breathed in the smell of summer, and of fear. Her fear had a sharp scent, a bit like vinegar, which reminded me of Papa's pharmacy.

Papa plunged into the living room. With one swift movement he picked up Elena and lifted me out from under Mama. Mama's hands and knees were bleeding where bits of glass had pierced her skin. As Papa dragged me down the corridor, I caught sight of my face in the console mirror. Blood from Mama's hands was smeared on my cheeks, my ears.

We went into the big bedroom. Papa tucked me and Elena under the bed and pushed a heavy walnut trunk in front of us.

'Whatever happens, do not make a sound. Do you understand me, my son?'

I nodded. I couldn't speak, even though I wanted to ask my father what was happening. They threw that rock at our window by mistake, didn't they? Then why are they smashing the windows in other houses? Nothing will happen to us, will it, Papa? We haven't done anything to anyone. Papa! You give our neighbours aspirins when they have a headache, you bandage their knees when they've fallen over – that's right, isn't it? They'll protect us, won't they? You remember how once when the baker's son, Ali, was fighting with Edip and Ali's head got hurt, you ran and helped him right away, Papa. You bandaged Ali's head. Papa, I beg you, tell me no one will touch us.

Papa had already left the room. I heard him saying quietly to Mama and Aunt Ismene, 'A bomb exploded at Ataturk's house,' then he closed the door. Elena and I were left by ourselves under the bed among the empty suitcases and baskets. I remembered something I'd seen when Mama and I had been hanging over the balcony. The baker's son, Ali, had been there with the men at the top of the hill. He was holding a huge rock in his hand and he'd smirked when he saw me. The baker was there too, waiting in the crowd with a club in his hand. Was that a good thing? They would not attack us. Then why had Ali raised the rock in my direction and laughed in that evil way? I tried to hug Elena from where I was lying under the bed. I put my hand over her mouth in case she cried.

The commotion outside had got louder. Forceful male voices were yelling in chorus, and it sounded like windows and doors were being smashed and heavy furniture was being dragged out from apartments and splintered into smithereens. The peal of the ever-loudening church bell was mixed with screams.

From somewhere near the back courtyard, an old woman was shouting at the top of her voice, 'Have you lost your mind, son? What are you doing, *vre?*'

Her voice was drowned out by a massive boom, as if someone had pressed all the keys on a piano at the same time. Our building shook as if in an earthquake. I didn't know then that they were trying to break down our door with axes and iron bars. The door of the room had opened with the tremor. Using the trunk Papa had pushed in front of the bed as a shield, I tried to see what was happening in the corridor. Mama, Papa and Aunt Ismene were struggling to move the marble console from where it stood in the entrance hall to a new position in front of the door. It was heavy. Men were battering, trying to force the door open. It sounded like they were beating it with axes and hammers, trying to get in. The wooden floor that Elena and I were lying on was rattling. Elena was glued to my hands, her eyes shut tight. She wasn't crying, but she was shaking as if spasms were passing through her body.

I was trying to think of what I could say to those men to save our lives if they killed Mama and Papa. I spoke Turkish very well. I knew all the words to the Turkish national anthem. I would say my name was something else. I'd say it was Mehmet. 'I am Mehmet. I came to this apartment to deliver medicines. Just as I arrived, a rock was thrown at the glass door.' But the baker and Ali knew me, and Elena too. 'Liar,' they would say. 'This one's name is Pericles. Off with his head!' I cried harder. They would not believe me.

A male voice on Temrin Hill Street shouted, 'Leave the child alone! Shame on you. It's a sin. Let him go!' There was another huge crash, very near us this time. The window in our room had fallen in. Shards of glass scattered under the bed, right next to us. The smell of burning filled the room through the pane-less window. They were setting fire to the neighbourhood. I was terrified. Dragging Elena by the hand, I managed to pull her out from under the bed. There was a huge cobblestone in the middle of the room. It was dark now and the sky outside had turned orangey-red from the flames of the building across from us.

I opened the bedroom door as wide as I could and shouted into the corridor, 'Mama!'

Mama was still in front of the console, which they had pushed against the front door. She saw me at the bedroom door and was about to run towards me when an iron bar shot through the front door and struck the far wall of the corridor. If Mama had taken one more step, it would have hit her in the face, or perhaps gone right through her. Aunt Ismene had grabbed her arm and pulled her back.

Hands wielding axes and clubs plunged through the hole that the iron bar had made in the door, and smashed at the marble console and its mirror. In a rush, Papa pushed Aunt Ismene and Mama down the corridor, gathered up me and Elena and shoved all of us into my room.

Mama wept as she clung to Papa's hands. 'Themis, stay in here with us! Themis, don't be crazy, *se parakalo*!'

Papa did not hear her. With his free hand he grabbed the cane and brandished it in the air like a whip.

'Lock the door from the inside, Alexandra.'

'Papa!'

The door closed. Aunt Ismene turned the key in the lock. Mama and I hugged each other. I was crying.

'Quiet,' murmured Mama. 'Shhh. Do not cry, *moro mou*. Quiet, my baby. They must not hear us.' I could not stop crying. This was not a nightmare; they were going to kill us. These were people who did not know that Papa helped everyone. Mama took me in her arms and sat on the edge of the bed. She covered my ears with her hands and began to rock back and forth. Like a broken record she kept repeating the same words. 'Shhh, quiet, *moro mou*.' Aunt Ismene had pushed Elena inside the wardrobe and was trying to hide her under my sweaters and coats. Elena was like a doll, motionless and glassy-eyed, buried under a mound of clothing.

Despite Mama having covered my ears, I heard everything: the repeated crashing of breaking glass, the smashing up of furniture, the pleas for mercy from men being kicked or beaten with clubs, the loud, coarse curses in response. The bells were silent. Dogs were barking like crazy. The smell of burning filled the room through the broken window and the sky was as red as a copper bowl.

'Mama, did they kill Papa?' I whispered.

Mama was holding me so tight I couldn't breathe. She must

have lost her mind. With a last splurge of strength I slipped out of her arms and charged towards the door to rescue my papa. Aunt Ismene sprang out from where she was keeping guard in front of the wardrobe.

Mama screamed, 'PERICLES!'

Just at that moment a gunshot exploded. With one hand on the key, I froze. Papa. They had shot Papa. I turned and looked at Mama. She wasn't rocking any more. Aunt Ismene had a long wooden stick in her hand, the clothes rail from my wardrobe. I could hear Elena, buried under clothes inside the wardrobe, whimpering. Mama slowly rose from the bed. She held my shoulders with trembling hands and pulled me close. Papa!

With the firing of the gun, all the shouting, crashing, smashing and cursing inside The Circle ceased. Our building fell silent. From the Temrin Hill Street side I could still hear the echo of crazed voices, the screams, the noise of breaking furniture. On one of the downstairs floors a male voice was speaking in Turkish. As his voice got louder, footsteps retreated from outside our apartment, and probably the whole building. I don't know how much time passed, but later we heard Papa's voice. He was tapping on our door.

'Alexandra, Ismene, children...'

Mama let out a scream, knocked away the chair and unlocked the door.

'THEMIS!'

We hugged in the doorway. Papa was alive! My prayers had been answered. He took me in his arms. 'It's over,' he said. 'It's okay, my son. It's passed. They've gone. They will not come back.'

I couldn't stop crying. Papa carried me to the big bed in their bedroom. Mama came too, and Aunt Ismene, carrying

Elena. We lay down with our arms around each other. Mama's bare arms were like ice. She couldn't even stroke my head. Papa said we had been saved, but we did not know where Uncle Stelio was. The violence had certainly not been limited to our street. We understood this. Still, it took time for us to grasp the extent of the events. We did not yet realize that the mobs had targeted not only the whole of Beyoglu but also homes and businesses all the way down the eastern side of Istanbul, the villages along the Bosphorus, the islands, the poor houses of Samatya in Kumkapi, and the neighbourhoods along the railway tracks on the western edge of the city.

It was Tahsin, the former apprentice of old Monsieur Panayiotis on the first floor, who had chased away the attackers with his gun. Tahsin often visited his old master, who had no living family, and helped him. When he heard that the shops of Greek people in Beyoglu were being looted, he grabbed his gun and raced to The Circle from his home in Tophane. It took him a long time to get to our neighbourhood through the crazed mobs. The thugs knew that Tahsin looked after Monsieur Panayiotis, so they did not touch the first floor or Monsieur Panayiotis himself. After they'd ransacked Madam Elpiniki's hat-making shop at the entrance of the building, they attacked Aunt Ismene's apartment on the second floor. By the time they'd finished there and were in the middle of breaking down the door of our apartment, Tahsin had arrived. From beside the lift on the ground floor he fired his gun up the stairwell. The looters fled before they reached the upper floors. It was a good thing they didn't make it to the fifth floor, where Yorgo's defenceless wife and daughters were shaking in fear.

Many women had been raped that night. For years we didn't talk about that. There were lots of things about that night that we didn't talk about.

The next day we went down to Uncle Panayiotis's apartment and hugged Tahsin. Papa, Mama, myself, Elena and Aunt Ismene all kissed his hands and cheeks. Uncle Stelio had managed to get home around dawn, when martial law was finally declared. He too went down to Monsieur Panayiotis's apartment.

'They would have had to step over my dead body to get to you,' Tahsin said, shaking his head as he stood there in the doorway. 'Unfortunately, I was late. I was not able to save your apartment, Monsieur Stelio, Madam Ismene.'

I couldn't take my eyes off Uncle Stelio. Something about him had changed. He wasn't wounded, but he looked different. Years later, I came to understand that the horror he had witnessed, and the pain of his situation, had warped his face. It would stay like that forever.

As Tahsin spoke, Aunt Ismene lowered her head and looked at the muddied fragments of broken teacups, the smashed copper pitcher and the shredded lace that she'd salvaged from the street. Papa went over to Uncle Panayiotis, who was sitting like a waxwork in his chair at the head of the table, and held his hand.

'Are you well, Monsieur Panayiotis?'

The old man did not reply. His eyes were fixed on the silent radio on the sideboard. They were a milky-grey colour, like a baby's.

'News came early this morning from the cemetery,' Tahsin said softly. 'They also attacked the Greek Orthodox cemetery last night. The scoundrels. They smashed up the tombstones and the marble crypts and scattered the skulls and bones of the dead. Monsieur Panayiotis's wife was in that cemetery.'

Within a month, Uncle Panayiotis was dead. Tahsin collected the bones from the cemetary and with his own hands built a solid marble grave for the two of them. He placed their wedding photograph at its head. Uncle Panayiotis had had no one except his wife and Tahsin. He left his apartment to Tahsin in his will. Tahsin, his wife, and their son Edip moved in. Papa and Uncle Stelio arranged a salary for him. And so Tahsin became The Circle's caretaker.

We did not give a name to the events of that night. We couldn't. We just said 'the Events'. Among ourselves we remembered it as 'Septemvriana', the Events of September 1955, when Greek, Armenian and Jewish shops in Istanbul were attacked and the homes of the non-Muslim minority looted. We did not speak of Septemvriana. We took upon ourselves the shame of the cruelty done to us. We lowered our voices. As the Greek community of Istanbul was forcibly uprooted and dispersed, the names of the streets and the apartment buildings changed. New residents moved in. What happened that night was erased from the city's memory. Our silence played a large part in this forgetting. But I did not forget, for forgetting means the defeat of humanity in its battle against evil.

Yorgo, the draper on the fifth floor, emigrated to Athens with his family. We stayed. Papa's pharmacy and Uncle Stelio's toyshop had been set on fire. Bottles of cologne, creams, and perfume imported from Europe had been smashed to pieces with hammers and trodden into the ground. The faces of those beautiful porcelain dolls that Uncle Stelio had not even given to Elena had been urinated on, their hair cut off. The toys I could never get enough of had all been crushed to bits.

'They should at least have taken the toys for their own children,' said Aunt Ismene. 'The children would have been happy.'

'We shall begin again,' said Papa. 'It is only material goods; we still have our lives.'

Silence. The mad shouting we'd heard while lying curled up on the big bed in the back room came to our minds.

'FIRST YOUR POSSESSIONS, THEN YOUR LIVES. DEATH TO INFIDELS!'

But no one said anything.

# Speaking in Silence
## of an Old Youth

Leyla rang my doorbell one evening in the second half of March. I was engrossed in reading over what I had written and was startled by the bell. 'It will keep you busy,' Berin had said about my writing, and she was right. I was hooked. After returning from my midday walk, I would eat the meal Vera had prepared for me, then shut myself away in the middle room and write. I would write until teatime, and at five o'clock I would go up to Berin's. Having something to occupy my mind stopped me from imagining the worst about this coronavirus that was holding the world in its claws and from obsessing about the fact that for some reason Leyla had not moved into the apartment.

It was Berin who provided me with the most reliable news concerning the virus, for she spent the whole day surfing the web. The World Health Organization had announced that the epidemic had become a pandemic and had advised that every country should now take more aggressive precautions. It had been ten days since Turkey had registered its first case of the virus. I had been very sad to hear from Berin that two of the people now in intensive care were pharmacists.

My colleagues were on the frontline of this dangerous new world.

When I went back downstairs to my apartment, instead of watching television, in which I had lost all confidence, I would read over what I had written that day with fresh eyes, from beginning to end. The youngsters at Istos Publishers were enthusiastic about the book. One morning several months earlier they had treated me to tea and buns at their office on the top floor of the Santa Maria Han building next to the Roman Catholic church. They had explained at length how they needed someone from Istanbul's Greek community to tell our story. With the passing of my generation, a chapter of Istanbul's history was coming to an end. To ensure that our experiences were not forgotten, it was important to record them. Being young Istanbul Greeks themselves, they were interested not in a romantic or nostalgic version but in a serious, heartfelt account that could only come from the pen of someone like me.

I had agreed, but I was far from confident that I would be able to write anything serious or heartfelt. For a long while I did not put pen to paper. Now, as I read over my notes, half in Greek, half in Turkish, I did not like my phrasing or my style. My inner critic was forever finding fault. Still, by the following day, I'd find that I was impatient for Vera to finish her work and go. If she fiddled around doing the ironing, decanting food from saucepans to Pyrex, separating out the glass bottles for recycling and such, I would shoo her away. I was keen to have peace and quiet as soon as possible, so that I could get to my notes in the middle room.

When I heard the doorbell, I stood up. I had been reading and correcting what I'd written for several hours by the light of my desk lamp and hadn't realized that the rest of the apartment was in darkness. Pressing the light switches one by one, I made my way down the corridor to the door. When I looked through the spy-hole and saw Leyla standing there, I thought my eyes were playing tricks on me. What do you expect, Pericles, I thought, when you spend hours reading and writing in such poor light?

Leyla obviously didn't trust my eyes either, for she called out softly, 'Monsieur Pericles, it's me, Leyla.'

I needed to lean against the console and catch my breath, but I was afraid she might go away if I didn't open the door right away. I unfastened the chain, turned the key and opened the door as fast as my clumsy hands could manage. The automatic stairwell light went out. Leyla spoke from the darkness.

'Hello. I'm not disturbing you, am I?'

In the two months since Leyla had bought the downstairs apartment, I'd lost hope that she would ever come and live in our building. Someone must have frightened her off. Yes, certainly, my apartment was a good investment, a good use of the money her father had left her. Not just good, outstanding. When Ferit saw me on the street, he still grumbled about it. 'What did you do, Uncle Pericles? You sold that beautiful apartment for nothing!' Acquaintances, relatives or friends must have advised her to keep the apartment she'd bought for a steal as an investment and to rent a house for herself in a safer neighbourhood. If Leyla had been my daughter or relative, that's what I would have advised her to do.

Would a single, thirty-year-old woman live by herself in Tarlabasi? Ours was not a respectable street like neighbouring Aynali Cesme, where intellectuals and artists lived in a protected bubble. On our street, gangsters who'd been trained by Nejat held the corners at night. All sorts of shady activity, from drugs to weapons, male and female prostitution and fake passports, was conducted on Kaymakcalan Street, in its empty lots. Bullets were exchanged in coffeehouses and at the exits of bars. New godfathers had emerged. They all wanted the abandoned houses around there. The construction mafia picked off Nejat's men one by one and collected the title deeds they'd hidden in safes. This was a new type of mafia, prepared to take on even Nejat's gang, who'd been calling the shots in our neighbourhood for fifty years.

Weeks had passed since we'd completed the paperwork at the Beyoglu municipal offices. And so, when Leyla laughingly told me that she had moved in and that she'd been living downstairs for two weeks already, I almost accused her of lying.

'But how can that be? I didn't see a removal van.' I hid from her the fact that for quite a while I'd rung her bell several times a day.

Leyla reached out and pressed the automatic light button. The stairwell lights came on. Since I'd last seen her, she had rested, her cheeks had filled out. Like a courteous gentleman, I invited her in, concealing my anxiety.

'No, I won't come in,' she said. 'I'm going shopping and wanted to ask if you needed anything. After tomorrow... um...'

It was obvious from my face that I had no idea what she was talking about. Leyla smiled. Her tiny white teeth sparkled in the dim light.

'I guess you haven't heard.'

I'd spent the whole day writing. I'd finally reached the point where I could write about the Events, which had been preoccupying me since the night I'd slept with the horse-head walking cane beside me. I'd got so absorbed in it that I hadn't even gone up to Berin's for tea. I'd not listened to the news nor looked at the internet or a newspaper. So it was from Leyla, as she stood in the doorway, that I learnt that from the following day those of us who were sixty-five years old and above would be forbidden from leaving our homes as part of the Covid-19 quarantine restrictions.

At my age, it can take my brain a while to process things, to understand what I'm being told. Just as when learning a foreign language, I sometimes find myself picking out the words I recognize and inferring the rest. Especially when talking to young people, who seem to have invented a new vocabulary that rolls around in their mouths; even their intonation is strange to me. When I telephone the bank, I'm afraid they'll ask questions that I won't understand. It's as if I'm feeling my way in the dark, grabbing at the walls of the world I know.

But on this occasion I grasped the situation immediately. Besides, Leyla spoke in clear Turkish, enunciating every word. Being in the category of an elderly neighbour who could not leave the house would give me unimaginable advantages. I asked Leyla, my thoughtful, beautiful neighbour, if it wasn't too much trouble, could she bring me some fresh coriander and a few limes from the fish market. The greengrocers there stayed open until late.

As soon as she disappeared down the stairs, I phoned Vera and told her not to come to me for a while. 'It's too risky, Vera. You travel here every day by bus and metro.' At first Vera laughed, telling me not to worry, that nothing would happen to her, but when I said that it was not her I was worried about but myself, she got angry. Only when I told her that I'd continue to pay her wages did she calm down. In fact she was happy. If I'd known she was in so much need of a break, I'd have given her one earlier. In truth, I was upset that she didn't ask who would do my shopping and prepare my food, that being her responsibility. Maybe she assumed that Tulin would look after Berin and me together.

My plan went like clockwork. First a few bagels, a loaf of bread, a couple of newspapers, then on the fifth day of house confinement I found myself hosting Leyla in the dining room of my apartment. I had laid the table with Mama's porcelain tea set.

The lemon cake she'd baked was too sweet and rather dry, but the hands holding the knife were dextrous. She squinted when she laughed, and when she was confused her eyes turned a deeper hazel. In spite of her haughty air, she was sincere. She listened to my explanation of the history of the apartment building with interest, asking the right questions. I told her that if one looked carefully, on the front of the building, directly over my balcony, one could see the bas-relief of two snakes swallowing their tails. The name of the building came from those snakes, from the Turkish word for 'The Circle'. The Italian architect loved the symbol of the snake or dragon swallowing its own tail – the mythical ouroboros, ancient symbol of infinity – and he put it on apartment buildings he designed in other districts of Istanbul, though ours was the only one that took its name from those snakes.

The building's name was one of things that had attracted Leyla to the building. It caught her imagination, she said. Circles were fundamental to the way both life and the universe operated – the circle of life, and so forth. Linearity was an illusion. If there was a god, he would be reached by passing through circles, she said. This wisdom was recorded in humankind's DNA. That was why temples were domed – just look at Hagia Sofia, the Neolithic remains at Gobekli

Tepe. She spoke of flying saucers, whirling dervishes, mystics, Hittite suns, yin-yang symbolism.

'And you? How did your family come to move here? Ferit Bey mentioned you were born in this building.'

Taking a deep breath, I reached for my tea.

'Yes, that's correct. My grandfather bought an apartment here just after the building was completed. His first child, my mother, had just been born and he thought it could be her dowry when the time came.'

'They arranged a dowry for a newborn baby?' Leyla said, her mouth still full of bagel.

I shook my head. 'It wasn't quite like that. My grandfather thought this apartment would be a good investment. His first child, my mother, was born that year. When she was a bit older, he transferred the title deed into her name. It was a clever move. When she got married, the apartment became her dowry.'

'Can one not marry without a dowry?'

'I didn't say that. My mother was very much in love with my father, and my father with her. They would have got married whatever the circumstances. But I'd imagine that having this apartment available made it easier for them to marry early.'

I looked at her with what I hoped was a mischievous grin. She was stirring her tea merrily and my dining room rang with the clink of spoon against glass. She hadn't asked for the rest of the story, but because I was enjoying her eyes trained on my face, I kept talking.

'My grandfather was a pharmacist. His pharmacy was in Tunel Square, on the corner, at the entrance to a lovely apartment. My father was his assistant. When my mother, her siblings and my *yaya* went out into Beyoglu together, they would stop by her father's shop. That's how they met and fell in love. *Papou* had no objections. It suited him fine. He would leave the pharmacy to his son-in-law and move to Buyukada. He was having a magnificent villa built on Cankaya Avenue on Buyukada and his plan was to take my *yaya* there immediately after his daughter got married, and have a wonderful life there on the island.'

I stopped talking, picked up my tea. The rest of the story was not pretty. The villa, into which my grandfather had sunk all his savings, would be confiscated as 'wealth tax', the unjust tax that the government levied from its non-Muslim citizens in 1942. The pharmacy in Tunel would also be requisitioned, as well as the building he'd bought on the island ready to use as a new pharmacy. My *yaya* would die of heartbreak. Saying, 'this country is going to burn us alive', my mother's siblings would emigrate to Australia. Almost overnight, my grandfather became an impoverished and lonely old man. It was into this world that I was born.

If Leyla noticed my silence, she didn't remark on it. When I am upset, my eyes immediately give me away. Ulker used to tell me that the blue of my eyes would darken when my spirits were low. During our final month together, that often happened. Back then, our homes had yet again come under attack, this time not from rocks and clubs but from bulldozers and diggers. Trees were being torn out by their roots. I was taking refuge in Ulker's bed, but the blue of my eyes was dark.

'If this building was constructed the year your mother was born, that must have been the 1920s, right?'

I had drifted off, so at first I didn't understand Leyla's question. Then I was surprised at how quickly she'd calculated the years.

'My maths is good,' she said with a shrug.

It was obvious that she didn't want to talk about herself. I didn't insist. Did Istanbul Greeks use to live in the houses now occupied by refugees and immigrants? In many of them, yes. Did they still have the title deeds? No, the deeds had disappeared. Where to? Better not to ask. Okay. Where did the name of the street come from?

'Kaymakcalan is the name of a mountain in Macedonia,' I said. 'But nobody realizes that. If they did, they'd surely change the name. The name of this building used to be "Kyklos Palace" – "kyklos" being "circle" in Greek. Then they made it Turkish. Anyway, it's nothing like a palace now.'

She raised her thick eyebrows in surprise. I was glad she didn't pluck her eyebrows. Eyebrows are where your intuition lives. If they're plucked, your intuition loses its home. That's what Aunt Ismene used to say. She wouldn't let anyone touch Markela's eyebrows.

'These bagels are so delicious. May I have another one?'

I had asked Tulin to buy the bagels for me. I had cut them in half, spread them with olive paste and put slices of cheese and tomato on top, then grilled them in the oven. I smiled to see Leyla devouring them hungrily.

'The bagels are from the Kaymakcalan Bakery. It's been run by the same family since I was a child.'

After finishing our tea, we moved to the living room. The sun had set and the sky on the Temrin Hill Street side had taken on that magnificent multicoloured hue. The weather was cool, but the window was open. Without saying a word, Leyla stood in front of it for a long time, gazing out until the colours faded. Then she drew the curtain. I switched on a lamp, giving the living room a mellow glow, and put on a Bob Dylan record. Hearing the crackles, Leyla turned and came over to the record player. She sat down on the rug in front of it.

'May I look at your records?'

I nodded. Watching her flick through them, I said, 'Records were already antiques by the time you were born, Leyla, yet I can see that you know how to use them. Did you work at a radio station?'

She glanced up at me and this time her eyebrows were raised, as if she'd heard something funny.

'I grew up in my grandparents' house and there was a record player there. Not a modern one like yours, a big bulky thing. When I was little, we used to play all the records in turn.'

She laughed, again revealing her small, perfectly white teeth, took the Jacques Brel record out of its sleeve and put it on the turntable.

I made a note of that comment because when we were at the tea table she'd given very curt answers to my questions about her family. Who was the 'we', I wondered, who played all the records in turn? She had no contact with her mother. She'd said that much, but no more. Her father had died of stomach cancer. I knew that already. He was a bohemian from Istanbul and he'd moved to Bodrum in the early 1980s. Leyla was born there. Despite that, she didn't know her relatives on her father's side. I wanted to know why she'd been brought up by old people but restrained myself. When the time came, she would speak.

While these thoughts were passing through my head, 'Jojo' began playing on the record player. This was one of Jacques Brel's songs. I hadn't heard it in years. All of a sudden, I felt crushed. My throat burnt and my eyes became moist, but I didn't understand why. The song held no special meaning for me. The record must have been Markela's. She loved Brel. When Leyla saw that I'd become emotional, she didn't take the record off but came and sat beside me on the sofa. We listened to the whole of 'Jojo' without speaking. Then she excused herself.

'I came for five o'clock tea and have taken up your whole evening, Monsieur Pericles.'

'Need we be so formal with each other, Leyla? After all, we are neighbours.'

'Agreed, Pericles. Tea at my apartment next time, then.'

Forgetting about the virus, we shook hands at the door. As she descended the stairs, one hand on the wooden bannisters, she turned and smiled. She was so adorable.

When I'd got into my pyjamas and was lying in bed, I recalled Leyla's tiny white hands breaking the bagel into pieces, the way she'd laughed, with her mouth still full, at my mimicking of Ferit the estate agent. She had opened a musty chamber in my memory and brought Ulker back to me. Or rather she'd brought back the feeling I'd had when I was with Ulker. I remembered the person I'd been when I loved her. There was a possibility I could be that person once more.

I may have been in love with that possibility more than with Leyla herself.

As I was drifting off to sleep, I tried to remember why 'Jojo' had shaken me as it did. If I'd had the energy, I would have got up and listened to it again. With the opening of that musty chamber in my memory where Ulker hid, there'd been awoken too, like it or not, memories of my poor wife. 'We speak in silence of an old youth'– were those the lyrics? My mind slid to the doorway and to Leyla's tiny hand disappearing inside my hand when we shook hands goodbye. Then I fell asleep.

# Narmanli Han

Ulker and I had met at Narmanli Han. It was the November of 1962. Papa was keen for me to learn German and was having me take private lessons. My tutor's name was Christoph Wagner. He taught at the German High School and liked his students to call him Christoph, but somehow I couldn't do that. Herr Wagner rented one of the little rooms in Narmanli Han for his private, after-school lessons. It was a warm room with a wooden bookcase that took up a whole wall, onto which he had pinned postcard scenes of Germany. There were film posters on the walls too, and during my lessons my eyes would repeatedly be drawn to Romy Schneider, dressed in a yellow gown in her role as the Austrian princess Sissi. A Milas rug, frayed but still colourful, was spread on the floor and a sofa that opened out into a bed occupied one corner. A desk that Herr Wagner had had a carpenter make was placed against the window. Because my German tutor brewed sugary Turkish coffee on the woodstove in the middle of the room, the room always smelled of burnt sugar and coffee.

Since the beginning of term in September, I'd been going to Narmanli Han every Friday afternoon for my lesson.

I was in my last year of high school at Zografeion, one of the Greek schools in Beyoglu. School finished at four and my lesson with Herr Wagner didn't start until six, so in the interim, instead of going home to eat or change my clothes, I used to wander around Beyoglu. Niko and Stephanos had a lot of freedom, and I would accompany them to the Saray Patisserie and watch girls. Probably because I was in my last year of high school, Mama didn't interfere in what I did so much. She didn't go around saying, 'Where were you? What did you eat? Did you do your homework?' like she used to. Sometimes I would skip classes on Friday afternoon and go to the 2.15 matinee at the Atlas cinema. When it was a Turkish film showing, I would sometimes sneak in anyway, hoping that no one had spotted me. It was the year my passion for going to the cinema by myself began.

As November approached, the days got shorter. When I came out of the matinee, it would be twilight already, and I'd walk towards Tunel Square among crowds of people dressed in suits, jackets and hats. After the Septemvriana – the pogrom of September 1955 – some members of our Greek community had emigrated to Athens, but the avenue was livelier than ever. The wounds of that time seven years before had been patched up and from their ashes the streetlights and sparkling shop windows of 1962 Beyoglu were born. Papa's pharmacy and Uncle Stelio's toyshop were as busy as beehives. 'We're back on our feet,' they were saying. 'The bad old days are over.' The seven years seemed like centuries to me. At the time of the Septemvriana I'd been a ten-year-old boy. When I met Ulker in November 1962 I was a young man, about to turn eighteen. For me, a lifetime had passed since that cursed September.

That year, our high school had been refurbished with an extra storey, central heating, a large auditorium and modern apparatus in our science labs. The school was so popular, they'd even opened a literary arts department. We could never have imagined that in less than two years' time our fathers would be forcibly exiled from their native land, our mothers compelled to give up their Istanbul homes and follow their husbands. Life's sharpest swerves always come when least expected, and never of one's own volition.

It was getting dark when I arrived at Narmanli Han for my German lesson. The lights in the little offices around the courtyard of the *han* had been turned on, and through the windows of the high-ceilinged rooms I could see heads bent over documents, pages and newspapers. A young man was pacing back and forth in his office with an open book in his hand, his lips moving, seemingly reading a poem aloud to his colleagues. In those offices literary magazines, poetry books, and a newspaper for Istanbul's Christian community were prepared and published. Famous writers lived on the upper floors. Their rooms were dark.

Ulker was kneeling on the steps outside Herr Wagner's room. In spite of the cold, she wasn't wearing a coat. Back then, I could tell just from the colour of a girl's uniform which school she went to. Since that girl wasn't wearing a uniform, she must have gone to Germaniko, the German School. When she saw me coming, she stood up. She was wearing glasses, was chubby and had a short fringe that made her look perpetually surprised. I guessed she was a middle-school student. She was holding a tiny kitten in the palm of her hand. It was trying to suck her little finger and creep inside her jacket. Greeting her with a nod, I passed by, taking the steps quickly with my long legs. I was sure the German School girl was looking at me, but I didn't expect her to grab my coat and pull me down as soon as my hand touched the door handle of Herr Wagner's room. I turned around in surprise.

Clutching the kitten against her chest, she smiled shyly. 'The teacher isn't available yet. Please don't go in.'

The kitten meowed weakly.

'But it's time for my lesson.'

'The lesson before you hasn't finished yet.'

I looked her over suspiciously. 'Herr Wagner doesn't have a lesson before mine.'

I knew that in the hour before my lesson, my teacher took a break, lay on his sofa and read a novel. This one-hour break was so important to him that when I turned up early once, he told me off. What was going on? Ulker walked over to the benches lining the wall of the courtyard, where she'd left her leather schoolbag, books and coat. She put on her coat and tucked the kitten inside it. With one hand she gestured at the place beside her on the bench.

'Sit and wait here. My friend's in there. She'll be out soon.'

I found her voice alluring. I was to learn later that she got this melodic style of talking from her film-star mother. She must have realized that I was getting impatient, for she added apologetically, 'Please don't be angry. Zeyno had an urgent question, but his session will finish soon, then you can begin your lesson. Or, if you're cold, there's a tea place in the *han*, over in that corner. They keep a stove burning. You can wait in there and I'll let you know when he's free.'

Without saying anything, I sat down beside her on the bench. In silence we watched the courtyard falling into darkness and the people behind the yellow-lighted windows hurrying back and forth with cigarettes and papers in their hands. I appraised the girl beside me out of the corner of my eye. I wanted to hear her voice one more time. She had charmed me with her affectations stolen from Yesilcam, Turkey's Hollywood. I can see that now, many decades later, but if someone had suggested such a thing then, I would have hit the roof. If a Yesilcam film happened to be playing at the Atlas or the Yeni Melek, then I would go and see it, but when I was with Niko, Stephanos and the girls from school, we made fun of Turkish films.

The kitten meowed weakly again and poked its black-and-white head out of Ulker's coat. Ulker stroked its nose with the tip of her finger.

'A car ran over its mother two days ago. The other kittens died right away, apparently. Only this one survived. I found it in that corner on a newspaper. The boy at the tea stand told me about it. They're expecting this one to die too. It cries all the time. But it stopped crying when I picked it up.'

'It must be starving,' I said. 'It's too small for solid food. It needs milk from a medicine dropper, and the milk needs to be diluted with water, otherwise its intestines won't be able to digest it.'

I sensed that she was looking at me with surprise and awe. I didn't know where I'd learnt what I'd told her, the words just came out of my mouth. As they spilled out, my self-confidence grew.

'Where can I find a medicine dropper now? I can't go far.'

'You could ask at a pharmacy.'

I heard her take a deep breath. 'I don't know. How could I find a pharmacy at this time?'

I realized what she was trying to say, of course. I nodded towards Herr Wagner's room. 'I can't go, unfortunately, but I can give you directions to a pharmacy near here that'll still be open.'

Ulker laughed. She dropped her film-star airs and became

herself. 'Wow, what a good student you are! You'll go to your lesson no matter what. Okay, fine, I'll go by myself. Only... Zeyno's business might take a while. She has some complicated questions which will require a lot of input from the teacher. If you see what I mean.'

She stood up, slung the strap of her leather school bag over her shoulder and turned on the heel of her loafer. As she walked down the lighted passageway from Narmanli Han to Beyoglu, she intentionally swished her ponytail behind her. No, I did not see what she meant. I got up and followed her because I was curious. Together we emerged onto the avenue from the passageway.

Much later, I discovered that Herr Wagner was having an affair with a high-school student, Ulker's friend Zeyno. Maybe the relationship began the evening I met Ulker. Realizing that there was no student waiting outside for him, did Herr Wagner offer Zeyno coffee in that warm room and then take her in his arms? Eventually they got married and moved to Germany. I learnt by chance from an art historian I met at a concert in a church years later that Zeyno's mother was a Greek woman who had hidden her identity. The art historian was Zeyno's niece. Hearing that I was Greek, she started the conversation by saying, 'Perhaps you know my grandmother.' When it turned out that I knew her aunt but not her grandmother, she laughed and laughed. She was a very attractive woman with a pale complexion and curly black hair streaked with grey. She flirted openly with me. I lost touch with her, unfortunately.

Looking back on my life now, I see that the little steps I took, the unimportant decisions I made, always served a greater scheme. It is not by happenstance that our Greek Orthodox priests use the word 'design' rather than 'fate'. There is no fate. God presents us with a design, and within the borders of that design we can go in any direction we want. Life's grand design is made up of our choices within this scheme. Life is like a genetic map. Our body's borders are set at birth, but the shape we give it is to a certain extent down to us. Likewise, if we'd changed even one moment of our past, our present would be different. We might not even be alive any more, or we might have missed out on our most meaningful discoveries. It is enough to glance back at the web of the past to realize this truth.

Ulker and I began to walk side by side in the direction of Galatasaray. I was free for the next hour. Mama would assume I was at my lesson with Herr Wagner, and Papa was at the pharmacy.

The avenue was crowded with cars, buses, shared taxis, women frantically doing their shopping, tradesmen keeping their stores open until late. Young lovers were escaping the evening chill by sitting in pastry shops and drinking tea and eating profiteroles. People were queuing in front of the sandwich shops beside the cinemas. Stars had appeared in the sky. All at once I felt very happy. This was my city. I was young. My life was just beginning. I was in my last year of high school. I was going to frequent these cinemas, cafés and clubs, meet new people, fall in love. The river of life roaring around me would sweep me along with it.

'You'll be able to get a medicine dropper in that pharmacy on your left,' I said.

We'd passed Papa's pharmacy a while ago. I pointed to the pharmacy in Galatasaray that used to belong to Monsieur Adonis. Monsieur Adonis and his wife, Dimitra, also a pharmacist, had left their shop to Turkish friends and moved to Heybeli Island.

Seeing me hesitate at the door, Ulker said, 'Come in with

me. I can't explain about the dropper and syrup bottle like you can.'

The new owner of the pharmacy didn't know me. He didn't even know Papa, but, still, I was reluctant to go in, to be seen with a Turkish girl.

Ulker was looking at me with one hand on the pharmacy door. 'Come on.' Again, I heard that Yesilcam inflection.

We went in together and acquired the medicine dropper and empty glass bottle with ease. I was prepared to use the money that Papa had given me for Herr Wagner, but the pharmacist didn't want payment. Ulker was messing around inside the shop, touching the cologne sprays and Tokalon beauty products, sniffing the air. Eventually, I dragged her out.

'I adore pharmacies,' she said. 'They smell so good – that mix of medicine, lemon cologne, mint and vinegar. And they're always cool. But I'm also scared of them. When I was little, they used to take me to a pharmacy on the corner of Asmali Mescit for injections. I can still feel that fear in my bones, but I quite like the sensation now. I get goosebumps. You know?'

I didn't answer. That pharmacy in Tunel Square where she had her shots was of course my father's pharmacy. I didn't tell her that.

'Now we have to find some milk from somewhere. We could ask at that stand that sells banana shakes. We'll mix it with water, and you can feed the kitten. Shall we turn back now?'

Ulker glanced at the traffic streaming down from Tunel to Galatasaray and on to Taksim, at the red and white lights of the cars and the crowds of behatted people walking beneath the streetlamps.

'Not yet,' she said. 'I'm cold and a bit hungry. Aren't you hungry?'

So instead of heading towards Tunel Square, we walked towards Taksim and turned left into Yesilcam, our Istanbul Hollywood. I'd heard of Bab Café on the corner, but I'd never been there before. With the familiarity of a regular customer, Ulker nodded to the man at the door dressed like a security guard and went in. It was vast. The seating was arranged back-to-back, like in train compartments, and the waiters didn't serve food at the tables. We went to the counter and chose what we wanted. I followed Ulker's lead and tried not to look too amazed at the size of the place. We selected hamburgers and French fries, and our order was marked on a card with a fluorescent pen. It looked exactly like the diners we'd seen in American films, from the bench seats to the jukeboxes. I felt like Tony in *West Side Story*. The first opportunity I got, I would definitely be bringing the beautiful Niki, a pupil at Zappeion School for Girls, there. If she was at church on Sunday morning, maybe I could invite her there afterwards and then on to a film.

As we made our way back to our table with our trays, Ulker stopped to chat and joke with some of the other customers, who were also eating hamburgers and drinking banana shakes. They were all 'movie-business drudges', she said. According to her, anyone who worked at her father's company fell into that category. We put our trays on the table and settled ourselves across from each other on the shiny red leather bench seats.

'Okay, what about the directors?'

'Them too. More than anyone, they're film-industry drudges. The directors have to do whatever the producer says, and the same with the screenwriters. The producer and the screenwriter write the film together anyway. The rough cut goes to Ankara, to the censors, and when it comes back, it gets cut and edited accordingly. If necessary, they shoot new link scenes where they had to edit bits out.'

I didn't know any of that. It thrilled me to discover that Ulker was the daughter of a famous Yesilcam producer, though I tried not to show it. The lighting was dim, but whenever anyone saw that it was Ulker, they would stop and say hello. I recognized an elderly actor who played grandfather roles. It was strange to see him in such a modern cafeteria. He stroked Ulker's cheek, shook my hand and scratched the kitten sleeping in Ulker's lap behind its ears. The kitten was content now that we'd fed it milk from the dropper.

After the elderly actor had settled himself at a crowded table in the back, Ulker whispered in my ear, 'He's come to get his money from my father. Who knows how many hours he's been waiting to see him. Dad makes no allowances for the man's age or state of health, he still makes him wait – a total capitalist.'

Not knowing how to reply, I looked into her face. She took a big bite of her hamburger and closed her eyes as she chewed.

'Mmm… I love the food here! Why aren't you eating?'

I took a little nibble of my burger. If I ate now, Mama would notice my lack of appetite. I checked my watch. I only had ten minutes until I was supposed to be coming out of Herr Wagner's lesson. I was going to be late home. If I asked Ulker, she'd find someone in no time to take a note to Mama. But I didn't say a word. We split the bill.

'Let's stop off at my father's office,' Ulker said. 'I need to get some money. I'm going to the fish market this evening to do the shopping. My mother has to be on set tonight.'

'Is your mother an actress?' I said excitedly.

Ulker stopped and looked at me. 'Are you interested in Turkish films?'

'No, not really. I can't even think of one.'

She couldn't believe it. She pouted.

'Not just my mother. I'm an actress too, and so is my big sister. I mean, we used to be. Now there's school. When we were little, my mother didn't have anywhere to leave us, so she'd take us to the set with her. They would use us for children's roles, which made it cheap for Dad too. It was a family business.'

I made no comment. We left Bab Café. Sahin Films was based in a two-storey, bay-windowed building on the right after you turned the corner. Inside, walk-on girls were sitting on the stairs complaining about Sahin Dermanli. When they saw Ulker, they poked each other in the ribs and stopped talking. The top-floor landing was full of people waiting outside Sahin Dermanli's office. Paying no attention to them, Ulker opened the door and went in. Seeing me hesitate on the threshold, she reached out her hand and drew me inside. Her other hand was holding the sleeping kitten inside her coat.

'Hi, Dad! Let me introduce you. This is my friend Pericles. Pericles, my father, Sahin Dermanli.'

From behind his large desk filled with files, photographs and reels of film, Sahin Dermanli raised his head and looked with expressionless eyes at Ulker, then indifferently at me. Two middle-aged film actresses were sprawled across armchairs on the other side of the desk, laughing and drinking coffee. They looked me over with condescending glances. Was it because of my Greek name, I wondered? Ulker had let go my hand.

Without even asking his daughter what she wanted, Sahin Dermanli opened a drawer and handed her a wad of money, as if Ulker was just another film editor or technician waiting in the corridor for their pay. She didn't seem to mind his cold behaviour. Leaning down, she placed a kiss on his fleshy red cheek. We left.

When we were out on the street, she said, 'My dad's having an affair with a young actress. He's rented her an apartment like a palace in Ayaspasha.'

'Does your mother know?'

'How could she not know? Everyone on this street knows about it, so there's no way he could hide it from Mother.'

I thought about my own mother and her raids on the pharmacy, those fits of jealousy that would suddenly come over her while Despina was fitting her for a new dress. They were the embarrassment of my childhood. What kind of woman was Ulker's mother, I wondered?

As we returned to Beyoglu, Ulker took my arm. It had turned colder. The tram trundled slowly past us. When I thought about Mama worrying about me, I felt guilty, but at the same time I was strangely happy. I was like two different people: the boy with Ulker on his arm, and Pericles, my mother's son.

Even now, walking with Ulker, I kept my eyes on the ground for fear of seeing someone I knew. The fish market was wonderful in the evening rush. The autumn produce – oranges, quinces, pumpkins – looked colourful under the lights, and bright-eyed bonitos shone alongside the rainbow-hued scales of bluefish. Vendors splashed water in front of their stands as they called customers over in a babble of the many languages then spoken in Istanbul. The kitten had woken up and was sticking its black-and-white head out of Ulker's coat, sniffing the air. Ulker was still holding my arm. She hadn't even let go while her olives and cheese were being weighed, or when the fishmonger scraped off the bonito scales with his knife for her. I pulled my grey tweed cap down over my face and hunched by her side. When the fishmonger threw the bonito guts onto the ground, several cats sprang out from beneath the stand and wolfed the fish down in seconds.

'We could leave your kitten here, if you like,' I said. 'It won't go hungry here; it'll be well fed.'

Ulker pouted, but this time I wasn't taken in.

'You do know you'll have to feed this kitten throughout the night, right? You'll have to wake up every two hours and give it milk from the dropper.'

That wasn't true, actually. The kitten was bigger than I'd initially thought and could probably last the whole night without food. But Ulker didn't know that. All of a sudden her bravado disappeared. Hooking her bag over her shoulder, she looked at me fearfully. The bright light from the bulb dangling over the fishmonger's stand fell on the lens of her glasses. She was trying to work out whether I was being serious or not. I didn't back down.

I took her bags of shopping and offered to carry the book bag too. Without saying a word, we walked to Tunel Square together. When we reached the front of her building, she finally let go of my arm. Taking the kitten out from inside her coat, she hugged it to her chest.

'I can't take it upstairs, Pericles,' she said. 'My sister has asthma. Just the cat hairs stuck to my coat will be enough to suffocate her.'

We stood facing each other. I put my hands in my pockets. My lesson with Herr Wagner was meant to have finished an hour and a half ago. Perhaps I'd bump into Papa on the street and we'd walk home together.

I was about to say, 'Oh well, goodbye then, Ulker,' when she asked, 'Could the kitten stay with you for a bit? And when it gets bigger and can stand on its own feet, we'll leave it at the fish market? What do you say?'

Mama would have a fit. She couldn't stand a speck of dust. Aunt Ismene was no different. It was very late and I really had to get home. Knowing the only way Ulker would let me go was if I took the kitten, I agreed. I would let it go in the back garden of the house next door, I decided. And then I'd tell Ulker that it had run away.

Her face lit up. She pulled on her fringe, stood up on her tiptoes and kissed me on the cheek. She smelled of sweet almond oil.

'Thank you so much, Pericles,' she said. 'You are a true hero.'

The kitten was small enough to fit in my cupped palms. It meowed when it left Ulker and I could see its little mouth pink in the light of the streetlamp.

'You're welcome. Well, good evening then,' I said. I sounded cooler than I'd intended.

'You'll bring it here tomorrow, won't you?'

'What?'

'The kitten. Will you bring it here tomorrow so I can see it? I'll find a box for it and a blanket and everything. We can meet at the German Pub if you like. In Galatasaray. We can drink beer and eat potatoes. My treat.'

When she laughed, she looked like a naughty child. She smacked the wad of money in the bag slung over her shoulder. I gave her the bags of shopping and took the dropper and the bottle of watery milk from her. I put the kitten inside my jacket and it stopped meowing; it felt warm. We promised to meet the following afternoon, but I'd already decided that I wouldn't go. She wouldn't be able to track me down. She'd wait and wait, then give up and go home.

As I walked through the dark, I hugged the kitten to my chest. It purred nonstop. What was I going to say to Mama and Papa? I climbed the stairs. Mama, Papa, Aunt Ismene and Uncle Stelio were in the living room. Mama didn't look as if she had been worried at all. With a quick hello, I disappeared down the corridor. I hid the kitten under my bed and found an old cardboard box at the bottom of the wardrobe that I filled with newspaper shredded into pieces. 'This is your toilet, little one,' I said. It scampered up onto the bed.

While I was washing my hands, I tried to hear the talk coming from the living room. Another friend of Papa's and Uncle Stelio's had been banished from the country. This had happened a lot in recent years. The Turkish authorities would accuse a rich Greek businessman of being a spy, then exile him to Greece. It wasn't only the rich Greeks of Istanbul that got deported. The young chap who'd repaired Aunt Ismene's curtains after they'd been ripped during the 1955 Events was accused of carrying information from the patriarchate to the Greek Consulate. He had been deported for that. His mother had come crying to Aunt Ismene. 'My son was carrying nothing but cloth, curtains. He is innocent. What will he do all by himself in Athens?' Clearly another similar incident had occurred that day.

I lay on my bed and tried to think about Niki. She'd been at the club the previous Saturday: we'd had one dance and then she left. But no matter how hard I tried, I couldn't focus on her. Ulker's flirtatious voice, her arm in my arm, the softness of her lips on my cheek when she kissed me goodbye, kept distracting me.

The kitten came out from under the blanket and settled on my chest. I petted the kitten and fantasized about seeing Ulker naked until I heard Mama's voice calling me to dinner.

# Ghostwriter

Leyla had placed a couch draped with white Bodrum cloth between the two French balconies that overlooked Kaymakcalan Street. She sat me there, gave me a cushion for my back and pulled a coffee table in front of me, then disappeared through the narrow service door between the living room and the kitchen. As I listened to the opening and closing of cupboards, the clatter of plates and glasses, I looked around me. She had moved Aunt Ismene's chocolate-armed armchair from the window to the far wall. The dining table that Mama had bought when she came to stay was cluttered with Leyla's laptop, piles of books, notebooks and paper. It took a while for me to register that the cupboard beside the service door was Aunt Ismene's white dresser with the screen doors. Bright red, blue and yellow cups were lined up along its shelves and a large bunch of lavender adorned the top. I was as pleased and surprised as if I had been reunited with an old friend. The apartment had never looked so full of life as it did now – not when it had been chock-full of Aunt Ismene's massive chestnut tables, mirrored sideboard and chandeliers, nor later when Mama had come to stay so that I wouldn't be on my own after Markela died, nor after our more recent refurbishment for our tourist rental business. Leyla had made it fresher and lighter. Of course, that was partly because the building on the corner had been torn down, letting in the blue of the sky on the seaward side. I wondered if Leyla had noticed the little aperture through which you now got a two-second glimpse of the ferry as it passed.

Leyla carefully carried the tea things to the coffee table. Her feet under the baggy black trousers she was wearing looked like a child's. Her ankles were hairless and slender. She had also bought bagels, but she hadn't prepared them as I had. I waited to see if she would sit beside me. She took a cushion from the couch, put it in on the wooden floor and sat cross-legged opposite me. A shaft of sunlight fell where she sat, making her hair, which was gathered loosely at her neck, glint red.

Unable to think of anything to say, I asked, 'Are you not cold, Leyla?'

The Circle had a central heating system which worked very well. The boiler room was behind Ferit's office. Edip had inherited his father's role as caretaker of the building and one of his duties was to collect the rubbish. He never failed at that. All of us knew that he took our bags of rubbish to his apartment and removed anything he could find a use for; because of that, we'd been separating our leftover food from our dry rubbish for years now. But he often forgot to light the boiler. In the autumn when the weather turned cold, Tulin would have to go and remind him. He would always light the boiler without complaint, then shut himself back inside his apartment, the door to which he never opened to anyone.

It was important that Leyla looked after herself, especially now, with so much sickness about. If her immune system got weak and she succumbed to the virus, I wouldn't be able to see her. I could not allow that to happen. 'Come and sit here, if you want,' I said, patting the empty space beside me. Motes of golden dust rose and danced in the air, falling on the sunlit wooden floor where Leyla sat.

'It's good like this, facing each other.'

So be it. 'The one beside me is a part; the one across is in my heart.' Mama used to say that, in Turkish even. It was now almost twenty years since she had died. I, a man whom children on the street called 'Grandpa', had still not come to terms with my mother's death. How many times had I picked up the phone to ask how she was doing? I still pictured her in her apartment filled with the smells and sounds of Istanbul.

Mama, Papa and their friends never became a part of Athens. Behind the closed doors of their new homes, they re-created the Istanbul that they remembered. When Mama heard the phone ring in the living room, she'd come out of the kitchen where she'd have been making peach torte for guests, wiping the sweat from her brow with the end of the gauze scarf tied around her head as she walked. 'Ha, is that you, Pericles *mou*?' she'd say in a weary voice, and then, settling herself in her rocking chair, she'd complain tearfully to me about her life, about this and that. She'd tell me how much she missed Papa, how upset she got when, opening her mouth to tell him something interesting she'd read in the newspaper, she saw that he wasn't in his usual chair.

As soon as I heard that Mama had been taken to hospital, I had taken the first flight to Athens. It was April 2002. Mama died while I was in the taxi to the hospital. I was neither beside her nor across from her while she was dying.

I saw Aunt Ismene's daughter Elena at the funeral. I hadn't

seen her in ages. She'd brought up two children since then. Her daughter was as tall as her and they had named her Ismene, as is the custom. The son was Stelio. Both of them had studied architecture. They were at Elena's side. The gathering after the funeral was held at their house. Ismene handed round glass bowls of *koliva* and Elena kept the cognac glasses topped up.

When Elena and I were on our own in a corner of the room, I thanked her for having organized everything.

'You took care of my mother and I of yours,' she replied.

Our mothers, on different sides of the same sea, had spent a lifetime missing us. Aunt Ismene had not come to Mama's funeral. She would not leave Istanbul. She could not leave it. She'd made halvah for Mama in her kitchen in Samatya, and she and her neighbour, Madam Ani, had distributed it to the neighbourhood tradesmen. Then she'd vanished. There was one last bowl of halvah left on her kitchen windowsill, but Aunt Ismene had disappeared.

Leyla noticed that I'd drifted off. 'What are you thinking about, Monsieur Pericles?'

'Ah, are we being formal again, Leyla?'

'Okay, sorry. It's going to take me a while to get used to.'

I was upset, but did not show it. What was it that would take her a while to get used to? Being friends with a man of my age? I would do my best not to dwell on it.

'May I ask you something... Pericles? Why did you leave this apartment empty for so many years?'

'How do you know it was empty?'

'The estate agent, Ferit, told me. He said you'd made it into an Airbnb more recently, but that before that it was empty.'

'Ferit knows why. He didn't tell you?'

Leyla tore off a piece of bagel and chewed on it for a

long time. As she chewed, she shook her head. I didn't know whether that meant yes or no. Finally, she swallowed down the bagel and took a big sip of tea.

'If it upsets you, let's not talk about it.'

'It's a long story, Leyla.'

When I said that, she gave me such a mischievous look. 'We have time.'

'It's actually not true that this apartment was unoccupied for long periods. Two elderly sisters lived here for many years. They were my mother's tenants. You see, a few years before you were born, vast swathes of this neighbourhood were demolished so that they could run the Tarlabasi Boulevard through here. Many beautiful buildings were torn down, a lot of them illegally. People were thrown out of their homes. Mama had been here on that night, and she felt very bad for two elderly women who'd been left homeless overnight. So she moved them in here. Some of this furniture belonged to them – the single bed and the wardrobe in the back room, for example.'

Leyla's eyes filled with tears. Through gritted teeth she muttered something like 'God damn them.'

'What's the matter? Have I said something to upset you?'

She waved her hand dismissively. 'No, no. It's just, I get all worked up when I hear stories like that, about how the residents of old Istanbul have been pushed out, their stories eradicated. I get too emotional sometimes. I'm sorry. Photos of old Istanbul feel so much more familiar to me, more recognizable, than the city I see today. I feel homesick for the Istanbul I never lived in. That's why I started looking for a house in Tarlabasi. Ever since I was a girl, I've wandered around here, believing that I'll find a clue left for me in a churchyard, a dark passage, in the ruins of a building. Do you know what I mean?'

She wiped her red-tipped nose with the back of her hand. Her eyes were shiny with tears. She looked so beautiful, I was speechless. I could not reply.

We were silent. I thought about what she'd said. So I was not the only one who still missed them. Leyla had chosen this old building hoping to find a passageway into that old world that she longed for. Thinking about The Circle, my thoughts went back to our looming eviction. They were going to tear down our walls – the walls that held so many stories – to make way for their ugly new building, all glass and concrete, a structure devoid of memory. As for us, the residents: what would remain? We were ghosts already, from a different time, hovering over a space that held our stories. It was too painful to think about, so I changed the subject.

'Are you a student?' I asked, pointing to the piles of books and notebooks lying on the table in the middle of the dining room.

From her cushion on the floor, she turned and looked at the table as if seeing it for the first time.

'Oh, those? Goodness. Me, a student, at my age?'

'What's wrong with your age? People do their postgraduate degrees and doctorates at your age.'

She frowned, then laughed. Her eyes lightened, making the yellow speckles more noticeable.

'I left university after my second year. I wasn't able to finish.'

She turned her head and stared out at the ruins of the building opposite. She must have given up when her father got sick. Like me, she was probably an only child. Poor girl.

With the tea glass in her hand, she stood up, sat on the wide sill of the window facing Temrin Hill Street, and drew her knees up to her stomach. She took a packet of cigarettes out from under the cushion. I was surprised. That evening at my house she'd not smoked at all.

'You don't mind, do you?'

She opened the window. The roar of the city had quieted throughout lockdown. Unbelievably, even the construction work had stopped.

'Let me have a cigarette too, then. Could you give me one?'

I stood up to take a cigarette from the packet she held out and lit it. Gazing out of the window, I inhaled the first puff. I used to smoke when I was with Ulker, but a lot of time had passed since then. The smoke clamped my ribs in a vice. I felt as if a bird was tearing chunks out of my lungs with its sharp beak. In my struggle not to cough, my face turned blood-red and just like when I'd smoked my very first cigarette at fourteen, after school, the ground began swirling beneath my feet.

Leyla had got up and gone into the kitchen. I was glad she hadn't seen me in that state. I moved to the couch.

Leyla talked from the kitchen. 'Bosphorus University. You asked which university. I was at Bosphorus University. I quit.' A pause. When did I ask her this? 'Those papers and notebooks you asked about, they're for my father's book.'

She put glasses of fresh tea on the table and came over to sit beside me. Leaning back against the wall, she sat cross-legged. She was next to me. By my side. My head was still spinning. I could hear her breathing. I took another drag of the cigarette.

'My father was a writer. Did I tell you that? He wrote detective novels and became quite famous. Especially in the last ten years.'

Interesting. So he'd been dealing with his cancer and writing at the same time. As soon as this thought occurred to me, I understood what Leyla was trying to say.

'Did you write his novels for him?'

Leyla nodded. Her cheeks reddened slightly. Reaching out, she stubbed her cigarette in the tea-glass saucer. I did not approve of that. I would have to bring her an ashtray from my apartment.

'Not all of them. When I was younger, he wrote them himself, of course. We didn't see each other then anyway. I was in Istanbul living with my mother's parents, as I told you. But in recent years, I mean after I moved in with him... And then he got sick.'

Interesting; I would ask her about that another time. I extinguished my cigarette in my tea saucer. An ashtray was required, as soon as possible. I could make her a gift of my blue Murano ashtray; it would suit her home very well.

'At first, I just made clean copies of Dad's handwritten notes. All his novels started in notebooks and were then typed up on the computer. By the time he got sick, I was so familiar with how it all worked, the detective-story formula, that I took over the writing. To start with we didn't say anything to the publishers, but later...'

She stopped. I turned and looked into her face. She looked back at me. Our faces were very close. Close enough for me to see the pale freckles on her little retroussé nose. Close enough to kiss those freckles. If our ages had been as close as our faces, I would have kissed her there and then, without any hesitation. I had kissed many women in the early stages of a relationship. What was the point in wasting time? And not once were my kisses rejected. But now I couldn't do it. The forty-five-year age gap had stolen my kiss and my courage. Is this what growing old meant? Getting stuck on obstacles?

'And then?'

Leyla laughed. She reached over, broke off another piece of bagel and spoke with her mouth full. Crumbs flew out of her mouth and onto her baggy black trousers.

'Later... umm... later, my writing... umm... began to sell better than his old books. One even broke a record. It was on the bestsellers shelf in bookshops for months.'

She told me its title, but it didn't ring a bell. Still, so as not to hurt her feelings, I said, 'Yes, I think I've seen that book in the shops.' She knew I was lying but didn't call me out on it, and that brought us a little closer. A warmth passed between us. I reached over and picked up a fragment of bagel that had fallen onto her lap and put it on a plate on the coffee table.

'In the three years of Dad's treatment, I wrote four books. Wait, I'll get them.'

She got up. Spraying crumbs everywhere, she walked barefoot across the wooden floor to the dresser with the screen doors. The shelf below the cups was lined with books. She took out four of them, as thick as bricks, and brought them to the couch. I recognized the colophon of a well-known publishing house. Her father's name was on the covers – even though every line of those novels had come from Leyla's hand? That was unfair.

'You should write your own books,' I said.

She didn't answer. As she opened the books one after the other, she moved closer to me. Our knees and arms were touching. Her hands and fingers brushed against mine as she leafed through the pages, pointing out lines. I wasn't listening to what she was saying. It did not occur to her that a man of my age couldn't read without his glasses. How nice. She'd forgotten about my age. I needed to forget about hers. My heart swelled with happiness.

Interrupting her, I said, 'Leyla, I'm serious. You have this talent, and as it turns out, I am writing my memoirs for Istos publishers. Could you assist me?'

She stared at me, open book in hand.

'Of course, you're busy now. Perhaps later, when you have some free time.'

'Nope,' she said with a smile. 'My dad's dead. What do I have to be busy with? There's just this one last novel, which'll be published as "the novel compiled from notes found after the death of the famous detective novelist Ufuk Duman". After that, I have no other work. Of course I'll help you. Anyway...' She squirmed uneasily, uncrossing and then recrossing her legs. 'Anyway, I'll need to find work at some point.'

Up to that moment I'd not considered how Leyla supported herself. I had seen that she didn't go anywhere in the daytime. After going shopping and coming back with her grocery trolley, she spent the rest of the day at home. No one came or went. It seemed she'd been spending her days writing this book. Did she live off the royalties from her father's books, I wondered? Even if they were bestsellers, how long could a person get by on royalties?

'Oh, excuse me. Do not misunderstand me, Monsieur Pericles. I mean Pericles. Do not think... If...' She blushed, looked straight ahead.

'I am offering you a job, Leyla. Do you think I'm writing my memoirs for free?'

She was still looking straight ahead, but I saw a smile spreading across her lips. She wanted to work with me too. She wanted to get to know me, to spend time with me. I was elated. Right there and then, I committed to giving her as a salary the rent from one of the apartments that I had inherited from my grandfather.

With no demurring, she raised her head and looked into my eyes. 'Agreed!'

She was a woman who knew the value of her work. Without getting up from where we were sitting on the couch, we shook hands. It seemed to me that Leyla's eyes lingered on my face, her hand in my hand, for a very long time.

# *Apelasis*

In 1964, thirty thousand Istanbul Greeks were condemned to exile. The decision was passed by parliament in a single night. Among those to be expelled were Papa and Uncle Stelio. We were in shock. It was true that in recent years many Greeks living in Turkey had been accused of treason and hastily banished across the border in a panic. We were aware of that. We also knew that a great injustice was being perpetrated. Those people forcibly deported were businessmen, owners of shops in Beyoglu, acquaintances, neighbours. After every expulsion the newspapers would write in one voice, as if by prearrangement, that the person who'd been thrown out of the country was a spy or a traitor who'd sent money to the Greek militia in Cyprus. Dragged off to a police station at night, roughed up and forced to sign a document confessing to their crime, these people were not interviewed. They were given no right to defend themselves. The paperwork was completed within forty-eight hours. The so-called guilty ones and their families, children studying in the same class as me, were forced to give up the city they had been born and raised in, their homes and their businesses, without even saying goodbye to those they were leaving behind.

Papa's face would turn pale when he read reports about friends he'd gone to school with having been thrown out of the country. His nerves were so frayed that eventually Mama forbade him from bringing Turkish newspapers into the house. The newspapers wrote that we Greeks were a corrupt tribe, devious, untrustworthy inheritors of Byzantine conspiracies, spies for Greece, sponsors of EOKA, the nationalist guerrillas in Cyprus. Papa did as Mama asked. He stopped bringing Turkish newspapers into the house. But every morning when he and I left the apartment to walk to Galatasaray, the first thing he did was stop by the newspaper stand on the corner of Balo Street and scan the headlines.

As I waited there, the same question always went through my head: if the editors knew Papa and Mama and me, would they still write like that about us? I wished I could sit them down and convince them. I even thought of knocking on the door of the *Cumhuriyet* newspaper, which was known for its relatively moderate editorials about Greeks, and saying, 'Look, we Istanbul Greeks have no ties with the Cyprus Greeks. Please, keep us separate from what is happening in Cyprus.'

I was too young and too idealistic to understand that the articles in the newspapers were all part of a larger plan: to prepare public opinion for what was to come, and to turn the Turkish population against us. We were paying the price for the rising tension in Cyprus.

'This will pass,' my good-hearted mama said. 'The newspapers will go mad for a bit and then they'll stop. The expulsions are isolated incidents. We don't belong to any committees or associations and we're not involved in politics.'

When she said that, she gave me a sideways look. I was in my first year of university; if anyone in the family was going to get tangled up in politics, it would be me. Youth activism and student movements were just taking off back then. But Mama had no reason to worry. I was not drawn to those movements. I went to my classes and to the labs, and I worked as an apprentice at the pharmacy run by Papa's friend Monsieur Dacat in the Hazzopulo Arcade. The rest of my time was spent wandering the streets with Ulker's ghost for company. She had left me the year before, gone to study at a university in Frankfurt. I still couldn't believe it. I kept hoping she would miss me too much and come back, that I would turn a corner and there'd she'd be, right in front of me.

The decision to expel all Istanbul Greeks who held Greek citizenship hit me harder than anyone. Of course I knew that Papa had a Greek passport, but that was an insignificant detail in the life of Istanbul Greeks like us, a mere stamp on a piece of paper. Papa had been born in Istanbul. He had Greek citizenship only because his father had immigrated to Istanbul from the Greek island of Andros in the years before the First World War. My grandfather had then married my grandmother, an Ottoman citizen, and the children of that marriage were given the father's citizenship. The Friendship Treaty signed by Turkey and Greece in 1930 granted Greeks the right to reside and set up businesses in Istanbul. Papa had never once used his Greek passport. He had never once set foot outside Istanbul. He was a true Politis, an Istanbul resident.

When we all gathered in our living room, I was furious. 'This can't be happening, Papa! How can they deport you? What do you have to do with Greece? When Greece takes a step back on the Cyprus issue, this ridiculous decision will be repealed. There are thousands of Greek citizens like you and Uncle Stelio in this city – what are they going to do, expel them all? Grannies, widows, tiny babies in nappies? Mama, say something, please. *Se parakalo.*'

It was the day after the decision had been made public in the *Official Gazette*, the journal that published all new government legislation. Having heard the news, I didn't go to university that day. It was an icy-cold morning in March and the Golden Horn had turned a milky-blue colour, the way it does before it snows.

The exiles were to be allowed only twenty kilos of baggage and two hundred lire of cash. They had to leave the country within forty-eight hours. We did not yet know that as they crossed the border they'd be forced to sign a document of confession, after which their right to sell any of their property in Turkey would be frozen, the money in their bank accounts confiscated. This was far worse than that terrible Septemvriana.

'Mama? Theia Ismene? Say something!'

Mama did not reply. She sighed, touching the tea service spread out on the dining-room table. She was worrying about what could fit into a suitcase weighing twenty kilos. The silver knives and forks, the tablecloth. Little did she did know that her silver tea service would be taken off her by customs control at the Turkish–Greek border.

Even though Mama was a Turkish citizen, she would go to Greece with Papa. She would not contemplate doing otherwise.

Aunt Ismene, sitting in an armchair by the window, was silent. Although her mother was Papa's aunt, her father was a Turkish citizen, from Imbros, so she was not on the list of deportees. Papa and Uncle Stelio were on the couch in front of the French balcony, drawing up a list of Turkish friends to whom they might be able to turn over their shops. Maybe in that way they could at least salvage some of their property.

Without taking her eyes from the window, Aunt Ismene said, 'I will stay in Istanbul until Elena finishes high school. After that, we will review our options.'

Uncle Stelio, pen in hand, stopped for a moment. This seemed to be a surprise to him too. But he quickly concealed his shock, nodded, and returned his attention to his list.

Mama walked over to the dining table and collapsed onto it, weeping. '*Ma ti les*, Ismene? What are you saying? For the love of God, how can you stay here? What will I do in Athens without you? Oh, what is happening to us? Why, oh why?'

I ran to Mama's side, put my hands on her trembling shoulders. I did not know what else to do. She did not hold my hand. She was bent over her silver cutlery service, crying.

In those days, for a woman of any community to have remained in Istanbul with her teenage daughter after her husband had been deported was extremely odd. Women went to Athens with their exiled husbands, as my mother did. My mother was hysterical. In an attempt to calm her, it was decided that after Elena finished high school and I finished university, we too would emigrate to Athens. I was a Turkish citizen by way of my mother. If I didn't leave the country immediately after graduation, I would be called up for military service. I promised that I would join them in Athens, and Aunt Ismene agreed with a nod of her head. Only then did Mama calm down.

The morning we saw them off, Sirkeci Train Station was packed with people. While those who were leaving either wept or stared out silently, those of us staying behind stood lined up on the platform in despair, trying to comfort our family members and friends as they hung out of the carriage windows. Whistles were blowing and hawkers selling sweets or bread rolls from trays balanced on their heads wandered through the crowd. Neither those of us on the platform nor those sitting in the carriages that would transport them to the border could believe this was happening.

This was surely all a bad dream. A huge misunderstanding, a ridiculous decision that would soon be rescinded. No Istanbulite with any conscience would accept their neighbour being thrown out of their house for no reason, surely? But that is where those toxic newspapers came in. Into the heads of the yogurt sellers and the bakers were dropped fabricated stories showing the Greeks to be an innately evil race.

We, the distraught crowd filling the station that cold March morning, understood nothing of this. We were people of this country. We were Istanbulites. We were Polites. Whatever our passports said, we were cosmopolitan citizens of Istanbul. Our roots were sunk deep in the city's soil, wrapped around its stones. We had found inspiration in the air we breathed; we had produced children, created businesses there, added our own souls to the soul of the city. And now we were being thrown out of our city, banished.

The word 'apelasis' rang in our ears. 'Apelasis' is one of those Greek words that kills several birds with one stone; with a single sound it makes a thousand heartstrings tremble. As I stood beside the train that had now loaded its cargo and was ready to depart, 'apelasis' described it all: 'thrown out', 'displaced', 'sent away', 'forced to leave one's home', 'driven out', 'exiled'.

Mama's entire torso was hanging out of the train window.

One of her hands was in mine, the other had grabbed Aunt Ismene. I was impatient for the train to get moving – I couldn't take much more of seeing her weep. Papa was in the seat next to the window, holding on to the skirt of Mama's coat. In his other hand was the spinach pie Aunt Ismene had made for their journey. Uncle Stelio was in the same compartment, but had already retreated behind his newspaper. Elena stood beside her mother on the platform, her head lowered. I thought she was crying, but her cheeks were dry. Years later, she told me she'd been so ashamed of what was happening that day that she couldn't look at anyone. She couldn't believe that humankind had sunk so low as to do this evil thing to each other.

Young people visiting the city from Buyukada and Burgaz Island, who had never set foot in Greece and were only in Beyoglu for the Easter celebrations, stared at the crowd on the train platform in bewilderment. Among them were kids I knew from school debates, girls I'd talked to on the island in summer. Children were weeping, aware that they were saying goodbye to their grannies and grandpas forever. Reminders and heartfelt wishes were exchanged. Some had left their plants with neighbours to be cared for; some had left cats, homes, jewellery.

Mama repeated the words she'd been saying for days. 'Ismene, you must come as soon as possible. Finish your school quickly, do you hear me, Elena? Once we've got our business settled, we'll all move into the same apartment building, with apartments one above the other. Be strong. Pericles *mou*, my son, my dear one, we are leaving Aunt Ismene and Elena in your care. Complete your degree in good heart. Your Papa will open a brand-new pharmacy in Athens and he will make you a partner. Study well, my dearest. Do not play around and lose a year. Let us be reunited as quickly as we can. Oh, Almighty God, ah, beloved Panagia, we do not question thy work, buy why is this happening to us?'

The train began to move, its wheels creaking on the track. Mama's black eyes grew wide and her lips retracted. Without letting go of our hands, she shouted, 'Pericles, do not forget your grandfather, my son! Go to the island from time to time to see how he is.'

How strange that in the last minutes my grandfather should come to her mind. Because Granddad was a Turkish citizen, he was staying in Istanbul. He did not leave his dark apartment in Buyukada, where he had shut himself away years ago, not even to say goodbye to my mother, his favourite child. I had not seen his face for many years. He had turned his back on us.

'Pericles, promise me that you will not neglect your grandfather.'

I nodded. '*Endaksi, Manoula*. Okay, Mama, you can rely on me.'

We were walking alongside the slowly moving train. Aunt Ismene and I were not the only ones who were holding fast to a loved one's hands. Everyone on the platform seeing their relatives off was doing the same. Hundreds of pairs of hands were reaching out of the windows, holding on to those left in the city, their one last hope. We, the scattering of people staying behind, were too weak, too defeated to hold on to them. Still, to comfort them we gave our promises. Of course they would be returning soon, and until then we would take care of their cats, their geraniums, their homes.

The train sped up, the whistle blew, the conductors closed the doors. One by one, hands were unclasped. The carriages leaving Sirkeci took with them our mothers, our

THE LAST APARTMENT IN ISTANBUL

fathers, our husbands, the sorrow of our people uprooted from their sacred land. One of the most painful things of all is to be driven away.

Aunt Ismene, Elena and I were left on the platform. Near us a lone woman, tall and slender, her grey hair gathered in a bun at her neck, stood like a statue. She was staring at the emptiness left by the departed train. The three of us must all have suspected the same thing: that she was going to throw herself onto the track. We all raced to her side, and Aunt Ismene grabbed her by the shoulders, pulled her back and held her in her arms.

'Do not give up, dear Anastasia. You have seen such days. Thanks to the blessed Panagia, your children are by your side. Irene's house, her cat are in your care. She too will return. The wheel of fortune spins, you know. Do not ever give up on yourself.'

The woman only held Aunt Ismene's hand. Her eyes were filled with tears. Looking at Elena and me, she tried to smile. We left the train station together, and while Aunt Ismene was putting the woman into a taxi, Elena whispered in my ear, 'That lady is an art teacher at the school in Fener. She hides the fact that she is Greek, uses a Turkish name.'

In spite of the rain, we joined the crowds crossing the Galata Bridge and walked to Karakoy. Life in the city was carrying on as normal. Nobody felt the absence of the thirty thousand people whom the train had taken away. Their consciences didn't burn. They were just working to put bread on their tables.

I looked at Elena. She had her hands in her overcoat pockets. She'd grown up so fast. At fifteen, she was already taller than Aunt Ismene. Her long, honey-coloured hair, parted in the middle, fell over her face as she walked. Because she wasn't wearing a hat, her little ears had turned red. At Karakoy we got on the underground funicular. Aunt Ismene was given a seat; Elena and I stood. None of us could look each other in the eye. The train leaving from Sirkeci had borne our sorrow away and we were left with shame. A huge chasm had opened inside us. Without them we were incomplete. If we looked into each other's eyes, we would bleed.

When we arrived home, we didn't take the lift but walked slowly up the spiral of marble stairs. Very slowly. Wordlessly, with downcast eyes, mother and daughter went into their apartment. I got out the key and opened the door of the apartment where I would now be living alone. The cat came running, rubbed against my legs, sniffed my shoes. For the first time in my life, it was just the two of us in that huge flat. It seemed stuffier than usual. I went into the living room with my shoes on. There was a silver soup spoon on the table. Mama had forgotten to pack it. I took it in my hand and stared at my reflection in its bowl, I had no idea for how long.

Less than two days later, we got the news. The state had confiscated the apartment where Aunt Ismene and Elena lived.

# Why Didn't I Know
# About All This?

'Why didn't I know about all this?'

Leyla was standing in the doorway, waving a sheaf of papers in the air. I ushered her in and closed the door behind us. She went into the living room with her house slippers on, sat down on the sofa next to the record player, and laid the papers in her lap. She was wearing a dark-green woollen dress that brought out the colour of her beautiful eyes.

'What? Why didn't you know what?'

'About this exile! This... what do you call it? This *apelasis* – in 1964. I had no idea such a thing happened. How could no one ever have told me?'

Hearing that, I smiled. Leyla's anger was real. Her eyes were wide and watery. I was pleased that this injustice, which I had long since become hardened to, had affected her so much.

'Almost nobody knows about the 1964 deportations, Leyla. It's not spoken of in Turkey or in Greece.'

'Why not? After I read your notes, I did some research. It said thirty thousand people left. Twelve thousand were Greek citizens and the other eighteen thousand were their families. Turkey used its own citizens as pawns. Banished them. Ninety-year-old grannies thrown out of the country as traitors. Thirty thousand Istanbulites! This city was finished that day. Now I understand.'

Moved by Leyla's anger, I stood up, lifted the needle on the record player and placed it on the Jacques Brel track that Leyla had chosen last time, a track that I had listened to continually ever since. Then I held out my hand to her. She looked at my outstretched hand in bewilderment. I sensed that never in her life had she been asked to dance.

Leyla's hesitation did not last long. Her eyes crinkled. She was smiling. She placed her tiny, cool hand in mine and stood up. 'Voir un ami pleurer' was playing. I put my free hand around her waist, sensing her embarrassment at her youthful inexperience. She didn't know what to do, where to step. Thank goodness I was an expert dancer. In two or three steps I managed to get her to give herself to the music. She stopped giggling. As Brel's song filled the room, the sounds of the street and the swaggering shouts receded. Here I was, twirling Leyla in my arms on the hundred-year-old wooden floor of our living room to songs that Markela and I used to dance to. If Markela's spirit was still wandering our building, I hope she forgave me.

When the B-side finished, the music stopped. The needle returned to its place. With a little bow, I kissed Leyla's hand. I was about to say, 'The past is in the past, Leyla. Your only life is in the present,' when we were interrupted by the doorbell. Someone was pressing it insistently; it rang five times as I was making my way to the door. It was Tulin who, when she saw Leyla, took two steps back. Then I appeared.

'Greetings, Tulin. Is everything all right? Is Berin well?'

Tulin looked Leyla over and cast a quick glance at the living room, where we'd been dancing. Then Tulin turned from Leyla to me.

'I am frightened, Monsieur Pericles. Did you hear the news? Another doctor died this morning. If they can't even keep doctors alive, what will happen to us?'

Her voice was tearful. I shook my head sadly. Men as strong as oaks were collapsing and dying. What could I say?

'What if something happens to Berin Hanim? They'll put her in an isolation ward and won't let me be with her. Old people suffocate and die in those wards. All alone.'

'Has something happened to Berin? Is that why you're here?'

'No. I stopped by Edip's apartment to ask him to turn up the heating – it's cold upstairs. While I was waiting for Edip to come back from the boiler room, I looked at Twitter. Another doctor passed away, and it's not even a week since the doctor from Chapa University Hospital died. So I wanted to ask your advice. They say it's possible to have an oxygen machine brought to your home. Since the morning I've been checking pharmacies online, but every single one has sold out. You're a pharmacist – you could find one for us, couldn't you?'

She spoke loudly, her voice echoing around the apartment. I began to suspect that Tulin was hiding something from me. Berin was a fit and healthy woman who didn't smoke, ate like a bird and wasn't on any medication. Her blood work looked as though it belonged to a healthy thirty-five-year-old woman and she was in her mid-seventies. I decided to go upstairs and see my friend for myself. With my writing and my conversations with Leyla, I had been neglecting her.

'Let me come up with you, Tulin. I will check Berin's blood pressure, and later I will look into the oxygen machines.'

As I made my way to the back room to get the blood-pressure monitor, Leyla caught up with me. Whispering so that Tulin wouldn't hear, she said, 'I don't think you should go.'

We went into the bedroom together. At least I had not neglected the housework in Vera's absence. I had made the bed, though dirty clothes were piling up as I'd not yet started on the laundry. I took the monitor out of the dresser drawer and turned to Leyla.

'Why not?'

'There must be a reason why Tulin's acting so strangely. What if Berin Hanim is sick?'

'Don't worry,' I said. 'Nothing will happen to me.'

I shouldn't have said that. She got very angry. Forgetting about Tulin, she raised her voice. Did I not read the news reports about all the people my age who were dying like flies in the hospitals? Just look at that successful doctor! Even his highly experienced students hadn't been able to save him. What did I mean, that nothing would happen to me? What kind of medical person was I? I was talking like those superficial conservative aunties who believed that educated people wouldn't get the virus!

I suppressed the smile that was spreading across my face, so that she wouldn't think I wasn't taking her seriously. I was so pleased that she was worried about me that I was even prepared to forget the 'people your age' designation.

'Leyla, Berin is a very close friend of mine. I will go up and reassure myself that she is all right. If necessary, I'll send Tulin to the pharmacy for some vitamin D to boost her immune system. Then I'll come back here. And anyway, Berin doesn't go out and no one comes to her apartment, so who could she have caught the virus from?'

'From Tulin, of course! You saw how she went down to tell

Edip to sort out the boiler without wearing a mask, and then she came to you. Totally irresponsible.'

We returned to the corridor. Leyla took a mask from the packet that she'd left on the console table in the entrance hall and put it on. She gave me one too, and handed a third one to Tulin. When Tulin hesitated, Leyla said, 'Either you put this on or we don't come upstairs.'

Tulin frowned. Behind my mask, I smiled. So she was coming upstairs too.

Leyla would not allow Tulin to get into the lift with me.

'You go up. Tulin and I will walk. Wait, let me wipe the handle. Use your handkerchief when you press the button.'

Our intimacy obviously surprised Tulin. A wave of anger passed across her face.

'I'm not sick. Berin Hanim is fine as well, as I told you. I just want to be prepared, that's all.'

I got into the lift. Through the mesh of the lift cage I could see Tulin and Leyla walking up the stairs with sullen faces. Tulin was huffing and puffing. Since she'd been staying at home so much recently, she'd put on quite a bit of weight. She was having trouble breathing. The lift shook as it came to a halt at the fifth floor. I opened the inside doors, pushed on the cage and stepped out onto the mosaic floor, which, up on this level, still looked glorious. The two bushy plants that Berin had placed at the entrance had grown large in the sunlight shining through the glass roof. In the shade of their leaves the dark red and blue strawberry design of the mosaics was very clear. I hoped Leyla would notice this beautiful feature.

Tulin had already gone inside. Leyla grumbled when Tulin reached to remove her mask. Suddenly she was a warrior. My Amazon.

We went into the living room. The whole place smelled of lavender. Berin was leafing through a book, and her tabby cat, Shadow, was running around the footed mirror, trying to catch her own reflection. Berin was surprised to see us.

'Welcome! What's happened? Is someone in the building sick? You have masks on.'

Then her gaze slipped to the blood-pressure monitor in my hand and she laughed.

'Oh, I see. Tulin's got you worried, has she? Because I coughed twice during the night, she's been looking for an oxygen machine since morning. I'm fine. There's nothing wrong with me.'

She did look good, in fact; slender and robust in a black turtleneck sweater and burgundy trousers, and she was even wearing a diamond brooch on her chest. She invited us to sit down on the navy-blue velvet armchairs on the Temrin Hill Street side. Berin's living room was full of sofa sets. Those on the Kaymakcalan Street side were draped in white sheets. They were for serious guests. We always sat on the smaller velvet set, near the dining room. To please Tulin, I took Berin's blood pressure. Typical for her, it was a little low: 90 over 60.

'Tulin, come over here. Sprinkle some cologne for Pericles and—?'

She looked at Leyla. Of course she knew who she was, but they had not been formally introduced.

Leyla was still standing. She waved. 'Hi. I'm Leyla. I live on the second floor.'

Perhaps because Berin nodded, or perhaps because she thought it unnecessary, Leyla did not say that she had bought the apartment from me, that she had been seeing me every day for the past week, that we had come to an agreement and that she was writing my book. No, she said none of that.

I looked at Berin. She had settled into her armchair beside the window like a queen.

Tulin returned with the famous lavender cologne from Rebul Pharmacy. She dabbed some onto our hands, then rubbed some onto her own wrists and put her palms over her face, inhaling the scent.

'Let me open the window. The room needs air, does it not, Monsieur Pericles? The most important thing is fresh air.'

'The most important thing is a mask,' grumbled Leyla from behind hers. Tulin had already removed hers. I took mine off as well and put it in my pocket.

Berin winked at me. Without waiting for my answer, Tulin opened first the net curtains and then the door of the French balcony that overlooked Kaymakcalan Street. Seagulls were shrieking somewhere. The curtains billowed in the breeze. Tulin tried to put a shawl she'd taken from the coatrack around Berin's shoulders.

'That's enough, Tulin! Do not treat me like a fragile baby, I beg you. I have not yet properly met this young woman.'

Tulin went muttering into the kitchen. Leyla sat opposite Berin on the sofa and I went to my usual armchair. Leyla could not take her eyes off the view. From Berin's apartment you could see all of Istanbul, from Maiden's Tower to the Golden Horn and out to the far islands. It was a bright, sparkling day. The wind was lightly stroking the surface of the sea and the winter sun was sprinkling its glitter across the open water. Thanks to lockdown, both sea and sky were deep blue, tranquil. People were saying that schools of dolphins were playing along the shore at Ortakoy.

Berin turned to Leyla, who was gazing out of the window with a dreamy expression on her face.

'So you are the young woman who bought Pericles's second-floor apartment. I am happy to finally meet you. It's important to have sensitive young people alongside us old folk in the struggle against the robbers who have set their eyes on our building.'

'I don't understand.'

'Did Pericles not tell you?'

'No… He didn't. Is there a problem?'

'I've not told her yet, Berin. Don't tire yourself. We can both explain the situation to Leyla later on.'

'What? What situation?'

Leyla looked angry, just as she had when she'd come to my apartment with my notes in her hands that morning.

Berin began explaining.

'The vultures have their sights on our building. They want to tear it down and replace it with a building of eighteen or twenty luxury apartments. Each of us would get two apartments or something like that. We have no intention of moving out, but the construction mafia has its eye on us. They want to demolish the building, no matter what. They are supposedly applying for a certificate of instability, but the buildings here are as stable as can be. Instead of pulling them down, they should restore them, should they not?'

Tulin brought in a tray laden with tea things. She had made me my favourite coffee with a dash of sugar. She'd put slices of cake on little plates. She handed Leyla a plate, put another on the tall table between Berin and me, and sat down beside Leyla on the sofa. Leyla looked uneasy but did not move away. She too had taken off her mask. I kept stealing glances at Leyla from over my coffee cup, which Berin noticed. I noted a slight upturn at the corner of Berin's mouth. She was laughing at the state of me.

Tulin spoke with her mouth full of cake.

'Up in the Taksim district they tore down buildings that were much older and more solid than ours. If the buildings round here were renovated, this area would be akin to Paris. That part of Taksim could have been like Venice, yet they razed it to the ground with bulldozers and diggers. Some of those buildings were very handsomely made. Next to them, The Circle has no chance. First they'll cut off our electricity and water, then they'll evict us, leaving us to go wherever we can.'

Leyla's eyebrows lowered further. I glared at Tulin to try and get her to shut up.

'But if they come for us here, they can't do anything, can they? I mean, we own three apartments. They can't demolish our homes without our consent. We'll tell them we're not leaving. Right?'

Leyla turned her questioning gaze first on me and then to Berin.

Berin gave her a reassuring smile. 'Do not worry your sweet soul about this just now, Leyla. Nothing has happened yet. Our lawyers are aware of the situation, so now all we can do is wait.' She tried to change the subject. 'Anyway, tell me a little about yourself. Where did you grow up? In Istanbul?'

Leyla's frown did not ease up. She gave me an inquiring look. It was only natural that she felt confused – angry, even. When I nodded in approval of Berin's last question, Leyla still didn't seem to relax much.

'I... I was born in Bodrum, but I suppose I grew up in Osmanbey, in the Sisli district, here in Istanbul. In a building a lot like this one. On Rumeli Avenue.'

Berin took a tiny sip of tea. 'Osmanbey is beautiful. Rumeli

Avenue was very fashionable at one time, though now it is noisy and chaotic. The backstreets are full of sweatshops. Do your parents still live there?'

Berin knew perfectly well that Leyla's father had died of stomach cancer.

'No,' said Leyla. She hadn't touched the cake on her plate. She too was taking tiny sips of her tea. 'That was my grandparents' home. I grew up with them.' She fell silent. Then, as if to answer the questions prompted by the silence, she hastily added, 'My mother was with us, of course. I was born in Bodrum, but then my father... It's a long story. My parents separated. My mother returned to Istanbul, moved in with my grandfather and grandmother, and took me with her. We lived there together until I left home.'

I looked at Leyla in surprise. We'd been meeting up every day for two weeks, but she hadn't told me any of this.

'Good,' said Berin. 'That's near here. You can easily go and visit them. What do they say about you living in this neighbourhood?'

Leyla shrugged and Berin did not pursue the matter. We spoke of Tarlabasi, of how this was not such a terrible place to live, of how, once you were known in the neighbourhood, you could relax. (This was not entirely true. We were often in danger. We had not told Leyla, but both of us knew that the construction mafia could cause us real harm if we didn't vacate our apartments and turn our building over to them. There was also the possibility of getting shot by accident, caught in the crossfire in one of the street battles waged by the mafia running illegal gambling houses. And because The Circle's front door didn't close properly, we were also vulnerable to thieves, who could strangle us as we slept in our beds. We lived in this neighbourhood despite knowing all of that. Since Leyla had bought an apartment here, she surely knew all of that too. Or did she?)

Just as we were resigning ourselves to small talk, Leyla said, 'I ran away from that house in Osmanbey.'

Berin's thinly drawn eyebrows rose in surprise. Leyla was smiling, lost in thought, as she stared out of the window between Berin and myself.

'I was nineteen years old. One evening I just slammed the door and left. I could not endure my family's hypocrisy. Back then, I didn't know that the world is founded on hypocrisy. I thought it was only my family who hid behind masks. It was snowing. I packed a backpack with my book, my notebook and a little money and traipsed through the snow for hours. Even though it was blizzarding, the snow hitting my face like a whip, I walked from Osmanbey to Taksim, then to Beyoglu, even as far as here. I was incredibly happy. I felt like I had achieved something great. Like a hero in a book, a freedom fighter. I booked into a cheap hotel here in Tarlabasi. I got into bed with my clothes on and slept the sleep of victors, as if I had conquered the world.'

She stopped. Her shoulders slumped. She looked at Berin. 'I haven't seen my mother or my grandmother since. There was another woman too, Kamile Hanim. She worked in our house for many years. I haven't seen her either.' Her voice cracked as she made that last comment. For some reason, I thought, it was clearly this Kamile Hanim she missed most.

Leyla continued to tell the story. It seemed that the mother, in her time, had also run away from that house in Osmanbey. When the mother was eighteen, she had moved into her lover's house in Bodrum. That was Leyla's writer father. Tulin nodded. There was no way she could fathom Leyla's story about booking into a hotel with just a couple of kurus in her backpack. But a love story – that she understood.

Her mother got pregnant right away, Leyla continued, which, according to Leyla, had been an attempt to trap her father. But things didn't turn out as her mother hoped. Leyla's father failed the class in fidelity. Eventually he went after an American woman, abandoned Bodrum, his daughter and his wife, and settled in Oregon. What could her mother do? She took Leyla by the arm and went back to Istanbul, to the house she'd run away from ten years earlier.

'So you and your mother share the same destiny,' Berin said.

Leyla's face darkened. 'What do you mean? I didn't run straight back to my father when I couldn't manage on my own.' Then suddenly she started laughing. 'Oh my God, that's exactly what I did! I might have tried to stand on my own two feet, but then I was right back at my father's side!'

Berin raised her tea glass in the air as if to say, 'You see?'

Leyla was shaking her head as she laughed. 'I'd never thought of it like that! You're right. How very strange. I always thought I'd gone to Oregon under my own steam, but without Dad, how would I have got a visa? Where would I have stayed when I first arrived?'

'Well, now that you've realized you have this in common with your mother, maybe you could contact her?' I noted that Berin was talking informally to Leyla now.

Leyla opened her mouth to say no but instead said dreamlike, 'Maybe. Maybe I will contact her.'

I was looking at Leyla in confusion. Oregon? America? Didn't her father die in Bodrum?

'Nope,' said Leyla, as if reading my thoughts. 'Dad stayed in America the whole time. I went to stay with him in Portland,

and that's where he died. After that, I came to Turkey to sell the house in Bodrum, and then suddenly I found myself here, at The Circle, on the streets I'd wandered all those years ago, when I ran away from home.'

Smiling brightly, she looked at each of us in turn.

'And you are very welcome here,' said Berin, with an equally bright smile. Even Tulin's face had softened; she was staring at Leyla with a mix of awe and curiosity.

The two of them bombarded Leyla with questions. Was Oregon pretty? Very. Were the people there cold? Definitely not. What work did Leyla do there? She worked in cafés, did babysitting, was a dog walker. What kind of job was that? A popular one. You had ten dogs on leads and took them for walks in the park. She helped her dad with his books. Did she come to Istanbul sometimes? No, never. Berin asked her grandfather's name. Leyla told her. He was a surgeon. He'd died a long time ago.

As they talked, my anger grew. I had told her about Mama's fits of jealousy, her raids on the pharmacy, the September Events when I'd lain trembling under the bed, the exile that had destroyed my family. She was ready to begin writing up from my notes the story of the day I met Ulker. I'd laid bare my weaknesses, my frailties. I'd even considered letting her read what I'd written about meeting Ulker again at the New Year's Eve party at Kemal's house. I had opened myself to her with all my heart so that she would know me and love me. And all along she'd been hiding herself from me.

I packed up my blood-pressure monitor and put it in its bag, then stood up. Leyla was in the middle of speaking. She was confused but also stood up and followed me to the door.

'Berin Hanim coughs at night. Should I buy some cough syrup?' Tulin asked.

'It is not necessary. Cut an onion in half and leave it near her head. Let her breathe that all night.'

'Do come again, Leyla,' Berin said, her voice very clear.

Shadow came to the entrance with us and walked into the kitchen with her tail held high. When Tulin poured cat food into a dish, she meowed. She wanted Berin to feed her. Leyla hurried to the living room and in a low voice said some final words to Berin. When she came back, she was smiling happily. Just as we were leaving, her eye was caught by the section of the living room on the Kaymakcalan side.

'May I ask one more thing? Is this living room the same size as yours and mine? It seems wider. It even fits a piano in. It couldn't be, but it is, isn't it?'

I didn't reply.

From the other side of the room, Berin called out. 'Come back another day and let's have a proper afternoon tea together in the dining room.'

I hadn't realized that Berin's ears were so sharp.

'As soon as I can. With pleasure.'

Once again, I remembered that jealousy was like a poison coursing through your veins. Nudging Leyla in the back, I left Berin's apartment, got in the lift and rode down to my apartment. I went inside and closed the door without waiting for Leyla. Besides, the telephone was ringing.

# 'Not a Minority, a Citizen!'

Two days after the train carrying Mama, Papa, Uncle Stelio and all the other Greeks who were being thrown out of Istanbul had left the station, the police rang Aunt Ismene's doorbell. The title deed to their apartment was in Uncle Stelio's name and the Turkish state was confiscating it.

On hearing noises from Aunt Ismene's flat, I went downstairs. The door was open. Two policemen – one young, the other middle-aged – had walked into Aunt Ismene's living room with their shoes on. They had their caps in their hands.

Seeing me at the door, Aunt Ismene looked relieved. 'Ah, come in, Pericles, my child. Gentlemen, Pericles will be my witness. You can ask him about it and he will tell you.' She sounded as if she were about to cry.

The police officers looked me up and down uninterestedly. The younger one was impatient. The one with thinning hair seemed more fatherly.

'What's happened? How can I help you?'

Aunt Ismene turned to me and spoke in Greek. 'Son, you talk to them – my Turkish isn't good enough. They're saying Stelio is from Greece. You tell them the truth, that his Greek citizenship is just a formality and he's no different from you or me. This is our home – are they going to throw us out of our home?'

'Speak Turkish! If you keep on like this, they'll send you and your son to Greece, so watch out. If you are a citizen, you will speak Turkish.'

The one with thinning hair was clearly not as fatherly as I'd thought. Aunt Ismene hung her head and sat down on the edge of the sofa. My Turkish was perfect, and even though I was only nineteen, I was taller than both of them. I looked them straight in the eye.

'This apartment belongs to Stelio Fotiadis. The Fotiadis family has lived in Istanbul for at least three generations. They pay their taxes. They are not involved in politics. You no doubt know of Stelio's toyshop in Hazzopulo Arcade, on the corner. Every child—'

The young policeman interrupted me. 'Don't bore us with this fairy tale, young man. You clearly know which members of the family you mentioned sent money to the Greek terrorists in Cyprus. We also have this information. Tell your mother she must leave this apartment within three days. Look what it says here about your darling toymaker.' The young police officer, clearly thinking I was Aunt Ismene's son, waved the papers he was holding in front of my face.

I read the document he shoved into my hand. Uncle Stelio, it said, had been exiled to protect the national security of Turkey. He was considered a traitor.

'See, he confessed. This is your husband's signature, is it not? Hey, lady, I'm talking to you.'

Aunt Ismene stood up, came over to me and looked at the spot the police officer was pointing to. I did not want her to read the document that Uncle Stelio had been forced to sign, but she saw his signature. She sighed and said in Turkish, 'They have chopped us into little pieces and made us into chicken feed.'

The policemen said nothing.

Aunt Ismene raised her head and looked at them. 'I will need a week to move my furniture out,' she said, her voice hoarse.

'According to the orders we've received, you must leave the furniture in the apartment,' said the middle-aged officer. 'You are permitted to take only what belongs to you personally.'

Aunt Ismene looked at the gap where the sideboard that had been smashed to pieces with an axe nine years earlier had stood, at the imprint on the ceiling from the chandelier that had been shattered with iron bars. She shrugged.

'This chestnut table and chairs were my dowry from Imbros. The bedroom furniture belongs to my daughter. You can have the rest.'

I found it strange that Aunt Ismene was negotiating with the police officers about her furniture. After receiving this painful news, surely she would forget about Elena's school and relocate to Athens?

But despite what I assumed, Aunt Ismene stayed in Istanbul, renting the ground floor of a two-storey, bay-windowed house in Samatya. The house belonged to Madam Ani, who lived on the top floor. She was Armenian and also on her own, and rented the flat to Aunt Ismene and Elena for a pittance. Into this flat they moved the dining table that seated twelve people (which took up more than half the space in the living room), Elena's books, the bedroom suite and all the bed linen she'd been able to save during the Events. The pair of them were squeezed into two small, dark back rooms. Aunt Ismene began to work as a nursing assistant at the Greek Hospital in Balikli. Elena had two more years at Zappeion, the Greek High School for Girls. Somehow, they would manage.

Papa's pharmacy remained ownerless for a while. When we tried to pursue this, doors were closed in our faces. All we were told was that 'all assets have been frozen until further notice'. Then one day, on my way home from university, I saw that a cheap pastry shop had opened where Papa's pharmacy had once stood. I braced myself for anger, maybe even a wave of despair, but when I looked inward, all I found was a deep, hollow numbness. It wasn't until years later that I understood: this was grief.

Uncle Stelio's toyshop was left empty for years, with the doors sealed up. The shop had been looted, the toys stolen. Even though the thick layer of grime on the windows made it almost impossible to see inside, I would still go into the arcade to look at a lead soldier left forgotten on the shelf. Weeds had sprouted in between the cobblestones of the arcade and the iron grille in front of the church door that opened into the arcade had been padlocked shut.

Whenever I found the time, I went to visit Aunt Ismene and Elena. I was continuing my apprenticeship at Monsieur Dacat's pharmacy. The Greek master apprentice had been exiled along with everyone else, but Monsieur Dacat himself, being Armenian, was still at work. I was going to train there until I graduated; after that, the pharmacy Papa had opened in the Nea Smyrni district of Athens awaited me.

When I visited Aunt Ismene, she would serve me tea at one end of the vast old dining table, while at the other end, Elena, scratching her head with a pencil, would be doing her homework. She had been awarded a scholarship to complete her high-school studies.

When I went one day in the summer of 1966, I was shocked

to learn that Elena wasn't living there any more. She'd gone to Athens to study law.

'What will you do here all by yourself, Aunt Ismene?'

I was actually more concerned about Mama than Aunt Ismene. In her letters, Mama wrote at length about how impatient she was for her friend to come to Athens. Things were slowly coming together for them. Any moment now they would be moving into their own apartment, having until that point been staying with relatives who'd taken them in. In less than a year I would be graduating from university, and Mama was sure that both Aunt Ismene and I would be joining them in the coming year. This prospect was keeping her going.

'What can I do, Pericles, my son? I will continue working, of course.'

I had thought that her work at the hospital, like her over-stuffed flat, was temporary. When she saw how surprised I was, she reached over the mountain of floury cookies and took my hand.

'I am fine. Don't worry.'

'You mean you're not going to Athens? What about Uncle Stelio?'

'Your Uncle Stelio is a grown man. He can take care of himself. Besides, Elena is with him now.'

And it was that evening, sitting at Aunt Ismene's tea table, that I decided I too would stay in Istanbul. We had not lost our home. Our apartment in The Circle belonged to Mama. If she ever wanted to see me, she could come to Turkey and stay there. A friend from university, Kemal, had suggested that the two of us open a pharmacy together after we graduated. We'd already seen a suitable place on Kurabiye Street. I could start again. And Ulker... Naturally, there was also Ulker. She had left me and gone to Germany, but she was due to finish university in less than a year. I was sure she would come back to Istanbul.

I was excited once again. My life's plan appeared before me; the pieces fell into place. I clasped Aunt Ismene's hand with both of mine.

'Then I will buy back your old apartment for you, Theia Ismene. It might not be possible straight away, but I will work very hard and I will get it back. I'm going to stay here too, in Poli, in Istanbul. I'm not going to Athens. We will be neighbours again.'

Aunt Ismene laughed. '*Trello paidi!* Crazy boy!' she said. She knew how hard it would be to buy back the apartment, no matter how much money I saved.

Our building – which around this time was renamed with its Turkish name 'Cember Apartment' ('The Circle') – had become quiet. Madam Elpiniki had closed her hat shop on the ground floor. Both Aunt Ismene's apartment and the apartment on the fourth floor had been empty for a long time. Tahsin, who had saved us all those years ago, had become the foreman of a company that procured marble for staircases and kitchen worktops, leaving Edip to act as The Circle's caretaker. A ghost-like young man lived on the top floor in the draper Yorgo's old apartment. We later heard that he was a writer. Whenever we met him on the stairs or at the front door, he would drop his head. We never knew what he ate, drank or did. I don't even remember his name now. He lived like a spirit in Yorgo's apartment for years and then one day, just as suddenly as he had appeared, he vanished. It was after this point that Berin and her husband bought the apartment.

The neighbourhood emptied out so much after the forcible exile of Istanbul's Greeks that at one point I thought Aunt Ismene and I were the only ones left of our community.

I had stopped going to church. The voices of the women who used to bring their chairs out onto the street and chat while they were preparing vegetables, the shouts of the children running from one end of Kaymakcalan Street to the other as they played hide-and-seek, the hopscotch lines chalked on the pavement – all of that had been wiped away. The hot yellow lights that I'd been accustomed to seeing behind curtains at night had now dimmed. The yogurt vendors, the hawkers selling vegetables from horse-drawn carts, and the scrap-iron dealers who stopped by houses with sacks on their backs now stood in the middle of the street, scratching their heads in confusion. No doubt they'd all been in favour of throwing out the innately evil tribe of Greeks who'd helped the terrorists in Cyprus, but they had not considered that those forced into exile would be the very same people they had talked to, done business with and forged deep connections with, day in, day out.

It was not just the name of our apartment building that had been changed, but also the foreign names of many districts and streets. At least the name of our street was Turkish, so they did not touch that. The Samatya neighbourhood became Kocamustafapasa. Every year when Elena, now a law student, came to visit her mother, she became angrier and angrier.

'This situation must be remedied. Justice must prevail. The apartment that my father bought with the sweat of his brow, the shop he paid taxes on without fail, they belong to him. What right do they have to freeze our assets? I'm not giving up. I have friends at university whose families are in the same situation and the day we finish our internships and take the bar exam, we're going to court. It won't be long now. We will get back our houses and our businesses.'

Whenever Elena talked like that, I bowed my head, feeling

guilty, like the survivor of a massacre. As soon as Elena sensed my survivor's guilt, she began to list all the things my family had lost. True, I wasn't one of those forced to leave Turkey with just a suitcase in hand, but had I forgotten my grandfather's pharmacy and the villa on the island that he'd had built with such attention to detail? My *yaya* had died of a broken heart. What was the difference between being dead and the life my grandfather was now living in his janitor's rooms on Buyukada? Had I forgotten the horrendous suffering we'd witnessed during the September Events?

Greece had turned Elena into a rebellious young woman, and the docility of Aunt Ismene and myself made her angry. Those of us who had remained behind were now prepared to put up with anything if that meant we could stay.

At one point, Aunt Ismene said, 'Elena *mou*, over there you have forgotten what it is to be a minority in this country.'

Eyes blazing, Elena was ready with an answer. 'You are not a minority. You are a citizen.'

For Elena, who had long since given up on Istanbul, nothing was more important than justice. She was ready to sacrifice her life to this court case. While Aunt Ismene went back and forth between the kitchen and the dining table, Elena lit cigarette after cigarette and went into great detail about the cases she and her friends were going to bring to court. Neither Elena nor the rest of us knew then that in the years to come Nejat and his men would buy and sell the property that the Greeks had been forced to leave behind and that, eventually, most of the buildings would be demolished, lost forever to bulldozers and boulevards.

# Hell is Within Us

Elena had been right to call my grandfather's place the 'janitor's rooms' – a description that strangely caught me off guard. Even I, his only grandchild left in Istanbul, hadn't been visiting him as often as I should. And yet Elena already knew how he was living on the island? I remembered Mama at the train window, her last words still echoing in my mind: 'Pericles, don't forget your grandfather!'

My *papou* was struggling on in his dank, dingy bedsit in the basement of an old villa on Buyukada. He was angry at the world. He had been a wealthy man, my grandfather, up until three years before I was born. His pharmacy had been in Istanbul's Tunel district, at the entrance to the beautiful Alvanopoulos Apartments. With the pastes he produced from sandalwood trees, the jasmine oil he extracted himself, and the special elixirs sent to him by an Indian jewel merchant living in Izmir, his pharmacy was more a place of healing than a dispensary. During the British administration of Istanbul at the end of the First World War, my grandfather also sold canned goods that had been smuggled into the country to the Englishmen living in the city. His rose and jasmine essential oils went on to become famous in Paris, and with the encouragement of a Levantine lady living there, he began doing business in France. During the first years of the Second World War his work continued without incident.

When his assistant Themis, whom he loved like a son, became engaged to his eldest daughter, Alexandra, he had a magnificent villa built on Buyukada. For his garden he ordered statues chiselled from pink and white marble and stone pools filled with gold fish. He was going to turn over his pharmacy in the city to his son-in-law, and he had bought a small two-storey building in the Kumsal neighbourhood of Buyukada for the pharmacy he would open on the island.

At the end of his first summer in Buyukada, his family was hit with the wealth tax. The pharmacy in the Tunel district went immediately. The small building in Kumsal was also sold for peanuts. When the fifteen-day grace period for paying the tax came to an end and my grandfather could not come up with the money (which amounted to one and a half times the value of all his properties and possessions), a soldier appeared at the door of the villa on Buyukada. Making no allowances for Papou's age – he was fifty-two that year – or health, the soldier threatened to send him and his son to a labour camp for non-Muslims in Askale. Hearing this, my uncle took the last crumbs of cash in his pockets, bought a ticket to Australia and fled. His twin sister, my aunt Kalliopi, followed him. The villa on Buyukada was sold. The wealth tax was paid. The only things they had left were a narrow, two-storey, stone house in the Cihangir district of Istanbul and the apartment in Kyklos Palace, which was in my mother's name.

They say that my *yaya* died of grief that winter, but actually she had consumption. She passed away in the sanatorium on Heybeli Island. After my mother and father were married, in a simple ceremony with no celebrations, my grandfather moved to Buyukada. He rented the basement floor of a dilapidated house on the hill leading up to the villa he'd built with such attention to detail, and lived there until he died. Not once did he come to Istanbul: not for my birth, not when Mama and Papa were being exiled, not to my wedding.

Once, at Markela's insistence, we visited my grandfather at his home on the island. We had not been married a year and Markela was in high spirits. There were no traces of her illness left at that point, or so we thought.

'The mimosa is in bloom – let's go and drink wine at the top of St George's Hill. It's Clean Monday, the beginning of Great Lent, so they'll be flying kites and cooking squid, mussels and shrimp up there. We can visit your *papou* as well.'

I thought I'd cured her. I took pride in this, which I tried not to show. My wife's family in Yenikoy praised me fulsomely. It was I who had rescued Markela from the deep well of depression; there would be no more hospital admissions, no more sessions with psychiatrists.

'You shouldn't be so modest, son-in-law,' said Markela's father.

Her mother clasped me in her neatly manicured hands, saying, 'Pericles, you have saved our daughter. You are our son now. Because of you, our Markela has come back to life. Ask of us whatever you desire.'

Her father immediately added, 'Why not move into an apartment in our building? You need only say the word and we will remove the tenant right away.'

This conversation was repeated each time we visited.

'You'll be right across from the sea, with a magnificent view of the Bosphorus from your balcony. Your spirits will be lifted, my children.'

Markela gave her parents a sweet smile in response. If she had wished, I would have moved to Yenikoy, but it was my wife who insisted that we stay in Beyoglu after we got married. That suited me, of course. I was able to walk to the pharmacy. At midday I would close up and return to The Circle. At that time Markela loved to cook. She and Rayiha would spend the morning in the kitchen preparing delicious dishes for me that she had learnt from her mother or from their cook, Janin. I would come home to find lunch ready on the table.

In those years Markela had energy for everything. She was always rushing around. She had the house whitewashed from top to bottom and the furniture that Mama and Papa had left repaired and polished. Her eyes glowed. As I raised the first forkful of food to my mouth, she would watch my face attentively. It was very important that I liked her food. For the first time in her life, she was the lady of the house. For the first time in her life, she had her independence. Perhaps that was why Markela was even keener to stay in The Circle than I was.

To Markela, who had grown up beside the Bosphorus, Beyoglu held a magical appeal. Her older sister had studied there, at Zappeion, the Greek High School for Girls, and Markela had gone to school out at Arnavutkoy, at the American College for Girls (though because of her illness, she never completed her studies). From what she had heard from her sister, Beyoglu was a magical place filled with chic shops, pubs, cinemas and nightclubs. At the time of our marriage, in the mid 1970s, no trace of that fun-loving Beyoglu remained, but Markela was stubborn and her family, knowing how sensitive she was, took great pains to give her what she wanted. They consented to her going to Tarlabasi as a bride, but they never missed an opportunity to repeat their offer of an apartment in Yenikoy.

The day Markela and I went to Buyukada to visit my grandfather, the weather was sparkling. It was Clean Monday, the start of Great Lent, and as was customary on that day, the islanders were flying kites off the top of St George's Hill. We disembarked the ferry hand in hand. It was the middle of March and both the market and the backstreets were empty. I gazed sadly at the café overlooking the terrace on the left-hand side of Clocktower Square. Like Uncle Stelio's toyshop, it lay derelict in the corner where it had been abandoned. The café owner, Kyra Panagiota, had been among those exiled in 1964. In the summers of my youth, whenever I walked past the café, I used to glance over at the poets and writers who frequented it, some of whom I was familiar with from the Beyoglu cafés like Baylan, Lebon and Garden of Paradise. Occasionally they would even recognize and greet me.

Markela knew the island like the palm of her hand. Her family had a three-storeyed wooden villa on Kadiyoran Hill Street, where, during the summer holidays, she and her two sisters used to be looked after by a nanny from Ethiopia. As we walked up the hill towards the Anadolu Club with our arms around each other, every nook and cranny gave rise to a memory that she related to me. She was full of energy. The island had pumped new life into my wife's heart and lungs. She gripped my hand and pulled me up the hill.

'Before we get the evening ferry back we must drop in on my nanny. She will like you so much! She won't believe that out of all us girls, it was me who caught the most handsome man. Although she didn't show it, Nanny loved me the most.'

'Your nanny is alive? And she still lives on the island?'

'Of course. She lives in an old wooden building on the Kumsal side. She's elderly now, just sits on her veranda and watches the comings and goings on the road. I haven't been able to travel to the island for many years, but... She's still alive, darling. If she'd died, we'd know.'

During the years when Markela had been in and out of hospital, her parents didn't come to the island. I understood. They needed to stay close to their daughter. Still, the state of the house shocked me when I first walked in. It had absorbed the dampness of the long winters and become mildewed. I had expected at least some maintenance of the garden, but the neglected space was now a forest. I kept forgetting how we, the Greeks of Istanbul, had lost everything, even the people who had once looked after our homes.

We weren't going to stay there overnight; we would return to the city in the evening.

'This summer we can open up the house and you and I can give it a good clean. Maybe your *papou* will come and live with us.'

Markela was still busy making plans when we reached my grandfather's house and pushed open the garden gate. His place looked out onto a small courtyard in the back garden, separate from the main building. We found him there, sitting beside the wall and picking through rice at a wooden table that had one leg shorter than the others. Not even a drop of sunlight fell into the courtyard. Markela put back on the blue coat she'd taken off while she was racing up the hill.

Papou raised his head and looked at us. He was wearing a dark-red, navy-blue and grey sleeveless jumper, leather slippers and beige socks. His face was unshaven. No light of recognition shone in his blue eyes. I visited him once a year because I had given my word to Mama at the train station, but I never stayed even half an hour with him. Visiting him always reminded me of Father Nektarios, and because I didn't want to think of the atrocities that had been wreaked upon the priest, my grandfather's friend, I avoided my grandfather. I was a bad person.

'Papou,' I said, 'it's me, Pericles. I've come to introduce you to my wife. This is Markela.'

My grandfather lowered his head over the rice he was picking through. Markela and I looked at each other. With my eyes I tried to say, 'See? I told you.' Because I knew it would be like this. Throughout my school years, Mama and I had come to this courtyard so many times and tried to talk to my grandfather, but he wouldn't even open the door to us. I'd told Markela all this every time she insisted that we invite my grandfather to our wedding. It was Markela who had expected something different. And now, it was she who pulled up a chair to the wobbly table and sat down.

'Kyrie Nikiforos, *harika poli*. I am very happy to finally meet you. We brought you some bagels and cheese pastries from the boat landing. They're still warm. With your permission, I will make us some coffee and we can eat together.'

A pungent smell of cat wee wafted over from the base of the wall. My grandfather stood up without saying anything, picked up the bowl of rice and went inside. Markela followed him. I sat on one of the tatty chairs beside the table and took in my grandfather's miserable surroundings. The courtyard was so dank that although it was winter, a couple of mosquitoes landed on my face. In one corner was a heap of wood scraps – no doubt picked up here and there to be used as kindling for the stove in winter – and some wire netting and steel rods. A tricycle was rusting away alongside them.

It was hard to picture this courtyard as it once had been, when my grandfather and Father Nektarios would set up their dinner table there and discuss life, destiny, God and the Holy Spirit while drinking red wine out of tumblers. They used to portion out the cornbread and sardines onto my plate too, and I would sit beside them and listen to their low voices. As the heat of the day withdrew, the courtyard would be suffused with the smell of earth and flowers. My grandfather had planted rosemary and lavender in two pots, one on either side of the door into the house. Street cats would gather round. The priest often praised the tranquil lifestyle of his friend. A good Christian showed their faith in God through humility and lack of greed. The Kingdom of God was not up in the sky, as was commonly thought, but inside us. Heaven was within us, and so was hell. A person who burnt with fear, doubt, envy or regret would find their hell on this earth. But a person who was satisfied with what they had, who was not consumed with ambition but was content with their life, was already living in heaven.

If Father Nektarios had known what was going to happen to him at the end of that summer, would he have described hell in that way?

I wanted to push those awful memories out of my mind. I wanted Markela to hurry back from the kitchen so that we could leave right away. But the two of them came into the courtyard, Grandfather in front, Markela behind, with cups of coffee in their hands. They'd not brought a plate for the bagels and pastries, so we opened the wax-paper wrapping out onto the dusty oilcloth that covered the table. My grandfather did not eat anything. Markela slurped her coffee and took only a few nibbles of her cheese pastry before putting it down, even though when we'd bought the pastries from the Greek bakery at the boat landing, she'd said, 'My mouth is watering. Put more than two in for me, please.'

'Kyrie Nikiforos, did you know that Pericles's pharmacy is doing very well? He extracts essential oils from flowers and makes pastes by pounding them with a mortar. You used to do that too, didn't you? He makes creams from that oil all the ladies are addicted to. Do you get news of your daughter? Their situation in Athens is improving. Pericles's father's pharmacy in Nea Smyrni is quite large. They're not living with their relatives any more. They've bought an apartment in Palaio Faliro...'

Markela was a courteous, thoughtful and naturally sensitive person. She did not say that my pharmacy was financed by her family's money. I would guess that she had no knowledge of my business dealings with Nejat.

My grandfather was mumbling something as he drank his coffee. Markela and I strained to hear what he was saying. Most of his teeth had fallen out, which may have been why he wasn't eating his bagel.

'Castles built on sand,' he was saying. 'They will destroy everything you build in this country. Like castles built on sand.'

'Don't talk like that, Papou,' I interjected. 'Turkey is changing. There are enlightened people here now. The new generation is open-minded. My Turkish friends and I protest against what is happening in Cyprus.'

Grandfather set his cup down noisily onto his saucer and gestured for us to leave. I looked away from him, not wanting to see the pain in his eyes. My gaze settled on the middle of the courtyard, where weeds had sprouted. I saw men with knives attacking Father Nektarios. It had been a heinous part of the September Events.

Grandfather had seen it too. He had lived it. They had made him watch the cruelty. First, they desecrated the holy icons which they had piled up in the middle of the church. Then they laid the priest on top of the filth and attempted to circumcise him.

Markela was looking at me. The smile had been erased from her pale face. She reached for her bag, which was hanging on the back of a chair. She was already wearing her coat.

'Get out of here!' said my grandfather. 'I don't want you here any longer. *Fygete! Fygete ap'do!* Get the hell out of here!'

His cheeks were flaming, his blue eyes glittering. He too was remembering. Remembering how his friend had been attacked by a mob of men in the middle of a church, and how he'd not been able to save him, had not been able to do anything, because he was too afraid. I was a painful reminder of his shame; he did not want me in his life.

Markela and I stood up. I took my wife's hand. It was ice-cold. We left the courtyard. Before turning the corner, I looked back at my grandfather one last time. He was standing up, leaning on the table. The bagels and pastries were as we had left them. He shooed me away again. 'Leave! *Fygete!*'

Hand in hand, Markela and I walked as far as Dilburnu without saying a word. Memories of the winter that had followed the Events flooded into my mind. We used to come to the island and Mama would bang on Grandfather's door; Papa would try to coax him out and I would cry. But he would not come. In time, the rosemary and lavender plants dried up and the cats stopped coming to the courtyard. Years passed. I tried to forget the whole thing. I had a beautiful wife and my whole life ahead of me.

Mimosa was blooming in the gardens surrounding the houses and along the roadside. The yellow flowers were very beautiful in the island's clear light. Markela didn't want to pick any. She didn't have the energy to climb St George's Hill. 'It's chilly and I'm cold, and the taverna won't be open now, in March. Let's take a carriage and go back to the boat landing,' she said. We found a carriage over by Lovers' Garden. I put my arm around her and she laid her head on my shoulder. Listening to the clip-clop of the horse's hooves and the sounds coming from the driver's mouth, we went down to the boat landing. I buried my face in Markela's beautiful hair and kissed the top of her head.

We took an earlier boat back to Istanbul than we'd planned. As the ferry approached Kinali Island, I remembered suddenly: Markela hadn't gone to visit her nanny.

'Forget it,' she said. 'She might be dead anyway. Or senile. She might not have recognized me.' She remained silent until we got to Istanbul.

My grandfather died two years later, in 1977, in the middle of summer. His landlord sent word. The funeral was held on Buyukada. Mama came from Athens. He was buried in Buyukada's Greek Cemetery on the outskirts of St George's. His wife's grave remained on Heybeli Island, so now they would lie facing each other across the water. I was in no state to deal with my grandfather's affairs that year. Markela's depression had recurred and I was forced to have her admitted to hospital. Nejat had starting coming to the pharmacy with alarming frequency, looking for a 'date rape' pill, Rohypnol, and various chemical stimulants. Our partnership was entering dangerous territory. The last thing I wanted to worry about was the death of my bad-tempered grandfather. I buried the memories of that awful night along with my grandfather. Such is the human condition: in order to continue living, one must sometimes forget the reality of the past.

# Pericles Efendi

I met Nejat while I was doing my military service in Ankara. I was a reserve officer in the medical corps. Nejat was a private. One night he was brought to the barracks infirmary unable to move his left side and with a temperature of forty degrees. The doctor in charge, Demir, used what we had in our medical supplies to try and bring down his fever, but Nejat was delirious, hallucinating and shouting out random, incomprehensible words. We needed to get him to a hospital urgently. Demir informed our superiors, but the decision was held up somewhere and somehow the paper authorizing the transfer of Private Nejat Canak wasn't signed.

Nejat spent the next two nights in the infirmary, during which time we came to hear a few things about him. He was a troublemaker. He had threatened his superior, which resulted in him being beaten up and forced to spend hours in the sun, breaking rocks. Demir suspected that Nejat was now suffering from a rare hereditary disease of the nervous system that had been triggered by the heat. I don't know how he managed to work that out, for even the doctors at the Military Medical Academy – where Nejat was eventually transferred – couldn't explain the partial paralysis he'd experienced. They called it sunstroke and sent him home for forty days of rest. I never ran into Nejat at the barracks again.

Three years after I was discharged from the army, Nejat found me at the pharmacy Kemal and I were running together. The two of us had set up the pharmacy as soon as we graduated. Kemal had managed it by himself while I did my military service, and then I took charge when he had to do his stint. Business wasn't bad. Turkish customers who trusted Greek pharmacists confided in me.

It was late afternoon, a Friday. We'd already locked the cash register and were preparing to close up. I recognized Nejat as soon he set foot inside the shop; when I saw him, I immediately headed for the area at the back. He was sporting a moustache with waxed ends, as was the fashion among right-wing men at that time, and it was obvious that the two young men who were pacing up and down Kurabiye Street had come with him. Right-wingers had always had a thorny relationship with Greeks; they believed all Greeks were communists and disseminated that falsehood widely. This visit did not augur well. It was 1971. The country was in a state of chaos and the military had recently issued its memorandum of March 12th, demanding that the prime minister bring to an end the anarchy and unrest that was plaguing Turkey. Incidents in Cyprus were also escalating. Nejat had not come into our shop by chance; he obviously had an agenda. I assumed he'd heard that one of us two pharmacists was a Rum – an Istanbul Greek – and had come to intimidate us. I didn't expect him to recognize me – he'd been delirious the last time we'd met – so I was surprised to hear my name from the other side of the curtain.

'Pericles Efendi, would ya come here a minute.'

My surprise turned to anger. 'Pericles Efendi' indeed! How dare he address me 'Efendi', as if I were a common yogurt seller he was summoning from the street?

Kemal understood the situation right away. 'Can I help you?' he said.

In the years since his discharge, Nejat had clearly become a real thug. I didn't want him to upset my partner, so I pulled back the curtain and came out.

'Good evening, Nejat. It's been a long time. How are you? Nothing wrong, I hope?'

He'd probably expected me to pretend not to recognize him. Surprise crossed his face like a shadow and I was reminded of how this 'Grey Wolf' had been in the infirmary, feverishly calling out for his darling mummy. I carried that image in my head from then on, which perhaps explains why I was never afraid of him, even though I knew he and his gang were responsible for all the dirty, immoral and illegal business that went on in our neighbourhood. He realized that too. Maybe the bond between us, which was based on a tacit understanding, had been established from the outset. We didn't see it like that back then. We were both too young and too arrogant to comprehend the intricate games of fate.

'Come outside and let's you and me have a little chat, Pericles Efendi.'

Kemal was agitated. I took off my white coat, and as I was hanging it up I put my hand on his shoulder. 'Nejat is a friend from the army, Kemal. I'll walk with him for a bit. You close up.'

The concern on my friend's face did not recede. Nejat's young heavies were now standing at the door, scowling through the glass.

We went out into Beyoglu and mingled with the crowds, Nejat and I in front, his bodyguards behind us. The avenue was gearing up for Friday evening. Men were gathering on the pavement and in front of the cinemas. Cars passed slowly on our left. Out of habit, I glanced at the tiny tables inside the narrow, train-like pastry shops. Most of them were half empty. A few elderly writers and poets were dotted in the cafés, stubbornly trying to keep the old Beyoglu places alive. Back then, I still held out hope that I might come across Ulker in a café or a pastry shop. She had not returned from Germany, or, if she had, she'd managed to evade me. It had been eight years since I'd last seen her.

When we were a sufficient distance from his bodyguards, Nejat spoke up.

'You said somethin' that night in the barracks. Somethin' about heredity.'

He thought I was the one who had diagnosed his illness. I played for time.

'You had a high fever, Nejat. You can't possibly remember.'

'Don't talk bullshit, Pericles Efendi. You know what I'm sayin'. You said the name of that illness that night.'

This illness had disabled his mother and eventually killed her. She had inherited it from her father. How had the doctor known his medical history at a glance, just like that?

'That wasn't me. It was Dr Demir.'

Nejat was so caught up in his own words that it took him a while to process what I'd said.

Enunciating each syllable carefully, but without raising my voice, I said, 'I am not the person who identified your sickness. I am a pharmacist. There was a doctor with me. You had a very high temperature. You cannot remember. It was he who identified your disease by name.'

Nejat stopped and turned towards me, his eyes flashing with anger. He put his hand on my chest and gave me a shove. 'What disease you talkin' about, buddy?'

Trying not to make it obvious, he glanced around for his bodyguards. I felt like laughing. In the middle of that bustling street we must have looked like Laurel and Hardy. Dark, stocky Nejat and tall, thin, fair Pericles. I was used to reading patients whose fear was masked by anger. I looked him straight in the eye. His boys must not know that he was sick. That was why he'd wanted to talk to me outside, on the crowded avenue.

I'd taken off my white coat when I'd left the pharmacy, but in my haste I'd forgotten my overcoat, and my head was hatless too. In those days few of us wore hats when we went out. We were letting our hair grow long. But it was April and the weather was cool. Hopefully we wouldn't be walking for very long, I thought. I was wearing only a shirt and a sleeveless jumper.

With the bodyguards trailing us, we went on to Galatasaray and stopped in front of the Church of Panagia. Nejat lit a cigarette but didn't offer me one. The boys waited at the entrance to Hazzopulo Arcade.

'Listen, you're gonna find that doctor.'

Demir had moved to Austria after finishing his military service. But when I told him that, Nejat growled threateningly. 'You're lyin', you bastard! What business does this doctor man have in Austria? Is he gonna work in a factory, shithead?'

I ignored him. His curses were just to impress his bodyguards, who were, at any rate, busy yelling lewd remarks at the Armenian girls going in and out of Hazzopulo Arcade. He could tell that I wasn't afraid of him. I took a slip of paper out of my pocket, wrote down Demir's surname and handed it to him. Demir was from Izmir, and some of his family members were Levantine. If Nejat didn't believe me, he could easily track down the family.

He threw down his cigarette, carefully ground out the butt with his round-toed, Cuban-heeled shoes, and put the paper in his pocket. He flashed a signal to his bodyguards and we began to walk back towards Taksim from Galatasaray. It had become quite dark. In the twilight, the street seemed very gloomy to me. It was now seven years since the deportations of 1964 and the shops that had been taken from us still stood empty. Their broken windows and dusty counters looked out at the crowds of sulky-faced men in shoddy clothes who'd recently begun hanging around the avenue. Some of the emptied-out buildings on the backstreets had been turned into cheap hotels. The cinemas were still in business; Yesilcam had not yet been defeated by television.

Nejat paid no attention to the changes on the avenue. He was busy cursing the entire medical profession. 'They killed my mutha. Do you know how many times they cut her open?'

I shook my head. I could imagine how much pain she'd endured. While Nejat continued his rant, arms and hands flailing, he was speaking in a voice so low that only I could hear.

'That doctor you call Demir, he knew what this disease was. I know he told you about it then. You two talked. Now you gotta find a medicine to make me well. If this disease does to me what it did to my mutha, you're gonna pay for it. D'ya hear me, Pericles Efendi?'

We turned into the street where our pharmacy was. Kemal was still inside. As soon as he saw us, he came to the door, his lips pale with anxiety. His concern made Nejat's hackles rise.

'If ya cross me, ya'll hear about it.'

The pharmacy was at the entrance of an old stone apartment building on Kurabiye Street. We had named it Kurabiye Pharmacy. Nejat looked at the sign and smirked. *Kurabiye* means 'biscuit' in Turkish. With his stubby finger he drew an imaginary '✚' on the wall. Kemal and I both understood that this was a reference to the sign of the cross, which had been painted on Greek buildings during the Events of 1955 to mark which ones were to be looted. Nejat's boys were too young to remember those days, but it was obvious from their appearance that they were more than ready for another Greek pillage. They chuckled unpleasantly. Then, walking behind Nejat, they disappeared in the direction of the French consulate.

Now that Nejat had me in his clutches, he was never going to let me go. I knew people like him. He was going to cause me a lot of grief – though it seemed he understood that I wasn't afraid of him. I might be able to use our cooperation to my advantage. I also sensed that my knowing about Nejat's illness was a possible trump card; I might be able to use it and have him take me under his thuggish wing.

I told Kemal that it might be time to dissolve our partnership. He was surprised, and rightly so. We were just at the beginning of our journey together. But from my silence he understood that this was about Nejat. He nodded. He wanted to go back to university and get his doctorate. The next time Nejat and his boys came to visit, the sole owner of Kurabiye Pharmacy was me, Pericles Efendi.

# Antidote for Grief

When I'd rushed after Tulin to check up on Berin, I'd forgotten to lock my door. The phone was still ringing inside my apartment. Leyla had gone down to hers and closed her door. Had she realized that I was angry with her? Had she considered that I might be jealous of her having confided in Berin? With these thoughts preoccupying me, it took me a while after I'd answered the phone to realize who was calling and what they wanted.

It was Elena on the other end. Stelio was coming to Istanbul. When I made no response, she felt the need to add that it was her son Stelio of whom she was speaking. Okay, madam, I'm not senile, I felt like saying. Her father Stelio, having passed from this earth years ago, was in no state to come to Istanbul. As I listened to Elena, my mood soured. She wasn't sure how long her son would be staying in Istanbul. Everyone was working from home now and because Stelio's work was done online anyway, there was no need for him to be in Athens. So he'd decided to realize a long-held dream of his – the dream of living in Istanbul. Could your son not come up with a more original dream, Elena? I wanted to say.

Elena, her voice scratchy from cigarettes, asked the question I'd been waiting for since the beginning of the conversation.

'If possible, I was hoping he might stay in our apartment. He would pay you rent, of course.'

'I've sold that apartment, Elena.'

Without giving her a chance to respond, I said that I was in the middle of some urgent work and hung up. Putting on my coat and hat, I went out onto the street. If that meant I was breaking the rules, let them be broken. If they caught me, they caught me. They could fine me. I couldn't care less.

I hurried out of the building. The street was deserted. Veli's coffeehouse on the corner had closed. The bakery was open but silent. I walked towards the church at a faster-than-normal pace. There were even more buildings wrapped in curtains of steel now. To the left, a beautiful three-storey building dating from the same period as ours had been emptied out. Its wooden shutters were dark; one was broken and dangled like a broken wing. Only on the ground floor was there seemingly still someone in residence, for through the open window came the sound of a television. Some idiot had again hung a rug out to dry on the fence surrounding the historic fountain in front of the church. And the paper-collector's cart was beside the wall as usual. I pulled the carpet down and threw it next to the paper-collector's dirty cart.

There wasn't a single person on the street. From between the buildings I caught a glimpse of the sky. It had rained earlier and the ground was shadowy and wet. The greyish daylight hurt my eyes and the smoke from houses heated with low-grade coal burnt my nostrils, but despite the gloom, it was good to be outside. I'd missed feeling the wind on my face, missed the dampness that made my bones ache, even missed the acrid smell of the rubbish that the street cats and dogs invariably scattered about.

Pulling my hat down over my face, I emerged onto Tarlabasi Boulevard and crossed it at the lights. No one was looking at anyone else's face. The shops were empty; the city was holding its breath. Everywhere was very dull. Although I was wearing my coat, I felt cold.

This Stelio had really picked his moment to come to Istanbul. Elena's son didn't even speak proper Turkish. If only his sister had been the one coming. Ismene, like the grandmother whose name she carried, was a clever girl. When Aunt Ismene disappeared all of a sudden, her granddaughter had come to Istanbul and stayed in the apartment in Samatya all by herself. She went to the Samatya police station so many times while she was there that she struck up a friendship with one of the officers and together they tried to track Aunt Ismene's movements, to no avail. It seemed that the earth had opened up and swallowed Aunt Ismene. Early one morning she had put her house in order and set off; she was never seen again in the neighbourhood. Her granddaughter waited a long time in that house for her *yaya*. At that time I said to her, 'Come, Ismene, my dear. You're my niece and the apartment below mine is yours. It's fully furnished. Your mother was born there, grew up there, and years ago I put the title deed in my name so that your *yaya* could live there. But that was not to be. Come and stay in it. A young girl like you will be bored in Samatya. It's not as dangerous as you think around here.'

Yes, I confess that I might have told Elena and her children back then that the apartment was theirs. In Athens, at the gathering at Elena's house after Mama's funeral, I had made extravagant promises. 'The apartment is empty now. Whenever you come to Istanbul, you must stay in your old home.' Mama's tenants, the two elderly Levantine sisters, had died a few years before Mama, within a couple of months of each other. During that time, Elena and her children would come to Istanbul often, squeezing into that small flat in Samatya.

Of their own accord, my feet took me to Yesilcam Street, erstwhile home of our once glorious film industry, full of production companies, editing studios, and coffeeshops frequented by directors and actors. For a while I just looked around me, unable to believe that this was where the old Emek cinema had once stood. Until very recently this street had been so vibrant; now it was nothing but a lightless corridor. To the right a dim wall stretched to Beyoglu Avenue. A dark ruin lay in the place of Bab Café, where Ulker and I had eaten hamburgers on the evening we first met. I stood in bewilderment, catching my breath. I had walked quickly and my legs ached. Staying at home for a long time did that to a person. With every step I took, my hip joints hurt.

Aside from a few people wandering about aimlessly with their hands in their pockets, there was no one around. I even missed the women of Abanoz Street, which used to be Beyoglu's red-light district. They would call out 'Hey, handsome, look over here!' as I walked past them on Sundays, hurrying to make the noon screening at the Cinepop or the Emek.

One night, after Ulker had deserted me for a second time, I was out drinking with Kemal when I had the misfortune of running into Nejat near the top of Abanoz Street. Back then, Nejat managed all the brothels and prostitutes on that street. He forced me to go into one of the brothels. (Though perhaps 'forced' is too strong a word. I was plastered. My wife had recently died. My lover had disappeared into thin air. Bulldozers were working day and night to raze my neighbourhood, my city, to the ground. My neighbours, whose houses had been demolished to make way for the grand new boulevard, had been left homeless. I was in a pitiful state.) I slept with a woman who was too elegant to be one of the Abanoz Street whores. Her name was Rose. She didn't want to remove her blouse while we were making love because her breasts were small and she was ashamed of them. By that point Nejat owed me, big time. He was in so much debt to me that even if he had my back for the rest of his life and treated me like a king, he would still never repay it. He was aware of that. He reserved Rose for me for the entire night. My body made the most of the opportunity; even though I wanted it to calm down so that I might fall into a deep sleep beside the woman, I just couldn't get enough of her soft curves and her warmth. In the morning I woke up curled like a child on a narrow, squeaky bed in a cold, shabby room with my head on Rose's puny breasts. She was stroking my hair, and my face was wet. I must have cried in my sleep. I extricated myself from her arms and climbed on top of her one last time. I didn't really want any more sex, but what else could I do? Making love to a woman you don't know is like licking a wound. It heals.

Returning from my memories to the quiet, ghostly Abanoz Street, I continued slowly home. The streets near Taksim had been hollowed out and were so cluttered with half-demolished buildings that they resembled a deadly labyrinth.

Back at The Circle, I telephoned Elena and told her that I would prepare a room for Stelio, and that he could come and stay with me for as long as he liked. 'I'll tell him,' Elena said, her voice cold. She was right to be cool, but I didn't try to make amends. We were both old and we both had the right to get angry. Stelio called a couple of hours later. He thanked me again and again for offering to put him up. He was very happy. Flights had stopped running, but Greek citizens were allowed to cross the border by car, so he was going to drive. When he got to Istanbul, he would self-isolate at a friend's house on Buyukada first, then come on to my place. If there was anything I wanted from Athens, he could bring it.

'Thank you, Stelio,' I said. 'Just come safely; that is all I want.'

There was nothing I wanted from Athens or from any other place on earth. The only thing that made me happy, that fulfilled me, was writing. The process of writing was helping me to re-live the past.

The fresh air and exercise had made me hungry. I opened the fridge. Leyla had bought big fat tomatoes. She didn't go out shopping any more either but ordered groceries for both of us online. The supermarket boy delivered both our orders to her apartment. With a mask on her face and surgical gloves on her hands, she took the bags from the boy and left them in her bathtub. The next day she wiped down every item with a vinegar solution and then brought them up to me. Before reaching my fridge, those tomatoes had been through all of that. Do I need to mention that I observed all her efforts with delight?

Tonight I would cook dinner for us both. Leyla had got me used to ordering in food from outside. For days now we'd been eating Chinese food, Japanese food, noodle dishes, pizza. Leyla picked up whatever we'd ordered from the front door with gloves on, threw it into a pre-heated oven and then brought it up to me. After we'd eaten, we'd look over my notes and work through the parts she hadn't been able to decipher. I would translate the notes I'd made in Greek and she would point out which sections still needed completing. Then she'd read out loud what she'd typed up on the computer. At first I'd found it strange to hear my story from her lips, but Leyla insisted we do it like that. That was how she'd written the book of her father's that had gone on to spend weeks on the bestsellers list. It was the only way to keep track of the rhythm of the narrative, she said. Anyway, poets always read their poems out loud. I acquiesced. As long as she was by my side, I would agree to anything. How wonderful it was! Leyla came to me of her own volition; she seemed happy to spend time with me. She told me that as soon as she'd completed her father's book, she would begin working on mine full-time.

I decided to make stuffed tomatoes – *gemista*, as we Istanbul Greeks call them, or 'dolma' in Turkish. Then I would invite Leyla to dinner. What did I need for the dolma? Onion, fresh mint, rice, spices. I had them all. I hadn't cooked that dish in years, but some things your never forget. We Istanbul Greeks don't put garlic in our *gemista*. Or sugar. I took the meatballs Vera had prepared out of the freezer. I smiled to myself, thinking how surprised Leyla would be at my cooking skills. I scooped out the tomatoes, set their tops to one side, stuffed them and arranged them in a roasting tray. Turks cook their dolma in pots, but we do them in the oven. I diced some potatoes to roast alongside them, splashed some olive oil over everything and put the tray in the oven. The smell made me forget my hunger.

While I was waiting for the stuffed tomatoes to cook, I went into my study. It had started raining and a flood of water clogged with branches and twigs was flowing down Temrin Hill Road into the streets of the poor, dilapidated Dolapdere neighbourhood. Istanbul had disappeared behind a grey curtain. Just the backdrop I needed. I picked up my pen and smoothed out the wrinkles in the pad of thin blue paper. As I wrote, I thought about Leyla more and more. As I thought about her, I wanted to write more and more. I found myself going round in a kind of circle. Maybe the antidote for grief was love.

# I Want to Go
# All the Way with You

Ulker and I got together the day after we met at Narmanli Han. I had not been able to hide the kitten she'd left with me from Mama and Papa. When I went back into my room after dinner, it jumped down from the bed and raced into the corridor. Mama almost stepped on it on her way between the kitchen and the pantry, but I got to it just in time. Standing at the pantry door with a container of lentils in her hand, Mama stared in surprise at the kitten nestling in the palm of my hand. Its eyes were grey, unclear, like a cloud. In anxious haste I tried to explain.

'I found it outside Herr Wagner's office, Manoula. All by itself. Its mother was killed by a car and nobody was looking after it. I couldn't bear to leave it like that in this cold weather so I brought it home. We can take care of it for a while, until it gets fatter, then we'll release it. Maybe we can take it to the fish market. They'll feed it there.'

I needn't have worried. Mama was already stroking its head, its black-and-white belly, with the tip of her finger. The kitten understood the situation and immediately crept across to Mama's palm and then onto her chest through the open neck of her sweater. Mama scratched its throat as it purred with happiness.

'Ah, where did you come from, *mikroula mou*, you darling little thing?'

I had not expected that, and was even more surprised the following morning when I saw Mama and Papa sitting side by side on the living room sofa, playing with the kitten. Papa, who always made such a fuss about getting to the pharmacy as early as possible every morning, was cuddled up on the sofa with Mama, watching the kitten having fun with a piece of string.

After I gave them an odd look, he said, 'Aristidis is going to open the pharmacy this morning. Don't wait for me.'

Papa and I used to leave the house together in the mornings and walk as far as the post office in Galatasaray, where he would turn towards Tunel and I would head for my school, Zografeion, across the street. Papa's old apprentice, Aristidis, was a grown man now and a partner in the pharmacy, but Papa still insisted on opening the pharmacy himself in the mornings.

It was a cool, bright day. Mama and Papa looked so young in the light coming in through the window on the Temrin Hill Street side that it seemed as if I really didn't know them at all. I had never before seen them loving a little creature, perhaps because I was an only child. Now they were sitting side by side on the sofa in front of the French balcony overlooking Kaymakcalan Street, laughing as they passed the kitten to and fro. As they tickled the kitten, their hands touched. They had slipped out of their parental role and become young.

'I fed it watered-down milk from a medicine dropper,' I explained, completely unnecessarily.

'You did well,' said Papa.

'My kind son,' said Mama, her eyes shining. Tired from the morning's play, the kitten had fallen asleep in Mama's palm. 'Themis, would you look at how adorable it is? Ah, *yavri mou.*'

She must have looked at me with a similarly loving gaze when I was a baby, as if she were witnessing a miracle. For a moment I wondered why they hadn't had a second child, but I was on my way out the door and had a thousand other things on my mind, including Ulker. I was almost eighteen by then, and didn't have much time to think about my parents. I left the house without waiting for Papa and set off for school. It only went on until noon on Saturdays.

After the fifth lesson, I went straight to the German Pub in Galatasaray. Ulker was not concerned that I hadn't brought the kitten.

'I knew it would be safe at your house,' she said.

We were sitting at one of the tables the pub had set out on the pavement. It was too cold to be sitting outside, but something kept us there. I didn't really want to walk through a door with Ulker, though I hadn't admitted that to myself yet. She was a Turkish girl and I was a Greek boy. Our Greek community was strict about cross-community dating. In the days that followed, I was reluctant to hold her hand while we were walking down the street or to go into one of the little pastry shops like Inci or Baylan with her, a reluctance that must have had its beginnings there at the German Pub.

We could see Galatasaray Square from where we sat. Sunshine was hitting the black hoods of the shared Chevrolet taxis to Harbiye, Kurtulus and Sisli as they waited in front of the school. Coming in the other direction, fully loaded 1950s Chevrolets were winding their way to Taksim. On Saturday afternoons people came to Beyoglu from all over

Istanbul, even from the islands, to shop, stroll around or go to the cinema. Those getting off ferries at Karakoy would take the underground funicular up to Beyoglu and from there disperse to all four corners of the city by bus or shared taxi.

At the table next to us four men who worked at the Swedish Consulate were telling stories and laughing loudly. They were wearing short-sleeved T-shirts, had red faces and obviously didn't feel the cold at all. Despite the frosty temperatures, we were drinking ice-cold beer. I looked at Ulker. She was trembling in her lightweight trench coat. I was seeing her in daylight for the first time. She had a light complexion and pale freckles. Her hair curled out from under the brown beret she was wearing, the light striking her curls and making them shine. I couldn't decide whether she was pretty or not. She wore glasses and was childlike. Compared with the Greek girls I'd danced with at the clubs in Elmadag or at school tea parties, she was short and a bit awkward. The hands clasping the fat beer mug were small but strong. Her nails were cut very short. I decided she couldn't be considered pretty. I drank my beer quickly, then finished off the fried potatoes that had come with it.

'Let's go to my house,' she said. 'We can listen to music and I'll make you some hot chocolate.'

That sounded appealing, maybe because I really was cold. While we were walking to Tunel Square, she again took my arm. I found an excuse to break away from her before we got to Papa's pharmacy, and hurried past Asmali Mescit without looking up. Finally we arrived at the place where we'd gone our separate ways the evening before, at the apartment building on the dark, narrow street that opened into Tunel Square. We climbed five flights of worn stairs, holding onto the old wooden bannisters as we went. Through open doors came the smell of onions, the sound of a woman scolding her child in Greek, a familiar melody being played on an out-of-tune piano. I was surprised that the film producer Sahin Dermanli lived in such a dilapidated apartment building with no lift.

Her sister Oya opened the door. She was very attractive, taller than Ulker, with green eyes. When you looked at Oya, you didn't wonder whether she was pretty or not. The answer was right there in front of you. Obvious. If the beautiful Oya thought it strange that her sister had brought a boy home, she didn't show it.

'I'm studying, so keep the noise down,' she said, wandering off into the darkness of the corridor.

Ulker hung her bag on the coatrack and took off her shoes, saying to me, 'Don't take your shoes off. The house is cold.' So I kept my beloved Cuban-heeled shoes on. While she went to the kitchen, I went to the bathroom. In a room at the end of a long corridor, Oya was indeed studying, bent over her books at a desk set in front of a window covered by a net curtain. Her backbone was prominent under her handknitted yellow sweater, her neck was long and white, and she'd gathered her hair into a bun on top of her head and fixed it with a pencil. She felt my gaze upon her and turned. Our eyes met. I looked down and hurried into the bathroom.

When I came out after having washed my hands in cold water, Oya had closed the door to her room. It was a small apartment compared with ours. Too small for the great film producer Sahin Dermanli. The girls shared a room at the end of the corridor, overlooking a courtyard. Years later, when I had found Ulker again, it was in this room that we would make love in the evenings. The bedroom next to theirs belonged to Sahin Dermanli and his wife Neriman. There was a small kitchen off the entrance hall, with another door opening onto the corridor. The other doors off the corridor were to the bathroom and a small toilet. It seemed Daddy Dermanli had spent all his money on the palatial apartment in Ayaspasha that he rented for his mistress, and considered this dilapidated apartment suitable for his wife and daughters. I was unimpressed.

In the kitchen, Ulker was standing in front of the stove stirring hot chocolate with a long spoon. She was wearing socks, and I noticed how thick her ankles were. Without saying anything, I went into the living room. Ulker came running after me and sat me down at a small table set against the wall on the left-hand side of the room. Throwing a couple of dry logs into the stove, she stirred the fire with a poker. The flames roared.

'Make yourself comfortable. I'll be right back.'

As I listened to the clatter coming from the kitchen, I glanced around the living room, which was dim even on that sparklingly bright day. For the first time in my life I was in the home of a Turkish family. They weren't a traditional family, of course. This was the home of a Yesilcam producer. There were huge rugs on the floor, armchairs, vases, tables, and a long, low, narrow sideboard that took up a whole wall, on top of which were whisky bottles, foreign cigarettes and photographs in silver frames. There was a marked mismatch between the wooden table beside the stove where Ulker had seated me and the rest of the room, which was like a filmset, obviously not lived in but designed to impress Sahin Dermanli's guests.

Ulker came out of the kitchen with a tray in her hands. She must have caught me surveying the room, for, gesturing at the small wooden table with her head, said, 'Mum, my sister and

I always sit there. It's close to the kitchen, easy to bring food, plates and everything. Mum comes home from the set really tired, so little things like that are important. And the stove is there. The front part doesn't get warm. That old apartment building beside Tunel Arcade blocks our sunlight. We roast chestnuts on the stove, listen to music, and if Mum's in a good mood, we dance.'

She poured foaming hot chocolate from the pot into my cup. After serving herself some too, she placed the pot with the remains of the cocoa in it on the stove. Immediately, the sweet smell of chocolate spread through the room.

'Shall we listen to a record?'

'Sure.'

She knelt down beside the record player, which was on top of the low sideboard, on the other side of the stove, chose a record and waved its cover in the air.

'Look! My dad brought this from France for me. It's not available in Turkey yet.'

It was a Platters album, a group that the girls at the school teas adored. When the record began to spin, Ulker settled herself on the rug. Her grey pleated skirt fanned out like a bell around her. The song that was playing was 'Only You', which would later become a staple at school teas and house parties. Ulker hung her head and closed her eyes, like the girls in Turkish films did. Her ponytail had come undone and her brown hair with the red highlights fell over her temples. I changed my mind. She was a pretty girl. She looked younger than she was. In a few years… She wouldn't be as pretty as her sister, but…

When the song ended, Ulker put the needle back to the beginning. The song's tempo was like a heartbeat, and my pulse had also sped up. I took a sip of hot cocoa. It was delicious. Ulker came over with her cup in her hand and sat down beside me on the divan, which was between the table and the wall. She took a tangerine from a bowl on the table, peeled it and dropped a segment into her mouth.

'Shall we go to a film tonight? At six thirty, say? *Monte Carlo* is on at the Konak. What do you think? Have you seen it? *The Geisha Boy* is also on. At the Atlas.'

'You're like the film page of a newspaper, Ulker. Anyway, it's Saturday night and we'll never get a ticket; they'll have sold out weeks ago.'

She handed me a segment of tangerine. 'Don't worry about that.'

She ate her tangerine without speaking. It was obvious that she expected a reply from me. When I didn't say anything, she got up and placed the peel on top of the stove. She opened the lid and stoked the fire. The smell of chocolate mingled with the clean, sweet smell of dried tangerine peel. The music had finished. She turned the record over. The B-side began to play. A tune that I would have made fun of if I'd been listening with my school friends made my heart ache there, in that corner of Ulker's living room.

Ulker turned towards me and took my hand. She leant her head on my shoulder. I didn't object. 'There's a box reserved for my dad in every cinema,' she murmured. 'We can't just go in there together, but we could find a seat in the main auditorium, then when the lights go out, we could slip in without the ushers seeing us.'

Hearing the word 'box', my body was immediately alert. It was possible that Ulker had said those last sentences knowingly. Back then, a box was where you took girls for heavy-petting sessions. Everyone knew that. I was seventeen years old and had never slept with anyone. Having realized that you could experience a degree of sexual pleasure alone, I had gratified myself. But I was dying to make love to a woman.

I lifted Ulker's head off my shoulder, removed her glasses and put them on the table in front of us. While the B-side track 'It Isn't Right' was playing, I took her face in my hands and kissed her on the lips. I knew how to kiss. I had kissed girls at school teas. Ulker didn't know how, but she learnt fast. Perhaps having grown up in Yesilcam was an advantage. Actually, there was no kissing in Yesilcam films, but the way she stroked my neck and my cheeks was skilful.

My heart was beating fast. I was both worried and excited by the thought that Oya might come out of the back room at any time. We were kissing insatiably. I couldn't touch any part of Ulker's body with my hands – my head put a stop to that – but kissing was free. Free and wonderful. We stopped, breathless, and looked at each other. Not knowing what to say, we began kissing again. Without her glasses, Ulker had become beautiful. Or I had gone crazy with desire. Ulker's mouth smelled of tangerines, like the room, and I caught the taste of cinnamon on her skin. Everything was so soft – her lips, the palms of her hands holding my head, her cheeks.

When the record-player needle started jumping, we pulled ourselves together. For a while we sat on the divan beside the table without moving. Then Ulker reached for her glasses and put them on. I shifted in my seat to stop the throbbing in my groin.

'I want to go all the way with you, Pericles.'

My throat was dry.

'Did you hear me?'

I nodded.

'I'm ready, and you're the one. I can tell.'

'Impossible.'

'Why?'

The dryness in my mouth had not abated.

'It's impossible. You see... Can we talk about this later? I mean, we've only just met each other.'

'Oh, you're going to play hard to get with me, like a girl!'

Hearing this, I took her in my arms with a sudden swift movement and kissed her more assertively. I bit her lips. I touched her nipples through her sweater. I was about to explode...

But then a thought came to my mind that made me get up, leaving her there on the divan, half lying down, while I flattened the wrinkles in my trousers with my hands. I was thinking about Mama. If she heard that I was going around with a Turkish girl, she would be so upset. 'We are a disgrace to the community,' she would say. She might even fly into a rage. Aunt Ismene would come upstairs, and while she tried to calm Mama down, she would mention so-and-so's pretty daughter to me. As if I didn't know the girls she listed from church, school debates and teas. Papa wouldn't say anything, but I knew he would be disappointed in me. I wouldn't be able to bear seeing the look on his face.

'I have other plans this evening, Ulker. We can go to a film next week if you like.'

She sat up and tucked her blouse back into her skirt. I felt good. Her cheeks were red, her eyes electric. She was smiling sweetly.

'Could you come on Monday after school, Pericles? I want to take you somewhere.'

The door to the back room opened. Oya's tall, thin silhouette appeared at the end of the corridor.

'What have you two been doing? You're so quiet.'

'We've not been doing anything. We listened to some music, drank hot chocolate. Pericles is leaving now anyway.'

Oya came and stood beside the coatrack. Her long, blond hair, released from its pencil, fell over her shoulders. She glanced at our swollen lips, dishevelled hair and slipped collars.

'Perfect. Ulker, go to the kitchen and make soup with the fish left over from yesterday. Mum will be exhausted when she gets home this evening. She's on four different sets today and one of them is at the airport. She won't have eaten anything but a sandwich the whole day, poor woman.'

'Why don't you make it?'

'I've got to study.'

Oya was aware that I couldn't take my eyes off her. She was obviously used to men staring at her like that. If she'd been the one wanting to go all the way with me, I wouldn't have cared that she was a Turk.

'My sister's going to be a lawyer. That's why she's studying so hard,' said Ulker with unmistakeable pride.

I thought she should be an actress. Their mother was probably equally beautiful. I had never imagined a Turkish family to be like that. How were they different from us? Their furniture didn't match. It was too big and more modern than the furniture in our houses. I could easily introduce Oya to my mother as my sweetheart. I would say she was Levantine, which would explain why she didn't speak Greek. It wouldn't enter Mama's mind that she was a Turk. I glanced over at the living room one last time, at the divan where I'd just been kissing Ulker, at the wooden table scattered with tangerine peel. Then, putting my grey tweed cap on my head, I bowed extravagantly to the girls. They both giggled. I was more pleased by Oya's giggles than Ulker's.

Leaving them, I went out into the Saturday evening liveliness of Beyoglu. The buildings were all lit up. People speaking different languages flowed past me, in cheerful spirits. The cafés Lebon and Markiz were full of intellectual, well-dressed people. I stared for a long time at a couple of pretty girls who were laughing as they passed me. I imagined following them and inviting them to Baylan. I inhaled the cold air and went into a cinema by myself. It was only after the film had begun that I realized the lead role was being played by Ulker's father's young mistress, the woman who lived in the enormous flat in Ayaspasha.

# The Leyla Incident

Hours later, hearing shouts coming from the street, I got up from the table. The dolma had finished cooking a long time ago; the automatic timer had turned off the oven. I'd been so engrossed in my writing that I'd committed cooking's cardinal sin: I'd put the dolma in the oven and left them. Food needs attention while it's cooking. The minute you ignore it, the food dries out, loses its flavour and becomes unpleasant, like a child raised without love. My dolma were angry with me. They'd sunk into the roasting tray. But there was at least a wonderful smell filling the apartment, and maybe Leyla wouldn't notice the effect my neglectfulness had had on the food. At any rate, it was now too late to invite Leyla up. While I'd been closeted in my study, I'd decided to write her a note on the back of an envelope, inviting her to lunch tomorrow. I would slip it under her door.

The sounds from the street got louder. It was probably another fight. I opened the door to the French balcony on the Kaymakcalan Street side. There was a crowd of twenty or thirty people in front of the bakery on the corner. Beneath the streetlight, they were pushing and shoving each other and yelling things. It had been a month since I'd seen any sort of gathering around here, and this scene was particularly odd, with almost everyone wearing masks, some of which would presumably end up slipping down onto chins or throats. I wondered what was happening. Just as I was retreating into an old, familiar fear, The Circle's front door opened and out came Tulin. I leant down for a closer look. With a large bag on her arm and the mask Leyla had given her on her face, she was walking towards the fractious crowd.

'Psst... Tulin...'

Edip's head appeared on the first-floor balcony. Instinctively, I stepped back behind the net curtain. I wasn't sure why. Maybe it was a reflex, something in Edip's tone of voice or the light in Tulin's face when she heard her name being called from the first floor. I could no longer make out what they were saying, what with the raised voices outside the bakery. If I ever give these notes to Leyla, she'll call me an 'unreliable narrator'. She uses terms like that; she's a bit of a show-off. She would prefer it if I said I was retreating behind the curtain because I was remembering the night when I was ten years old and Mama and I stared down from the balcony at the crowd of men with clubs in their hands. Much more meaningful.

Hearing Tulin's voice, I came out from behind the curtain and stood on the balcony. She was speaking to Edip.

'They just announced a weekend curfew. No one will be allowed out, so I'm off to buy bread. Lower your basket and I'll buy you a couple of loaves.'

Edip drew back his head. Catching sight of me on the balcony two floors up, Tulin was momentarily surprised, but she composed herself quickly.

'Monsieur Pericles, I'm getting you some bread, okay? Do

you need anything else? We'll be stuck at home all weekend now. It was announced on television a little while ago.'

As if we ever went anywhere anyway. I didn't even know what day it was. I'd stopped buying newspapers several years ago, and rarely turned on the television, but since I'd become so caught up in my writing, my connection to the outside world had been severed. I checked the growing number of Covid cases on Twitter and that was it. After thinking a bit, I realized that today was Friday, which meant the curfew would begin tonight. I checked my watch. It was 10.30 p.m. Tulin had said they'd announced the curfew just a short while ago. How long ago, I wondered? You could see why people were at each other's throats.

Just then, Edip's head reappeared. 'Don't go out into that crowd, Tulin! It's very dangerous. Don't you dare go out!'

Tulin bristled like a lion. 'Don't you worry.'

'Tulin!'

With a flirtatious wiggle of her body, Tulin joined the crowd outside the bakery. I closed the balcony door, musing: Could dear old Edip and Tulin become an item? Why not? They were both lonely souls, each craving connection. In each other's company perhaps they might find solace, or even a quiet solidarity. Isn't that after all, what we, the residents of this building – or indeed, of life itself – were seeking? A touch of connection, a simple sense of belonging.

The Circle had turned into quite an enjoyable place since the lockdown. And when Stelio was added to the mix... A dark cloud suddenly settled over me. When Stelio came... He would definitely fall in love with Leyla. I felt as though my insides were being twisted. I collapsed into the orange bergère. What if Leyla liked Stelio? She surely would like him. He was a good-natured, energetic young man. Not as young as Leyla but not as old as me. I suddenly wanted to cry, like a child whose toy had been taken from him.

With sudden decisiveness, I stood up, put on the oven gloves and took the dolma out of the oven. The tomatoes had shrivelled up and the tops of the potatoes were burnt. I spooned the lot onto a plate, returned the meatballs I'd been defrosting to the fridge, went downstairs and stuck the pages I'd just written in my scratchy, pharmacist's handwriting under Leyla's door. Then I picked up the plate of dolma, grabbed Berin's key off the nail and got into the lift. With the sleeve of my sweater I pressed the button for the fifth floor.

'Are you not a grown man? You're acting like a child. Why did you leave so suddenly this morning?' said Berin as soon as I opened her door.

I didn't know how she knew it was me and not Tulin, for she was sitting at the piano with her head bent over the keyboard. Every evening she played the piano, to keep her mildly arthritic fingers from getting worse. She turned on her stool. When she saw the plate in my hands, she smiled.

'Ah, things are serious. I see. Let's sit at the table. Tulin heard about the curfew so now she won't be back until midnight. She'll walk all the way to Beyoglu.'

That's what you think, I thought to myself. If Tulin wasn't at Edip's on the first floor right now, with her bagful of bread, my name wasn't Pericles.

Berin rose from the stool. She was wearing a pink quilted dressing gown. She took the plate from my hand. I was glad she'd not yet gone to bed.

The table was already laid for breakfast the next morning. Two plates, silver knives and forks, cloth napkins in napkin rings, placemats. This was how Berin liked it. She did not eat an evening meal but had Tulin lay the table for breakfast after afternoon tea. Taking a trivet from the sideboard, she placed it in the centre of the square table and put the plate of dolma on top. We sat across from each other.

'Since you cooked, let's eat. It smells delicious.'

She slipped the napkin onto her lap. It pleased me that she was ignoring one of her rules for me and eating this late. She served one tomato onto her plate and another onto mine.

'I googled your Leyla.'

I stopped with a forkful of food halfway to my mouth and stared at her, even though I was very hungry.

'I beg your pardon?'

'Why didn't we think of that earlier? We really are getting old, Pericles.'

'How? How did you do that?'

'I typed her name into Google, darling. You told me her father's last name was Duman, so I typed "Leyla Duman" and pressed the search button. What else would I have done?'

'Did anything come up?'

Berin laughed. She closed her eyes as she chewed. 'Your dolma is delicious,' she said. 'Health to your hands. It'll be a lucky woman who gets you.'

'Don't be funny, Berin,' I said sharply.

I hated myself for getting so angry, but for years now I'd stopped caring what others thought of me. I'd turned into a bad-tempered, impatient old man with no sense of humour. I pulled myself together.

'Thank you. It's my mother's recipe. I slightly overcooked it, unfortunately. I could teach Tulin how to make it for you.'

Berin waved her hand in the air, meaning 'Forget it.' We

laughed. Tulin was no chef. Even after all these years, she still cooked under Berin's supervision, following her instructions. Even Shadow didn't like Tulin preparing her food.

Berin dabbed the corner of her mouth with the napkin and set her fork down on the edge of her plate.

'What did I find? Bits and pieces of information. I did some detective work.'

'And?'

I had a feeling that something bad was going to come out. That this Leyla had lied to us. That she had no dead father, her money was dirty, she was using my apartment to launder the money. She had bewitched me, and here I was having her write my memoirs. A series of scenarios, each one darker than the last, flitted through my mind.

'About ten years ago, your Leyla became the subject of gossip in the media.'

Just as I'd thought. Or even worse. My heart constricted.

'Why was that?'

'It was nothing, darling. No reason to turn so pale.'

'Tell me, Berin! Don't drive me crazy!'

'I'm going to tell you, but you've become so sensitive that I'm not sure you'll be able to take it.'

I wasn't sure either.

'Didn't you just say it was nothing?'

'She had an affair with a well-known businessman.'

Was that it?

'I googled the man as well. He's since become extremely rich and is very tight with the government. If I tell you that he's in the textile business, you'll know who I mean. He owns several shopping malls in Bursa.'

'Is Leyla in trouble?'

Berin shook her head, took a potato from the plate.

'No. I don't think she's in trouble. It wasn't a major incident. Leyla's name still comes up in the archives of some newspapers. Some magazines. A few smart-alecky writers have tried to analyze the state of our society through the incident with Leyla, but no one has said anything meaningful.'

'What incident?'

'"What incident?"'

'You just referred to the incident with Leyla.'

'Oh, yes… This businessman was married – when he had the affair with Leyla, I mean. They claimed he took Leyla as a second wife in a religious marriage ceremony.'

'He married Leyla?'

I couldn't reconcile this idea at all. A Muslim businessman – and Leyla?

'If you don't believe me, see for yourself.'

Berin got up from the table and went to the living room. She handed me the tablet she'd left on the piano. I followed her, glancing at the window as I passed.

Against the dark night, Istanbul seemed brightly lit and strangely silent. The fight in front of the Kaymakcalan Street bakery had come to an end, or the noise of it didn't reach the fifth floor. At some point Mansur Bey had had double-glazed, aluminium-framed windows installed in their apartment. I lodged a complaint with the municipality, but I was ignored. There were planning regulations for old buildings like ours, and you couldn't simply change the frontage just because you felt like it. On several occasions, Nejat offered to waylay Mansur Bey on the street and rough him up, but I said it wasn't worth it for aluminium window frames. The windows of the fifth floor didn't attract attention anyway.

I suddenly felt very alone. Berin and I were like a couple of buoys stranded and forgotten in dark waters under a starless sky. We had no one left in Istanbul except our neighbours in this building.

I gazed dejectedly at the tablet Berin handed to me. There was a photo of Leyla on the screen, looking almost like a child. 'Don't read it,' Berin said. 'It's disgraceful. The businessman's wife created a huge fuss, went all out to try and shame our girl. It must have been after this that Leyla ran away and took refuge with her father. The businessman's wife was both an influential person and a vile individual. As public opinion began siding with the wife, Leyla didn't have a branch to cling to. This girl was a tart, the woman said, who had led her husband astray. With TV ratings in overdrive, she raced from one morning show to the next. She kicked up quite a storm.'

I looked at the tablet screen once more. Leyla was smiling at me. She was wearing a black hat and her red hair curled over her shoulders and arms. It was ten years ago. She'd lost a lot of weight in the interim. There was no trace now of that childlike robustness.

Berin continued filling me in. The businessman and his wife had a happy marriage now. They'd moved to a villa in Beykoz and had two sons. No one remembered Leyla any more. Since then, the man had probably changed his mistresses as often as he changed his underwear. He presumably married each of them in a religious ceremony, and then, saying, 'I divorce you', sent them away again. Who knew how heartbroken Leyla had been. She was still a university student back then. Maybe she'd even covered her hair for him, or the man had forced her to, knowing full well that this would infuriate her secular family. Then the son of a bitch had left her high and dry.

Whenever Berin got started on men's mistreatment of

women, she found it hard to stop. As I was putting the tablet down on the coffee table between us, I noticed how much Leyla resembled Ulker. I picked up the tablet again. Not the Ulker I'd found later on, but the Ulker of Narmanli Han, when I first met her. My heart almost stopped. What if...? Then I remembered Leyla's date of birth. 1990. I took a deep breath, put the tablet down.

'Pericles, my old friend, what's up with you? You're not looking well these days,' said Berin.

Berin knew about the women in my life. She knew about my first sexual experience. She'd heard from my own mouth my memories of making love to my Levantine sweetheart in Buyukada's Splendid Hotel. She'd known Markela personally, of course. Markela and I were already married when they bought the apartment on the fifth floor. When Mama, Aunt Ismene and I returned to The Circle after Markela's funeral, Berin and Tulin stopped by to offer their condolences. Mama gave them bowls of the *koliva* she'd made for Markela's soul. Berin knew most of my heart's secrets, but she didn't know about Ulker. For some reason I'd not been able to tell her about my first love, the greatest love of my life. When I talked about the old days, I carefully avoided the Ulker periods. That's why, in order to complete the story, I had to write it down.

I stood up.

'Goodness! What now? We were just having a chat. Pericles, I'm serious. You don't look well.'

'You keep the dolma, Berin. Tulin will eat them. I've just thought of something. I need to go home and get it done.'

I stuck my elbow out at Berin.

'What's this?'

'This is how it is now. I learnt it from Leyla.'

We bumped elbows. Berin laughed.

'You are clearly besotted, neighbour. May God grant you a happy ending.'

I collided with Tulin at the door. Her bag was full of bread; her eyes were shining. Instead of accusing me of being in love, Berin should be taking a look at Tulin's face.

I took the lift to the second floor. Bending down as far as I could, I checked under the door. Leyla had taken my pages of notes. I pressed my ear against the door. There was no sound. I returned to my own apartment. With the faces of Ulker and Leyla in my imagination, I fell into a deep and dreamless sleep.

# Garden of Paradise

Ulker had said, 'Come after school. I want to take you somewhere,' but once again, I had no intention of seeing her. Her fearlessness scared me. She was going to seduce me and then I'd be stuck with her. I could never be the one to take a Turkish girl's virginity. It would be a huge risk. I hadn't asked Ulker how old she was, but since she was in the last year of high school, she had to be seventeen. If her family came and banged on my family's door, my poor mama and papa would be on the receiving end of their accusations. 'Your son seduced our underaged daughter.' How would I get out of that? As if my being a Turkish girl's lover wasn't enough. No, I couldn't let that happen. I would not see her again. I would put her out of my mind.

When the bell rang at the end of the school day, I followed my two closest friends, Niko and Stefanos, to Baylan patisserie. They'd arranged to meet some girls from Zappeion, including Sofia. Sofia and her family had recently moved back to Istanbul from America. They'd fled to the States after the September Events, but now that things had settled down, they'd returned to Istanbul. Sofia had gone to middle school and high school in

America and was now at Zappeion. Her American education had been deemed inadequate, so she'd been put into the year below. Niko and Stefanos could think of nothing but Sofia.

'Mate, the girl is eighteen – say no more... She turned into a real American while she was there. You missed out on Saturday night, Pericles. You should have seen Sofia at the club. She wears these tight sweaters, dances with anyone who asks her. And when she dances, she's not like our girls with no touching. Does she touch! Cheek to cheek. *Yavri, yavri!* What a sweetheart. What a *yavri*.'

We walked all the way from Galatasaray to Taksim talking about Sofia's legs, her lips, her bottom, her carefree ways. It was a cloudy day but unexpectedly warm for November. A couple of blocks before Baylan, combs were taken out of back pockets, and in the windows of parked cars, brilliantined hair was smoothed back. Jacket collars were turned up. When we got to Baylan, my eyes were drawn to the billboard for the Atlas across the street advertising *The Geisha Boy*, one of the films Ulker had promised to get me into. Her father's box in the cinema came to my mind.

Niko pushed on the door into Baylan. We were about to go in.

'I'm not coming, guys,' I said, with one eye still on the Atlas.

Stefanos pulled my arm. 'Mate, are you nuts? At least get a look at Sofia's face. She's a kindred spirit. Mature.'

'Not today. There's something I have to do.'

I pulled away from Stefanos and turned back towards Galatasaray.

Niko came over to me. 'Mate, I know you're a bit of a James Dean character, but what is this uncivilized behaviour? You're going to a film, aren't you?'

I had to get away from my friends. 'No, I have something else I need to do.'

'Pericles, look, I need to tell you something. The girls love you, but they're spreading rumours about you always going to the cinema by yourself.'

'What? Why? What do they say?'

'They've seen you, fella. You've become hooked on Yesilcam films, watching those Turkish melodramas one after another.'

'What a joke.'

Niko was staring at a light-blue Chevrolet sports car on the road. 'Come inside with us,' he said. 'Maria will be there. And Niki. Don't you like Niki anymore?'

'Niki pays no attention to me.'

'She's just playing hard to get. The poor girl was pretty upset when she didn't see you at the club on Saturday. She'd come all the way from Cengelkoy to Elmadag on the ferry. She was so sweet. Even though she was sad, she still kept a smile on her face. If it was me, I'd ask Niki to be my girlfriend right away.'

I pictured Niki's tanned face. She resembled Audrey Hepburn, with her thin neck and her fiery, coal-black eyes. I felt not the slightest twinge of emotion.

'Ask her then,' I said jokingly, unsure whether I was addressing Niko or Stefanos. 'I'm off.'

Leaving them in front of Baylan, I mingled with the crowd. My long legs quickly covered the distance to Galatasaray. Ten minutes later I was in front of Germaniko. When she saw me, Ulker stood on her tiptoes and kissed my cheek, then took my hand in happiness and slung her school bag over her shoulder. She didn't look as if she'd ever doubted that I'd turn up.

'Where are we going?'

'To Paradise.'

She pulled me back onto the street. The clouds had darkened. Ulker was wearing a beige trench coat, but I wasn't wearing anything over my school jacket, nor had I brought an umbrella. I thought of using the rain as an excuse for going home. As we passed Papa's pharmacy, I dropped her hand. If this upset her, she didn't show it. I made something up and crossed the street so as not to be seen by my friends sitting in Baylan, then I slowed down in front of the Atlas.

'I think it's going to rain, Ulker.'

She didn't stop, even though I'd wanted to remind her about the box proposal. Despite all the decisions my head had made, my seventeen-year-old body was burning with fantasies about what might happen in that box. We wouldn't need to go all the way. There were various stages beyond kissing but still far from making love that would give my young body great pleasure.

'Are you hungry? Should we stop in at Krystal Bufe? Have you ever been? They make great hamburgers and they have a special sauce. It's delicious.'

Krystal Bufe had opened that year, and the queue in front of it stretched past the corner, as far as Tarlabasi. I'd never been, but if we were to go there together now, there would for sure be someone in the queue who recognized us.

'I'm not very hungry. Let's just get a bagel from the street.'

Actually, my stomach was growling. If we walked towards Elmadag I would get a salami sandwich, I decided. Familiar faces passed us right and left. Ulker greeted her acquaintances but didn't stop to talk. She was a true Yesilcam princess. As for me, I buried myself in the crowd, as far as my height would let me. Whenever I spotted someone I knew approaching, I quickly lowered my head.

We got to Taksim Square and Ulker grabbed my hand again in front of the Ankara Market. As we passed Pamuk Pharmacy, whose owner knew Papa, I lengthened my strides, not even slowing down for the shop next door, where I loved to rummage through the 45-rpm records and the foreign magazines. At the bus terminal we turned towards Gumussuyu. I suddenly began to suspect that she was taking me to the apartment of her father's mistress, that famous film star. What if she'd arranged for her father's mistress to leave the house for a few hours so that we could make love there? Was such a thing even possible? Of course not, but just the thought of it made me so excited I could hardly breathe. Was it because I'd be going to the famous star's house or because I'd be making love to Ulker there, on the star's bed? My hand was sweating as it held Ulker's tiny hand and my breathing didn't calm down until we got to where Ulker was taking us. 'Garden of Paradise' was written over the entrance.

Like everyone, I'd heard of the Garden of Paradise, but I'd never been there. Elderly, well-known writers and poets frequented it, as they did Baylan. It was an outdoor tea garden, and that day, no doubt because it was cold, there weren't many people there. The upper tier of its terrace of clean white pebbles was empty. One or two university students were studying at round, marble-topped tables. My eye was drawn to the lovers who were secretly embracing as they sat in wicker armchairs beneath white umbrellas in the private bowers along the edges. Ulker and I were the only customers of high-school age, and the waiters wandering between the wooden chairs with trays in their hands cast mocking glances at us. I wanted to get out of there as quickly as possible, but Ulker was talking to an elderly woman sitting alone at a table to the right of the coffee stove. The woman had a book in her hand and was drinking tea. Praying that Ulker wouldn't call me over and introduce us, I sat down at the first table I found.

A minute or two later, Ulker scampered over.

'Sorry I couldn't introduce you, but she doesn't like to be disturbed. Do you recognize her? She's a famous writer. She's written the scripts for several of Dad's films.'

I looked over at her out of the corner of my eye. She was wearing a woollen beret and was wrapped up in her coat. She'd returned to the book in her hand. Our tea arrived, along with some delicious pastries. The wind had picked up and the pages of the books the students were studying from were turning of their own accord. Ulker rubbed her hands together. She was cold.

'How's the kitten?'

'Good. It's a girl. My parents treat her like she's their new baby. They've named her Mitsy. She's having bread mixed into her milk now, and pretty soon my mother's going to start cooking liver for her.'

Ulker smiled dreamily and tugged at the curls falling across her forehead.

'So, did you mention me to your mother? I mentioned you to mine. She wants you to come over one day.'

'What did you say to her?'

'I didn't say anything, but Oya couldn't hold her tongue. As soon as Mum came home on Saturday evening, she spilled the beans.'

'What beans?' I said, more sharply than I'd intended.

The writer glanced up from her book. She had prominent cheekbones that spoke of a once beautiful face, and sad-looking, wide-set, black eyes.

Ulker didn't answer my question.

'Did you think about what I said?'

I stared at the writer. Was she listening to us? The woman smiled and lowered her eyes.

'I'm Greek, Ulker.'

'As if I didn't know! What does that have to do with what we're talking about?' She stopped, smiled mischievously. 'I don't think it's an obstacle. In that way, I mean.'

Seeing how serious I was, she stopped laughing and said, 'Look, my mother's family is Circassian. My grandmother and all her family were exiled from the Caucasus. They call it the second exodus. The journey here was miserable. When they first arrived, they lived in tents in Adapazari. My grandmother still remembers it.'

'It's not the same thing.'

'Why isn't it the same thing? If you're Greek, we're Circassian. Nobody's family is from here anyway. Everybody came from somewhere else. Also, don't forget, we live in Tunel Square. Our tailor, our greengrocer, our pharmacist, they're all Greeks. We deal with them every day. My grandmother lives on Rumeli Avenue. She buys all her stuff from Tanas, the delicatessen there. Big chocolate bars, Mozzarella cheese and everything... Actually, I think he's Armenian. Do you know if Tanas is Armenian? You know, the man with the delicatessen in the basement?'

I was nervously twirling the tea glass in my hand. Ulker's words had opened a wound inside me. I felt the pain, but I could not find the words to explain it to her. It wasn't a language issue. It was something that couldn't be articulated, even in my native tongue. Ulker's ignorance had touched a nerve. Armenian or Greek? To her, the difference was inconsequential; to her, the minorities were all one and the same. All the Greeks she knew were tradespeople. But what really hurt was her saying that everybody had come to

Istanbul from somewhere else, when, in fact, my mother's family had been in this city for seven generations. My paternal grandmother was from the oldest family in Fener. It was said that our family tree went back to the Byzantines. Without even thinking about it, Ulker had simply assumed that we couldn't be natives of Istanbul, that we must be foreigners.

But that wasn't the only thing that made me angry. She and I had nothing in common. There was nothing equal about the pain of her grandmother coming from the Caucasus and that of my *yaya*, who, unable to bear the agony and persecution, got tuberculosis and died. When Ulker and her mother were in a tram or when she was walking down the street with her sister, nobody ever grabbed her arm, pulled her around and said, as if they were spitting in her face, 'Citizen, Speak Turkish!' The ground beneath the feet of her film producer father was solid.

'Look, let me try to explain the inequality between us like this. If a Greek girl was sitting at that table next to us today with a Turkish boy, and the girl said to the boy what you said to me...'

I looked over at the writer. She was definitely listening to us from behind her book. I lowered my voice.

'Let's say the Greek girl said, "I want to go all the way with you" and the boy agreed. When the Greek girl's family learnt of it, they wouldn't be able to confront the boy's family, tell them that their son had deceived an underage adolescent, used her. If they went to the police, they'd be laughed at. No, don't interrupt, please. Let me finish what I'm saying. But if you and I get together, at your request and with your consent, and your father finds out about it and bangs on my family's door or goes to the police, if he declares that his daughter's honour has been compromised, there's no way we'd be able to defend ourselves. Is that clear?'

Ulker finished her tea and threw a lump of sugar into her mouth. 'I'm eighteen,' she said, as the sugar melted. 'I did two years at the Austrian School before coming to the German School in Year 7. I'll be nineteen in two months.'

She smiled victoriously, as if that was our problem and she had solved it. But she hadn't understood the real issue, the one that was making my gut ache. In despair, I looked at the university students sitting at the tables around us, the self-confident men and women holding hands. I imagined them in bed together. I imagined Ulker and myself in the same way. Those soft lips, the fingers that stroked the nape of my neck so expertly, were just a taster of the pleasure I'd experience when I had hold of her entire body.

Years later, after Ulker had studied philosophy in Germany and returned, she spoke to me once again about this conversation. 'I knew I was in a privileged position, so I was trying to erase the inequalities between us by looking for similarities. You resented that.' Then she hugged and kissed me. 'But I was so very much in love with you. What could I do?'

'I've fallen in love with you,' said the young Ulker at Garden of Paradise. Her eyes filled with tears. Despite the trembling hands and fluttering eyelashes, this time there was no trace of that Yesilcam posing. I reached across the round marble table, took her tiny hand and kissed her fingers, frozen from the cold. What else could I have done? The writer had put her book down on the table and was watching us like a film.

'Come on,' she said. 'Let's go for a wander around Asiyan. What do you say? Come on. Don't let me down.'

I paid our bill. Hand in hand, we jumped on a bus from Gumussuyu. The rain started as the bus was passing between Dolmabahce and Besiktas. I put my arm around Ulker and she leant her head on my shoulder. I held her hand as we gazed at the dark, choppy waters of the Bosphorus, at raindrops falling on the ferry boats carrying tired workers home, at the wings of wet seagulls. For the first time a girl had declared her love for me. I felt both powerful and responsible. We got off at Emirgan. At the point where the Bosphorus opens out towards the Black Sea, we stopped, embraced and kissed. The sudden deluge had emptied the streets. Sitting side by side on wicker stools beside a stove in a coffeehouse in Baltalimani, I touched Ulker's cold, damp knee under the low table, without the waiter or the handful of fishermen inside noticing. When she didn't make a sound, I slid my hand a little further up, stroked the inside of her thigh. Her skin was as soft as cream. She had taken off her fogged-up glasses and her beautiful hazel eyes looked straight into mine. For a moment I felt that I knew her, that she was familiar to me from way back in the past, from the beginning of time.

In the months that followed, I took Ulker in my arms and kissed her many times while we were walking in Taslik Park or on the slopes of Asiyan. Sitting under a tree, I would slide my hand under her skirt, feeling with my fingers for the first time a woman's warmth and wetness. But I could not go any further. After school, if it was good weather we'd sit at the Taslik Café with its magnificent view and sip fizzy drinks. If it was raining, we'd go to Lebon and sit among the elderly writers and poets. We would smoke cigarettes and drink cup after cup of coffee while we discussed books and films and dreams. But we never, ever talked about 'us' again. The winter of 1962 and spring of 1963 passed in this way. With Ulker. Somehow, I could never find the courage to give her what she wanted. Then, one day at the end of the summer, when I rang her doorbell, Ulker was no longer there.

# Lockdown

On the Saturday that lockdown began, Leyla came upstairs early. I'd put on one of Leonard Cohen's records and was making toast. I'd woken up before daybreak, taken a bath and had a long shave. The shirts and trousers that Vera had ironed were still hanging in rows in my wardrobe. I was on form. Writing about Ulker had energized me and given me focus, like an arrow heading for its target.

As for Leyla, it was obvious that she'd not slept. She took one look at my ironed shirt and trousers and said, 'You're dressed up very fancily. Are you going somewhere?'

Without waiting for an answer, she flopped down onto the sofa. I'd never seen her so tired. I recalled what Berin had found out about Leyla online. What if this girl was having clandestine night-time rendezvous with that businessman? What if the money for my apartment had come from him?

What awful things I was thinking. I went into the kitchen, took the bread out of the toaster and wrapped it in a cloth napkin. I put some olives, jam and butter on two plates, took them to the living room and placed them in the centre of the coffee table. From where she lay on the sofa, Leyla eyed my breakfast offering.

'We Greeks don't put on a huge spread at breakfast,' I explained. 'You have to wait until lunch for the big meal of the day.'

'I'm all for that.'

She sat up, leant over the table and popped an olive into her mouth. I brought out our coffee and handed her a napkin to spread across her lap. Since she was tired, I would spoil her. Perhaps she'd not even noticed my bad temper the day before. I didn't know whether to be happy or sorry about that. Had she simply put me down as a grumpy old man? At any rate, I had to be solicitous of her now. How did one behave solicitously? The music finished. I turned the record over again, to the A-side. For a while we listened to 'Suzanne', which I love, without speaking. When the song finished, Leyla yawned.

'I worked all night. Because of the lockdown, the publishers have decided to print Dad's book a month earlier than planned. Apparently there's been a rush on detective novels in the past month. I'm handing it in on Monday.'

I didn't say anything.

Pushing back the hair that had fallen over her face, she looked at me and laughed. 'Are you upset? This will be better. Once I've submitted Dad's novel, I'm going to dedicate all my time to your book.'

'Why would you think I was upset? I'm just angry that they treat you like a slave.'

She took off her slippers and brought her legs up under her. With the mug of coffee in her hand, she leant back. Her eyes had turned green in the light coming through the window on the Temrin Hill Street side. I recalled the photo I'd seen the previous night on Berin's tablet. The rosy-cheeked, smiling, child Leyla. Who knew how badly Leyla's heart had been broken by that scoundrel? Entice a nineteen-year-old girl into your bed, then throw her away when you get bored.

'You're scowling.'

'Not because of that.'

'No?'

She was smiling at me now. Looking at her pale face, her puffy eyes, her dishevelled hair, the blue, handknitted sweater wrapped around her thin body as if she were cold, something stirred within me. It was hard to pinpoint exactly what it was – a nameless emotion rippling quietly across my chest. Picking up the empty plates, I went to the kitchen, turned on the tap and waited beside the sink.

Leyla called out from the living room. 'What's up? Pericles?'

I was feeling a spark I hadn't felt in years, a warmth spreading through me, unexpected and consuming. I wasn't even sure the sensation was connected to Leyla. It seemed to emerge from the maze of my memory, something long-buried stirring awake. Maybe it was simply life force running through my veins again.

'You aren't having a heart attack or something, are you?'

Or maybe that was it.

Leyla was looking at me from the narrow doorway between the dining room and the kitchen. I turned to her and tried to smile.

'Are you all right, Pericles? Why is the tap running for no reason?'

Leyla put her empty coffee mug in the sink and turned off the tap.

'It's nothing. For a moment I felt... I mean...'

'What?'

She brought her face very close to mine. At this point, I

must put this in writing. I am a tall man. Despite my age, I was looking down at Leyla from a head taller. Leyla was a small woman, no more than 160 centimetres tall. Her shoulders were narrow, her hips wide, and her torso as slender as a stick. As we stood side by side next to the counter, I was pressing my hands on the edge of the kitchen sink and bending down. Meanwhile, she had to crane her neck quite a bit to see me close up. Once again, the gods had set the scene for me to kiss her, but then I caught a faint smell. It was coming from her stomach. Most probably she'd not been able to digest some raw onions. Who knew what she'd eaten the night before while Berin and I were feasting on dolma?

'Come, I want to show you something.'

Actually, I didn't know what I was going to show her. I just needed to change the subject. Like a child, she believed me.

We left the kitchen and walked to the end of the corridor. Guiding her gently between her shoulder blades, I nudged her into the dark room on the right, the one that overlooked the scrap-iron-filled back garden of the next-door building and the backs of the apartment buildings on the lower street. I turned on the overhead light and my nose filled with the scent of dust and wood, reminding me more of Mama than of Markela, even though this was the room Markela had shut herself up in for those last years.

Leyla must have understood that I was thinking about my mother, for she asked, 'Are you going to show me your mother's letters?'

That had not even crossed my mind, but I nodded and opened the wardrobe next to the window. The smell of Mama wafted out. When I married Markela and finally moved into Mama and Papa's bedroom, I hung all of Mama's clothes in this wardrobe. Until she died, I didn't touch so much as a button. Moths ate her sweaters and her leather shoes dried up. Two years after Mama's death, Vera could stand it no longer. 'Monsieur Pericles, there are a lot of people who'd be interested in buying the clothes in this wardrobe. Would you like me to sell them? You'll be keeping Madam Alexandra's memory alive. The camphor's not working any more, and the moths from this room are slipping out and making nests in your jackets and sweaters now too.'

Vera was fanatical about things that didn't get used. She would throw away a broom if it went unused for a season. I would scold her when I saw that she'd thrown away the plastic bags, string and rubber bands that I'd been saving in the pantry. We'd had our biggest row when, without asking me, she'd given a carpet sweeper to the scrap-iron dealer. It was true that I was a hoarder. Maybe I was no different from Edip, who filled Monsieur Panayiotis's apartment with cardboard boxes, bits of paper and bottle tops. Okay. But what was left to us other than our things? When even the memory of our presence had been erased from the city, was it too much to want to keep your cleaning implements? If I were to tell Leyla about that, she wouldn't even know what a carpet sweeper was. But it reminded me of Markela – I had grown accustomed to seeing it in her hand. That's why I sent Vera after the scrap-iron dealer to buy back the carpet sweeper.

To Vera's surprise, I gave her permission to sell Mama's clothes. 'Surprise' wasn't the word; she was overjoyed. I said I would give her half the money, but in the end she probably only brought me a third. If the young people paid the sort of money Vera claimed they did for second-hand clothes, Vera must have made a fortune from the sale she held in the apartment. Throughout the weekend young women and stylishly dressed kids came and went from The Circle, disappearing around the church corner carrying plastic bags filled with jackets, skirts and sweaters. I watched it all from the window of my apartment on the third floor. The wardrobe was emptied in one weekend. I prevented her only from taking the hats. At one point Vera had come to me saying a little gentleman from the National Broadcasting Company had asked about them, and had offered a high price. I chased her away with an umbrella in my hand.

The wardrobe was now full of hats and boxes.

Leyla had forgotten about her question and had plunged into the boxes. She was picking one hat up, putting on another, looking at herself in the mirror. None of them became her as they had become Mama. She wore most of them backwards anyway. I didn't interfere. I had emptied a full box of Mama's letters onto the single bed of my childhood. After Leyla tired of the hats, she sat beside me on the bed.

'I think it would be good to include a couple of these letters in your book.'

Leyla passed her hand over the envelopes spread out over the bedspread.

'Gosh, what a lot of letters your mother wrote to you!'

I nodded. 'She liked to write. My dear mama should have been an author. She would spend hours writing to me, to Aunt Ismene, to her friends here, her relatives in America.'

'And you are fulfilling her unfulfilled dream.'

'What do you mean?'

'You are writing a book now.'

I laughed. 'Not really. I'm only making notes. You're writing the book.'

She didn't say a word. She picked up one of the envelopes, opened it and looked at the faded black ink on the crinkly paper. Disappointed, she blurted out, 'Oh, but this is in Greek!'

'What did you think? That I spoke Turkish with my mother? Are you that much of a white Turk, Leyla?'

The words that came out of my mouth surprised me. I had heard the expression 'white Turk' from Berin, as shorthand for the urban, secular, modern Turkish elite, but this was the first time I'd used it myself.

Leyla flushed and dropped her head. 'You're right. I'm so sorry. I can be thoughtless sometimes. Forgive me.'

I reached out and took one of her hands. 'It's not important. Really. What I said was uncalled for. As you know, I'm of the generation that had to endure the hurt of the "Citizen, Speak Turkish" campaign.'

She nodded. She did not withdraw her hand from mine. 'We should write about that.'

'About what? The "Citizen, Speak Turkish" campaign?'

'Yes. About all the bad things. The ordinary bad things that are blind spots for white Turks like me. Because we can't see them, we continue doing them, reinforcing them. I think your book will be very important. It will wake people up.'

What a dreamer she was!

'Your mother's letters would play an important part in that. If only someone would translate them into Turkish – or English would do, then I could put them into Turkish.'

'Maybe we can do that.'

She looked at me with curiosity. Her beautiful eyes were shining. 'How? Would you do it?'

'No. I... I couldn't manage. But... a visitor is coming soon. You know about Aunt Ismene now, from my notes?'

She nodded. A shadow seemed to fall across her face.

'Her grandson, Stelio, is coming to Istanbul. He will

stay with me. Elena is my second cousin, so Stelio could be considered my nephew. I'm going to prepare this room for him. I was going to ask if you would help me.'

She was frowning. I explained that Stelio was coming by car and would self-isolate on Buyukada for two weeks first.

'He said he'd be very careful, Leyla. He's a sensitive boy.'

'We can't know that. It's men who are spreading this disease. They don't wear masks or wash their hands. Couldn't this Stelio find somewhere else to stay? I'm not happy about this.'

She was bristling again. I gathered up the letters to take to my study and stood up. Leyla didn't move. She remained sitting there, like a child, staring at the slippers on her feet.

'Come, Leyla. We'll ask Stelio to translate at least a few of the letters into English, as you wish. His Turkish isn't good, but I imagine his English is.'

Hearing that, she gave a little laugh. 'That's something, at least. He won't understand us when we speak Turkish to each other.'

I couldn't quite work out what she meant. With a bunch of Mama's letters in my hand, I stopped at the door of my childhood bedroom and looked at Leyla, who was stubbornly continuing to sit on the bed. She raised her head.

'The thing is, I just don't want a stranger coming here. We're working together so well now, and this Stelio will be an intrusion, he'll put a dampener on our productivity.'

When I heard that, I felt such overwhelming happiness that I turned off the light and went out into the corridor so that she wouldn't see the smile on my face. She followed me into my study.

'Sorry. I get childish sometimes. I'm a bit tired today.'

She looked at the pile of papers on my desk where I'd

put the letters and grabbed the notes I'd written early that morning.

'Are these new? See, you never tell me anything.'

'I wrote a bit when I woke up this morning.'

Standing up, she began to read them. Then, giggling, she looked up from the notes. 'Playing around in Asiyan, eh? Like they do in Turkish films. It seems Pericles's guilty pleasure was like a Yesilcam movie.'

Laughing, I shooed her out of my room.

'These notes are great! I'm going downstairs to write them up now. Dad's book will have to wait for a bit,' she said, walking to the door.

'There's an envelope here,' she called out. 'Somebody put it under the door. I'm leaving it on the console. I'll come up again in the evening. *Efharisto poli* for breakfast. Thank you very much.'

I walked to the end of the corridor, wondering who could have delivered an envelope on a lockdown day. Leyla had already gone down to her apartment with my notes in her hand and closed her door.

# Circle of Fortune

It was in 1974 that Nejat brought the cleaned-up title deed for Aunt Ismene's apartment to me in the pharmacy. Nejat's illness had not yet affected his ability to walk. His balance was still OK. He had the beginnings of a slight limp, which only I could see. That was all. His thick hair, which he oiled and slicked back, was still a shiny black. He was getting a paunch, but since he was short and stocky anyway, it wasn't that obvious.

Leaving his bodyguards at the door, he came into the pharmacy waving the title deed in his hand. One of my regular customers, Karin Hanim, who was waiting to have a bottle of cologne refilled, immediately dashed out, but Nejat didn't even notice her. He threw the deed onto the counter.

'What kind of title deed is this, Pericles Efendi? It made my mutha cry. Whatever. I fixed it. Here you are. Clean as a baby's bottom. We did every single thing, all the way up to the place where they record this business. The apartment is yours. Use it to the max. If anythin' goes wrong, we can fix it again. You won't forget this favour I've done you now.'

I would not forget. Nor would I forget the US dollars and

German marks I'd counted out into his hand for the past three years in order to get Uncle Stelio's deeded apartment put into my name. I had illegally prescribed him medicine to slow the progress of his disease. I had stuck penicillin injections into his buttocks and given him countless antibiotics so that he could try the alternative treatments he'd heard about from Demir. Thank goodness I'd not gone to jail for handing out those sleeping pills like sweets to his boys. Who knew how many women they'd knocked out with those. I didn't even want to think about what else they'd all done.

I thanked him. As was expected of me, I took Nejat and the boys to the restaurant next to the churchyard. I loaded the table for them and they ate as if they'd just come out of a famine. They got me drinking as well. We were celebrating the title deed. I'd closed the pharmacy in the middle of the day to do that for them. Since Kemal and I had parted ways, I'd been running it by myself. I couldn't even afford an apprentice. Besides, I didn't want anyone questioning all the medicine I was secretly giving Nejat. Everything I had went to Nejat anyway, so where would I have found the money for an apprentice or an assistant?

'I've got a project in mind, Pericles Efendi,' said Nejat once he'd filled his stomach.

A large bottle of raki had been consumed, and Nejat was slowly finishing up the last bit in his glass. He lit a cigarette and offered me one. I too lit up. A gardener was hoeing in the churchyard. It was March and behind the high wall of the consulate buildings the almond and plum trees were in blossom. One of Nejat's bodyguards had gone outside to sneeze. The other one followed him. Because he was afraid of catching a cold, Nejat always sent his boys away if one of them had a runny nose.

When we were alone, Nejat leant towards me over the dirty plates.

'I'm thinkin' of a nightclub.'

I nodded.

'A fancy place. Classy. Like a discotheque. With an American bar, a silver ball hangin' down from the ceiling, a reinforced dancefloor, neon lights, loudspeakers from Europe, dancers, performances. Huh? What d'ya say?'

What could I say? He was talking about the alcoholic drinks, the stage, the backstage equipment, this and that that he had come up with. I waited to see where I would be affected. Nejat certainly wasn't going to give me the title deed for the apartment on the second floor for the measly antibiotics, sleeping pills and cash I'd given him so far.

'What d'ya say about the basement floor of The Circle? There's lots of space. We could handle the boiler room. There's a separate door that opens onto the hill. It wouldn't bother the people livin' there. We'd put mufflin' on the walls for soundproofin'.'

So that was it. At that time, I was the chair of the homeowners' association for our half-empty building. Berin and her husband had not yet bought the fifth-floor apartment – the pale, silent young writer was still living there. Nejat had obtained the title deed to the fourth floor and a distant relative of his who had relocated from Sivas had moved in there with his large family. Throngs of children raced around the flat above me morning and night. Edip was below me. So that meant I was the only owner in the building, and only I could give permission for the nightclub.

'The place is yours, Nejat. Enjoy it.'

He clinked his almost empty raki glass with my more than half-full one.

'I wanna offer you a partnership, Pericles Efendi. It'll be a nightclub like in America. Ultra-modern. Society kids from Levent and Etiler will come and dance. Eh? What d'ya say? Nightlife is slidin' into Taksim now. I'm thinkin' 'bout somethin' like the Parisienne or Club 55. Let the feet of Turkish kids turn towards Taksim and Beyoglu. Your people ran away, but rich young Turkish kids can move into the houses your people left behind. Ten years ago this district of yours was like Paris: crowded streets, fancy, decorated buildings, angel statues, mosaics and all. Young folks today give importance to stuff like that. Some of 'em have seen Paris. They'll move in slowly. The insides of your houses are in good shape. They even have furniture, some of 'em. I don't know much about furniture and that, but if I brought an antiques dealer over and he did some valuations, we could all get rich.'

My people did not run away. They were exiled, thrown out of their homes. That furniture was smashed into pieces with axes, the glass shattered, and then it was repaired, patched up. It stayed upright with difficulty. Do not speak as if our people left the city of their own volition, Nejat. You have squatted on the property they left behind and now you want to make me a partner.

Oblivious to my rage, Nejat got to his feet. Christo, formerly a waiter at Baylan patisserie, rushed over to help him with his jacket. I too stood up. We went into the churchyard, where the gardener's wife was planting geraniums in pots. The roses wreathed around the grapevine were in bloom and the gardener was hoeing around their roots. We walked down the cobbled path and out onto the street. Nejat put his hand on my shoulder.

'I'm gonna come to The Circle tomorrow. We'll look over that basement together. You're a man of taste. You'll give us some ideas 'bout where to put the bar, the stage, what kind of wallpaper, all that shit. So goodbye for now. Think about a name too. Somethin' that fits our club. Not somethin' foreign soundin'. Somethin' modern but local, like us.'

Hearing that, I couldn't stop myself from laughing. His dreams were so ridiculous.

'If there is to be a nightclub in the basement of our building, Nejat, its name will have to be "Circle of Fortune".'

His hand was still on my shoulder. He only came up to my chin. He let out a sudden guffaw, a real deep-chested, childish guffaw. The bodyguards hurried over in consternation.

'I swear, Pericles Efendi, aren't you somethin'! Beneath that gentlemanly facade, what a rascal you are. "Circle of Fortune", ha! That's it, decided. I'm gonna get a neon sign made tomorrow. Boys, take a good look at this man. From this day on, Monsieur Pericles is my partner. Don't make him say nothin' twice, ya understand? Enough! Stop smirkin' like a pair of boiled sheep's heads. Scram! See ya tomorrow, partner. Circle of Fortune!'

Before Nejat turned towards Beyoglu and disappeared from sight, he hung an imaginary sign in the air. With his finger he showed me the colourful letters winking on the imaginary sign: 'Circle of Fortune'. It was comical seeing that poor excuse for a mafia thug acting like a child. Once again, the image of him in the barracks infirmary calling for his mummy came into my head. I smiled involuntarily. This new partnership was no bad thing for me. The Cyprus incidents had been escalating and in the previous month my pharmacy window had been smashed twice. Nejat and his boys could help me stay afloat in Istanbul. Being a partner in a nightclub wouldn't hurt me.

Since I'd closed the pharmacy at midday, I decided I'd

go and give Aunt Ismene the good news. I flagged down a taxi. It was a cool, clear afternoon. As the taxi crossed the bridge over the Golden Horn, I felt within me the stirrings of a happiness that I had repressed for a long time. Things were going to work out. Aunt Ismene would return to The Circle, to her home. Perhaps those who had been exiled would be allowed back, their assets released. The court cases that Elena and her friends had launched would be settled in our favour. Nejat could even buy back Papa's pharmacy. I had a good feeling inside. At that age I did not yet know that I should never, ever trust my feelings.

I got out of the taxi at the Greek Hospital. Three or four patients, wearing overcoats or wrapped in shawls and with woollen socks and slippers on their feet, were sitting on benches under the giant, thick-trunked trees in the hospital courtyard. With running strides, I dashed into the building via the double doors with tall windows that opened onto the garden and hurried up to the psychiatric ward where Aunt Ismene worked. I was young and my legs never tired. I took the stairs two at a time.

The white-coated guard sitting in the little cubicle in front of the locked doors to the psychiatric ward knew me. I used to come by every so often with special mixtures I'd made up for the hospital's faithful old pharmacist, and, anyway, our community of Istanbul Greeks was very depleted now and we all knew each other. Without questioning me, he came out of his cubicle, took a key from the pocket of his white coat, and unlocked the door. The high-ceilinged corridor and hardwood floors smelled of apple vinegar. I found Aunt Ismene, white cap on her head, in the third room on the left, giving some medicine to a patient lying on a bed set in front of a window overlooking the courtyard. This was a woman's ward with six or seven beds, but being a pharmacist I was able to stride confidently from one end of the ward to the other. Most of the beds were surrounded by worn pink curtains. When Aunt Ismene raised her head after taking the cup from the patient's hand and saw me there, she was surprised. In the months since I had last seen her, she seemed to have aged. Looking back now, I realize that she was only fifty-four or fifty-five at that point. She wasn't a widow, but she wore black, and the grey hair under her cap was cut short. She looked like a strict schoolmistress, no longer the young aunt of my childhood, pushing Elena in the pram as she chased up and down hills after my mother. Noticing this, my urge to make her happy intensified.

'Theia Ismene,' I said rather too loudly, forgetting about the patients behind their curtains, 'come and look at this.'

'Shhh, son. Don't shout. The patients are resting. How did you get in here, anyway, waving your arms around like that?'

I lowered my voice. 'Forget about that now, Aunt Ismene. Look what I've got.'

'Gracious! What is it, Pericles, my boy?'

She took the title deed from my hand, which was shaking with happiness and excitement. Putting on the glasses that hung from a chain around her neck, she read the document. For a long, long, overly long time she stared at the precious piece of paper. I felt the need to explain.

'This is the title deed to your apartment, Aunt Ismene. I finally got it. Don't you remember? I promised you I would, and I did it! Now you can come home again.'

Aunt Ismene touched my shoulder gently. She gave me back the title deed and began pushing the medicine cart through the ward. I followed her. Maybe she hadn't understood. Maybe she was too old. Ah, the arrogant presumptions of youth!

'This title deed is legal, perfectly legal, Theia Ismene. There's the right to sell, the right to reside. It's registered in my name. There's no outstanding tax. The state can't confiscate it. There's nothing left to worry about. You can come back to your home.'

Aunt Ismene drew back the pink curtain of the next bed and I found myself staring into the big brown eyes of a young woman propped up against the pillows of her bed. She was reading the book that was open on her lap. Her neck was pure white. I couldn't take my eyes off that neck. When I realized I was staring, I was embarrassed. She didn't seem to notice, but Aunt Ismene did. She glared at me. The young woman took her medicine, thanked Aunt Ismene and obediently drank some water. The small bedside table at her head was piled with books. When my curious gaze alighted on them, without saying anything she showed me the cover of the one she was reading. It was in English. Then, as now, I didn't know much English. Smiling evasively, I turned to Aunt Ismene.

Aunt Ismene wasn't really listening to me anymore. Eventually she said, 'Pericles, my son, I am happy in Samatya. I don't want to move anywhere at my age. That apartment is yours now. You can rent it out. In the future you will have children and they can live there. You can make it your daughter's dowry.'

I laughed at that.

'I swear, Aunt Ismene, you really are counting the chickens before they've hatched. Look at you, arranging a dowry for my daughter.'

I met the gaze of the young woman on the bed. With her long nose and pale, thin face, she looked like a woman out of a classical Greek painting. There was something noble about her. I wondered who she was. I'd never seen her anywhere, even though she had to be about my age. She wasn't one of the Greek girls I'd met at school teas, church, weddings, or picnics on Buyukada. I looked at her again. Did I know her?

'Hello,' I said quietly.

Her face was still, as if it had been dipped in wax. It was hard to believe she was in a psychiatric ward. She was so calm.

'Hello.'

Pushing her cart full of medicines, syringes and syrups, Aunt Ismene left the ward. I raced after her. I could see that she was not going to change her mind about the apartment. I was angry. I wanted to tell her everything I'd endured to return the apartment to her. But she was an eccentric woman. She was not going to listen to me. I would bring up the subject another time. For now I wanted her thoughts about the young woman in the ward.

'She is not for you. Put her out of your mind,' she said.

'I've never seen her before. Is she Armenian? Then what's she doing in the Greek Hospital? Is she Levantine?'

I was about to follow her into the next ward, but she stopped me, took my arm and pulled me over to the green-painted wall of the corridor. Lowering her voice she said, 'That young woman is not for you, Pericles.'

I laughed. Aunt Ismene frowned.

'Don't even think about it. I'm telling you, listen to what I'm saying.'

'You're making her seem very attractive now, Aunt!'

Much later, when I learnt the young woman's last name, I understood why I'd never met her before. She was the middle daughter of a wealthy Greek family living in Yenikoy. I vaguely knew her two sisters, whom I'd see in the pastry shops of Beyoglu. Her family had not been exiled in 1964. They were still wealthy and they still lived in Yenikoy. But they had not presented their middle child to society. She was unwell, had a nervous disorder. Back then, psychiatric illnesses were not talked about as openly as they are today. Today, patients with conditions that are easily diagnosed and treated can lead a normal life. But in those days such patients were hidden away in their houses, and when they could no longer be kept hidden, they were shut up in a hospital.

'Pericles! This is not a laughing matter.'

'Okay, Aunt Ismene. Anyway, seeing as she's reading a book in English, she must be a graduate of the American College, so what would she want with me? At least tell me her name.'

'Son, you need to go. Come to my house on Sunday and I'll cook for you. You've lost weight. Come on, dear. I've a lot of work to get through.'

'If you don't tell me her name, I'll go and ask her myself.'

Laughing, I made a move towards the ward we'd just come out of. Aunt Ismene grabbed my arm.

'Don't you dare! Don't disturb the poor thing. She's confused enough as it is. Don't you make it worse.'

Except for her neck and her books, that poor, pale-faced young woman didn't really hold much appeal for me, but Aunt Ismene's response had piqued my interest. How well fate knows which strands to weave into its web!

Aunt Ismene sighed as she wheeled her medicine cart into the second ward. She spoke softly. 'Markela,' she said. 'Her name is Markela. Now, go! Come to my church on Sunday morning and we'll go to my house from there. I'll make you a cheese pie.'

I left the hospital laughing, even though I should have been disappointed by Aunt Ismene's lack of interest in the apartment business. On the bus from Yedikule to Taksim

I kept looking at the title deed in my hand. But when the bus pulled up outside Galatasaray High School I realized that it wasn't the new apartment that I'd been thinking of all that way, but Markela. I jumped off and went home.

I didn't go back to the pharmacy that day, even though I risked being fined for not opening. Besides, I was now a partner in a nightclub. I went home and listened to Leonard Cohen's new album while I sketched the plan of our basement on a piece of paper and thought about where we would put the kitchen, the bathrooms, the bar and the dancefloor. I hadn't danced with anyone for such a long time. If the Circle of Fortune became the classy place that Nejat was dreaming of, I decided I would take Markela dancing there.

# Demolition Permit

The envelope that Leyla had found under my door as she left was sealed with Sellotape and had my name written on it. There was no postmark or stamp. Someone must have delivered it while Leyla and I were in the back room. Curious as to who it might have been, I walked back to the living room to look out of the window. Inside the envelope was a note in what looked like a child's handwriting. I put on my reading glasses. It was full of misspelled words and grammatical errors, but what it said was clear. Zulfu, the man in whose name Nejat had registered the title deed to the fourth-floor apartment, had lost the apartment in a gambling game. He begged my pardon and asked for my blessing. It was time for him to leave the neighbourhood. I folded the note and put it in my back pocket. For a time I gazed out of the window on the Temrin Hill Street side, taking in the ruins of the next-door building. A section of its stone walls was still standing, waiting patiently in the dust and dirt. Time had stopped on the empty streets. There was no traffic, not even in the distance.

I knew very well what the note in my pocket meant. The Circle was losing its criminal protection. We'd been expecting this ever since Nejat had gone to Canada, and it was something of a miracle that it had taken so long. And, worse luck, the new owner of the fourth-floor apartment was none other than the contractor who had his eye on our building. He'd obviously found out about Zulfu's gambling addiction. Even children knew about the illegal casino on the second floor of an old mansion on one of the lower streets. He must have found Zulfu there. Very soon the man would apply for a demolition permit and have our building torn down. Then he would construct the luxury apartment building he wanted. I'd heard from Ferit that he was thinking of putting three apartments on each floor. We would be imprisoned in boxes. He would turn the basement floor where Fortune Nightclub used to be into a gym for the young people of the neighbourhood. His sensitive provincial soul would even think of that.

Taking the key from its nail on the wall, I went up to Berin's in my slippers. She was drinking coffee in the navy-blue armchair beside the window. On the sofa in front of her, Tulin was holding the tablet on which I had seen the photo of Leyla the previous night and reading out the news.

'Good morning.'

'*Kalimera*, Pericles. What do you think about the news?'

After the 10 p.m. announcement that there would be a lockdown all weekend, people had besieged the bakeries and markets. The argument outside our bakery had turned into a fight. With people pushing and shoving each other outside grocery shops, virus precautions had been thrown aside along with masks. Now, the Minister of the Interior had taken responsibility for the chaotic clashes of the night before and tendered his resignation.

Tulin looked up from the tablet. 'The president has not accepted his resignation.'

Sitting down in the armchair across from Berin, I handed her the note I'd taken from my pocket. Tulin stood up to make me a cup of coffee.

'Not now, Tulin. You sit here with us.'

Berin put her glasses on and slowly read the scratchy writing. When she finished, she folded the note and placed it in her lap without comment. With her coffee cup in her hand, she stared out at the horizon, to where the sun and the waters of the Golden Horn were flirting with each other. There was not a sound in the whole neighbourhood.

'What happened, Berin Hanim? What does that letter say?'

'Read it.'

Tulin opened the note where she was standing, behind us. Moments later, she let out a scream.

'Fuck him! Zulfu gambled away The Circle? Goddamn the bastard! We knew this would happen.'

She threw herself on the sofa.

'Sorry.'

In a thoughtful voice, Berin said, 'Don't just lie there, Tulin, go and get Leyla. We need to talk through this together.'

Tulin did not reply. She was still looking at the note in her hand. My eyes lingered on the scar running down her left cheek. How had that happened? Was it a birthmark that got removed or something? I couldn't remember. It was depressing that my memory was so poor. Why did I forget things I'd so recently learnt? My memories of events that had happened fifty or sixty years ago were clear, but whatever I'd seen and heard over the past twenty years was seemingly crammed into a drawer in my mind marked 'unimportant'.

'Tulin! I am speaking to you!'

Tulin shook herself.

'Go! Go and get Leyla.'

'Sorry, Berin Hanim. I was so shocked that... Of course, I'll get Leyla right away.'

Once Tulin had left the room, I was keen to find out what Berin thought about Edip, but my neighbour was not one to enjoy idle chatter before noon. Finishing her coffee, she placed the cup gently onto its saucer. Shadow came and rubbed herself against my feet. I wanted to take her onto my lap, but she ran off, stared at her reflection in the gilded, full-length mirror for a while, then disappeared behind it.

Leyla was wearing a mask. Seeing me with my mouth and nose exposed, she frowned. She was right. Tulin had mingled with the crowd outside the bakery yesterday. This was no laughing matter now. I was starting to hear of the deaths of some of my former colleagues. Pharmacists were being hospitalized. I had to be careful.

'Before you sit down, Tulin, could you bring me a mask, please.'

'We don't have any, Monsieur Pericles. They've stopped selling them in the pharmacies because the state's going to hand them out. Yesterday I made do with the one Leyla gave me. Anyhow, I'm as strong as an ox.'

Hearing that, Leyla rolled her eyes. She sat light as a feather in the armchair that Tulin had flopped into a short while earlier. Shadow jumped out from behind the mirror to prey upon the belt of Leyla's sweater. Berin gave Leyla a quick summary of the situation. Leyla listened calmly, then asked the question that Berin and I had frequently discussed.

'Since they want to tear down The Circle and replace it with a multi-apartment building, and since it appears that it is enough that only one owner applies for a demolition permit, why doesn't the construction company just buy the ground-floor apartment and go from there? Remember the first place realtor Ferit showed me? The one that used to be a hair salon?'

Tulin nodded, confused. She'd never considered that possibility.

'We aren't their first priority, that's why,' said Berin. 'This is still an impoverished neighbourhood. When they finish with the Taksim district, they'll come for us. I don't think they're quite ready for that yet, but since the fourth floor has fallen into their laps, sooner or later they'll turn their attention on The Circle. They've been waiting for us to give our consent, to move out, to acquiesce, to kiss the three kurus they will count out in our hands. That's what they've been hoping for. But we have stood our ground. Now we must decide what to do.'

'What can we do? You mentioned that lawyers were involved.'

Berin nodded. 'That was yesterday. Today we have lost one apartment.'

Seeing Leyla looking so unhappy, I felt the need to explain. 'If this building is torn down, you will have the right to a share in the new building.'

She turned to me in anger. 'As if I care about that! This beautiful building will be razed. Even if they paid me a fortune, I wouldn't accept it. It still makes my heart flutter to see the stained glass above our front door, the mosaics, the pattern of the wooden flooring, the decorative plasterwork on the ceilings... And what will become of the bas relief of the snake eating its tail? The bas relief that the architect loaded with such symbolism? They'll come and tear it down. These monsters have not the least respect for things of beauty or elegance.' Her voice was suddenly tearful. 'Oh, I am sick and tired of these gangsters taking over the world!'

She leant her elbows on her knees and buried her face in her hands. Berin turned towards the window. Tulin was nervously rubbing her fingers over the velvet of the armchair. I wanted to take Leyla in my arms, kidnap her and whisk her away from this place of thugs to a city in Europe where beauty and elegance were still valued – to Vienna or Rome.

She raised her head and turned towards me. 'Your... that friend, Nejat, the mafia one, the one in your notes. You said he stuffed his safe with the title deeds of houses left from the Greeks. Couldn't he do something?'

Tulin's hands stopped. Berin stared at Leyla.

'Nejat died,' I said. 'Fifteen years ago. He went to Canada and passed away over there. The apartment that Zulfu gambled away used to be Nejat's. Before he went to Canada, he put the title deeds into the names of the boys he employed.'

'The first floor was Nejat's as well,' Tulin explained to Leyla.

'What do you mean?'

'Edip's father, a long time ago, used to take care of an elderly Greek man. That apartment on the first floor belonged to him. What was his name, Monsieur Pericles?'

'Panayiotis. Edip's father, Tahsin, was an apprentice at Monsieur Panayiotis's marble workshop. When the poor man couldn't get around, Tahsin would come in the evenings to help him.'

'Oh, yes, Uncle Panayiotis. Edip remembers the old man fondly. Before Uncle Panayiotis died, he told Edip's father that the apartment was his, but he never actually put the title deed in their name. A while later, Nejat took that one too. The title deed is in the name of one of his men now. Galip.'

Berin sighed.

'Okay, who is this Galip? Would he be helpful to us?'

Leyla was looking straight into my eyes. Her hopefulness seared my insides.

'Nope. He won't do anything,' Tulin answered for me.

Galip took control of the drugs trade after Nejat left. When Nejat used to come to the pharmacy for his raw materials, he would bring Galip, just a teenager then, so that Galip could learn the business. I suspected that Galip was his own son. In spite of his illness, Nejat had relations with many women. I don't know whether he was in working order sexually or not, but it struck me that he was more attentive to Galip than to the other boys. With his black, slick-backed hair and short stature, Galip also looked a bit like Nejat.

Before Nejat went to Canada, he and I used to meet for lunch at a beer garden in Galatasaray, at the place known as the Flower Arcade. After our long years of tacit understanding, we were relaxed in each other's company. The Circle of Fortune had not worked out as a discotheque; it had evolved into the Fortune Nightclub. Nejat would come to the beer garden in a wheelchair. Galip, Zulfu and the other boys he'd trained were now great big men. Wearing black sunglasses and black jackets, they would enter the arcade like an army, pushing their godfather's wheelchair. By that time, Nejat's chin was sagging, his eyes and cheeks were red, his hair dyed black. They would settle him across from me, then withdraw and wait, guarding all three entrances to the arcade. One of the restaurant's tables had been specially adapted, with one of its struts removed, so that Nejat's wheelchair could easily slide under it. If someone else – a confused tourist group or some young people attending the film festival – happened to be sitting at our table at midday, they would immediately be relocated.

'If I came through that door on my two legs and wanted

to sit at this table, those hippies would give me a hard time and force a man to get tough. But with this thing under me, before I've even turned the corner, they'll stand up and do whatever I want. What d'ya say to that, Pericles Efendi?'

Nejat made up some story about the deep state and a super-confidential secret service report when questioned about his trip to Canada. There might have been some truth in that. Around the time of the high-profile and highly explosive Susurluk scandal, during which lots of dark connections between the state, the police and the mafia were revealed, Nejat was absent for several months. After that, he showed up in his wheelchair, saying that his legs didn't work anymore because he'd taken a bullet in the spine while slugging it out with a gang leader who had impugned his honour. I was the only one to whom he confessed that he was going to Canada for experimental stem-cell treatment. The treatment didn't work. After he'd been living in Canada for four or five years, Nejat died.

Nejat's army were respectful of me. They knew I'd been a silent partner in Fortune Nightclub. After Nejat left, I withdrew from the partnership, but whenever I met Galip or Zulfu or one of the other neighbourhood thugs, they would pause their bullying and come over to kiss my hand. It was because of them that I had been able to hold on there for so many years. The drugs trade had long since moved on to other things, so they no longer required the raw materials I used to supply them with, but Galip would still stop by from time to time to pick up some green prescription pills for his friends and relatives. When Berin's husband died, I called Galip and he arranged the death certificate from the doctor, the funeral and the burial business. Could Galip do anything about the demolition permit? But then again, why would he?

He would prefer to get his share of the property money. Not everybody was like Leyla.

'If they issue demolition permits on the grounds of a building's safety, or lack of it, couldn't we get an engineer to issue a certificate of sound construction?' asked Leyla. 'Our building being perfectly sound, I mean.'

Nobody answered. Leyla looked stubbornly into each of our faces. I felt guilty. The contractor who had his eye on our building had for months been sending his drug dealers to do their business on The Circle's front doorstep, encouraging glue-sniffers to sleep on our stairs. Before the coronavirus epidemic, he'd forced male and female prostitutes to work on the desolate Temrin Hill Street in front of Ferit's estate agency. He did all that so that we would find it disgusting and sell our apartments. Berin and I both knew that. Everywhere was quiet now, but before the lockdown, those shameless men in their vans used to turn up almost every day, blocking the mouth of Kaymakcalan Street and playing loud music. They were in cahoots with the construction mafia. In the first few days after Leyla moved in, Edip used to go to his window and shout at the men in the vans to turn down the music. They responded with such whopping curses that I would pray that Leyla was out of earshot in one of the back rooms. Leyla considered these things to be just part of the neighbourhood's unique character. She hadn't realized that the residents of The Circle were under siege. And we hadn't disabused her. What we did was unconscionable.

'Without someone high up to help us, we'll be squeezed into a corner,' said Berin. She was looking straight into Leyla's eyes. I immediately understood her plan and hated her for it. 'Do you know anyone in Ankara, Pericles?'

She knew I didn't. What kind of relationship could a

seventy-five-year-old Greek man have with the government? I was just grateful that I was allowed to live in this country. Aunt Ismene's old neighbours in Samatya and Kumkapi were being found strangled or stabbed in their homes.

'Um… maybe… maybe there's someone I could call.' Leyla had taken the bait. 'I don't know whether he can help us, but I have someone in mind. Don't let me get your hopes up, though. I might not be able to contact him. It's been a long time.'

My eyes blazed with fury. Berin's eyebrows, drawn with a thin pencil, lifted in feigned surprise. Tulin took a chair from the dining room and sat across from Leyla. Now everyone was looking at Leyla's mouth, as if the fate of The Circle lay in her words.

'Why not?' said Berin. 'It's worth a try. We have nothing to lose, at any rate.'

I hated the smile that appeared at the corner of her lips. I stood up, saying that it was time for my medication, even though I wasn't taking any. Which Berin was fully aware of.

# Hopeless, Helpless and Bereft

Now, looking back after many years, I can see that when I met Markela I was a broken man, exhausted from following the trails of those I had lost. When I first saw my future bride in the hospital, it had been eleven years since Ulker had gone to Germany without saying goodbye. I couldn't confide in anyone and so, while I waited for Ulker, I tracked my memories of her around the city. I, who had at first not been that interested in Ulker, who had never invited her to my home to meet my parents, even though she'd begged me to, went crazy when I heard that she had gone to study in Germany.

It was autumn and I was about to start university. 1963. I'd spent the summer holidays on Buyukada. Mama had rented a house on the island near my grandfather, as she did every summer. During the week, Papa was in Istanbul at the pharmacy. He would come to the island on Friday evenings and return to the city by ferry on Monday mornings. My grandfather continued to suffer in the dank basement flat that opened onto a dank courtyard infested by mosquitoes. Perhaps he and my mother talked to each other, I don't know. I had long since stopped knocking on the door that my grandfather had closed on us. I was young and needed to get on with my life; in order to do so, I had to forget what my grandfather had experienced during the Events.

The island was full of my friends. As a reward for having graduated from high school, Papa left me to my own devices. In previous summers he'd kept me at the pharmacy two days a week, to learn the work, wash the windows, sweep the floor. But that summer I was free. I was surrounded by beautiful women and girls. I had a brief affair with a woman quite a bit older than myself. She was a Levantine from Izmir staying at the Splendid Hotel. Her husband was away at sea and she took me under her wing. It was she who taught me the finer points of lovemaking, how a woman should be touched. During the day I would go swimming, have races with my schoolfriends Niko and Stefanos, play tennis. Sofia, the American, was the best at tennis. We were never able to beat her. The loser had to buy Sofia profiteroles from the pier – it's possible we sometimes lost on purpose. She was as warm and friendly as ever and her body language made it clear that we could give her more than profiteroles. In the evenings large groups of us would go for walks in the pine forest and picnic at Dilburnu.

Sometimes Niki would come to the island for the day. I would take her to the Akasya Hotel for ice cream. She'd be wearing a flowery cotton dress made by her mother and worn-down sandals. As we walked past the front of the Splendid Hotel holding our ice-cream cones, my Levantine lover would flash me secretive smiles from the terrace. Niki never noticed that. She was busy being jealous of American Sofia. Suddenly Niki, whom everyone likened to Audrey Hepburn, began to seem too dark and too thin in my eyes.

After eating the evening meal with Mama in the garden of the rented house, I would rush over to join my elegant older lover. We would drink champagne and eat shrimp cocktail on her balcony as Istanbul winked at us from across the dark water. In those years, Buyukada's entertainment venues – its nightclubs, hotels, tavernas on the boat landing, outdoor cafés – used to stay open until morning. The dawn breeze, wafting in through the open door of the balcony along with the sound of laughter and music, would caress our sweaty skin as we lay on the bed and we would hold each other even tighter.

At the beginning of September, Mama and I returned to Istanbul. Aunt Ismene and Elena were still on Imbros. Uncle Stelio and Papa were following the violent events in Cyprus with apprehension. Both the Turkish and the Greek newspapers carried photographs of wretched people whose families had been slaughtered, their children lost. Each community believed that it was the side who spoke their own language who were the real victims, that the opposite side were the cruel aggressors. By the end of the year Cyprus would be divided in two, along a 'Green Line' which had been sketched by an English general. The line identified the north of the island for Turkish Cypriots, the south for Greek Cypriots. With this line, the fate of we Istanbul Greeks – who lived so far away – was determined. The Greek population of Istanbul was used as a bargaining tool during the Cyprus crisis. In the end, my family and friends paid the price for a negotiation that happened far away and had nothing to do with them. They were deported with nothing but a single suitcase in their hands.

Having spent my summer holidays in the lap of desire and pleasure, I'd had little time to think of these things.

I also realized that I'd spent very little time thinking about Ulker. When I returned to our apartment in Istanbul, I threw my bag into a corner of my room and immediately took a book of poetry from the shelf, stood in front of the window overlooking the courtyard and began reading a poem I had chosen at random. It was then that Ulker came to my mind.

Mama was in her bedroom, unpacking suitcases, hanging our summer clothes in the wardrobe. I hugged her, kissed her cheeks. Then I set out for Beyoglu from Galatasaray. In a heartbeat I was at Lebon. Ulker would definitely be inside, chatting with the old men as they smoked. Lebon was closed, whether temporarily or because it was the end of the summer holidays, I didn't know. The door was locked. I glanced at the fashionable people inside Markiz, though I knew Ulker wouldn't have gone there. I slowed down in front of Tilla's pastry shop and Inci. Ulker was in neither, even though she used to beg me to go with her to both places. Our going in and mixing with other lovers – who were sitting side by side eating profiteroles or peach melba from the same spoon – was out of the question. I never took her anywhere except Lebon, where the old people went, the Garden of Paradise, with its secluded bowers, or the little fish restaurants along the Bosphorus. The man in the guard's uniform at the door of Bab Café looked me up and down and then refused to let me in, even though he knew me. Ulker and I had gone to Bab's many times together. I'd been introduced to several football players there and had sat at the same table as a famous singer. This fellow had witnessed all of that. But here he was, saying I couldn't enter without a partner.

Anger fuelling me, I reached Ulker's building in no time. The street door was open. I ran up the five floors.

Oya opened the door. Feigning surprise, she said, 'What,

you didn't know, Pericles? Ulker's gone to Frankfurt to study. She must have told you she'd applied to go to university there. She spent all last winter and spring studying for the entrance exam. She was overjoyed when she heard at the beginning of summer that she'd been accepted. We sent her off last week. She's moved into a student hostel. She sent us a telegram. She's in good spirits.'

She stopped. 'I thought she'd told you.' She hadn't opened the door wide. We were speaking through a crack.

'I wasn't in Istanbul. I was on Buyukada. I haven't heard from Ulker for a long time.'

'Oh,' she said, shrugging. She pulled the door towards her, almost shutting it in my face. I pushed it open again.

'Give me her address, Oya.'

'I can't.'

'Let me come in. I'll explain. I didn't call her because...'

'Impossible. My father's here.'

She said that in a whisper. I quickly glanced in the direction of the living room. I didn't believe her. I had come and gone from that apartment often enough to know that Sahin Dermanli was never at home during the daytime. Oya had to be hiding a lover in there.

'Just write her address down on a piece of paper.'

'If Ulker didn't leave you her address, then I can't give it to you.'

'Please, Oya.'

'Look, I'll tell you this, Pericles. You're too late. Much too late. Goodbye now.'

With a strength I wouldn't have expected from her slender arms, she pushed the door shut in my face. I was left outside Sahin Dermanli's apartment, in the stairwell that smelled of onions.

In the years that followed, particularly after Mama and Papa were forced to leave Istanbul, my life was spent tracing footsteps. At first I was hopeful that I'd run into Ulker somewhere. If she didn't have enough money to come to Istanbul at Christmas or Easter, she would surely come for the summer holidays. I stopped going to the island so that I could instead spend my time at the Garden of Paradise, beside the Bosphorus, on the slopes of Asiyan, in the bars of Bebek and at the coffeehouse in Emirgan – places we'd gone to together – in the hope that she would be there. I was consumed by regret for having neglected her the previous summer, when I'd been indulging in the island's carefree pleasures. Back then I thought that was simply what youth in Istanbul did – abandoning their winter lives in the city, only to circle back to old loves as summer waned. I didn't realize that this was not the case for Ulker and her family. They had spent the summer in town, and life continued without interruption.

The longing I had felt as I stood at my bedroom window with a book of poetry in my hand intensified with each passing day. Ulker and Ulker alone could fill the great emptiness I carried like a pain in my gut. I would spend hours on the bench in Narmanli Han where we'd sat the day we first met. Passing time with the Narmanli cats, I replayed over and again my first encounter with Ulker, remembering the way Mitsy (who was still living with me, since Mama and Papa couldn't take her to Athens) had poked her tiny black-and-white head out of Ulker's coat, the way Ulker had turned on the heels of her loafers, swinging her ponytail, and headed for the courtyard exit, her pitiful Yesilcam posing. I remembered it all clearly, in minute detail. But it wasn't the same me who had experienced all that. When I first met Ulker I was a carefree young man, living with my parents, in my last year of high school. Now

I was like a snake that'd shed its skin. I was a completely new person.

As time passed, I became aware that it wasn't Ulker that I was searching for. It was the life I had lost, a life that had slipped away very suddenly, like a wet fish from my hand. Mama and Papa banished from the city, Aunt Ismene in Samatya, Elena studying law in Athens. Papa had been offended that instead of going to join him in Greece I was going to open my own pharmacy on Kurabiye Street with a Turkish friend. He hadn't written me a single line since I told him. The thing I was looking for, whatever it was, was just over there, so close, like a dream, like a word that skittered across the tip of my tongue. But as I pursued it, it raced away from me.

Markela came into my life just as I was preparing to accept defeat. Her family believed that I had saved their daughter, but actually it was Markela who saved the helpless, hopeless, bereft Pericles from the despair he'd fallen into.

# Ulker was the Past, Markela the Future

In the first years of our marriage, when I believed she'd got better, and her family and even Aunt Ismene were also convinced, Markela and I would go to the fish market together. We would buy all sorts of spices, herbs and roots I didn't know the names of, and if the greengrocer or the herb seller didn't have what she wanted, we would order them. Then we'd go home and Markela would dive into the kitchen, throw slices of onion, tomato and pepper on top of a sea bass and put the lot into the oven, cook a pilaf with pine nuts and currants, and fill the table with mezze dishes and all kinds of salads – broad bean puree, yogurt with cucumber, Russian salad, dandelion salad. 'Who's going to eat all this, girl?' I would joke. My wife ate like a bird. But she was in good spirits. There was still a long time to go before she'd start spending the entire day perched on the windowsill overlooking Temrin Hill Street, pulling at her hair, a long time to go before she'd shut herself away in the dark room at the back because she was frightened of the street. We were happy to begin with.

Looking back on it now, I realize that when I first began

visiting Markela in the hospital, it was not love I was seeking but heroism. I was going to rescue Markela – both from the hospital to which her family had consigned her (they were ashamed to have their daughter seen in public), and from the sorrows and tricks that her mind played on her. The hospital was giving Markela a lot of different tranquillizers. At university we hadn't been taught that clinical depression was an illness; in fact, we'd never been taught about it at all. I thought that when the chemicals in a person's brain were out of balance, the person could be cured with love, care and kindness.

Aunt Ismene lost no time in letting my mama in Athens know that I had started visiting Markela every week that spring of 1974. In her letters to me, which became more frequent during those months, Mama would write: 'That young woman is mentally unbalanced, Pericles. I know her family. The poor thing couldn't even finish school because of her nervous breakdowns. You don't know this, but her parents came all the way to Papa's pharmacy to ask if he could get them some medicine from Europe that might help. They begged him, wept, but what could be done? Son, this young woman is not for you. Stay away from her, Pericles, I beg you. Do not ruin your future. Come, my darling, do not distress your poor *manoula*, your dear mother. I can't sleep a wink at night for worrying.'

I did not reply to Mama. Instead, I sat with Markela in the hospital courtyard under a chestnut tree and we discussed books. She was sad that she hadn't been able to finish her education at the American College for Girls. She found American literature comforting. I would bring her Greek poetry books – Cavafy, Elytis, Seferis – but because she'd been at the American school all the way up to the second year of high school, her Greek was not as good as that of the girls who'd studied at Zappeion. She had trouble with the Greek alphabet. So I would take the book from her and read the poems aloud. She loved Elytis. I would read 'The Mad Pomegranate Tree', or his epic poem 'The Axion Esti', just a little each time. If anyone were to come over from Athens, I planned to ask them to bring as a present for Markela the record of 'The Axion Esti' that the composer Mikis Theodorakis had set to music.

Nobody was coming over to visit from Athens. Not because they were upset with me, but because that year everyone was preoccupied with what was happening in Greece. The previous autumn, a student protest against the military junta at Athens Polytechnic had been violently suppressed. The junta had been oppressing the Greek populace for seven years – political parties had been shut down, freedoms curtailed, and opposition politicians and citizens tortured, exiled and killed – and the student protest quickly became a huge resistance movement. At three in the morning the junta's tanks opened fire on the protestors, killing some. The junta was also secretly supporting EOKA, the far-right Greek nationalist organization in Cyprus, and tension on the island was escalating. All of this meant that in the spring of 1974, relatives and children who still lived in Istanbul were forgotten. There was only a handful of us left anyway.

Amid the violence in Cyprus, hostility toward Istanbul's Greek minority escalated. Our shops were stoned and, when Greek schoolchildren came out of school at the end of the day, they were beaten up in Beyoglu. If I hadn't been under Nejat's protection, my pharmacy would never have survived. Our Greek community was falling apart.

Markela and I did not speak of love in the hospital garden.

I didn't know if we would even see each other after she was discharged. In that courtyard, under century-old trees and among the nurses and patients, we were far removed from the chaos of the world, disconnected from geography and time. During those hours spent side by side, there was nothing else. This must be love, I used to say to myself. Love was the force that kept you deep in the present, with no before and no after. I tricked myself into believing that what I'd felt for Ulker, before she left for Germany, was not love but unfulfilled desire – or, not even that, my yearning to catch the thing that got away.

That summer, when the sun was strong enough for me to have to close the pharmacy's blinds, out of nowhere came the vision of Markela. With a desire that was different from what I'd felt with Ulker – calmer, steadier – I imagined making love to Markela. I'd have to teach her, this woman who'd never learnt how to find pleasure in life, what surprises lay hidden in the depths of her body. My heroic fantasies did not let up, nor did the warnings that filled my mother's letters.

As we sat on a bench under the chestnut tree on one of those early summer days, Markela told me about her childhood in Yenikoy. She spoke briefly and softly. She'd been very sad when they'd torn down their old wooden three-storey mansion, with its spacious garden, and had built in its place a modern apartment block with large balconies opening onto the Bosphorus. She'd grown up hiding in the secluded spots smelling of figs in that garden.

While she was speaking, she was brushing her long black hair. Sunbeams slipped through the chestnut leaves and fell on us and for the first time I noticed the red sheen to Markela's hair. Sparks wound around her head. Unable to resist, I stroked her. Gently at first, afraid of frightening away the sparks. She glanced up at the hospital windows. Aunt Ismene's eyes were always on us, but somehow that Saturday there was no one spying on us.

Markela dropped the hairbrush in her lap and lowered her head. I thought I saw the hint of a smile on her face. I imagined her in The Circle, brushing her hair in front of Mama's trifold dressing table, and suddenly I felt a desire sharper than ever before. The nape of her neck was pure white and very long. I gently pressed my fingers into its protruding vertebrae, one by one. Holding her hair with one hand, with the other I stroked the place where her neck connected to her skull. It was the first time I had touched her.

Right then I understood: Ulker was the past, Markela was my future.

'Do you think these stones were taken from graves?' she said softly. 'The churchyard is like that.'

She was showing me something on the ground with her bare foot. Her black hair was again falling over her face. I hoped her pale cheeks were a little flushed. Or had my desire not affected her at all? Had my caresses not made her heart beat faster? Why was she still talking about marble and graveyards and stones?

'The courtyard of the nunnery down the road is paved with old gravestones, did you know that? I'm talking about the church with the holy spring underneath it. The names of the deceased were carved on the gravestones. They were Karamanli Greeks. Their trades were also represented – a pail for a milkman, a notebook for a clerk, a saw for a carpenter. Do you think these stones were taken from the graves of Karamanli Greeks as well?'

I bent right down to the ground, very near Markela's slender white foot. The skin of her ankle was very white.

The veins appeared green. If I reached out and touched them, I wouldn't be able to control myself. I felt the eyes of the other patients in the courtyard upon us, looking at us with curiosity and interest, as if they had been waiting for this moment. Being centre stage, surrounded by them, I had no choice. I had to play the role I had been assigned. Without leaning towards Markela's ear or taking my eyes off the ground, off her ankles, I said, 'Will you marry me, Markela?'

My voice came out hoarse; it must have been from desire.

Pulling on her hair, Markela again glanced up at the windows. Then she mumbled, almost inaudibly, 'Are you serious, Pericles?'

I finally raised my head and looked into the languorous black eyes of my future wife. Roses had bloomed on her cheeks.

'Yes,' she whispered. 'Yes.'

I suddenly felt wonderful. I was a real hero. I thought I heard the patients surrounding us clapping. Smiles appeared on their careworn faces as they celebrated our love. I was sure of that. Too sure.

# Poison

I didn't see Leyla until early evening on Sunday. I was caught up in my writing. If anything could match the anticipation of seeing her, it was writing. Knowing that Leyla was waiting at the other end of the text spurred me on. Ultimately, I was writing to her, so that she would know me not as this old person whose joints creaked when he rose from a chair but as the real Pericles, the man who dreamt, loved, deceived, envied, pursued petty arguments and performed acts of heroism. Pericles was more than the pieces that had made it this far and I wanted Leyla to know that.

Somehow, when I saw Leyla for the first time, I understood that hers were the ears which would give life to the voice inside me. Her sincere curiosity, her eyes that could see deep inside a person, had been reflected in Barbaros's mirror. They curled up and settled into the gap in my soul. The joys of creativity and love were bound together, inextricable. If it had been someone other than Leyla conjuring stories out of my notes, I would not have been writing. And had I not been writing, I would not have been so drawn to Leyla.

At noon I ate a tomato, ham and cheese sandwich standing

up in the kitchen. Having taken the last bite, I was about to lie down when the telephone rang. It was Stelio. He'd just crossed into Turkey.

'I was going to leave the car in a car park somewhere near you, then take a taxi to the ferry landing. But when I crossed the border, I discovered that Turkey's in lockdown this weekend. Cars with foreign number plates are not subject to any restrictions, but do you think I'll be able to find a car park that's open? Are the ferries to the islands running?'

He was supposed to be staying at a friend's place on Buyukada for fourteen days. That's what he'd planned. I yawned. These young people had no respect for the quiet hours of the afternoon. In the past, we'd stop talking and moving around as soon as the clock struck two. No one, and especially not an elderly person taking a nap, was to be disturbed until four thirty or five o'clock. Who would dare make a phone call? But this clearly hadn't occurred to Stelio, for here he was at lunchtime, waiting for me to say, 'Come and take a rest up here.'

'Listen, Stelio, your mother said you were going to take a Covid test before coming to Istanbul. Is that right?'

'Yes. *Malista*. Of course. I did a PCR test at the Bioiatriki Clinic in Athens. I was expecting them to ask for it at passport control, but nobody bothered. There were so many trucks waiting at the border that private cars like mine were—'

Okay. No need to drag it out. 'Your room is ready. After such a long drive, don't bother parking the car, finding a taxi and getting the ferry. Once you've settled in here, you can go to the island whenever you wish. While you're here you'll be free to wander around the city. It's not like Athens.' In Athens everybody was confined to the district they lived in. Anyone caught outside their district was fined. I wondered how the protest-loving people of Athens were taking this arrangement. I'd have to get Stelio to tell me about it when he arrived.

Silence. Why wasn't he saying anything? Had he fallen asleep at the wheel?

'Are you there, Stelio? Have we been cut off?'

'No, I am here, Monsieur Pericles. But, I don't know... I can't be sure... I mean... Are you sure it's okay with you?'

'I am expecting you, Stelio.'

I heard the engine growl. He must have stepped on the accelerator. He shouted with happiness. I held the receiver away from my ear.

'Thank you! *Efharisto poli*, Monsieur Pericles. Uncle Pericles. That's wonderful. It really takes a load off my mind.'

I hung up. Speaking Greek had tired me out. He should not start calling me 'Uncle Pericles'. Although I might be his distant uncle, 'Monsieur Pericles' was better, and he could use the formal form of 'you'. Don't let him get cheeky. I walked down the corridor to my bedroom and closed the curtains on the Temrin Hill Street side. The weather seemed to have turned all of a sudden. I stretched out on the bed and pulled a plaid blanket over my feet.

Lying in bed, I began to outline the chapters of my book, my thoughts drifting to Beyoglu Avenue, back when the street hummed with shared taxis, private taxis, trolley buses and trams. I was with Mama, Aunt Ismene and Elena, standing on the corner where the avenue met Balo Street. Me. Young Pericles. The real Pericles. It was the year I started high school. 1960. That autumn was different. It was beautiful. Martial law had been declared, but we were hopeful. The trials relating to the September Events were to be held on Yassiada and those found guilty of robbing us of our homes, our sense of security, would be punished. The intervening five years seemed like centuries to me. Shops had been repaired and their window displays had reappeared, the wounds of the lost had been covered over. I walked down the avenue with confident strides, my head held high.

It was a Saturday afternoon and Beyoglu Avenue was always crowded at that hour. The tram driver was ringing his bell as the tram passed between the taxis, buses and three or four private cars. We were going to the 4.30 matinee. Marilyn Monroe's *Some Like It Hot* was on at the Melek and I'd bought tickets for the four of us a few days earlier. The box tickets were sold out, but so what? We would sit in the grand auditorium.

I'd grown a lot that year; my voice had changed, got deeper, and an Adam's apple had appeared in my throat. I was often clumsy, not knowing what to do with my arms and legs. Mama must have been thinking about Papa, for she found an excuse to drag us over to Tunel Square. Not knowing exactly what we were looking for, we wandered in and out of the arcades there, the big old buildings with streetlamps dangling from their upper floors, the alleyways behind Papa's pharmacy.

As we were passing through an arcade with a high, glassed-in roof that let the light through, Mama and Aunt Ismene both suddenly stopped dead. They were staring at a young woman browsing the books piled up in front of a bookshop window. Elena and I looked at them, then at the woman, with curiosity. The woman had a long black plait hanging down her back like a village girl and was hatless. She looked up and, seeing us, she hurriedly put down the book she'd been leafing through and headed for the arcade's Sishane exit. As if a switch had been flicked, Mama and Aunt Ismene immediately hastened after her, leaving Elena and I behind at the entrance to the arcade.

'That was Despina,' murmured Elena.

'Who?' I must have heard wrong.

'Despina. Yorgo the draper's eldest daughter. Don't you remember? They used to live in our building. They fled to Athens after the Events.'

Despina! My childhood love. The beautiful neighbour who used to hem Mama's dresses. Despina, who used to smile at me in the mirror with her mouth full of pins while I lay on the big bed watching her. When she smiled, firecrackers would burst inside me. 'Son, don't jump on the bed!' Mama's jitteriness contrasted with Despina's simplicity and calmness.

It had been five years since Yorgo and his family had left Istanbul. That was a very long time for a fifteen-year-old boy. The past had long since been lost in the fog. Although I'd experienced the full terror of the Events, it was as if the child who'd lived through them was someone else. That child, whose father had hidden him under the bed while thugs banged on the door with iron bars and axes, was the hero of a story which had been told to me over and over again.

Mama caught up with Despina and grabbed her shoulder. She turned around and looked at Mama and Aunt Ismene with eyes that even at a distance were huge. I realized why I'd not recognized her at first. She'd changed, lost weight. Her cheeks were sunken and her chin longer. The face that had once smiled at me so sweetly was now twisted, hard. Mama drew her close and hugged her. Despina did not yield immediately but stood stiff in Mama's arms, like a broomstick. Aunt Ismene joined them and together they stroked the young woman's hair, rubbed her back. Then Elena went over as well. They encircled Despina and gradually she relaxed and softened, surrendering her body to the women embracing her.

They sat Despina down on a thatched stool. The poor woman was weeping. Orders rained down on the men who were standing watching in front of the shops. Coffee arrived from somewhere, and a bottle of lemon cologne from somewhere else. Elena was kneeling down beside Despina, holding her hand. Handkerchiefs were taken from handbags, arms encircled; jokes were made and laughter followed. Everyone forgot about me, standing at the Asmali Mescit end of the arcade. I felt more awkward and useless than ever.

They put Despina on a trolleybus back to her home in Kurtulus. Afterwards, while we were walking to Galatasaray, I tried to understand what had happened from what Mama and Aunt Ismene were saying.

'The poor girl's name was even erased from the church registry,' Aunt Ismene said.

'What our people did was absolutely vile. Her husband didn't even make it a condition that she change her religion. She kept her Greek name. He even said he would get baptized if they wanted him to.'

'What a good man he must be! God bless him. After all the things that happened to that girl…'

'Mama, why was Despina crying? Was it because they erased her name from the church records?'

'Yes.'

They were walking unbelievably fast. Elena caught up with them.

'But she's married, and everybody gets married in a civil ceremony nowadays. Her husband is a good man, isn't he? So why was she crying like that?'

'She got a little emotional.'

'*Yati?* Why?'

'What a lot of questions you're asking today, son. We just told you. Our community rejected her because she had a Turkish husband. People would cross the street to avoid her. When your mama embraced her, not caring what anyone might say, she got emotional.'

Mama cut in. 'If you carry on dawdling like this, we're going to miss the film. We won't have time for a banana milkshake now.'

Working our way down the Beyoglu pavements, we arrived at the movie theatre. When we'd taken our seats, Elena leant over to me.

'When Despina was coming home from her father's shop during the Events, they cornered her in a courtyard.'

The second gong sounded and the auditorium went dark. I stared at the screen for a long time without taking in what I was watching. Even when Marilyn Monroe, the object of my adolescent fantasies, appeared, I couldn't concentrate on her. In the seats around me, people were fidgeting, whispering to each other and laughing.

Elena leant over once again.

'It wasn't just one man, do you understand? There were lots of them, one after the other. She was unconscious when she was found and they thought she was dead; they even covered her face with a blanket. She recovered, but when her parents went to Athens, they didn't want Despina to go with them. So she married this Turkish man. That's why she was crying.'

I rested my head against the back of my seat. I had no energy for the film. In the scenes racing through my head, Beyoglu was burning. Flames were rising from furnishings, fabric, toys, furs, clothing, fridges, windows, shattered glassware, everything all piled up. The howls from that fateful September night filled my mind once again. I heard the screams of the women that had sounded in my ears while I lay in the darkness with Mama and Papa in the big bed after Tahsin had chased away the men who'd attacked our building. Women begging 'No! No!', followed by cruel male laughter. I was very young and I didn't know what those screams meant. Now, in the horrifying film playing in my head, I saw women cornered in courtyards, in arcades, in their own homes. All of them had Despina's face. Despina's smile, reflected in mirrors, was being broken, shattered by rough hands. This scene was repeated in every face. Laughter rising from the crowd around me made me sick to my stomach.

It was evening when we left the cinema. I was silent as Mama, Aunt Ismene, Elena and I walked slowly to Kaymakcalan Street. They were talking about the film. I couldn't remember a single thing about it. That night I was feverish. I vomited until morning. Mama thought the banana milkshake I'd drunk so quickly before going into the cinema was to blame. While she changed the cloths soaked in vinegar on my forehead, she kept saying, 'You were poisoned, my son.' She was right. The image of men in a blazing courtyard climbing on top of Despina had poisoned my mind. Remembering, I vomited again.

# Somebody Else's Story

The doorbell was ringing. I reached out to the bedside table and checked my watch. Stelio, presumably. I got up slowly from the bed and smoothed my hair with my hands. I felt nauseous. The memories that I thought I'd forgotten long ago weighed heavily on my heart. Even discovering that it was not Stelio but Leyla at the door didn't cheer me up.

'Sorry,' she said. 'Did I come at a bad time? Were you asleep?'

She had her laptop under her arm. I motioned for her to come in. Whatever she saw on my face kept her from flopping down on the sofa as she usually did. She came gingerly into the living room, sat down on the orange bergère, opened the computer on her lap and moved her fingers swiftly over the illuminated keyboard. I glanced out of the window. Clouds had settled over the unusually silent neighbourhood.

Leyla raised her head from the computer and appraised me warily. 'Seriously. I can come some other time.'

I was standing up, leaning against the wide windowsill.

'Aren't you going to sit down?'

'Please read it. I'm curious to hear the new sections. I can hear you better from here.'

The doorbell rang again. Stelio. Leyla jumped up, put the computer down next to me on the windowsill and opened the door without asking who was there. My heart felt even heavier. In sadness I looked at the words, at my story on Leyla's computer screen. Who did I think I was, anyway?

'Please keep your mask on,' said Leyla. 'Leave your suitcase outside for now.'

This was the first time I'd heard her speaking English. The old sense of inferiority that I used to get around Markela's books returned. I couldn't compete with these young people. I could understand what was being said, but I couldn't speak English with them. From my spot by the window, I observed Stelio's gentle entrance into the corridor. He was bespectacled, with a smiling face, and his curly hair was streaked with grey. Leyla had got some spray from the kitchen and was trying to disinfect his suitcase outside the door. They were joking together already.

With difficulty, I walked to the door.

'*Geia sou*, Stelio. Welcome. How are you? All well?'

Let Leyla not understand what we were saying. Let her be the outsider for a while.

'Monsieur Pericles! You look great. Fit as a fiddle!'

'*Efharisto*, Stelio. Thanks. I try to look after myself.'

Leyla was rummaging around in the drawer of the console table. Stelio was observing us, trying to figure out who Leyla was, what her role was in my house. I hadn't introduced her. I could have said she was my neighbour, my assistant, my young friend, but I didn't. It wasn't necessary. They'd already introduced themselves at the door, bumped elbows. 'I'm Stelio.' 'And I'm Leyla.' Titles and last names had lost their importance in today's world, and with the simplicity of English, the formal and informal forms of 'you' were irrelevant. Hopefully, Stelio didn't think Leyla was my carer. I prayed – oh, yes, with all my heart I prayed – that he thought she was my lover. Ridiculous. Impossible? Impossible, of course. Still, I prayed like crazy that just for a few seconds this possibility had crossed Stelio's mind. What would he have thought of that? Maybe he'd be disgusted by me. Maybe he'd admire me. Fit as a fiddle, Monsieur Pericles, and with a slim and graceful woman in the prime of her life. Come to your senses, *vre* Monsieur Pericles!

Having handed out masks and disinfected the bags, Leyla was now flitting down the corridor like a butterfly on the wing. First she showed Stelio the bathroom.

'*Signomi*, I'm sorry, Stelio,' I said. 'Because we thought you would be staying on the island, we haven't made up the bed yet.'

I used the word 'we' quite happily, knowing that Leyla didn't understand what we were saying in Greek. 'We' hadn't made up the bed. Leyla and I. Stelio didn't seem very interested. He was focused on whatever he was looking at out of the window.

'This was my childhood room,' I explained. 'The garden below belongs to the neighbours; it's full of scrap iron. The whole neighbourhood is being torn down. We are to be rebuilt from top to toe.'

'*Telia*. Very nice,' Stelio said, finally turning towards me. Then he continued in English. 'It will be a real Istanbul experience.'

He took his laptop out of his backpack and plugged it into a wall socket. His computer was like Leyla's – metallic-grey. He put it on Mama's dressing table. Kneeling down, he opened his suitcase. Leyla walked to the door and I followed her.

'Get some rest,' we both said in two different languages at
exactly the same time. We laughed.

Stelio began taking shirts from his suitcase and hanging
them in the wardrobe where Mama's dresses had hung in the
past. He turned and looked at us in the doorway.

'Thank you,' he said in Turkish.

Leyla giggled. It seemed that Stelio had taken Turkish
lessons. He would be grateful if Leyla would speak Turkish with
him. Just what we needed! We were stuck there in the narrow
doorway, side by side.

Suddenly Leyla did an unexpected thing: she held my
hand. Then she said to Stelio in Turkish, 'Pericles and I are
going down to my apartment, one floor down. We'll make
something to eat and bring some up for you.'

I don't know how much of what she said Stelio understood.
He was looking at our joined hands, our interlocked fingers. He
nodded. There was a smile on his handsome face.

We didn't mention Stelio when we went down to Leyla's
place. Although we counted him in while we made spaghetti
with tomato sauce, we didn't talk about him. 'Do you have
any red wine? It's good to add a couple of spoonfuls to the
sauce,' I said. She didn't have any, but she did have vinegar, so
we used that instead.

We strained the spaghetti, rinsed it with cold water, dumped
half of it onto a platter left from Aunt Ismene, and poured the
sauce over the top. Then the other half went onto the same
platter with more sauce. Leyla was hungry and in a rush to
eat. I had to teach her that it was the small details and many
layers that touched a person's soul.

We could not set the table. Since I'd seen it last, it had
gotten very cluttered. Leyla had bought a lot of new books
– books on the Events of September 6th and 7th, about the

exiles of 1964, research books, novels, poetry books, books about Cyprus. She was taking my work seriously. I realized that she was trying to earn every kurus I gave her. I wondered why she'd left university. Would she tell me about her past one day?

We placed our steaming platter on the coffee table in the living room. Leyla filled her plate and took her place on the windowsill overlooking Temrin Hill Street. I sat on the divan. The apartment smelled of tobacco and sandalwood. Leyla must have been burning incense in the daytime. The only light in the living room came from a large white globe on the floor. The place on the ceiling where Aunt Ismene's crystal chandelier had once hung was empty. There was a lamp among the papers on the dining room table. What with it being so quiet outside, the muted lighting made everything seem peaceful.

'Mmm, mmm,' Leyla murmured from her perch. 'This is wonderful. Such delicious layers of flavour on my tongue. Magnificent!'

I was pleased with myself. Invigorated, I said, 'Let me bring some wine down from upstairs. We'll have a glass each, shall we?'

She shook her head. 'Wine makes me sleepy. I want to do a bit more work on these sections with you. But don't worry about me – you go ahead. I'll go and get it, and I'll leave Stelio's plate in his room.'

'I'll go.'

I stood up from the hard divan at a speed that astonished even me. Leaving my plate beside the books on the dining table, I went upstairs. There was no sound from Stelio and no light under his door. He was probably sleeping.

By the time I got back downstairs, Leyla had finished

eating and was rolling a cigarette. She saw that I'd brought two glasses down with the wine, but she didn't say anything. I filled mine. She'd rolled a cigarette for me too, which she handed to me. I lit it and inhaled. This time my lungs didn't seize up. We sat side by side on the couch. When she opened the computer on her lap, the white light was reflected in her face. Puffing on her cigarette, she began to read. As I sipped my wine, I gazed at her tiny nose, the movement of her fine lips as she read my story to me, her neck protruding from her sweater.

When she finished reading, she asked, 'How was that?', her voice anxious.

'It was good.'

'That's it? I thought the part where you met Ulker on New Year's Eve was particularly well written.'

'You're right. That part is strong.'

'But…?'

'It's like I'm reading someone else's story. When it comes from your pen…'

'Okay. Do you like this other person's story? I mean, does it move you? Are you affected by it?'

'Yes, of course. Even more than when I lived it.'

Gathering her legs under her, she turned to me. In the dim light, something like lightning shone in her hazel eyes. Happiness made her voice go higher.

'That's great! That's very, very, very good news. Do you know why this last part is so good?'

'Why?'

'Because you've finally opened up. You aren't hiding from me, from your reader, any more.'

I felt as embarrassed as a child. I didn't know what to say. For a man to open up was not laudable, not something to trumpet. I took a big gulp of wine. Then another. I changed the subject.

'What about you, Leyla?'

'Me?'

'When are you going to open up to me? You've just said that I've opened my heart to you. But you…'

She leant over and stubbed out her cigarette on the tomato-stained plate. Mine had gone out by itself between my fingers.

'We aren't writing my story, are we? And, anyway, my life isn't book material.'

I wished then that I could list all the things that we had found out about her online – her becoming a conservative businessman's mistress when she was nineteen; abandoning both her home and her university and running away to America's most remote state; removing herself from the world; her mother, with whom she wasn't on speaking terms, a mother who had herself run away from home when she was eighteen only to eventually give up and return with her daughter… just because this was the stuff of novels, it didn't mean I should put pressure on Leyla to tell me.

I finished the wine in my glass and refilled it. The bottom of the bottle was visible now. It was a wonderful thing to rest there, to live one's life in that softness. I thought of Ulker, of our lovemaking in her apartment in Tunel, of how much I missed her. More than anyone, it was always Ulker whom I missed the most.

Leyla pulled the computer onto her lap.

'Let's carry on then. With… what? Do you have any notes from yesterday?'

'No notes. This time I'll talk and you can type.'

I was going to talk about Ulker. About when I found her again. About our love.

'Agreed,' said Leyla. 'That's also good. What year are we in?'

'1960. The year I started high school.'

Leyla typed into the blank document she'd just opened.

'Which month?'

'October.'

'Place?'

'Beyoglu.'

Once again, there was a gap between what I was intending to say and what I actually said. I tried to speak about Ulker, but what came out instead was the story of our running into Despina that Saturday afternoon.

Without saying a word, Leyla transposed what I'd said onto the blank page in front of her. A story was being woven from my memories.

At one point her fingers paused over the illuminated letters.

'Despina, Despina, Despina...' she murmured. Was she singing a song or trying to remember something? Then, as if the needle in her mind had leapt over whatever was obstructing it, she nodded and returned to her computer.

We continued well into the night, sitting side by side on the couch as I talked and she typed. Every so often she'd read out what she'd written and I'd add things. I polished off the wine. When we'd finished, we sat silently for a time, thinking about Despina's painful fate.

'There so much evil in the world. And all because of people,' murmured Leyla.

I thought of saying that it wasn't 'people' but men. Most acts of cruelty were perpetrated by my own sex; I felt the burden of this deep inside me. At the same time, my head was spinning. I wanted to forget about my age. I reached out and took Leyla's hand. She laid her beautiful head on my shoulder. A while later I felt her breathing getting deeper. My beauty had fallen asleep on my shoulder. I looked at our hands locked together. What did Leyla see in me? The father she had lost? The grandfather who raised her? Though I knew my back would hurt intolerably the next day, I leant my head against the wall behind me and closed my eyes.

When I woke up at around dawn, I was lying alone on the divan, covered in a thick navy-blue blanket left from Aunt Ismene's time. Even in my drowsy state I hoped that Stelio, upstairs, had woken up and noticed that the bed in my room had not been slept in.

Fit as a fiddle, Monsieur Pericles. Yes, indeed.

# The Wedding is Mine, the Marriage is Yours

A week after my marriage proposal, Markela was discharged from the psychiatric ward. I took it as my success. Her love for me, and the joy of our upcoming wedding, had healed her. Although Dr Lefteris had warned us that she should not get over-excited, her family in Yenikoy immediately rolled up their sleeves to prepare for our wedding celebrations. We were to be married without delay, that very summer, and a magnificent affair was planned. First there would be a ceremony in the Greek church in Yenikoy, and then a wedding feast at the very fashionable Grand Hotel in Tarabya. Guests would come from Athens, and for those who would not be staying with relatives, my future father-in-law had reserved rooms in the hotel. Our wedding was to be the gathering of the Greek community that we'd been longing for.

I kept putting off telling Mama and Papa the news. I had asked Aunt Ismene to hold her tongue too. Mama needed to hear it from me. That's not what happened, of course. Most of the Istanbul Greeks in Athens lived in the same neighbourhood and socialized exclusively with one another. The news that the middle daughter of the Stathopoulos family, the daughter who'd never yet been seen in society, was marrying Pericles Drakos landed like a bomb in the Palaio Faliro neighbourhood, where they all lived. It would be the first big party that those who'd fled Istanbul in 1955, and those who'd been exiled from the city in 1964, would attend as guests.

When they finally heard the news, Mama refused to come to the wedding, and Papa was forbidden from entering the country. He was, in any case, still angry with me for having abandoned him and his new pharmacy. He cut short our telephone conversations and whenever I went to visit them in Athens he went to bed early.

Markela was staying in her parents' apartment in Yenikoy, where she spent her days reading on the balcony. While her mother and sisters busied themselves with every aspect of our wedding, from the bridal dress to the menu, Markela would look up from her book only to watch the fishing boats chugging up and down, the brightly lit ferry boats travelling their evening routes or the children jumping in and out of the water. Looking back now, I can still recall the glow on her face, the way the Bosphorus reflected in her eyes. She was peaceful, content in her quiet, Markela way.

Meanwhile, I was happy with my life. Yenikoy was far for me. It took an hour to reach Markela's house. But I assumed my future father-in-law would buy us a car as a wedding gift. If Markela was to live in Beyoglu at The Circle, she wouldn't be taking public transport to visit her parents. The thought of the car gave me a sense of relief. I felt a spark of excitement about our married life. Markela and I would live together in joy and plenty.

The apartment block that had replaced the mansion and garden in which Markela had grown up was a very pleasant three-storey building with a garden. All the flats were occupied by relatives or acquaintances. We used to have our evening meal of wine, mezze, fish and raki at a long table in the jasmine-scented garden. Markela's older sister, her husband Yanni and their three-year-old daughter Maria would join us at the table, along with other relatives who lived in the building. Sometimes Markela would go into the kitchen with Janin, their Armenian cook, and prepare fish roe salad, broad bean puree and fresh pinto beans in olive oil. Once she and Janin even cooked *topik*, a fancy Armenian dish made with chickpeas. Her younger sister Tasoula was a lively girl. She was studying sculpture at the Arts Academy and after dinner she would take up her guitar and sing. Markela's father would ask her mother to dance, and I too would grab Markela's hand. While we danced, I would kiss her cheek, and a tiny little dimple would appear on her waxen face. Seeing that dimple, her mother's eyes would fill with tears of joy.

As I gazed at the stars reflected in the shining waters of the Bosphorus, I felt happy. Perhaps I had found my home. Those merry evenings made me forget the cruelty of the world, the fact that at any moment the rug could be pulled from under our feet.

Markela and I both knew that our wedding celebration was more about presenting the Stathopoulos family's middle daughter to society than blessing our union. They were going to prove to everyone that their daughter had finally been 'cured'. This party was Monsieur Stathopoulos's show. He didn't hide this from us. When we raised our glasses in a toast at the long table, he would say, 'The wedding is mine, the marriage is yours, young ones.'

In the eyes of Markela's father, I was an orphan whose parents had been exiled to Greece. Since we had not had an engagement party, there was no harm in the bride's family hosting the wedding celebration. That was fine by me. The only people concerned about whether Mama and Papa would be coming or not were Markela's mother and sisters, for they were organizing the seating arrangements for the feast at the hotel. If the groom's family didn't come, there would be two empty places at the main table. May this be your only problem, mother-in-law, I thought to myself. I asked them to reserve seats at the family table for Aunt Ismene and my grandfather. I hoped my grandfather would not refuse such an invitation. (It would be another year before he would throw Markela and me out of his dank and dingy courtyard on the island.) In my naivete, I assumed that even if he wasn't bothered about my wedding he would at least not pass up the opportunity to enjoy a meal at Tarabya's Grand Hotel. Markela's father was going to have a car and driver pick him up from the Bostanci ferry pier. The Bosphorus Bridge had recently been completed, making it easier to get to Yenikoy.

Markela's family were very well-mannered people. They didn't ask me anything about Mama. Even so, I told them that Papa had a heart problem. That wasn't a complete lie. He had been diagnosed with a heart irregularity. Mama couldn't leave him on his own, which was why, unfortunately, she would not be joining us for the wedding ceremony. What else could I say? Should I have said that my mother could not accept my marrying a girl I met in a psychiatric hospital? I suggested to Markela's family that we could all go to Athens in September or at Christmas and celebrate our marriage over there as well. The in-laws could meet each other then. Markela's family accepted my proposal, though we all knew it would never happen.

Two days before the wedding, Aunt Ismene came to see me

at The Circle. In years to come, when Markela's illness came back, Aunt Ismene would spend every day at our apartment taking care of Markela. But this visit, just before the wedding, was the first time she'd been back to her old home since the day she was thrown out. The main door was open as always, so she came straight in and rang my doorbell. Seeing her there, I was suddenly overcome with emotion. The wounds I thought had healed began to bleed, slowly, softly. Mama's refusal to come to my wedding, the stamp in Papa's passport that forbade him from entering the country, his anger at me for having opened a pharmacy without him, the pain of Mama having not come to see me, all gathered force like an avalanche. I almost wept, even though it was one of my last nights as a bachelor and I was getting ready to go out and have some fun. I was going to meet my friends in Beyoglu – friends from university as well as other, more recent friends who were filmmakers, writers and cartoonists. I had showered, shaved and put on some cologne.

Aunt Ismene paid no attention to my smart appearance, nor my sudden surge of emotion. Neither was she thrown off by the fact that this was her first visit to The Circle in ten years. She walked straight into the living room in her black dress and worn-down shoes, put her handbag on the couch beside the record player and confronted me. Her grey-steaked head only came up to my chest, but I felt small as she fixed me with a hard stare. I immediately sat down in the orange bergère. She got a straight-backed chair from the dining room and sat directly across from me.

'I've come to warn you one last time, Pericles, my son. Do not marry poor Markela. You are my responsibility and that young woman is no good for you. *Ela*, come on now, give up on her before it's too late.'

She knew I wasn't going to listen to her. I guessed that it was because of Mama that she'd come such a long way. Mama would have insisted and Aunt Ismene would not have wanted to let her down. I made a joke of it.

'Theia Ismene, I'm marrying into a rich family. You should be happy for me. Markela's father is going to help me open a pharmacy in fancy Nisantas. He says Beyoglu is finished, and he's right. He might buy us a car as well. I'll be able to take you and Markela to restaurants along the Bosphorus in the evenings, to Bebek and Tarabya. Now that the new bridge has been completed, we can drive across it in our car and look down on Istanbul from up high. Will that be so bad?'

Aunt Ismene shook her head sadly. There was no point in wasting any more words, but I continued with my speech nonetheless. I told her how hot water ran from the taps in the apartments in Yenikoy, I described the family's mansion on Buyukada and I talked about the place I'd reserved for her at our table in the ballroom of Tarabya's Grand Hotel. As I talked, I got excited. I stood up. David Bowie's *Hunky Dory* was on the record player. I put the needle on 'Life on Mars?' – a track I'd been listening to on repeat for days – grabbed Aunt Ismene's hand and with difficulty pulled her up to dance with me. She resisted at first, but she must have seen the joy in my young face, felt the heat of my feverish body, for she eventually sighed and surrendered to my arms. I twirled her around the armchairs, the sofas, the coffee tables. I made her laugh, pressed an invitation to the wedding into her hand and sent her home, away from The Circle.

As I walked from Tarlabasi to Beyoglu, the sadness that had stabbed at my heart when I saw Aunt Ismene at my apartment door dissipated. You made the right decision, Pericles, my boy, I said to myself. You saved her life; now they're going to save yours. At my age there's no reason to be coy: the wealth of Markela's family had dazzled me. As the son of a family accustomed to losing out, I had never tasted a life of luxury. While my family were not poor, we were always wary. At any moment everything could be taken away from us. We had to stash our money away in nooks and crannies. Our apartment was our only possession that had survived the wealth tax. It was etched into my soul that I must grow up as quickly as possible, become a pharmacist and be a support for Papa. Ever since I'd decided against going to Athens, I'd worked very hard. This feeling of having nothing, of having nobody to protect me, was the reason I had gone along with Nejat's illegal activities and becoming a partner in his Circle of Fortune nightclub. I was hoping that after I'd married Markela and moved my pharmacy to Nisantas, I'd be able to free myself from him. Once I'd left Beyoglu, I'd no longer have need of the protection he and his boys gave me. I was marrying into a wealthy, established family. At last I would belong to something stronger, something larger.

My friends were waiting for me at Kilim, a club frequented by film people and art students. They cheered when I arrived. All of the friends I'd made since I'd been living by myself in Istanbul, including Kemal and Betul, were there, together with four or five of my old friends from high school, the last remaining members of our Greek community in the city.

After Kilim we jumped in cars and went to an American bar in Bebek. Others joined our table there. Girls I used to be sweet on came too. They raised their glasses cheerily, telling me they were going to miss me. No one was jealous of anyone else. Someone gave me a ride and we all went to a house in Nisantas. The house had a fantastic record collection, so we dimmed the lights and danced. Joints were passed around, bottles of imported whisky too. The beautiful women around me made my head spin. Towards morning I went out onto the street. Day was breaking, the stars were fading. I was very drunk and foolishly happy. I don't remember how I got from Nisantas to Tarlabasi.

Nejat was crouched in a dark corner beside the entrance to The Circle. When he suddenly materialized in the half-light, I didn't turn a hair. I was staggering by now. He took me by the shoulders and shoved me into The Circle. The automatic light switch was broken again and the whites of Nejat's eyes shone in the darkness. He was looking straight into my face, his hands still on my shoulders. I felt like laughing at his seriousness.

'If you wanna, I can get you to Greece right now,' he said.

'Me?' I said, trying to find the right words. 'I'm getting married, Nejat. Our wedding is in two days. No, wait. Not two days. What day is it now? It's morning, right? Tomorrow. Our wedding is tomorrow. You should come, Nejat. You wouldn't look so good in the church, but afterwards... In Tarabya, we're having a magnificent—'

Nejat shook me by my shoulders. 'Boy, are you crazy? What weddin' you talkin' 'bout? What church?'

'My wife, Nejat... such a beautiful girl... She's got long black hair. And my father-in-law is going to buy—'

'Oh-hoo. You don't have a clue, do ya?'

He stopped and looked me in the eye, then shook me again. My head spun.

'We've invaded Cyprus, boy! Do ya hear me, idiot? We've invaded Cyprus! Prime Minister Ecevit's on top of you Greeks. You're finished, Pericles Efendi. Finished. They won't let you breathe here now. Pack up your stuff. I got a car to get you over the border. I'm gonna shove you in it.'

I pulled my hands free. 'Mind your own business, Nejat!'

'We're at war, I'm tellin' you, boy. Don't you hear what I'm sayin'? Blood's gonna spill on that island.'

The lift wasn't working either. Swaying, I walked up the worn marble stairs to the third floor. Nejat seemed to stay watching me for a long time, and then, muttering a few swear words, he turned towards the street.

Even when I was inside my apartment, his invective flooded in through the open balcony door.

'Oh well... Don't take my advice, you idiot! You bastard idiot of a Greek! You've had it now. You're all finished. Cyprus is Turkish and Turkish it's gonna stay!'

The next day, when I woke up at noon, Markela called to confirm the news of the Cyprus invasion. The Turkish army had occupied the northern part of the island the night before. Our wedding party at the Tarabya hotel was cancelled. We got married in the autumn, in a simple ceremony at the church in Yenikoy – no party, no guests. When I brought my bride back to The Circle there was no pleasure in it for either of us. From the very beginning the shadow of the war in Cyprus hung over our marriage. When Mama came to Markela's funeral twelve years later, she whispered in Aunt Ismene's ear that our marriage had been cursed from the start.

# Breakfast

Stelio was standing by the windowsill that Leyla loved to perch on, drinking coffee and looking out onto Temrin Hill Street. I was elated by this, for that meant he'd got up early and realized that I'd spent the night at Leyla's apartment. I looked into his face. He was wearing black jeans and a dark-cherry cashmere sweater. With his greying hair and thick-framed glasses he was – why should I lie? – very handsome. He showed no trace of the ill-natured character of the grandfather whose name he had taken. He had a smiling face and was very polite. Seeing me, he reached for the mask in his jeans pocket. I motioned with my hand for him not to bother, then put on my house slippers which were in the entrance beside the console table.

'Don't worry about that, Stelio. Relax. You can't be walking around under the same roof as me for two weeks with a mask on.'

'I can put it on. It's no problem.'

I retrieved the basket on a rope from under the console table, took it into the living room and went out onto the French balcony overlooking Kaymakcalan Street. Samiha, the sister of Veli who owned the coffeehouse, was in the queue outside the bakery. She cleaned The Circle's common areas. I called out to her. When a loaf of bread and three of our sesame-encrusted, ring-shaped rolls – simits – had been placed in the basket, I hauled it up by its rope. Stelio, coffee cup in hand, had come over and was watching the ascent of the basket with a mixture of surprise and wonder. I hoped that Leyla would notice it passing her window. The third simit was for her.

As I lifted the basket inside, Stelio said, 'Let me make you a coffee.'

'I will take a bath first. Then I will have coffee.'

I didn't say anything else. Let him understand that I was still wearing yesterday's clothes. I took a long bath in the footed bathtub. I looked at the white hairs on my chest in the mirror. My arms were still strong and my flesh had not turned to flab. Genetically, I was fortunate. I hadn't put on weight or acquired a potbelly. I shaved meticulously, rubbed on some cologne and combed my hair back. In my bedroom I put on a navy-blue, Italian, wool sweater and corduroy trousers.

Of course, this Stelio didn't know what a proper breakfast table entailed. As an Istanbul host, it was my duty to show him. I made the tea and left it to steep in the kitchen. I set out the feta, black olives, butter, honey, jams and peeled and sliced tomatoes sprinkled with thyme on the marble counter in the kitchen, and Stelio carried everything through the tall, narrow service door to the dining-room table. I poured the tea into thin-waisted glasses, then wrapped the simits and several slices of fresh bread in a cloth napkin and placed them in a basket.

Stelio was even hungrier than I was. He set to everything at once, stuffing his mouth with simit, tomatoes and feta.

At the risk of burning his tongue, he took a sip of the hot tea and closed his eyes.

'Mmm, mmm! I've not tasted anything this delicious since the breakfasts I used to have at Yaya's house in Samatya, Monsieur Pericles. *Gia sta heria sas*. Health to your hands.'

Seeing Stelio had made me think about Aunt Ismene again. I was reminded of the day she walked out of the door and never returned. What season was that – spring or winter? I was surprised that I didn't remember. I'd just come back from Mama's funeral. Madam Ani's voice on the other end of the phone was muffled. I couldn't quite understand what she was saying, but it was something to do with Aunt Ismene, that much was clear. I had hailed a taxi and gone to Samatya. Aunt Ismene's house, stuffed with mismatched furniture, was neat. It was 2002 and Aunt Ismene would have been over eighty, but she was still strong and active. On her own two short legs she did her shopping and went to the bank and to the telephone office to pay her bills. Every Friday she'd go to the Four Seasons restaurant in Tunel for a meal by herself.

'Your *yaya* was a wonderful cook. She had a deep affection for the food simmering in the pot, and that love added a special flavour to her dishes.'

'She used to run away from home when she was young,' Stelio said, smiling as if he had heard my previous thoughts on Aunt Ismene. 'She'd jump on a bus, not knowing where it was going, and wander around the old neighbourhoods of Istanbul.'

I nodded. I knew this. That was why I used to send her home with a friendly taxi driver when she'd spent the day watching over Markela. The taxi driver would wait at my elderly aunt's door until she'd gone inside her house.

'What did your mother tell you about that?'

Stelio took a piece of bread and spread it with the quince jam that Vera brought when she last came. To avoid having to watch crumbs being scattered all over the tablecloth, I went to the kitchen to fetch the tea. Stelio immediately jumped up and followed me. He grabbed the teapot and brought it to the table, talking all the while.

'When Yaya ran away, she used to take Mum with her. That was before Mum started school, which makes it... when? Probably the early 1950s. Mum was very little. She doesn't know which neighbourhoods they went to, but she remembers seeing old courtyards with fires burning in the middle of them and little children with their hair cut short standing around the fires trying to warm their hands. When they saw my mother and grandmother at the entrance to the courtyard, they'd start crying. Mum and Yaya must have looked so incongruous among all that misery and squalor.'

We returned to the dining room. I refilled our tea glasses. Stelio lowered his voice.

'I'm trying to write a story about this running away from home. Mum's told me a lot, but it's you I need to talk to. You're the person who spent the most time with my *yaya* in Istanbul. You witnessed the last forty years of her life most closely. I want to make use of your knowledge in my story.'

Ha, that was all we needed! Two writers in one apartment – three, if you counted Leyla – was too many.

'I didn't know you wrote,' I said.

He laughed. With a hunk of bread he mopped up the juice from the tomatoes, the thyme and the last crumbs of feta from his plate and threw it into his mouth. Then he leant back.

'I'm writing this story for an anthology,' he said.

I didn't like the arrogant expression on his face and

immediately decided that I wouldn't ask him about it or answer his questions about Aunt Ismene. But he carried on regardless, as if I'd requested that he tell me more. At least this time he'd remembered to finish his mouthful before speaking.

'I have this friend. She's compiling an anthology of short stories and asked me to write something about my *yaya* after I mentioned her one night.' He paused. 'This friend... She's sort of the reason I came here.'

He was showing his true colours from day one. He was here for love. Good. We would understand each other. He told me how the woman was married. They had made love in a hotel room one night and then the woman had gone back to her husband. Stelio had been chasing her ever since. The house on Buyukada belonged to her.

'I thought you were going to stay there by yourself,' I said, taking inexplicable pleasure in finding inconsistences in his story.

'I was. She – my friend, I mean – is in Athens.'

The plot was thickening, but I wasn't interested. Stelio, the sensitive young man he was, noticed my lack of interest.

'Anyway, that's why I'm here. To write the story, in the hope that she'll be impressed by it. Which is ridiculous, of course, but life's all about taking risks and chasing impossible pleasures, isn't it?'

He placed his tea glass in the saucer and looked directly into my face, as if seeking my approval.

I nodded. 'You're right, Stelio.'

He smiled, presumably encouraged by my reaction. Raising his voice, he said, 'I'm going to explore the ancient temples of Byzantium – the ones in the ramparts, the ruins. I think they're going to inspire me.'

Aunt Ismene came to my mind once again. The police had

searched for her corpse along the old city walls, in the ruins of its old Byzantine churches. At that time elderly Greek women in Samatya and Kumkapi were being strangled for the gold they'd supposedly sewn into their petticoats or the family fortunes they were said to have hidden beneath their houses. Several corpses had been discovered alongside the walls of long-forgotten churches, but no one found Aunt Ismene's body. Stelio was hoping to unearth traces of his grandmother as much as he was hoping to impress his lady friend. That's why he wanted to go to the old city, to the half-buried churches.

I was about to ask Stelio again about Ismene when he said, 'Leyla stopped by while you were having a bath.'

I hurriedly took out the pit of the olive I'd thrown into my mouth and put it on the edge of my plate.

Stelio smiled. 'She's very devoted. You're lucky to have a neighbour like her.'

I cleared my throat, reached for my tea. 'Very devoted', was she?

'Given your closeness, I thought Leyla had lived here for a long time. But I understand that she's only recently moved into the downstairs flat.'

I wondered what else Leyla had told him, chatting in the doorway. I'd been in the bath for quite a long time.

'Eh, *vevea*. I understand. During lockdown, when you're so cut off, a week can seem like a month, of course.'

'What did Leyla want?'

'Nothing. She was worried about you. You left her apartment so early this morning.'

I smiled.

'I mean it. She's really protective of you. When she saw me walking around the apartment without a mask, she fussed at me. She's so cute.'

I stood up, gathered up the napkin I'd spread over my lap and shook the breadcrumbs onto my plate.

'Stelio, with your permission, I will have a little rest now. I didn't sleep much last night. Could you clear the table? I don't have a dishwasher, so you'll need to do the dishes by hand.'

Without waiting for a reply, I went into my study overlooking Temrin Hill Street and closed the door. I wanted to write, and in writing to remember, in writing to forget, in writing to live.

# Bloody May 1st

By the time I saw Ulker again at the New Year's Eve party at
Kemal's house, Markela and I had long since been sleeping in
separate beds. In the twelve years that separated our wedding
in the shadow of the Cyprus invasion and that New Year's
Eve, Markela had been hospitalized several times. The first
few times, she chose to admit herself to hospital as soon as she
heard the footsteps of a major depression in a dark corner of
her brain. Just as a patient can anticipate a migraine, Markela
could sense the change in her brain chemistry. She would
pack her suitcase. In the hospital she'd be given medicines
not found in my pharmacy. But it wasn't enough. The liquid
injected into her veins made her sleep but did not make her
well; asleep, she was merely free of pain for a while.

I talked with Dr Lefteris many times, bombarded the poor
man with questions. Could something have happened to
Markela in her childhood? Her sisters were well-balanced,
happy, loving women. The parents were devoted to their
daughters. She'd had a happy childhood in a wealthy home.
Why was it that my Markela had been having nervous

breakdowns since she was fourteen years old? Why didn't she get well even though I was giving her everything?

'You should view Markela's illness as a medical condition, Pericles. There are so many things we don't know in the field of psychiatry. Some people are born with a hole in their heart or only one kidney, others fall prey to diseases that progress over the course of many years. You've got to think of Markela's depression in that way.'

Even as Dr Lefteris talked to me about the chemistry of the brain, fluids, glands and hormones, I stubbornly persisted in searching for something traumatic in Markela's past. When he got fed up with me, Dr Lefteris interrupted, saying, 'Any Istanbul Greek who grew up in this city will have experienced enough trauma to cause them psychological damage in later life, but your wife's condition cannot be ascribed to that alone. Otherwise you'd expect most of us here to be suffering from serious depression, wouldn't you? But no, we've managed to supress our fears and get on with our lives.'

When Markela came home from the hospital that first time, she was happy. The crisis had been averted. She congratulated herself for having nipped it in the bud. I took her to Athens for the Easter holiday. I wanted to prove to Mama and Papa that my wife was a healthy, well-balanced individual. We did not stay at their house in Palaio Faliro but at a house lent to us by my high-school friend Niko. He gave me the keys to his little stone house in an olive grove on the outskirts of Plaka and it was there, in the spring of 1977, that Markela and I had the honeymoon which for one reason or another had eluded us until then. We woke in the morning to the twitter of birdsong and made love for a long, long time inside our white mosquito netting. We talked about having a baby.

Because of the Cyprus crisis, Markela's father's business was not going well. He was on the verge of bankruptcy. Turkish businessmen had terminated their partnerships with him because he was Greek. They were applying a covert embargo. The car we'd been given as a wedding present had been seized by enforcement. If we were to have a child, how could we take care of it? Should we move to Athens like everybody else?

The tavernas on the narrow streets of Plaka were packed. Greece had at last seen the back of wars, coups and military juntas and had turned its eyes towards freedom. The houses lining the road to the Acropolis were painted in bright, shiny colours, and red, pink and white geraniums bloomed in the windows. Daisies dotted the grass of the ancient agora and the marble of the Temple of Zeus shone pink in the setting sun. Perhaps we should raise our child there, I thought. But first we had to make our child. Laughing, we fell to lovemaking again, sometimes in the middle of the day, without even taking off our clothes, on the kilim in the living room of the little stone house or on the kitchen's marble counter.

After those days of abundant lovemaking in Athens, nothing went our way. As soon as we returned to Istanbul, she suffered another bout of depression, just when we least expected it. Markela was sure she was pregnant. She hadn't been to a doctor, but her period was late.

'I can feel it. A new life is beginning inside me, like a delicate pulse. Put your hand here. It's like the purring of a cat. Can you feel it?'

I did not feel it, but my wife was happy. On our return flight from Athens, as the plane flew low on its approach to Istanbul and we gazed down at the Sea of Marmara and the Princes' Islands, we both reflected on our place in Istanbul.

Life in Greece was easy. People were warm and friendly and everyone spoke our language. If we lived there, we wouldn't need to be in perpetual fear that our jobs, our home, might be taken from us. We wouldn't be consumed with anxiety that with every new political upheaval our child would be roughed up when they came out of school at the end of each day. Papa had aged greatly in ten years, but his anger had almost passed. Mama had been reserved with Markela, but would grow to love her in time. The picturesque stone houses with olive trees growing in their courtyards and the streets of Athens lined with citrus trees would make an ideal place to raise a child. All of this was true. But the truth was, we couldn't give up on our city. We were going to stay in Istanbul. As we stared down through the little windows of the plane, our interlocked hands were like a seal. In spite of all the difficulties, we were bonded to our Poli.

When we got home, Markela's downturn began with a flow of menstrual blood. 'I'm losing our baby,' she cried.

When I tried to comfort her, she got more upset. There might not have been a baby there at all, I said. Perhaps her period had been late because of the travelling, which could upset a woman's cycle. Taking one's body out of its normal environment could cause it to temporarily stop ovulating; now that her body knew it was back home, back in The Circle, back in its routine, it had relaxed and her hormones had resumed their old rhythm. There was nothing to get upset about.

'*Ohi!* No! No!' cried Markela. 'Our baby was there. He was alive. I felt him. Now he's slipping away and I can't hold onto him.'

Three days after that, five hundred thousand people, who had gathered in Taksim Square in Beyoglu to celebrate

May 1st, International Workers' Day, were opened fire on. Shots were fired at the crowd from the top of the Waterworks Building and from various floors of hotels in the vicinity. Panicked people raced into side streets, where they were met by military tanks and police vehicles. The moment we heard bombs exploding, Markela and I shut ourselves in the back bedroom. We sat on the floor between the wardrobe and the bed under which Papa had hidden Elena and me years earlier, and hugged each other. From outside came the sound of screams, sirens and bombs exploding one after the other. We didn't know then that they were stun grenades. Markela was curled up like a foetus in my arms. We should have stayed in Athens, I thought frenziedly. Now they're going to come and break down our door and drag Markela from my arms... I held her tighter. Some people must have run all the way to our street, for there were screams coming from right below us.

Hours later we listened to reports about what had happened on the radio. Helicopters were flying overhead and the police and ambulance sirens were nonstop. I went to Kurabiye Street to open the pharmacy. Markela wanted to come with me, and I didn't object. I would need an assistant. Many people had been trampled in the crush. Word that our pharmacy was open spread rapidly and Markela and I spent the whole night tending to the wounded. We cleansed the shoulder and leg injuries of young girls, bandaged up as best we could the workers whose faces and heads had hit the edges of pavements in the crush, treated academics with dislocated bones. Shortly after midnight, Kemal came in. His arm was in a sling, his head bandaged. Although he'd narrowly escaped being killed, he was smiling. He'd been in the throng that had tried to leave the square via Kazanci Hill. A truck was blocking the way, causing the thousands of people fleeing the bullets to pile on top of each other. They trod on Kemal's head and carried on. It was a miracle that he'd escaped with only that much damage. I hugged my friend and looked around for somewhere for him to rest in the pharmacy that he and I had started together ten years earlier.

'What rest, Pericles, my friend? I came here to help you. Forget about the hospitals – they're all full to bursting. In the emergency rooms they've got two people to each stretcher. Some fascist doctors are purposely making people wait, and children are lying there with open wounds. Kurabiye Pharmacy is on the lips of all the walking wounded: "Kurabiye Pharmacy is open and they're bandaging people up for free. Don't go to the hospital, go to Kurabiye Pharmacy." When I heard that, my friend – what can I say? – I wasn't surprised. I said, "Yes, that's my lion-hearted Pericles." I immediately raced here to help. However...' Kemal turned to Markela and smiled. 'However, I see that you have a very attractive assistant.'

Somehow, I'd not yet found the opportunity to introduce Markela to Kemal, though of course he knew about her. Markela held out her thin white hand. They shook hands. The pharmacy had filled up. Kemal put on a white coat. His left arm was out of action, but he could clean wounds with his right hand. The three of us treated the wounded together until morning. From somewhere in the distance we could still hear shots and explosions, but we were used to night-time fighting by then. Everybody was shooting everybody at that point. So much blood was being shed in the country.

After that bloody May 1st, Markela's condition deteriorated. One night I awoke to find her standing in front of the bedroom window, her eyes closed, the old shirt of mine that she wore to sleep in open at the neck. She was facing into the breeze. We'd been sleeping with the window open so as to breathe in the fresh air of early summer. The tails of the shirt – which barely covered Markela's bottom – and her long black hair were dancing in the seaweed-scented breeze. It was a southwest wind, a *notias*, as we call it, the one they say drives people crazy. My wife's magnificent legs shone like two columns in the darkness – a beautiful sight. I was drowsy with sleep, hovering between dreams and reality, unable to distinguish between the two right away. But when she sprang like a grasshopper onto the windowsill, I realized she was intending to jump. I don't recall how I got up from where I was lying. In my memory's next scene, Markela has fallen into my arms and is crying.

'Let me go. Oh, let me go. My chest is tight, I can't breathe. Don't you understand? Let me get some air into my lungs.'

I called Aunt Ismene. We put Markela in a taxi and took her back to the hospital. Dr Lefteris said that we could try electroshock therapy, which had had a positive effect on Markela in the past. Since Markela was now a married woman, my permission was all that was needed. I couldn't tell him that this was the first I'd heard about that. Markela, my wife of three years, had hidden from me the fact that she'd undergone that horrifying treatment. I must have looked very confused, for the doctor felt the need to explain, saying, 'Don't worry, in this hospital we administer electroshock therapy under general anaesthetic and we give muscle relaxants too.' When I first met Markela she'd been having that treatment three times a week, and after the seventh session they'd observed a sudden improvement.

It took me a long time to process the shattering news. In the months that I'd visited Markela in the hospital every Saturday afternoon, her brain was being subjected to regular bouts of this terrible treatment. The real reason her face had been placid and unemotional was this therapy. I'd believed it was my increasingly frequent visits that had cured Markela, that I was making that poor, broken young woman well with my love; that I was a real hero. What a fool.

Dr Lefteris was a tall, thin man, a few years older than me. He knew Markela's family from Buyukada. Lowering his voice, he said, 'We've seen some good outcomes in seriously depressed patients with suicidal tendencies like Markela.'

Markela was sitting there so hopelessly, on her iron bedstead in her room overlooking the hospital garden, that she was ready to do whatever Dr Lefteris recommended. But despite her apparent calmness, I saw the fear in her eyes as the nurses, led by Aunt Ismene, stretchered her out of her room. Aunt Ismene reiterated that everything would be fine. She would go to sleep. When she woke up, she would be free of the shadow that absorbed the light of her brain.

And for a while Markela did cope all right. But she was never again the woman who'd made love to me under the white netting in the little stone house in Athens. We still slept together, but I knew she was only doing it to make me happy. She didn't even come close to passion. The electric shocks took away all pleasurable sensations, all desire.

Then, right after the military coup of 1980, Markela separated our bedrooms.

# Hotel Rooms

A few months after the military coup of 1980, I ran into my childhood sweetheart Niki at the funeral of our high-school literature teacher. She was still gorgeous, but it was clear she was extremely troubled. Her husband had been arrested. After being tortured, he had confessed to a crime he had not committed and had been sentenced to seven years' hard labour.

'Couldn't you have gone to Greece?'

In the late 1970s, when people of different political ideologies were killing each other on the streets, many left-leaning Greeks had fled to Greece, which meant they weren't around when the military coup happened.

'Engin – my husband – is Turkish,' Niki said.

I suggested we go for a drink after the funeral. We ended up talking late into the night, and as memories from our former life flooded back, one thing led to another.

She didn't want to sleep with me in her house in Sisli, so we began meeting in hotels in the afternoon. Occasionally I'd feel guilty about taking advantage of a lonely, desperate woman whose husband was in prison, but Niki was very beautiful.

She generously offered her slim, dark, curvaceous body to me. To begin with, I was able to leave Markela at home by herself; it wasn't yet necessary to have Aunt Ismene be with her. Since the night when I'd seen her at the window, she'd not made another suicide attempt. She told me repeatedly that she'd not been thinking of taking her own life that night; she'd really only wanted to get some air. I let myself be convinced.

Whenever I went to meet Niki, I would leave the pharmacy in the hands of my apprentice, Aydin, whom I had trained. He was a recent pharmacy graduate and knew the work well. He probably also knew about my partnership with Nejat, but as long as I paid his salary regularly, he wasn't about to say anything.

The market for heroin in Europe was growing and Nejat was not one to pass up an opportunity. He had links with the organized crime gang who trafficked the heroin and morphine coming out of Afghanistan and Iran into Europe. Turkey was a key point on the international heroin route. A small portion of the heroin stayed in Nejat's hands, which he then sold to the rich kids of families living in Bebek, Levent and Nisantas. He would often offer me some of the heroin to 'make Markela happy', which I vehemently refused. In those years Nejat would often stop by our apartment. Using the nightclub as an excuse, he'd come up to us on the weekends, stretch out on the sofa and watch films that Markela had rented from the video shop with her. It seems strange to look back on, but ultimately, Nejat was an ill and lonely mafia godfather and ours was the one place where he could relax. He was aware of my wife's depression. While I paid no attention to his offer of heroin, when he had some good Afghan weed, I would occasionally buy some, and I would smoke it with Niki in the hotel rooms where we made love in the afternoons.

Beyoglu was in a miserable state. Yesilcam was finished. Some of the cinemas I used to race to after lessons were over had closed down. Others survived by showing porn films. The stars of the Turkish films whom I had adored in my high-school years were now forced to take roles in those porn films; that included Ulker's father's young mistress. When Niki and I walked to the hotels on Mis Street or to the ones behind Asmali Mescit Street I would see the doe-eyed actress's bare breasts and buttocks on film posters. Strangely, I never went to see the sex films that she, the woman who'd decorated the fantasies of my youth, was in. The thought of watching the men and women whose faces were familiar to me from the Yesilcam films I used to secretly sneak into making love made me feel sick.

Niki could no longer walk down Beyoglu Avenue unaccompanied. The hordes of men who'd poured into the city from every corner of Turkey would not leave a slim, elegant woman like her alone. The moment she stepped onto Beyoglu Avenue, men swarmed all over her. Spurred on by one another, they'd tap her on the shoulder, grab her bottom or her leg, try to touch whatever part of her they could lay their hands on. Even before she got to my pharmacy from Taksim, there'd be at least one man following her. The men gathered at the entrances to the cinemas would scratch their crotches and look Niki up and down with dark eyes, even if I was with her. The pastry shops and cinemas of our youth, where we used to meet our classmates and have such fun, were gone from Beyoglu now. Niki and I were like a pair of dinosaurs. Beyoglu had become a place for poor, angry young men. The coup of 1980 came upon us in this darkness, only increasing the sadness and pessimism.

The hotels where Niki and I made love in the afternoons

were used by clandestine couples like us and by women who had sex for money and the men who paid for it. We could have gone to better hotels. Was it essential that I bring my beautiful lover from her house in Sisli to Beyoglu, to my doorstep? We both had money. We could have gone to the Bosphorus. We could have escaped to the Polish village on the weekends. We could have made love in my downstairs flat. But no. Both of us loved to demean ourselves in those cheap hotel rooms. Niki felt guilty for cheating on her political prisoner husband. I didn't feel guilty about anything. I was a man whose wife slept in a separate room. It was my right to have sex with a beautiful woman who desired me. The grotty hotel rooms excited me. The cheaper and more vulgar they were, the greater the erotic pleasure I experienced with Niki.

We never went to the same hotel twice, even though we only ever used them for a couple of hours at a time and there was never anyone there to remember us. Niki would bring clean sheets from her house because for some reason she was afraid of catching scabies, a fear that always made us laugh. We needed to laugh. We needed each other. It was as if in all of Istanbul there were only the two of us left, out of all our classmates. There had to have been others around somewhere, one or two friends who'd managed to hold on to life in the city. Surely not everyone had fled to Greece, had they? We would ask each other: is Niko in Athens? Where is Stefanos? Where did Maria get to? And what about American Sofia? Everyone had scattered to distant corners of the earth.

Niki and I would lie stark naked, holding each other, in a dingy hotel room on a Beyoglu backstreet, on a bed with squeaky springs, atop lavender-smelling sheets she'd brought from home. I loved to run my fingers along her spine and her dark, narrow back. Unlike Markela, she was a woman whose skin was responsive to touch, who knew how to take pleasure. She was as hungry for sex as I was. If necessary, she would make love to me several times so as to attain the orgasm she desired. As she climaxed, she'd bury her face in a pillow so that her moans wouldn't pass through the thin walls of the hotel room. We laughed about that too. 'Yours is the only genuine orgasm to pass through these walls, Niki,' I'd say. Closing her big eyes, she would lie back on the bed beside me.

As we lay naked in bed, our room behind the faded curtains would be filled with the clamour of the Beyoglu backstreets, the deafening sound of megaphones on trucks selling onions and potatoes, the cries of yogurt sellers. The architecture and interiors of some of the hotels were still lovely: lion-footed bathtubs and bronze taps in huge bathrooms, floor mosaics that, if cleaned, would have been breathtakingly beautiful. But all of them were deteriorating from neglect. Niki claimed that our choosing these places for our lovemaking was a charitable act. Maybe some owner with taste would realize what a treasure they had in their hands and restore the building. This would be our contribution, however small.

Niki's hopes were not realized. Day by day, the hotels became more rundown. Repairs were carried out with cheap, plasticky materials – vinyl or asbestos tiles on top of mosaics, old wooden floors covered with synthetic carpeting, lion-footed bathtubs ripped out and showers with disgusting curtains which stuck to your body when you were washing installed in their place. Breaking our rule once, we returned to a hotel in Tunel because Niki had particularly liked the woodwork there, only to find that they'd since installed aluminium window frames. She gripped my arm and began to cry. After that we gave up on Beyoglu and went to hotels in Sirkeci, near the train station, instead.

My relationship with Niki lasted for five years. We would meet on Tuesday afternoons at Sirkeci Train Station, hurriedly have a sandwich and an orange juice at a stand, then go to the hotel we'd chosen for that day. After satisfying our bodily needs, we would lie in bed and chat. When we left, Niki would get in a shared taxi from Eminonu to Sisli and I would walk across the Galata Bridge and go up to Beyoglu on the funicular. The smell of coal would burn my nostrils, make my eyes stream. The waters of the Golden Horn were lead-grey. When the south wind blew, I felt nauseous.

For all those years we never once skipped our arrangement, until one Tuesday afternoon Niki did not come to Sirkeci Train Station. It was the autumn of 1985. Niki had never talked about her husband to me, but at one of our last meetings she had mentioned the possibility of an amnesty. So it seemed that Engin had now returned to his home and his wife. At the same spot where I had once bid farewell to Mama and Papa, amid trains arriving and departing, passengers disembarking, porters scrambling to grab suitcases and conductors blowing their whistles, I waited for my lover in vain.

Strangely, I never saw Niki again. I never ran into my lover of five years at church or funerals or in the cafés of Beyoglu that in the 1990s returned to their former state. Our secret affair that no one knew about and my lover who looked like Audrey Hepburn became like a dream. A dream that you recalled when you woke at midnight but that by morning had vanished from your mind.

I didn't tell Markela about my affair with Niki and she didn't ask. Did she know? She must have noticed that I didn't ask her for sex any more. No doubt she knew that a forty-year-old man could only suppress his sexual needs up to a point.

I always came home in the evenings and we'd eat together; the meal would have been prepared either by Markela, if she was in a fit mood, or by Rayiha if she wasn't. We'd moved the sofa in front of the television and after dinner we'd sit there side by side, peeling oranges. Markela read the TV page of the newspaper carefully and always knew when there was a good film on. As she watched the film, she'd doze off and her head would rest on my shoulder. Then I'd put my arm around her shoulders and stroke her beautiful black hair. Not with passion but with love and tenderness. With the inner peace of a man who had taken his pleasure from another woman's body. No, I felt no guilt as far as Markela was concerned.

Which was why, when I met Ulker again at the New Year's Eve party at Kemal's house, I didn't mention that Markela was waiting for me at home. 'My wife and I are separated,' I said. 'We'll be divorced soon.' Perhaps I too would be causing irreparable damage to my poor wife's psyche. But once I'd found Ulker again, what else could I do? Ulker wasn't my past as I once thought – she was the one I could never move beyond. The moment I took her in my arms, I made the decision to divorce Markela. Later, no one believed me, but that really had been my intention.

# Chain of Losses

Once the final novel written in her father's name had been turned in to the publishers, Leyla worked like a bee on my book. In three days she finished three chapters. On Friday evening she called me down to her apartment. She didn't want to read what she'd written out loud in front of Stelio. I had never seen her so excited.

'Come and sit here,' she said, pointing to the divan beside the wall.

She settled herself in her customary place on the windowsill overlooking Temrin Hill Street. The last of the day's sunlight was withdrawing from the living room's wooden floor. I reached out and turned on the fat white lamp in the corner. Leyla opened her laptop, cleared her throat. I leant back against the cushions and prepared to listen to the story of my life. Leyla's voice cracked from time to time; she would take a break, have a sip of water. Her eyes kept flitting back up to me. The more involved she was in her work, the more importance she gave to my reaction.

When she finished, she remained facing her open computer. Her eyes were shining like a cat's in the white light reflected from its screen and her cheeks seemed flushed for some reason. In describing my first kiss with Ulker she had embellished the scene, lengthened it, and in a strange way had managed to make it exactly as it had been.

'Where did you find the Oya part? There wasn't much about her in my notes.'

She ran her fingers over the letters on the illuminated keyboard. 'You think there wasn't?'

Up till then, we'd always followed the same pattern. Leyla would make a rough draft from my notes and then, before reading it to me, she'd ask for certain details, which she'd then include. Could the sound of soldiers drilling be heard from The Circle? What about church bells? How tall was Markela? What day of the week was it when we saw Mama and Papa off at Sirkeci Train Station? What happened to the hat maker, Elpiniki? In the last chapters about Ulker, however, she'd gone beyond my notes and invented all the details herself, from start to finish. Now I understood why she was so excited. It was extraordinary how the scenes she'd written without consulting me, the specifics she'd included, were so similar to how I remembered them. It was as if a passage had been opened into my past and Leyla had journeyed back into those years. Although I hadn't mentioned it to her, she had guessed that I initially liked Oya more than Ulker. I'd tried to get her attention, but she couldn't have cared less. She even made fun of my interest in her. I didn't want to say this to Leyla. That would have been too mean. But clearly the truth had emerged nonetheless. Leyla was very perceptive.

Leyla closed the lid of her computer. Darkness settled over the room.

'Let me buy you a lamp, Leyla.'

'I like it like this. I'll light a candle.'

She jumped down from the windowsill, lit a log-like candle and placed it on the coffee table between us. Leaning over, she lit a cigarette from the flame. I looked sadly at the baggy, low-slung trousers of her grey sweatsuit. If Vera hadn't sold Mama's dresses, how those narrow-waisted suits and flowery summer dresses would have become Leyla!

She sat down on the floor in front of me. 'What happened to the kitten?'

'She lived with me for years after my parents left to go to Athens. But one day, when a friend was driving overland to Athens, I put Mitsy in their car and that's how she crossed the border. Little Mitsy, the kitten from Narmanli Han, lived in Athens with Mama and Papa. She was almost twenty when she died.'

'I'm glad. Finally, a happy ending.' She waved away the cigarette smoke.

'What do you mean? Why do you say "Finally"?'

She averted her eyes.

'I mean... Just look at the story. While the young Pericles is still a university student, the Turkish Republic decides to exile his father. His mother chooses her husband over her son and goes to Athens with him. There's a grandfather who's dealt such a blow with the wealth tax that he falls to the ground, never to rise again, after which he witnesses a horrible incident that makes him turn his back on life. His wife, unable to bear the pain of having the fortune they'd worked for all their life taken from them, dies of tuberculosis. Aunt Ismene, who had taken the young Pericles under her wing, leaves her house one day and vanishes into thin air. Before that, Markela has died. Ulker abandons you. We haven't written about it yet, but it's obvious that soon she will abandon you for the second time. You have one male friend. He's a mafia godfather with multiple sclerosis and he also dies in this story. If Yesilcam hadn't been wiped out by the arrival of television, they would have made a series out of your book. Amid so much loss, the kitten's happy ending makes me glad.'

Having rattled off all that without taking a breath, she stopped talking and started picking stray strands of tobacco off the divan with the tips of her fingers. I hadn't told Leyla that I'd decided not to give my book to a publisher. In truth, until that moment I wasn't even aware that I'd decided that. When Leyla held up a mirror to my life, I suddenly understood that I didn't want anyone else to read my story. But I would keep writing until the end so that Leyla would read it. After that, I could die in peace. There would be one person who had borne witness to my life. This witness business is particularly important for childless people. We all want there to be someone left behind who knows we existed.

Leyla circled the table, holding her extinguished cigarette in her fingers. She came and sat beside me and put her arm around my shoulders. With happiness I watched the candle gutter.

'I didn't mean to make you sad when I said all that. Are you upset?'

Her young body was warm and soft as it pressed against mine. I didn't answer, in the hope that she'd stay like that a little longer.

'Pericles?'

The fingers gripping my shoulder gave me a nudge.

She leant a little closer, sighed and relit her cigarette with a lighter she took from the pocket of her sweatpants.

'My life is also, to a certain extent, a chain of losses. What else, anyway, is this thing we call life?'

I stayed still. Without taking her arm from my shoulders,

she kept her eyes on the candle flame. I could feel the touch of her fingers on my shirt. I took an almost imperceptible breath.

'When I was a child, we lived in a village near Bodrum. My dad was an alcoholic even then. He smoked weed too. Mum was in her twenties and suffered from a narcissistic personality disorder, eternally her father's little girl. As you can imagine, no one paid any attention to me. At school the other children made fun of me, didn't invite me to birthday parties or anything. The place Dad called his office was actually somewhere for him to conduct his affairs. One tourist woman would come, another would go. Eventually, he followed one of them and abandoned us. Without telling me anything, Mum packed up my shorts, shoes and books and put us both on a night bus to Istanbul. We moved into the family home she'd run away from nine years earlier. It was a gloomy, dusty, dark apartment in Osmanbey. You could tell it had been elegant once, but by now it was falling apart. A despotic grandmother, a grandfather who had pledged to punish my mother with his silence. A new school. This time I had to deal with the daughters of men my mother was flirting with. In Cihangir, in Taksim, Mum... It was like the past nine years hadn't happened. She went back to her youth and devoted herself wholeheartedly to enjoying the nightlife.'

Leyla leant back against the wall, drew her knees up to her stomach. She'd withdrawn her arm from my shoulders. She took one last puff on the cigarette that had burnt down to nothing in her fingers.

'That's it.'

I turned and looked at her. She'd laid her head on her knees. Our shadows cast by the candlelight on the wall between the two French balconies were enormous. She smiled. She had meant to comfort me by telling me all that. She was a child unaware of her own wounds, her own loneliness.

'You mentioned that you ran away from that house, your grandfather's house. What did you do after you ran away?'

Leyla bent down and stubbed out her cigarette in the blue Murano ashtray, which I had given her. Pushing her hair out of her face, she looked at me. With her eyes shining brightly above her prominent cheekbones, one hand holding her long, dishevelled hair on top of her head, she looked wild and beautiful. But for the first time I felt not even a pinch of passion. I just wanted to hold her, to wrap my arms around her.

'I was defeated,' she said.

'You were defeated? By whom?'

'The whole system… Everybody. Above all, by myself.'

She must have been referring to her former lover, the scoundrel for whose sake she had covered her head and been tricked into a religious wedding. Berin said that the conservative businessman had sorted out his marriage after Leyla and was now the father of two children. Oh, was my beauty the sort of woman to let herself be crushed by an evil man? If her family hadn't effectively abandoned her in all those different locations, would she have rushed into the arms of a married man? Perhaps she thought she'd been defeated by the conservative businessman's wife. I was suddenly furious.

'You were not defeated, Leyla. Please don't ever say that again.'

A surprised smile passed over her face. 'What happened? Who did you get so angry with all of a sudden? Nobody did anything to me – I mean, if that's what you think.'

'I'm not angry. I want you to see the truth. You are a

wonderful person and you're still at the beginning of your life. You're talented, smart, beautiful...'

She must have heard such sentiments many times, but she didn't look as if she had.

'You think I'm beautiful?'

Ah, women! Why did they always get stuck on the same subject? Even the most beautiful ones, like Leyla, could never be told enough times.

'You are very beautiful, Leyla. Don't ever doubt it.'

She took that as a joke. 'Oh, well, coming from a Casanova like you, it must be true then.'

She giggled as she stood up and walked to the door. The doorbell must have rung. I hadn't heard it. She'd called me a Casanova. I couldn't stop smiling. Casanova! I suddenly realized why I found her so attractive. Despite my age and appearance, Leyla flirted with me. She'd done that from the very start. She'd brought the possibility of desire back into my life. What attracted me more than my desiring her was the possibility that I was desired by her. This possibility, which would never be fulfilled, was powerful enough to carry me willingly and enthusiastically to the end of my life.

Tulin plunged into the living room.

'Monsieur Pericles!'

She was sobbing.

'What's happened, Tulin? Did something happen to Berin?' I stood up.

Tulin grabbed hold of my hand. 'Ah, Monsieur Pericles.'

'Out with it, Tulin! For the love of God, tell us!'

'Edip... Monsieur Pericles... Edip is dead!'

She collapsed onto the divan where Leyla and I had been sitting. Shouts were coming from within the apartment building. I heard a deep male voice. Leyla opened the door, stood on the threshold and listened to the voices coming from Edip's apartment. Some instinct told her that we shouldn't get too close to Tulin, and we felt bad about that. Tulin's mask had slipped down. Her mouth and nose were exposed.

'They just came from the Department of Health. Those people downstairs. They took Edip to the hospital last night. The ambulance came after everybody was asleep. I didn't hear it. They took him out on a stretcher, like a thief, like a ghost... Veli and Samiha saw them leaving the building from their house on the corner. This evening... He's gone. Edip. Gone. Finished. Who knows how much he suffered... Ah! Ah!'

Leyla raced to the back room and brought me a mask. I hurriedly put it over my face.

'Don't stay here, Pericles. Go home and close your door.'

Right then, for the first time, I thought I was going to lose my life. I saw myself dying, breathing my last in a hospital ward, isolated from the rest of the world, with other dying patients in beds beside me. They had put my body in a black bag; they were taking me in a truck to a distant burial place; they were throwing me into a hole that they'd dug. No children, no priest, no funeral service, no grave where one day Leyla might come to visit me. I took two steps back. Leyla opened the windows and balcony doors and handed Tulin a new mask to put on. The living room immediately turned cold. The candle on the coffee table went out.

'Tulin, have you been to Edip's apartment recently?'

Tulin was crouched over on the divan where I'd been sitting a short while ago. She was looking at the extinguished candle and weeping.

Leyla raised her voice. 'Tulin! You need to tell us the truth. It's a matter of life and death. Have you been face to face with Edip?'

Taking off her glasses, which had misted up from the mask, Tulin looked at us with teary eyes. She shook her head.

'No. He wouldn't let me inside.'

If Tulin had caught Covid, how could we protect Berin? Or was it already too late? We didn't know anything about this damned virus.

'You, then... the two of you... did you see each other through a crack in the door?'

Tulin shook her head again. Behind her mask, she muttered something in a hoarse voice.

'No, no. I don't have anything. I'm sure of it. I didn't even know Edip was sick.'

The previous week, when the lockdown had been announced at very short notice, Tulin had gone out to buy bread and hadn't come back to Berin's for a long time. I assumed she'd been in Edip's apartment, but it would have been inappropriate to question the poor girl right then. Someone knocked on the door. Leyla opened it. Two officials entered, dressed from head to toe in protective gear, one a woman, the other a man. They looked like astronauts. It was hard to understand what they were saying from behind their masks.

'We've come from the Department of Health. There's been a death in your building. Covid-19.'

Hearing this, Tulin began sobbing noisily again.

'Have you had any face-to-face encounters with the resident of Apartment 2, Edip Yalovali, in the past two weeks? On the stairs, in the lift, at the front door?'

'No.'

'No.'

They turned to Tulin, sitting on Leyla's divan.

'You?'

'No. I just told you that, downstairs, when you were sealing off Edip's apartment,' said Tulin. 'Oh, God, I swear on the Koran I didn't speak with him. The man wouldn't open his door! You're all talking like you don't believe me.'

'We are placing this building and its residents into a fourteen-day quarantine. You must inform everyone you've been in contact with. The sanitation team will come and disinfect your building.'

Tulin began to cry again. I left and went outside to try and catch up with the health officials on the stairs.

'Excuse me, I'd like to ask you something. Who called the ambulance that took Edip to hospital last night?'

They didn't answer. They were wearing such thick clothing that they might not even have heard my question. I opened my apartment door with the key and ushered them inside. I explained the situation to Stelio, who'd heard the noise and had come to the door. He nodded. The male official heard us speaking Greek with each other.

'Are you foreigners? Let's have your passports.'

'My guest has come from Greece. I am a citizen of this country.'

'I need to see both of your passports.'

Stelio took two steps back, clearly afraid. I took my new ID card from my wallet and handed it to the health official in the astronaut outfit.

'Why is your name foreign? Passport?'

'I am not a foreigner and I do not have a passport.'

'Where are you from? Your nationality?'

The woman official took charge. 'If he has a Turkish ID number, write it down and let's move on, please.'

The man was twirling my identity card around and around. May my name be our only problem, I thought.

Before handing over his passport, Stelio started to ask why they wanted it, but I stopped him. They noted down a few things on the papers in their hands. As they left, the woman official cautioned us to be on the alert for fevers and respiratory symptoms.

'Shaking, bodily aches, sore throat, diarrhoea, nausea, vomiting – these can all be signs. Telephone your district health service immediately.'

'Madam, I'm a retired pharmacist. Please give me detailed information concerning Edip's condition. For how long was he ill at home? Someone must have had close contact with him, since an ambulance was called last night. If that person is living in our building, we have a right to know.'

Elena came unbidden into my mind. The Elena of the year she became a lawyer, at Aunt Ismene's house in Samatya, at the tea table where she puffed on cigarettes. *You are not a minority. You are a citizen.*

This man was not about to give in. 'Since you've worked in the health sector,' he said, 'you must know that by delaying us here, you're putting our lives in danger.'

They went out into the stairwell and headed to the fourth floor.

'That flat's empty,' I called out behind them.

But then the door opened in the apartment above me. I walked to the head of the stairs and looked out.

'Good evening, Uncle Pericles,' said a familiar voice.

'Put on your mask,' said the woman health official from the floor above.

I didn't have my glasses on, but it wasn't difficult to figure out who the voice belonged to. Who could it be other than our estate agent Ferit? He was the only one who called me 'Uncle Pericles'. (Stelio had attempted, but I had soon put an end to that.) So, it seemed that Ferit was also mixed up in the construction mafia, since he had moved into the fourth-floor apartment. I wasn't at all surprised. Ferit had had connections with Nejat's boys for a long time.

'Uncle Pericles, you've heard about Edip, haven't you? May he rest in peace, poor fellow. I found him in his apartment last night. He was lying on cardboard boxes. The state of that apartment... Don't ask me to describe it to you.'

'Please go inside, put on your mask and close the door. Have you had face-to-face contact with Edip Yalovali in the past fifteen days?'

'Eh, what have I been saying for the last five hours? I was the one who found him. The man was suffocating. He'd wet himself. The place was a tip. Oh, forget about all that – close contact doesn't bother me. I'm telling you the truth. Uncle Pericles, I'm so happy for you. Your son has come from overseas. As soon as you sold the downstairs flat, he suddenly appeared, right? That's always how it goes. I told you that when you sold that apartment for nothing.'

I went inside, closed the door behind me, threw my mask in the bin and washed my hands in the bathroom for a long, long time. I brushed my teeth, gargled with salt water and looked at my face in the mirror. My eyes were bloodshot. You are tired, Pericles Efendi. I put on the lamp in the living room and a soft yellow light fell across the furniture. I sat down on the sofa, turned on the television and stared vacantly at the daily Covid statistics. Everyone was lying and we all knew it. The number of cases was much greater than what was being reported. Looking at the situation around the world, even a child could see that. I turned off the television.

Not a sound was coming from the apartment downstairs. Tulin must have gone up to Berin. Wasn't that risky?

But then, whatever was going to happen was already in process. There was nothing to do but sit and wait. The health official had said that if we'd caught the virus, the symptoms would appear in two or three days. Until then, should we not even see each other? Not knowing what to do in the middle of this enormous unknowingness, I reached for the telephone and called Berin. The health officials had come to her door too. They'd been polite. Tulin couldn't stop crying.

'So where do you think Edip picked up this virus, Berin?'

'From Ferit, of course. Tulin knew that he'd moved into the fourth floor. She didn't tell us because she didn't want to worry us. Ferit has had his eye on Edip's apartment for a long time. "We're going to get you out of here," he said to Edip. "Galip isn't the owner anymore; they can't keep you here." And so on and so forth.'

I didn't ask where Tulin, who had allegedly not seen Edip, had learnt all this. I suddenly felt exhausted. I hung up and lay down on the sofa.

Stelio came over to me. He'd filled a fat wine glass with two fingers of Metaxa. He held it out to me, then took another glass for himself. He stood in front of the window overlooking Temrin Hill Street and gazed at the ruins of the building opposite.

'We're finished now, Stelio,' I said. 'We've had it. They've got us in their claws.'

'They'll come and test us, won't they, Monsieur Pericles?' he asked. He thought I was talking about the quarantine. I didn't answer. We both buried ourselves in our own silences and listened to the night.

# Love

Ulker had come back from Germany after exactly twenty-three years. She had finished university in Frankfurt, got her doctorate in philosophy and then found work as a member of the faculty. She had married, but the marriage had not gone well. Her divorce and the offer of a visiting professorship at Bosphorus University had come at the same time. After twenty-three years she returned to Istanbul. Her father had died prematurely, Oya was living in Italy and her mother had moved to Erenkoy, passing the time by giving lessons at a theatre school. This was her summary of the years we had been apart. To tell the truth, I couldn't have cared less. She was staying in the apartment in Tunel Square. Ulker would only be in Istanbul for a year and had no intention of tying herself down. I needed to be clear about that from the start. It seemed clear to me, therefore, that it was meaningless for me to keep saying I was about to divorce Markela.

'But maybe you'll stay, right?' I said during one of our post-coital chats. 'If Bosphorus University made you a permanent member of the faculty, then what would you do?'

She didn't know. She didn't want to know. The divorce had

been amicable, but it had still worn her down. She needed to be unfettered for a while, to not be tied to a place or a thing. Her husband – her ex-husband – had been adamant that he wanted children, but having a child had never been on Ulker's agenda. This had been a bone of contention between them from the start and when Ulker turned forty the arguments became more frequent, eventually leading to their divorce.

'I couldn't deprive a man who wanted to be a father. Now he's gone and found a German woman with two children. My guess is that a third is on the way. Some women like being pregnant, even if they don't adore their children.'

Ulker was modest about her professional achievements, but at the New Year's Eve party at Kemal's house I established that she was a successful academic. She had published two books on existential phenomenology and had written reams of articles. I didn't even know what this philosophy she wrote about was, but just as she didn't know what ingredients went into which medicines, I didn't need to understand her work. At any rate, she spent the whole day teaching at the university and in the evenings sat writing at her desk at home, so she had every right to stick to light conversation when she was with me. She wanted to go out in Beyoglu – to Inci, the only pastry shop still there from the old days – to eat profiteroles; to the cinemas where the woman at the ticket window and the old uncle showing us to our seats in the dark auditorium would shout for joy on seeing her and press her to their bosoms; for a drink with old friends.

I was no longer reluctant to be seen with her at Inci. Sitting across from each other at a round, marble table, we would even hold hands. I knew that the elderly pastry makers behind the counter were giving us sidelong glances. Markela had barely left The Circle since the military coup of 1980, so perhaps they'd forgotten that I even had a wife. Or maybe they thought this was a second wife. It wasn't important. As we age, we stop caring so much about what others think. Good. Anyway, we weren't old. We were both in our prime. Our bodies were strong and we had shed youth's lack of confidence. We were like a couple of peaches at their most delicious – no longer hard and raw, but not yet soft and flabby. The time for living was now.

'I used to think you had a beautiful Greek lover. When you went to those school teas together... There was that dark-haired girl. We bumped into her in front of Baylan once and you didn't introduce me.'

'I didn't introduce you to anyone. I was a fool.'

'Most of all I wanted to meet your mother and father. I was curious about your house.'

'Why was that?'

'Probably because it was a Greek house. I don't know. I thought it might have a different atmosphere, a different smell to ours. When you're young, you always see other people's houses as happy places. And my family were sort of like foreigners in Beyoglu. How many Muslim families lived in Tunel back then? I felt like your house would be the real thing, an authentic neighbourhood home. My family was incomplete; yours was whole. You'd been there for a long time, whereas we'd somehow never been able to fit in. Thinking about it now, that all seems absurd, but we were children of course.'

Two days after we'd bumped into each other at Kemal's house, I took Ulker for a meal at the Russian restaurant, Rejans. With its dreary, dilapidated buildings and neglected, muddy backstreets, Beyoglu looked as if it was trying to climb out of a hole it had sunk into. Nobody was talking about the demolition at Tarlabasi yet. At Rejans we drank wine and ate filet mignon with sauce beneath the Christmas and New Year's decorations in the dimly lit dining area filled with dark, heavy furniture. Ulker was wearing a purple turtleneck sweater. I gazed admiringly at her fine-featured face, her cheekbones prominent now that she had lost her teenage plumpness, her large hazel eyes no longer behind glasses. On the one hand, she was an old friend from my youth, someone I knew well; on the other, she was a brand-new woman. When I least expected it, love had appeared in front of me.

That night, I held her hand when we left the restaurant. It was snowing. The city was quiet after New Year's Eve and there were only a couple of cars driving through Beyoglu. We went to her apartment in Tunel. The back room where I had once seen Oya studying was now Ulker's bedroom. There was no sign of Oya's desk. Without letting go of her hand even for a moment, I dragged Ulker to the bed and pulled off the purple sweater. The apartment was cold, but Ulker's bare skin was warm. I undressed her from head to toe. Then I undressed myself. We got under the heavy cotton quilt and, like children discovering sex for the first time, we made love, shivering partly from the cold, partly with pleasure.

'Do you know how crazy I was when I heard that you'd left me and moved away? I searched for you for ten years, in all the places we'd ever gone to together. Why didn't you come back?'

She was lying naked in my arms. There were freckles on her shoulders. The nape of her neck, exposed by her short hair, was sweaty. She reached for her glass of water. I hadn't realized how beautiful her breasts were. Were they always so big and full? I touched them with my fingertips.

'Why didn't you come back?'

She handed me the glass, shrugged. 'Because I really liked Frankfurt.'

'More than me?'

'Don't be ridiculous! You were a crazy, mixed-up kid then. Okay, I had fallen for you, but I had to forget you. You were a dead-end.'

'Is that why you left without saying goodbye?'

'Of course. I had to let you go.'

I sighed. She was right. What could she have done with me? I had even been too scared to make love. What an idiot. I could have taken this beautiful woman in my arms. But what did it matter, she was mine now. Or was she? Back then, I was the one who wouldn't commit; now the roles were reversed. I understood that immediately after our first lovemaking. I hoped it would pass, that she would become attached to me, would fall in love with me. It had happened once; it could happen again. The possibility that at any moment she could slip away from me made my heart tight.

'And, anyway, I assumed you'd been exiled in 1964. It's not that I didn't think of writing to you when I heard about that. There were a couple of students at Frankfurt who'd come from Greece. Istanbul Greeks. I asked them about you, but they didn't know you. To tell the truth, it didn't even occur to me that you might have stayed in Istanbul.'

'I stayed,' I said in a low voice.

It was exactly the right time to say, 'I stayed for you.' Hadn't I dreamt about this moment for years? 'My father was exiled and my mother went with him, but I stayed on, thinking you might return.' But I couldn't say a word. Was it even true? Had I really stayed in Istanbul because of Ulker? As life for us Greeks became increasingly difficult in the years that followed – embargos, 'dirty infidel' taunting, Cyprus incidents, being fired from jobs, having property confiscated, seeing our ancient places of worship destroyed – did I continue to remain in the city because Ulker might return one day? I wasn't sure.

'You didn't write either,' she said. She snuggled up to me again.

I rubbed my face in her rosemary-scented hair. Her skin was so soft. 'Your sister wouldn't give me your address! Was she afraid I'd go knocking on your door? It was only after you left that I realized how important you were to me.'

I threw off the quilt and got on top of her. As if making up for last time, I kissed her full breasts, stroked her bounteous buttocks. I had not made love for more than three months, ever since Niki didn't show up at Sirkeci Train Station at our usual meeting time. As snowflakes stuck to the branches of the grapefruit tree in the back courtyard, I surrendered the entirety of my pent-up desire to my lover – that night and through the weeks and months that followed. Winter and spring passed as I made love to every centimetre of Ulker's beautiful body. Her skin became my home, her breath my hearth.

Ulker had missed Istanbul. Leaving the pharmacy to Aydin in the afternoons, I would explore the city with her. She had driven a blue Mini Cooper over from Germany, by herself. She was very proud of that car. We would cross the bridge, go to Kandilli on the Asian side, and I would close my eyes as Istanbul's cool, moist wind filled the car through its open windows. Colourful fishing boats were tied up in front of faded and neglected waterside mansions. We ate fresh, silvery fish at the restaurant beside the pier, dipped bread into our salad. As the sun set, we'd sit at a tea garden in Kucuksu and watch the waters of the Bosphorus change colour. The weary workers and students, passengers on the commuter ferries that passed in front of us, glanced at us with indifference. We walked along the Goksu River, the 'sweet waters of Asia', holding hands and talking of old novels, past the riverside workshops of skilled metalworkers, potters and printers. As I looked at the calm, quietly working people, I would squeeze Ulker's hand. I was so happy to be with her. With her there, Istanbul had changed, become more colourful, more expansive; it had turned into a magical, multi-dimensional place. Walking down Beyoglu Avenue, we would suddenly turn onto the backstreet behind a building I knew like the back of my hand, go through a passageway and find ourselves in the courtyard of an Armenian Catholic church. I'd be totally confused. As we strolled past an abandoned apartment building that was becoming more dilapidated by the day, Ulker would point out the ivy and rose bas-relief on its facade. The building that I'd been walking past my whole life would suddenly come alive with history and romance.

Places remain fresh, vivid and unchanged in the memories of those who return to them after a long absence. Ulker remembered better than I did where long-closed Baylan, and Tilla, now under new ownership, had been. She could recall the places on the street where I had dropped her hand, the elegant bars of now demolished Krepen Arcade, the apartment buildings that had contained the chicest flats. All the changes had blocked my memory, but as she described the Beyoglu of twenty years earlier, it gradually resurfaced in my mind, like buried treasure revealed in an archaeological dig.

The coffeehouse in Emirgan that we'd frequented in our youth was still there, as was the plane tree. We sat under that tree as if we'd rediscovered an old friend. I didn't tell Ulker that I used to go all the way there every evening in the hope of finding her. It seemed so childish.

Across from us, a sculptor was still at work. We lit a cigarette. Weird-looking people were coming and going from the record shop in Herr Wagner's old room. We watched them. Cats kept rubbing against our trouser legs, trying to get up onto our laps, and we tried to guess which ones might be related to Mitsy. Remembering her little black-and-white head sticking out of Ulker's jacket, sadness washed over us.

When I got home in the evenings, did Markela notice the smell of cigarettes on me? I had no idea. But Aunt Ismene, who stayed with my wife when I was not at home, was aware of everything. During the winter months, when I returned from Ulker's house to The Circle, she would put my jacket and scarf on the radiator so that the smell would evaporate. We never talked about where I'd been. No matter the time, Aunt Ismene would be up.

The apartment on the second floor was still empty. If Aunt Ismene had wished, she could have moved in there. I had to call her every evening to sit with Markela. I couldn't bear to go a single day without seeing Ulker. The hours she was at the university seemed too long to me, and I was scared senseless that she might then spend her evening with her old friends instead of me. When she met up with her friends, Ulker didn't want me there with her. The moment dusk fell on Kurabiye Street, my hand was on my telephone, calling her. I learnt her timetable. I knew which buses took how long from the university to Tunel. If she took an Eminonu bus, she'd get off in Karakoy and take the underground up to Beyoglu. If she took a Taksim bus, she could stop by the pharmacy on her way home. I took everything into account. My hand was on my telephone, my eyes on the clock.

Aunt Ismene was aware of all of that. Yet she continued to stubbornly refuse to move into the downstairs flat, her old home, and instead suggested that I get my affairs in order and either sell it or rent it out.

'Who else besides you or me would live here, Aunt Ismene?' I replied, teasingly.

Families from the Anatolian interior, from the country's east, had moved into all the abandoned houses in the vicinity. Some of them had been there so long they'd even had the title deeds put into their names. From morning till night the streets resounded with the yells of little boys with shaved heads and little girls with patched dresses and tangled hair.

'That's what you think,' Aunt Ismene said, 'but look at the family that's bought the top floor. They're a wealthy, well-mannered husband and wife. Before you know it, our Beyoglu will again become the fashionable, cosmopolitan district of old, our historic Beyoglu. The name has changed, and when a wave crashes over it, the place falls to its knees, but things will improve, and the ladies and gentlemen will return.'

The well-mannered couple Aunt Ismene referred to were Berin and her husband. I didn't tell her that right then it was impossible to sell an apartment in our building. A rumour was circulating about an unbelievable plan for a boulevard. If the plan went ahead, thousands of buildings, including The Circle, would be demolished, some of them of historic significance.

When I told Ulker about the huge boulevard rumours, she shook her head in sadness. We were grilling meat on the terrace of the building in Tunel Square. Spring had arrived.

Judas trees were blooming on the slopes of the Bosphorus, and almond and plum blossoms were opening in the back gardens of apartment buildings and in unexpected corners.

Ulker waved her raki glass at Maiden's Tower. 'In the last twenty years the city has changed so much, has got so ugly that... most probably they will build that road you're talking about.'

'And some of the buildings are genuine works of art. The Council of Monuments should be the one to make that decision.'

Nobody except us used the terrace of Ulker's apartment building in Tunel. As evening fell, purplish-pink clouds passed over Sarayburnu. Lights on the Princes' Islands came on one by one. When the moon was full, it rose like an orange cannonball behind Uskudar. Ulker had acquired a penchant for grilling meat from fellow Turks in Germany. She turned lamb chops marinated in thyme and salted olive oil alongside mushrooms, onions and tomatoes. She cooked them to perfection, not letting them dry out.

'There are people living in those buildings.'

She shrugged.

'They'll expropriate them.'

'They can't expropriate them. They're historic.'

'They can do anything.'

'Not that much.'

She hadn't changed the know-it-all attitude of her youth at all. It made me angry. How did she know that? How could she be so sure? But later we clinked our raki glasses in a toast. Seagulls were flying overhead. Ferries were shuttling to and fro in the open sea over by Maiden's Tower. Fishing boats were pulling in under Galata Bridge. The sky turned pink, then dark blue. The cool sea breeze blew Ulker's cigarette smoke my way. I love life, I thought to myself. No matter what it brings, I love life. This is living, I said to myself. This is love. What makes a person love life is love itself. How did I endure this life without love? The awe-inspiring beauty of Istanbul was inextricably entwined with the beauty of Ulker in my eyes. Until that point, I'd looked at Istanbul as a conundrum, trying to understand why it was like it was, where and why things had gone wrong. But when I was with Ulker, I realized that there was nothing to figure out. Life and the city were spectacles, to be viewed. When I was looking at my lover and at Istanbul, I was fully alive. I was in the right place; I was at home.

Noting the expression on my face, Ulker said, 'Don't you dare try to tie me down, Pericles. I am only passing through. Even if I were to stay, I'm not ready for a relationship. And anyway, you're a married man. Don't do anything rash.'

I poured water on the grill and dragged her down to her apartment. Before we'd even made it to bed, crows had stolen the lamb chops from our plates and flown off with them. Breathlessly, I made love to Ulker. I pressed her hands to the bed so that she couldn't escape. I kept up our lovemaking for as long as I could so that she could climax. Even when she collapsed, laughing, into my arms, I felt uneasy. My heart was burning. Still, I comforted myself that she had loved me once, so she could love me again. This slice of life that we were sharing was unique. It couldn't have been experienced with anyone else. She had to be aware of that too.

With her head on my chest and her legs interlaced with mine, Ulker fell into a brief sleep. Our bodies nestled into each other with the familiar closeness of a couple who'd been sleeping together for years. I could have stayed like that until morning, intertwined like ivy. I could have stayed like that forever. I could have forgotten about Markela at home with Aunt Ismene and stayed in that warm nest, with Ulker in my arms, until I died.

# Edip's Funeral Ceremony

The day after Edip's death I wrote from morning till evening. At midday I dined in my room; I ate the chickpea dish that Stelio had made along with a couple of slices of the previous day's bread. We had forgotten to put the dish in the fridge the night before, so the juices had been absorbed and it was very tasty. I'd already moved the coffee machine into my office, right after Stelio had arrived, and I only used the bathroom when I knew Stelio was in his room with the door shut. I spent the whole of that locked-down Saturday writing, immersed in the past.

It was pitch-black when I finally came out of my room. The apartment was in total darkness except for the light seeping out from under Stelio's door. From the far end of the corridor I eyed the entrance hall and the door into the living room. I didn't feel like staying at home, but leaving The Circle was not an option. For one thing it was a Saturday; for another thing, our building had been quarantined. The day before, I'd heard that ridiculous line for the first time on TV – 'Everything you need from life can be found at home' – which only served to intensify my longing to go out and socialize. Everything you need from life cannot be found at home. The authorities were treating us like children, trying to trick us into wanting to stay put. As someone with the greater part of his life behind him, someone who's spent his whole life in the same neighbourhood, on the same street, in the same apartment, I know that life happens outside. Life happens when you're among people and animals, in nature and in cities. Home can make us happy temporarily; it's a refuge, a shelter. But you cannot find everything you need from life inside an apartment. No. Life happens where others gather; we get together, we broaden our horizons, we change. If it weren't for Leyla, lockdown would have been unendurable. I would probably have flouted the restrictions every day.

I picked up my notes and went down to Leyla's. She wasn't at home, but she must have guessed I'd be round because she'd stuck a message to her door. I took my glasses from my shirt pocket and read it:

'I'm bored. I'm going to visit Berin Hanim. If you read this note, come too.'

I took the sticky note off the door and put it in my trouser pocket.

As the lift approached the fifth floor, I heard Berin's piano. The sound got louder when Tulin opened the door. Tulin's shoulder-length hair was wet, her eyes still red.

'Come in, Monsieur Pericles. They're in the living room,' she said, disgruntled.

It crossed my mind to say 'Why aren't you sitting with them?', but I stopped myself. Perhaps Tulin had been quarantined within the quarantine and had been sent to the back room. I went into the living room. The music stopped. Berin turned on the low piano stool and greeted me with a nod. She looked lovely. Tulin must have dyed her hair and pencilled in her eyebrows. She had the air of a real concert pianist in a long-sleeved, black dress with a diamond brooch sparkling at the collar. Her hair was gathered in a bun on top of her head. Leyla was sitting on the two-person sofa that faced Temrin Hill Street, Shadow on her lap. The ceiling chandelier illuminated Berin's furniture-filled living room like a ballroom.

Since we were quarantined, the time for masks was over. If this ship was going to sink, we would sink in it together. So be it. I too removed my mask and put it in my pocket.

Without withdrawing her hand from Shadow's chin, Leyla greeted me with a nod. I felt as if I were attending a chamber music recital. Seeing that I was seated, Berin turned back to the piano and began to play a gentle, familiar piece. I looked at Leyla. Her eyes were shining. She too was wearing an old-fashioned, long-sleeved, black velvet dress, with tiny blue flowers on its collar. Like Berin, she'd put her hair up in a bun. I guessed that the dress was an old one of Berin's. They must have spent the whole day trying on clothes. Leyla was eyeing the notes in my hand with curiosity, but couldn't say anything for fear of disrupting the recital. I put them down beside me on the sofa, and Leyla, with one hand still stroking Shadow's head, used the other to quickly flip through my handwritten pages. Her head nodded in acknowledgment of my words as she read.

I knew the piece Berin was playing. I'd heard it before. It was one of Mozart's piano concertos. Berin had played it on the day Mansur Bey died, after the police officer and the death-certificate-issuing doctor arranged by Galip had left. I knew Berin only slightly back then, as my neighbour on the top floor. We'd been neighbours for a long time, but we merely exchanged greetings at that point. That day, it was Edip who broke the news that Mansur Bey had died. The late Edip, who had opened car doors for VIP guests, not at the Temrin Hill Street entrance to Fortune Nightclub but at the main apartment entrance. Who had rejoiced at the tips he put in his pocket.

Mansur Bey died in the bath. It was his custom once a week to fill the tub with hot water and take a bath. He died with a thud, but it took Berin and Tulin some time to realize what had happened because he tended to stay in the bathroom for quite some time, leaving the tap running a little so that his bathwater wouldn't get cold. After an hour, perhaps an hour and a half, they noticed that Mansur Bey was being quieter than usual. Thankfully, the door was not locked. They went in and what did they see but...

Edip had stood in my doorway and recounted the story in fits and starts. When Edip was young, his father had made sure his head was shaved, but the adult Edip had let his hair grow long. It was black and stuck out like a brush. As Edip stood stuttering in front of me, I thought about how, in spite of his advancing years, his hair had not turned grey or fallen out. He must have seen from my expression that I'd not understood anything of what he was trying to tell me.

'Pe-Pe-Pericles Bey, Berin Hanim is asking for you,' he finally said with difficulty.

It was the first time I had been to Berin's apartment. The lift stopped at the fifth floor. In the landing light I saw that the mosaic floor in front of her door had been immaculately preserved. Healthy, large-leafed pot plants stood beside the door and a few vintage film posters hung on the walls. The door was open. Tulin was crying outside the bathroom. Berin was pacing the length of the corridor, up and down, her hands on her hips and her eyes on the ground. Seeing me come in behind Edip, she strode over and shook my hand.

'Monsieur Pericles, we've asked you here because we're in a delicate situation. Please forgive us. Mansur Bey, my husband – may he rest in peace – has unfortunately died in rather awkward circumstances. The doctor did warn him. As you know, for a man in his seventies with a weak heart, it's risky to bathe in hot water for a long time.'

I nodded. Berin clearly knew that I was a pharmacist. But everyone in the neighbourhood knew that. I was aware that Mansur Bey and Berin had come from Ankara in the 1980s, that he'd been the manager of a state bank, had retired, and that they had bought the apartment from Despina. As for Berin Hanim, what did she do? I wasn't sure. She was an intelligent and well-educated woman, I knew that much. She was staring straight at me, but I did not immediately understand what she wanted.

'I do not wish for my husband to be found in this state in the bathroom. He was a high-ranking government employee. I thought that with your help we could get Mansur Bey out of the bath and onto his bed before the doctor arrives to certify his death. Tulin and I will dry him and dress him in something appropriate, and then the police and the ambulance can come.'

As I opened my mouth to object, my eyes met Tulin's. There was a scar on the girl's left cheek, running from top to bottom, as if sliced by a knife. When she saw I was staring at it, her hand went to her face and she looked away. Berin continued holding my gaze. She seemed extremely calm for someone whose husband had just died. A great shock can sometimes have that effect on a person.

Mansur Bey's body had shrivelled up like a prune in the

bath. His eyes were open and his head was tilted in a strange way. Edip and I were both strong men, but we struggled to lift the corpse out of the water. His arms and legs were as stiff as planks of wood. When Edip and I got him out of the water, Berin and Tulin rushed to wrap him in towels. Together we carried Mansur Bey's body, swaddled in yellow towels, to the bedroom. It was a real struggle to get him dressed in the trousers and shirt he'd left on a chair, so much so that my eyes frequently sought out Berin's to question why we were going to so much trouble. The ambulance team would take the body to the morgue after the doctor had written the death certificate and could just as well have taken him straight from the bath. What was wrong with them seeing Mansur Bey's lifeless body naked? It would have been a routine situation for them. But I couldn't say any of that to Berin, who was trying to put a sock on Mansur Bey's purple foot. Just like Edip, I was doing the job I'd been asked to do without questioning it.

'All right,' I said. 'Don't worry, I will handle it. We will organize the death certificate.'

She reached out, touched my shoulder and looked into my eyes. 'Thank you, Pericles.'

Since Nejat had gone to Canada, I contacted Galip. The police and doctor business was completed straight away. It was a heart attack, nothing suspicious about that, so there was no need for a coroner to do a post-mortem. Mansur Bey had eaten a large serving of kebab, accompanied by two double rakis, in a restaurant. He had come home, taken a bath and lain down to rest. It was at that moment that his heart, already weak, stopped. Berin thrust Mansur's death certificate into Edip's hand and sent him to the municipality, the mosque and wherever one went for a funeral. Then she sat down at the piano and played a Mozart piece.

Now, after Edip's death, she was playing the same piece.

When Berin finished the piece, she turned on her stool.

'Wonderful! A beautiful rendition,' said Leyla softly. 'You play with such expressiveness. You know exactly which notes to play with intense feeling. You have a real talent.'

'Thank you,' said Berin, lowering her head.

'You should have been a concert pianist, Berin,' I said, just to say something.

'They wanted her to be one,' mumbled Tulin distractedly. She had come in while Berin was playing and sat down in the armchair opposite me. Instead of her usual grey cotton dress, she was wearing a dark-red turtleneck sweater and black trousers. I realized then that this was a funeral ceremony for Edip. The women had dressed up and fixed their hair in his honour. That Mozart piece was Berin's funeral march.

'Didn't they want you to play the piano in an orchestra, Berin Hanim? Where was that – Munich?'

'Berlin,' said Berin. 'I wouldn't say they wanted me, but, yes… The year we lived in Berlin, I was bored and began taking piano lessons. My teacher said that if I worked really hard, I might get to join the Berlin Philharmonic. I was very young, of course. I got so excited.'

I'd not heard that story. I knew that when Berin and Mansur Bey were first married they'd lived for a short while in Berlin, but this Philharmonic part was new to me.

'Then what happened?'

'What could happen? The teacher shared his opinion with Mansur Bey. Mansur Bey said, "Is this fellow in love with you or what?" and the lessons were stopped.'

Leyla scowled. Berin got up from the piano stool and came over and sat beside her. Shadow immediately moved onto her owner's lap and sat there arrogantly, looking into each of our faces in turn.

'Do you remember, Monsieur Pericles, when Edip was a barman at Fortune Nightclub?' Tulin said.

'Really?' said Leyla, with a sweet light in her face. She looked at me expectantly, like a child waiting for a fairy tale.

'Really,' said Berin. 'We went down to the nightclub to have a drink served by Edip.'

As soon as Berin said that, the scene in my memory became clear. After Mansur Bey's funeral, I began socializing with Berin and Tulin for the first time. It must have been at the beginning of the 2000s. It seemed like centuries ago. I laughed.

'You're right! Galip prepared a centre table for us. What was our waiter's name – was he Bulgarian? There was even fried liver.'

'Edip made me a cherry vodka sour,' Tulin said proudly. 'He used Smirnoff, not Turkish vodka.'

Details of the scene surfaced bit by bit. Edip was dressed in a stylish suit. When Nejat had gone to Canada I had given up my partnership in Fortune Nightclub. Because they no longer had enough money to pay their staff, they hired fifty-seven-year-old Edip as a barman. He endlessly wiped and polished the copper bar. There must have been a list hidden under the bar that he consulted when making the drinks; how else would our Edip have known how to mix cocktails? Anyway, there were fewer customers by then and those that remained were more likely to order raki, whisky or vodka on the rocks than a fancy cocktail. It was only when Berin asked for banana liqueur that he got confused. I ordered a beer to make it easy for Edip, but Galip got mad, went behind the bar and made Edip fix me a fancy drink.

A photographer had been wandering around with a young girl selling roses. He couldn't take pictures of the weary-faced men who were trying to make overripe women laugh at the dark tables in the back, so he was pleased to find us. Two foreign tourists were sitting at the table next to ours. We couldn't understand how they'd found their way to that bar. They were stout, blond and drunk. The photographer, having concluded that he wouldn't be getting any business from them, took a lot of photos of our group sitting at the big round table in the middle of the nightclub. At the end of the night he left an envelope with our photographs in it on our table. Courtesy of the establishment.

Leyla was excited to hear that. 'Do you still have that photo?'

Berin stuck out her bottom lip. 'You'll have to ask Tulin. She's the archivist of the house. I throw everything away.'

'Let me have a look,' Tulin said, getting up. She seemed slighter than usual.

When she'd disappeared down the corridor, Berin looked first at me and then at Leyla. 'How do you like Leyla's dress?'

'It looks very good on her. Is it yours?'

Leyla squirmed uncomfortably and smoothed the shiny velvet skirt of the dress with her hand. What a beautiful woman she was.

'1972, Berlin. I had it made by a tailor there. The fabric is exactly as it was when he cut it. Look at it. It's a maxi dress, even though in 1972 everyone was wearing skirts so short you could see their bottoms. But that German tailor insisted on making me a long dress. How's that for forward thinking?'

Or maybe, I thought, Mansur Bey had forbidden his wife from following the mini-skirt fashion. My eyes met Leyla's and I realized that she was thinking the same thing. But

I didn't say anything. Let Berin hold on to her memories. Besides, when you were talking about the past, was it ever possible to be certain about what was and wasn't true?

Tulin came back with envelopes in her hand. She sat on the arm of my chair.

'I found them.'

She gave me one of the two envelopes marked 'Ates Photographic Studio' and handed the other to Berin and Leyla, who were sitting side by side on the sofa. Smiling, I looked at the faded, poorly printed photo. There was the Fortune Nightclub I had forgotten, with its red velvet walls. There was Berin, sitting upright at the centre table, seventeen years ago. She was younger but had the same air about her. I was beside her. My hair was thick; streaked with grey, but thick. Tulin was a young woman. How happily she was smiling. She was wearing a pink blouse with puffy sleeves and her hair was long. The stage was visible in the background, with some young man playing the lute and next to him that lovesick-voiced... what was that girl's name?

'Tulin, what was the name of that poor girl with a melancholy voice? Look, you can see her at the edge of the picture.'

'You mean Zishan? She wasn't a poor girl at all, Monsieur Pericles. You know, she—'

As she passed the photograph to Leyla, Berin said teasingly, 'Tulin didn't like her because she flirted with Edip.'

'Why do you say that, Berin Hanim? What does that have to do with it? The girl was Galip's mistress.'

Leyla giggled. Then she sighed. 'I see that I missed The Circle's heyday. Look how handsome Edip was. I only saw the top of his head a few times when he leant out the window.'

We all laughed. With the photos still in our hands, we

looked at Edip again. A black suit, a tie, and hair slicked back and as shiny as jet. He was standing behind us, one hand on my shoulder, the other on Berin's. Who knew, perhaps he saw himself as the guardian of those of us who lived in the building, as his father Tahsin had been. All at once a lump came to my throat. Edip was gone. Dead. We'd exchanged no more than a couple of words, had never reminisced about the past, and yet he'd been a silent witness to almost my entire life. Like the house-cat who sits in the corner observing the unfolding of life's most momentous events, he was always there, a perpetual presence.

Everyone was silent. At that moment Edip's spirit was flying over The Circle, bidding us farewell, I thought. A warmth that resembled happiness spread through me. I'd felt something similar when Markela died, which I'd felt guilty about. As Markela lay dead in her room, I should have been grieving, but instead I was suffused with a warm glow. I couldn't forgive myself, not for what I'd done, but for not feeling sad that she was dead in the back room. But now, as the same warmth filled me once again, I understood that this was not about me but about the dead who left this world behind. I understood this because Leyla, Berin and even Tulin, as they all bent over the photo, were smiling. That warmth was Edip's spirit. When her time had come, Markela had also paid me a visit and then gone away, leaving her warm farewell with me.

Berin broke the silence that had descended on the living room.

'I spoke to Ferit today.'

Leyla turned to face Berin. The photo from the envelope was still in her hand.

'I hope he didn't come here.'

'No, he didn't come here. Nor did we go to him. I phoned to ask how he was. I was expecting him to say "I'm fine; nothing will happen to me". He was very pleased to hear from me, said he'd been planning to contact me. Apparently he'd tried you, Pericles, but couldn't get through. In short, he says this construction company is now the legal owner of three flats in our building: the ground-floor flat, the flat on the first floor where Edip lived, and the fourth-floor flat which Ferit is supposedly renting. Ferit is mixed up in it, of course. He says lockdown will be lifted at the beginning of June and that that's when they'll present the demolition permit. After that, it'll be like a sock unravelling, he says. They'll organize somewhere for us to stay while the construction's going on – the company owns some comfortably appointed buildings, apparently, so we'll move in there and wait for the new apartment building to be finished. The demolition and rebuilding will be completed by the new year at the latest.'

Leyla looked at Berin and then at me. 'What do you mean? Are we giving up and abandoning The Circle to the construction mafia?'

'Ferit said the new building will remain faithful to its original design. There'll still be one spacious apartment per floor, and the frontage will be preserved.'

'And you believe them?' Leyla's eyes were flashing as she looked from my face to Berin's.

Tulin stood up, walked to the window and gazed down at the ruins of the next-door building. Shadow stretched in Berin's lap, jumped down and passed in front of the gilded, full-length mirror.

'What frontage? They'll stay faithful to the original – ha! You two have been in the apartment for so long you've forgotten what an atrocious state that boulevard's in. They build a frontage like a film set and behind it it's as hollow as a rotten tooth. Nobody's buying those newly constructed apartments either. The project has blown up in the faces of its contractors and financiers, so now they're turning their eyes on us to try and make up the shortfall. And you're fine with the fact you're going to live in a cell?'

'Don't be so angry, Leyla. We've already explained the situation to you. Now that Edip's gone, there's almost nothing left in our hands. The government is right behind the construction sector, so they'll be full steam ahead. Even if they can't sell The Circle, they'll want to tear it down. Clearly, there are wheels turning that we don't understand. We're not strong enough to fight them. We've done everything we can, but we're just not powerful enough.'

Berin clasped her hands in her lap and fell silent.

'I thought you studied law,' Leyla snapped at her. 'You must have a way round this?'

I turned my head away from Leyla, towards the view from the window. Above the darkness of the Golden Horn, properly dark because there were no ferries, ships or boats passing by, the sky was velvety soft, like the dress Leyla was wearing. How silent the city was.

'I am saying all this precisely because I am well versed in the legal system and its loopholes, Leyla. At this point we can't expect the law to come to our aid. In fact, there are some laws that are blocking us...'

Leyla stood up. 'I'm going downstairs.'

She left my notes on the coffee table. I got to my feet.

'I'll come with you.'

She shrugged, opened the door and got in the lift – her hair was in a bun and she was still wearing Berin's old-fashioned black velvet dress that came down to her ankles. Wishing

Berin and Tulin a good night, I caught up with her. Tulin followed me and locked the steel door from the inside.

'You tricked me,' Leyla said as the lift began its shaky descent. 'You said we would fight for this building together, but now you've changed your mind.'

'Leyla, we three apartment owners can't stand up to the monster that's swallowing the whole city. You heard Berin. Believe me, we've been trying to fight this for years, both legally and with the help of Nejat's gang. But it hasn't worked. Even the old mafia have given up on this neighbourhood. You've seen how they've withdrawn.'

The lift stopped with a shudder at the third floor.

'Come to my apartment for a bit and we'll look over my notes. I spent the whole day writing. Stelio made a chickpea dish. We can eat together.'

Leyla didn't answer. The heavy cage door closed when I let it go. Leyla pressed the button for the second floor. Inside the lift, first her dress, then her frowning face and last of all the red hair gathered on top of her head vanished from sight. I heard her blow her nose as she turned the key in the lock downstairs. My beauty was crying. I had disappointed her. I was very upset. She was right. I had tricked her.

Avoiding Stelio, I shut myself inside my study. I had nowhere else to take solace except the past.

# The Happiest Summer of My Life

The summer after I found Ulker again and fell head over heels in love, things became easier than I could have hoped. Aunt Ismene took Markela to Imbros. I don't know how my wife, who never even left her room, agreed to the trip, but one morning in the middle of July I found her in the living room waiting for Aunt Ismene. She had packed the maroon leather suitcase she'd borrowed from her sister years earlier, when we went to Athens. She was wearing a yellow, flowery, mini-skirted summer dress from a decade back, which surprised me, as for years I'd seen her in nothing but nightdresses, pyjamas and sweatpants inside the apartment. I'd forgotten how beautiful she was. I'd basically forgotten that she was a human being. During her long period of incarceration in the dark back room, I'd come to view Markela as no more than a rare plant that I had to water regularly, a house plant that I couldn't leave outside. I'd stopped worrying about what might be going through her mind, what she did at home without me, and since that New Year's Eve I'd begun to resent her for tying me down.

The morning when I saw her in the living room wearing

her yellow dress, I thought she was leaving me, and, to tell the truth, that filled me with joy. If only Markela would do what I hadn't been able to and end our marriage. No matter how many times Ulker said, 'Don't you dare end your marriage on my account; you can't depend on me – I might go back to Frankfurt at the end of the summer; I'm also in touch with a university in America,' and other such things, deep down she was committed to me. If I asked her to marry me, she would accept happily. I felt that.

Markela sat down in the armchair next to the record player and crossed her legs.

'I'm waiting for Aunt Ismene. She's invited me to stay with her on Imbros,' she said.

I looked at her long white legs and made a decision. When she returned from this trip, we would get a divorce. Since she had got up, got dressed, taken the old suitcase down from the top of the wardrobe and packed it, since she had the energy to take a bus and then a ferry with Aunt Ismene, she could manage without me.

I went and sat across from her but could find nothing to say. As always, she was silent. From time to time she would get up, look down from the balcony on the Kaymakcalan Street side, then return to her place. Markela did not get bored. She could sit for hours without doing anything, staring vacantly at a single spot. In the past, in the first years of our marriage, I had loved this unique characteristic. A quiet woman was a rare jewel, I thought. Not once did Markela give me an order; she didn't interfere with how I dressed; she didn't pack my suitcase; she didn't hold the telephone to my ear, saying, 'You might want to say hello too.' We were like two trains that had started off at the same place but had gradually gone in different directions and now had no idea where the other one was, which stops we'd passed or where we'd ended up. Ever since I'd found Ulker again, I'd become so close to her that every other woman, including my wife, seemed like a stranger to me. Markela couldn't guess what I was thinking. We had lost our common reference points long ago.

When customers from the pharmacy bumped into me by chance on island ferries, on the subway going down to Karakoy or at the theatre, at first they'd be confused. They'd struggle to recall where they knew this man from, this man with such a familiar face. They were used to seeing me at the pharmacy, behind the counter, wearing my white coat. I thought about that as I looked at Markela sitting in the living room. If I were to see her outside the apartment, with the big dark circles under her eyes, her black hair that fell to below her waist, the hollow of her collarbones, visible above the neckline of her dress, perhaps at an open-air cinema on Imbros or at a taverna set up with drinks and musicians in the shade of a plane tree, would I recognize her?

Then, suddenly, I was angry. My wife had made secret holidays plans! Aunt Ismene and Markela had put their heads together, packed the suitcase, talked about what they would do on the island, built castles in the air. If I had woken up a bit later or had left the apartment at 8 a.m. to open the pharmacy, Markela would have left without telling me. The moment I opened my mouth to call her to account, a car horn tooted on the street. Markela stood up hurriedly and walked to the window. I got to my feet and blocked her path.

'How long do you plan to stay on Imbros?'

She shrugged.

I'd got used to being with Ulker, whose head only came up to my chest, but my wife was tall and her purple-shadowed eyes were level with mine. She met my gaze directly and there was no shame in her expression, no guilt, no embarrassment.

The taxi driver was getting impatient. I picked up the suitcase and went downstairs. I opened the boot. Aunt Ismene was sitting in the back seat of the taxi. I held the door open and Markela got in without looking at me. She knows about Ulker, I thought. Just as she'd known about Niki. In the hope of seeing that in her eyes, I leant through the open door of the taxi, but Markela had put on large round sunglasses that covered half her face and was staring straight ahead. As I stood leaning into the taxi, I expected Aunt Ismene to extend me an invitation. But no. As if hiding this trip from me was not enough, they said not a word about me joining them.

What did I expect? I'd effectively been sharing my life with Ulker those past seven months, since New Year's Eve, so why would Markela include me in her world? That was the obvious rational conclusion, of course, but it didn't immediately soothe the pain at having been excluded. And Markela looked very beautiful and mysterious, with her face hidden behind sunglasses and an expression that gave no clue as to her thoughts. She was tall, slender and very elegant. The shepherds on Imbros would be stunned at the sight of her.

I felt dazed as I watched the taxi disappear down Kaymakcalan Street. Nejat came up from Fortune Nightclub, walking with a pronounced limp. He too stared for a long time at the taxi taking Markela and Aunt Ismene away.

'Eh, Pericles Efendi, now what ya gonna do?'

I lingered at the door of The Circle for a while without answering. Istanbul's humid heat was banishing the morning's coolness. The sun had risen above Beyoglu's buildings and was striking our street. The garbage stank. I went inside. Nejat followed. The entranceway was cool thanks to the thick walls that kept both the heat and the cold outside. As I waited for the lift, I watched the play of colourful shadows cast onto the mosaic floor by the stained-glass fanlight above the door.

There was some money of mine in the nightclub's cash register. I asked Nejat for it.

'You goin' somewhere?' he asked.

He had come upstairs to my apartment with me and plopped himself down in the armchair where Markela had sat with crossed legs a short while earlier. He still visited our apartment very often. He spent Sundays on our couch, munching on pistachios. Towards evening he would call out, 'Come on, all of ya, get up. We're goin' out to eat. There's a new restaurant on the Bosphorus. You're gonna love their shrimp cocktail, Markela. And what a soufflé they do!' Markela barely ever left the apartment. She would smile at Nejat. Our mafia godfather was in need of friends. Sometimes I would accept his offer of a fish dinner beside the Bosphorus; on very rare occasions, Markela and Aunt Ismene would come with us. The Bosphorus restaurants Nejat chose always served us the freshest fish, the most varied mezze. The wine was never warm and the raki supply was endless. Our car door was held open as we got out, jackets and coats were removed from our shoulders, warm towels proffered for our hands.

While I was preparing my bag, Nejat was watching a video in the living room.

'You need a car? I can get one for ya.'

'Not necessary.'

Ulker definitely wouldn't want to drive anything other than her Mini Cooper.

'Markela and Ismene Hanim went to Imbros? Why'd they take a taxi? I would have sent a chauffeur.'

I didn't answer. I zipped up my bag, then watered the plants.

'I'm leaving, Nejat. Come on.'

I knew he was hoping to stay at our apartment. Although he had masses of money, Nejat didn't have a proper home. He never had. He would stay in an apartment that he was doing up, then stay in some woman's apartment for a long time, then disappear. He had a bed in his office in the back of Fortune Nightclub where he would sometimes stay for months on end. Since he was now gazing around our apartment like a little puppy, I knew for sure he wanted me to turn the place over to him. He'd sit numbing himself in front of the TV, pockets full of everything from hash to heroin. In his dreams!

Locking the door, I left The Circle and parted ways with Nejat at the corner of Kaymakcalan and Temrin Hill streets. It had suddenly got hot, and the reek of garbage had intensified.

I spent the rest of the summer at Ulker's house in Tunel Square. In August I left the pharmacy in Aydin's care for fifteen days while Ulker and I went to Bodrum. We stayed in a small bed-and-breakfast in Gumusluk. In the jasmine-scented sunset we would climb up the cliff behind Rabbit Island and drink wine. We would make love on the divan on our balcony in the dark of night, then skinny-dip off the beach in front of the bed and breakfast. Kemal, Betul and friends were staying in Turkbuku and some evenings we would join them for raki and mezze and endless rounds of fiery political debate. When Ulker contributed with clever arguments, I felt very proud. I would stroke the skirt of her long cotton dress. 'This is my woman,' I would say to myself. 'This brilliant, profound woman is my lover.'

Kemal and his friends accepted us as a couple. When Kemal and I were alone, I told him that I had separated from Markela and divorce procedures would begin in the autumn. Kemal didn't say anything. He had met Markela on the night of May 1st, but they'd not seen each other since. I had continued to get together with Kemal and Betul, eating and drinking with them at Aynali Arcade, at Yakup's, at the Cumhuriyet Pub, but Markela never joined us. Kemal knew my wife had been in and out of hospital. Seeing me so happy with Ulker pleased him, or at least that's what I wanted to think. Markela had as good as left me. As soon as she got back, I was going to take her by the arm and drag her to court. Wherever she went after that was up to her. I no longer worried about where she might live or with whom. For all I cared, she could move in with Aunt Ismene or go back to her parents' house. She was a thirty-eight-year-old woman who had gone to Imbros without her husband. She could do whatever she wanted. Without realizing it, Aunt Ismene had freed me from Markela.

When she got sunburnt, Ulker's freckles became very pronounced, as they had been in her youth. It was as if the intervening years hadn't happened, as if we'd spent a lifetime together. Ulker was not the past, she was now and forever. When I was with her, time did not so much move forwards as inwards. The present moment gained significance. When I kissed her salty, freckled shoulder, I thought that everything I'd experienced up to then had been preparation for that moment. I was filled with gratitude. Because of all the pain I had endured, fate had decided to reward me at last.

That summer was the happiest of my life. But that was before the 1986 demolition of Tarlabasi Boulevard. All it took was one night for bulldozers to enter our street and, along with the beautiful buildings, destroy everything I cared about.

# I'll Block My Ears
## and Tear Tarlabasi Down

They began tearing down the neighbourhood from the upper street.

It was October. I awoke to an incomprehensible roaring noise. Half asleep, I put my slippers on and crossed the corridor. The roaring got worse as I entered the living room, and when I stepped towards the balconies facing Kaymakcalan Street I realized that the building across from us that had been there forever – since my childhood – had gone. It had been pulled down. Its rubble was shrouded in dust, like a bombed city. Packs of uneasy dogs wandered around amid the fallen marble columns and twisted iron railings of the balconies. Unsupervised children were yelling and confused birds flitted between the ruins. An ominous cloud of dust settled over us from the upper streets. The roaring sound that had woken me up was coming from all corners of the neighbourhood. Stupefied, I stood in front of the balcony door with my hand on the knob.

So they'd finally done what they'd said they would and were making that infamous eight-lane highway connecting Taksim to Golden Horn a reality. Since the beginning of the summer words like 'demolition' and 'evacuation' had been bandied around. For months now, members of the Chamber of Architects had been wandering around our mostly dead-end streets, assiduously taking notes on the ornamental features of our buildings, fountains, doors and balconies. From them we learnt that our streets, the ones strung with washing lines full of multicoloured clothes, had the only examples of buildings constructed in that style in the world. Several meetings were held in which the architects informed us of our legal rights and property values. We were not going to let our homes and shops be razed to the ground.

On my way to Ulker's flat I would deliberately take the small side streets all the way to Tepebasi so that I could talk to neighbours sitting on the marble steps in front of their buildings and shop owners standing outside their businesses. When my elderly Armenian neighbour who owned the delicatessen where I bought wine, cigarettes, ham and cheese had shown me the official document in his hand, I had confidently insisted, 'They can't do that sort of thing. It's not that easy to throw us out of the homes we've lived in all these years, the shops we've established.' It was illegal to tear down the apartment buildings at Tarlabasi.

Whenever I said things like that, the old women shopping in the delicatessen, the greengrocer and the café owner would all listen in. After all, I could be considered one of Beyoglu's longest-standing residents. Touching the brim of my hat in greeting, wine bottle under my arm, carrying the various snacks I'd bought for our picnic in bed, I would leave them there and walk to Ulker's flat in Tunel. The only thing missing was my whistling a tune. That autumn I was a man in love. I had not been expecting to wake up one morning to a war zone in front of my apartment. Which was why I stood there with the doorknob in my hand, staring at the upper street that no longer existed, unable to comprehend what I was seeing.

Markela crept to my side as quietly as a ghost. I was startled when I heard her voice.

'They knocked down the old orphanage last night. You know, the one with a little church in its courtyard. A cat had made its home there in the quiet and its kittens were buried under the rubble. They cried and cried.'

I opened the balcony door. A roaring like the buzz of a giant vacuum cleaner filled the apartment. Markela stepped out onto the narrow French balcony. I stood beside her. She was trembling in the cardigan she'd pulled around herself, even though it wasn't cold. It was an October morning as sweet as syrup. Out of the corner of my eye I was watching to be sure she wasn't about to do something crazy again. After she'd returned from Imbros, she had shut herself away in her room and almost never came out. She didn't speak to me. She didn't confront me about Ulker. When her depression came back, I couldn't bring myself to drag her to the divorce court. Aunt Ismene took trays of food to her in her room and persuaded her to have a bath once a week and get her hair washed and her body scrubbed. The Imbros holiday had not helped Markela as I'd hoped it would.

I tried to comfort her.

'The kittens would have run away. Cats have strong intuition and at the first sound of a bulldozer, they would have scarpered.'

She turned to me in anger and looked me up and down as if she'd just noticed I was there.

'They couldn't run away. The kittens cried all night long, I'm telling you. The mother searched for her babies under the rubble. I heard it myself. What would you know about it?'

She was right. How could I know? I'd come home late, very late. It was two in the morning before I'd been able to tear myself away from Ulker, to separate my skin from hers.

I tried to take hold of Markela's thin shoulders and propel her inside. A bulldozer and a digger were making their way down our upper street, which no longer existed. One was knocking buildings down as it went and the other was scooping stuff up and piling it some distance away. Markela's face was ivory white. Her waist-length hair was a mess of uncombed tangles. The expression in her eyes was vacant, the words coming out of her mouth incoherent. Her blank stare was the mirror of an inner world disassociated from reality, a mind in turmoil. All the signs pointed to her having entered a phase of deep depression, but I had no strength left to deal with it. I wanted to run to Ulker as soon as possible. I had looked after Markela for years. If things deteriorated, Aunt Ismene could call her mother, father or one of her sisters and they could have her hospitalized. I was worn out.

I was immediately ashamed of myself for thinking like that. I closed the balcony door and tried to put my arms around her. She turned and stared at the ruins of the destroyed buildings. The bulldozer and digger attacked the next building in line, an old bay-windowed house that had been derelict for a long time. The fig tree in its garden had reached through the glassless windows and spread into the rooms. Children called it the Haunted House. Years earlier, an alcoholic man and his daughter had lived there. In 1964 the man was taken out of the house on a stretcher. He was one of those who was accused of being a traitor and exiled. He had a bad turn on the train and never made it across the bridge, so I heard, and the building had been empty ever since. The title deed was in Nejat's safe, of course, but no one had ever wanted to rent it, not even refugees from the war in the east, maybe because of its reputation. That had been good for the neighbourhood kids, who would sit on its marble front steps for hours, discussing who might be brave enough to enter the Haunted House, playing games and telling stories about magic charms, genies and fairies.

The Haunted House put up a fierce resistance to its destruction. The repeated thwacks of the bulldozer made the windows of our apartment shudder. If they kept that up, it would be only a matter of time before our windowpanes broke free of their wooden frames and shattered. I went to the bedroom, tipped a tranquilliser out of a bottle in the dresser drawer and filled a glass with water. Hoping she wouldn't push me away, I placed a pill between Markela's lips. She swallowed it without objecting. Holding the glass of water in her hands, she remained rooted to the spot as she watched the demolition. With every thump of the bulldozer, the purple shadows under her eyes appeared to grow darker. Veins showed under the transparent skin of her face, on her cheekbones and forehead.

The door opened and Aunt Ismene came in, using her key. She was sweating. In front of the console table in the entrance she brushed off the dust that was sticking to every bit of her and said, 'They're finally going to kick us out of here. We've clung to the stones, to the earth, and now they're taking that too. I ask you, if the streets are destroyed, what will be left of this city, of Poli? Only, *mono*, ruins. Nothing more.'

Having taken off her shoes, she came into the living room and saw Markela. She looked at me. She understood that we were on the brink of a new crisis. Just then there was a large explosion. In an instant the Haunted House crumpled and turned to dust, as if it had been made of flour. Bewildered pigeons fluttered out of the glassless windows and dispersed into the sky. The glass of water slid from Markela's hands to the ground. Wet shards scattered across the wooden floor, under the coffee table. Aunt Ismene and I both sprang up at the same time and caught Markela by her arms. She was trembling more than ever. She was as light as a feather. We took her to her bed. One pill would not be enough; I wanted to give her a tranquillizing shot as well. She wrapped her cardigan tightly around herself, shaking. At first, she refused to have the injection, but after she'd calmed down, Aunt Ismene was able to turn her over, face down. Markela didn't make a sound when I stuck the needle into her buttocks. As she fell into sleep, I left the apartment.

Veli was sitting on his usual wicker stool in front of his coffeehouse, watching the bulldozer trying to yank the fig tree out of the Haunted House garden. As its roots clung to the friable earth, the huge machine roared ever louder. The coffeehouse windows were rattling. I strode angrily towards Veli.

'Did you not form a cooperative to save this neighbourhood, Veli? What good did it do? The Chamber of Architects? The High Council of Immovable Monuments and Antiquities? All those experts strutting around writing reports, all that pomp and frantic activity, and for what?'

Veli put the prayer beads he'd been running through his fingers into his pocket and got to his feet. He was confused.

'How would I know, Monsieur Pericles? The mayor said, "I'll tear them down and take the consequences." What can we do? They started late yesterday afternoon.'

'*What?* What did he say?' I hadn't been able to hear clearly above the noise.

Veli raised his voice. 'When the mayor heard that the Chamber of Architects would be issuing a formal complaint, he said, "I'll block my ears and tear Tarlabasi down." Every newspaper ran the story. See here. Yesterday they had an opening ceremony with a marching band. In just a couple of hours they pulled down several enormous buildings with great thundering booms.'

I must have looked at Veli strangely, for he took my arm and steered me away from the noise.

'Come, let's walk around the upper street so that you can see it face on. A Chernobyl explosion couldn't have done more damage to Damacana Street.'

Veli and I entered the upper street side by side. Floral bas-reliefs, angel faces, intricately decorated wrought-iron railings, doors and lion-headed doorknobs were scattered all around the demolished apartment buildings. Multicoloured fragments of stained glass crunched under our feet. My bewilderment turned to anger, then to deep sadness. Yet again I was left feeling helpless, a victim of the despotic power and macho evil of faceless people determined to take my home from me. The streets of my city were being attacked in a fit of blind rage. *I will tear Tarlabasi down.* Our Poli was now in the hands of these merciless bullies. We were watching her suffer and die and there was nothing we could do about it.

I collapsed beside a flower-embossed marble column that had been tossed aside. My legs would no longer support me. Someone grabbed my arm.

'Pericles Efendi, what you doin' here, boy? Get out of the way. Good God Almighty! You gonna get hurt.'

Turning my head with difficulty, I saw Nejat. I stood up, dusted off my trousers in vain. In the background I could see

Nejat's boys going in and out of the empty houses. Who knew what they were after.

'Yesterday we came. You wasn't at the pharmacy.'

Markela's accusing eyes and scornful words came to my mind. *You? What would you know about it?* The previous day I'd left the pharmacy early and gone to Ulker's house.

'I'm sure Aydin helped you. He knows what to give you. Did he do something wrong?'

Nejat pulled me over to the front of the abandoned houses on the pavement behind. He was limping obviously now, but out of stubbornness would not use a walking cane.

'You can rest easy in that department. Aydin's got a brain. He's smart as a genie. Good you found him. He handles whatever we need, don't ask us nothin'. Not out of kindness, ha. He's a real businessman. And you hang out with your chick...'

'Nothing gets past you, Nejat.'

'Nothin'.'

He took a toothpick from his pocket and started fiddling with his teeth, looking at the apartment that the bulldozer was trying to demolish.

'You lookin' low, Pericles Efendi. What's goin' on? Everything okay at home? How's sister Markela? Her health all right nowadays?'

He was the one who looked low. With my head I indicated the apartment building that was somehow resisting destruction. The bulldozer was trying to pull it down with steel cables that they'd tied around its supporting columns. I saw Pharmacist Dacat's son in the distance. He had set up a tripod and was taking pictures of the horrible scene. He greeted me with a nod. I didn't even have the strength to raise my hand.

'Don't go over there! Get away from there, son!' shouted a

police officer. Children were still trying to play games on their street. When they paid no heed, the officer blew his whistle and approached them. Just then the columns gave way and the beautiful, finely ornamented five-storey building folded, one floor on top of the other. Everything vanished behind a dirty yellow cloud of dust. A dog howled. Perhaps Markela was right that cats and dogs which had made their homes in the abandoned houses were dying under the rubble.

Nejat turned to me.

'You listen to me, Pericles. You can't think about this stuff too much. This construction business is just beginnin'. Two hundred, three hundred buildings are gonna come down, I'm tellin' ya now.'

'It can't be that many, Nejat. Every one of these is a historic monument.'

'No matter what, that road is gonna come through here. The stakes are high. You wait and see.'

He took the toothpick from his mouth and chucked it in the direction of the destroyed building. Zulfu, Galip and the other heavies who'd been loitering in the background took this as a sign and immediately appeared at his side. They greeted me respectfully. A black-haired, black-suited, solarium-tanned army. Sweeping their godfather along with them, they walked to the navy-blue S-class Mercedes parked on the corner and opened the door for him.

Seating himself in the back seat, Nejat rolled down the window and lowered his voice. 'You know, they're thinkin' of making this road pass through Kaymakcalan. Your canny upstairs neighbour has already sat down to negotiate with the municipality. Don't worry, we will handle it. You and I can talk on Sunday. See ya later! Give my greetings to sister Markela and Ismene Hanim.'

I caught my own reflection in the window glass as it closed. My eyes were bloodshot, my clothes crumpled. I'd put on yesterday's clothes when I left the apartment. Were they really going to flatten our building? The canny upstairs neighbour Nejat referred to was of course Mansur Bey. When had he sat down to negotiate with the municipality? We'd never even received any official documents about evacuating our apartments.

I started in the direction of the pharmacy, but I couldn't walk two steps. I should have got a ride in Nejat's car. There'd been something odd about Nejat's behaviour. He'd been a bit subdued. Who knew what machinations were being played out behind the scenes with this Tarlabasi business. Maybe even Nejat had had to bow down to the multinational monopolies that controlled the capital.

I felt dizzy. I looked around for a grocery shop to buy a bottle of water. All the apartments, stone houses and shops had been emptied. They looked like hollowed-out caves. An old woman holding a pot of geraniums on her lap was sitting on the marble steps of one of the houses, her head resting on the wall behind her. I approached her anxiously. Was she dead? I reached out and touched the arm of her black woollen dress. She looked at me, her pink scalp visible under her scant white hair. A few words came out of her toothless mouth. Was she speaking Turkish or Greek? I couldn't tell. I leant down and looked carefully into her face. Then I recognized her.

'Madam Elpiniki? Is it you, Madam Elpiniki? It's me, Pericles. Do you remember me?'

Madam Elpiniki, who'd had a hat shop on the ground floor of The Circle when I was a child. The talented designer whose hats had been cut to shreds and scattered on the street during the September Events. The tweed cap that used to look so good on me had been her creation. Madam Elpiniki was crying in front of her home, which was vanishing under a cloud of yellow dust. Tears were rolling down the wrinkles of her face.

Madam Elpiniki had been an old woman even back when I was young. She used to complain about her rheumatism. She must have been ninety by now, or older. I raised my head and looked up at the flaking paint and broken windowpanes of her building. Papa used to go there to give her injections and he brought me with him a few times. I remembered her lying face down on the sofa with her dress pushed up. Her living room had been filled with dusty sideboards, mirrored consoles, and bookcases with hundreds of framed photographs lined up on them. I didn't know she was still living in the same house, one street up from ours.

I bent down so that she could see my face, trying my luck one more time.

'Madam Elpiniki, *kalimera*! I am Pericles, Pharmacist Themis's son. Themis Drakos. Do you remember? My mother, *mama mou*, was Alexandra. Nikiforos's daughter. Nikiforos Proodos. My grandfather. He was also a pharmacist.'

She narrowed her eyes, cloudy like a baby's, and gazed at me. Her wrinkled jaw moved from left to right. No, she didn't recognize me. Taking her by the arm, I helped her up and took the pot of geraniums from her hand. It wasn't good for her to be sitting there all by herself. We walked down a corridor with sticky flooring and into the living room. Without saying a word, Madam Elpiniki withdrew her arm from mine and sank into a satin armchair. Although it was a bright October day outside, the apartment was dark. The furniture was just as I remembered from my youth. Strangely, the tick-tock of the cuckoo clock on the wall could be heard above the noise outside. An officially stamped document was lying on the dining-room table. This was a notification of the pending destruction of the building and its compulsory evacuation. The same notice had been passed from hand to hand throughout the summer and affixed to the frontages of some apartment buildings. The paper guaranteed Madam Elpiniki ten million lira for moving out of the three-hundred-square-metre place she owned and asked that the old woman vacate her house within two days.

I put the geranium on the windowsill. She reached out and pulled it onto her lap. She wasn't crying any more. She might even have smiled at me. Did she have children somewhere? Could I send word to them? At that time ten million lira couldn't buy even a one-bed apartment, even though Madam Elpiniki was the owner of three apartments in the building they were appropriating – four if you counted the ground floor.

I could not endure heaping further sorrow on the mountain of woes already towering inside me. The old wound, a product of searing cruelty and injustice, had lost its scab and was bleeding. Leaving my old neighbour with the geranium in her lap, I walked away.

Two days later, when I stopped at Madam Elpiniki's on my way home from the pharmacy, I found the door wide open. Construction workers were removing the windowpanes in the living room. Children playing ball on the street ran over to me, shouting and yelling that the old madam had been found dead in the house the morning before. Municipal officials had come for the evacuation and discovered Madam Elpiniki lying lifeless on the sofa. They covered her with a blanket and took her out on a stretcher. Where to? Where was the funeral? They stared at me in bewilderment, as if I were speaking a different language. I pushed open the door and went into the house. At least I could take the geranium.

'They emptied out the house,' yelled one of the shaven-haired boys behind my back. 'Junkman Ihsan came from Cukurcuma. He loaded all Madam's furniture on his truck and took it away.'

# Kilyos Beach

The following morning I went straight to Ulker's house, without even stopping at the pharmacy. When I let myself in, she was sitting at the kitchen table wearing a dressing gown, drinking coffee and reading the newspaper. She got up immediately, came over and wrapped her arms around me. I buried my face in her auburn hair. My hands found the curve of her waist under her robe. I stroked her collarbones and her beloved round buttocks. Kissing, we moved to the bed and rolled onto the wrinkled sheets and white cotton blanket that smelled of sleep. We'd not yet said a word to each other. I loved Ulker's silence. Hers was not the kind of silence that left one desperate, not like Markela's; it was a silence that comforted, calmed, held one tight.

In spite of Ulker's caresses and the sensual moves of her lithe body that still carried the drowsy warmth of night, I couldn't find the energy to make love to her. I had no appetite for anything that might arouse me. I had lost my libido. I curled up beside her. Ulker took no offence at my having stopped our lovemaking. Covering her legs with the yellow nightdress that had bunched up around her waist, she lay down beside me and placed her hand on the knife wound of pain on my side, on that ache right under my ribs that had returned as I'd stood all alone in Madam Elpiniki's empty house. How well she knew exactly where my pain was. Her palm was soft and warm, like the inside of a loaf of bread fresh from the oven.

I don't know how long we lay there. I had closed my eyes. I could hear the growl of shared taxis leaving Tunel Square, the shouts of street sellers, the bells of the Catholic churches along the avenue. As I hovered in that limbo between sleep and wakefulness, Despina came to my mind. That Saturday when we had bumped into her in an arcade in Beyoglu, her instinct had been to run from us. Her long black plait hung down her back, her big black eyes were anxious and sad. 'Unlucky Despina,' Mama and Aunt Ismene used to call her in private. 'They erased her name from the church registry.' Back then, I thought the community had ostracized Despina because she'd married a Turk. That was the reason given on paper, I'm sure. A member of our Greek Orthodox minority who married a Muslim was no longer considered a part of the community. But now, lying on Ulker's bed and listening to the heavy rhythmic thuds of the bulldozers as they drowned out Beyoglu's familiar morning sounds, I realized that Despina had been cast out because she'd been raped. Instead of taking her shame and going somewhere far away with her family, to Athens, she had stayed in Istanbul and carried on with her life, not even changing her name. Seeing her walking around in plain sight had obviously upset people's peace of mind, for it reminded them of all the women who'd been raped on that fateful day.

Ulker slipped out of my arms and got out of bed. 'Come on, get up!'

I didn't answer.

'Pericles, get up. Let's go and get some air, you and me. It's noon already.'

I forced myself to open my eyes. The noise of the demolition reverberated all the way to Tunel, leaving my head throbbing. Every thwack and thump of the machinery against the condemned buildings echoed down the narrow passages of the Flower Arcade, the fish market and Aynali Arcade before reaching Ulker's bedroom and landing like hammer blows inside my brain.

'Look, here's what I suggest. Let's jump in the car and go somewhere far away for the day. What do you say?'

I eased myself to sitting. Ulker knew better than I did what I needed. I had to get out of that neighbourhood, away from Beyoglu's dark buildings, shadowed streets, inclines with steps that came to a sudden stop, abandoned homes. I had to distance myself, if only for a day, from the place that had been the centre of my universe for my entire life.

We got Ulker's Mini Cooper from the car park above Asmali Mescit Street. Beyoglu was calm. We stopped at the corner of Kurabiye Street and I raced into the pharmacy to glance over the accounts.

'Don't worry about anything, Monsieur Pericles,' Aydin said. 'You should rest this afternoon. You look tired.' His sweet-faced fiancée, Mina, was arranging make-up items on the shelves. We were selling cosmetics and toys now. The tiny bells we had hung on the door jingled. A ten-year-old girl who wanted her ears pierced came in with her mother. I drew Aydin behind the counter.

'If Nejat comes in this evening, or Galip...'

'I have prepared what's required. It's in the depot in the back.'

I gave Aydin a friendly pat on his white-coated shoulder.

He was a sharp guy. Respectful too. I left. As the door shut behind me, the bells jingled again. White-capped traffic police had turned their lights on at the corner of Kucuk Parmak Kapi and were approaching Ulker, who was waiting for me in the car, to issue her with a parking ticket. It took my long legs just two strides to cross the street. Before the police could reach us, I jumped into the front seat, hitting the glove compartment with my knees, and we sped off, mingled with the Taksim traffic and disappeared. From Gumussuyu we went down to Dolmabahce, then past Besiktas to Ortakoy, and from Kurucesme to Arnavutkoy. In the honeyed October light, the sea had turned dark blue. The little boats out in the open water shone green, red and yellow. I put my hand on Ulker's knee. How grateful I was to her. She reminded me that Istanbul was bigger than just Beyoglu.

'They're going to build a road here too.' She said this cautiously, afraid of making me even sadder. 'Two lanes. They'll hammer piles into the seabed. It'll pass in front of the houses.'

'They can't do that!' I said. 'These Bosphorus mansions are a century old. Would people allow it? These—'

I stopped mid-sentence. They could, of course. Without even giving it a second thought. I turned my eyes to the bridge being constructed. One bridge had not been enough to smother the Bosphorus, so they were now building a second one. From Ulker's terrace we had watched the fireworks when the Japanese firm had begun work. It had been a glorious celebration.

Ulker accelerated. We passed Asiyan, Baltalimani, Istinye. It seemed to me that she went a little faster at Yenikoy, where Markela had grown up and where her parents still lived. North of Yenikoy, as the Bosphorus suddenly opened up and got broader, the harsh wind coming off the Black Sea hit my face through the open windows. Ulker lit a cigarette and passed one to me. I didn't want it. Leaning my head against the back of the seat, I watched the city silently slipping by until I fell asleep.

When I woke up, we'd reached Kilyos Beach. Dark clouds were lowering over the northern parts of the city and the wind was whipping up the sand. Making a screen with a rainbow-coloured umbrella from the boot of the car, we sat beside the sea. We kissed. Sand found its way into Ulker's tousled short hair, onto her bare neck, into her small ears. There was no one on that limitless Black Sea beach but us. Two shepherd dogs, tugging on a stick, bounded over to us. They were large but it was obvious from their playfulness that they were still very young. Their eyes were circled as if with black mascara. Ulker gave them the meat pie she'd bought from Sariyer. They swam in the sea and came back to us, shaking themselves off. When they got tired, they slept beside us, their tan-coloured bodies resting against Ulker's legs. The foamy waves softened on the horizon, where the deep-blue sea mixed with the sky and made a paler blue. I wanted to rest my head on Ulker's lap like the shepherd dogs and close my eyes. I lay lightly back on the straw mat we had spread on the sand. The straw rustled.

'Pericles, I need to tell you something,' Ulker said.

At first I didn't understand what she'd said. 'Hmm,' I murmured. The rest of what she'd said was like the buzzing of a mosquito in my ear.

'My period is two weeks late. I mean, I don't think anything's going to come of it, but... I'm forty-two years old, so I'm not taking it very seriously. It's happened before, after all. Doctors say such irregularities are normal before the menopause.'

We hadn't been taking precautions, that was true. We'd been making love since we met at Kemal's house on New Year's Eve. Ulker had had her periods for ten months. They were short, just a little blood, normal for a woman of her age. She carried on with her life and we just stopped having sex for two or three days, that was all. Even though I knew how regular her cycle was, it had never crossed my mind that she might fall pregnant.

I sat up and turned towards her. She was watching a tanker passing by in the open sea. One hand was on the shepherd dog's head. I looked at her little retroussé nose, the freckles left from summer, the moles on her neck, her auburn hair tossed by the wind, and suddenly I was filled with joy. If we could have a daughter... a child like Ulker... a little person, cute, sassy, hazel-eyed. A bit of Mama, a bit of Ulker, a bit of the beautiful Oya, and a bit of *yaya*, whom I had never known. Could we be good parents at our age? Why not?

'Ulker...'

She turned her face to me and smiled, shrugging slightly. I put my arm around her, drew her close and kissed her head, her hair. In my shock, I somehow couldn't find the words. She spoke in my place.

'It's nothing. It's happened before.'

I was confused but didn't say anything.

'If I am pregnant, the first three months would be really difficult at my age. The chance of a miscarriage would be very high.'

I held her tighter.

'Don't think about such things now.'

I was glad that some words had at last come out of my mouth. Don't think about such things now. Think happy thoughts. Our little daughter... The life we would live together.

We'd move from Beyoglu to a little house in Bebek or Etiler or Levent. Whatever we could afford. Markela would return to her mother and father. I had not one but two apartments to sell and we would rent out Ulker's apartment in Tunel. I would open a new pharmacy. It was easier to import goods now. All sorts of toys, cosmetics, vitamins and health and beauty products were flowing into Turkey from Europe, the USA and China, and there was a growing new social class ready to consume such items. I'd sell my share of the Fortune Nightclub to Nejat. I could get along at work without him now.

Like every man on the threshold of being a father, I spent those first moments appraising our assets. Yes, really. What else could I think about? That I was married to another woman? Would Markela's family declare war on me, vowing to take everything I had in alimony? It wasn't that those things didn't cross my mind, but right in the middle of that circle of feelings and thoughts was joy and the fresh bud of hope. I understand now that the one thing I needed to convey was the existence of that bud of hope. I'd assumed that Ulker had sensed how happy I was. Did my joy not radiate off me in waves as I leant into her, my arm around her shoulders? Was it not obvious how much I wanted to have a child with her? No. She saw, sensed and understood only the anxiety that was clouding my eyes.

I did not know that for the rest of my life I would regret not having proposed to Ulker that day on Kilyos Beach. Let us have a child. If not now, then next month, next year. If it doesn't happen naturally, let's try and make it happen. Medicine has made advances. Let us bring a person into the world. I did not say to her: this news you have given me, this tiny possibility, is the one seed of hope in a soul that otherwise lies in tatters. I did not say anything. If Ulker was offended, she didn't show it.

We got up, gathered up our umbrella, rolled up the straw mat, picked up our bags and put shoes and socks on our sandy feet. Ulker unwrapped the paper from around our meat and spinach pies and put them in front of the dogs, who were cuddled up together, asleep on our beach towel. Let them have the towel, we said. Holding hands, we walked to the car. The subject was closed.

Dusk was falling. We were hungry. We found a drinking place on a hilltop overlooking the sea, with two or three tables thrown out onto a makeshift terrace. They only had Greek salad, bread and fresh bonito left. We ordered it all. And a bottle of raki. There was another couple who by the look of them were having a secret rendezvous. They glanced at us out of the corner of their eyes. We smiled at each other. The fish was fresh, the salad smelled like a tomato garden. Dipping the fresh bread in the juices, we ate. We drank the raki. Quite a bit. To the point of oblivion. Then, to clear our heads, we walked arm in arm along a dark forest road. I had no idea where we were. I wanted to make love. The back seat of the car was too small – when Ulker stretched out on it on her back, there was room enough only for her, no space for me. We thrashed about in the dark forest, then dozed off. When we woke up, it was past midnight.

On the way home Ulker didn't speak at all. Her eyes were closed. She must have been asleep. I drove the car slowly to Tunel. Sometimes the dark waters of the Bosphorus swelled at a curve, sometimes they flattened, sometimes they became a shining current. Fishing boats lit by kerosene lanterns spread like stars from Besiktas to Dolmabahce, from there to the open waters of Maiden's Tower, and on towards the Sea of Marmara. In spite of everything, Istanbul was too beautiful to give up on, I thought in my tipsy state. Those who were violating her must be blind.

We left the car in the Asmali Mescit parking lot. I accompanied Ulker to the door of her apartment and waited on the street until the cage lift had reached the top floor. Then I walked to The Circle. The construction work had stopped. A couple came out of Fortune Nightclub, holding on to one another. They were drunk. They had roses in their hands and were laughing and kissing. They disappeared from sight down the unevenly cobbled Temrin Hill Street leading to Dolapdere. There were lights on in Edip's flat and a dim light like a candle flame seeped out from the fourth floor where a group of ten or twenty dishwashing boys were staying at that point. The rest of the building was dark.

I found Aunt Ismene on the divan in my office. She was asleep under a pink wool blanket. There was no sound from Markela's room. I got undressed and lay down. Thinking of that tiny possibility growing in Ulker's womb, I fell asleep.

# A Story That We Think
## of as Being Our Life

On Monday morning I woke up on the divan in my office. I was wearing the corduroy trousers and sleeveless maroon jumper of the day before. The collar of my shirt was awry, the sleeves wrinkled. I'd spent the whole of Sunday writing, furiously jotting down notes in my book so as to get down on paper the memories that were flowing through my mind in a flood. The notes, half in Turkish, half in Greek, would have to be rewritten neatly before I turned them over to Leyla. I had stretched out, saying, let me just close my eyes for a couple of minutes, and then I'll continue. When I opened them again, it was after eleven the next morning.

Stelio was in the kitchen trying to close the pressure cooker. I went in and helped him. He was making chicken soup. He had filled the cooker with vegetables. He should have cooked the chicken first, taken it out, cooked the vegetables in its broth, deboned the chicken and then added that to the vegetables, but I said nothing.

'*Kalimera*, Monsieur Pericles. How are you?'

Because I wasn't used to waking up after sunrise, my head hurt, and because I'd slept on the divan, my back hurt.

'Let me drink some coffee and I'll be fine.'

He turned on the gas under the pressure cooker and stepped aside. I took the Turkish coffee pot from its nail on the wall and set about making my coffee. Stelio silently left the kitchen. It was a dark day. Clouds hung low over the antenna-strewn rooftops and it was drizzling. My mind was full of the sentences I was going to write, and I was impatient to have Leyla read the chapters I'd already written. I poured the hot, foamy coffee into a cup, took a dry biscuit from a jar and headed for my office.

Stelio was staring out of the balcony window. Just as I was closing my door, he shouted out, 'Ah! Ah! Monsieur Pericles, isn't that Leyla?'

Returning to the kitchen, I set my coffee down on the counter, spilling some of it into the saucer and ruining the froth, and went through the dining room and into the living room. Stelio had opened the balcony door. I went over to him and together we looked down. A black, official-looking car was waiting at the corner of Kaymakcalan Street and Temrin Hill Street. The chauffeur closed the back door, then took his place at the wheel. The car glided down Kaymakcalan Street then vanished into the rain.

'So where is she?'

'She went out to the corner, got in the car and left.'

I looked over at the spot where Kaymakcalan Street ended and the church street began. The black car had disappeared. I heard thunder in the distance.

'Come inside. You'll catch cold,' said Stelio.

We closed the balcony door and I paced up and down the dining room for a while, scratching my unshaven cheeks, before eventually coming to a standstill in front of Stelio.

'Did that car come for Leyla? Are you sure it was Leyla you saw?'

The boy was surprised. He took off his glasses and wiped the lenses with the edge of his sweater.

'I don't know. I thought it was Leyla – she came out of our building, after all. She was wearing a tan trench coat. The driver held the door for her, she got in and they left. You saw the car too.'

'Are we not in quarantine?' I said heatedly. 'How could the girl just go marching off? What kind of irresponsible behaviour is that?'

Stelio looked at me in bewilderment. I'd obviously gotten too agitated. Taking the key to the downstairs apartment from the nail beside the door, I went down to Leyla's apartment. As I put the key into her lock, I hesitated for a moment. Maybe Stelio had been mistaken about what he'd seen. I rang the doorbell instead. There was no sound inside. I rang it again, longer, more insistently. No, Stelio had been correct. Leyla had broken the quarantine and gone out. But where?

I let myself in. The cream-coloured curtains in the living room were drawn. The whole place smelled of incense. I went and pulled the curtains wide open. In the dull grey light of the street Leyla's living room looked dirty and in disarray. Tobacco had been spilled and a bowlful of pistachio shells had been left on the floor, forgotten between the sofa and the coffee table. I counted three empty coffee mugs on the windowsill where Leyla loved to sit. The midnight-blue Murano ashtray that I had given her had been emptied but not washed. I went into the dining room. My nose, which had got used to the smell of incense, now smelled cigarette smoke. Had Leyla spent a sleepless night, I wondered? Or had there been someone with her?

It seemed I was going to have to accept the unpleasant possibility that had been niggling away at me since the moment I'd seen that damned official car. That married man had spent the night with Leyla and in the morning his chauffeur had come to pick them both up. Perhaps the man was taking Leyla to a luxurious hotel. 'This is the way to live, my princess, the life you deserve, a five-star hotel, one hand in butter, the other in honey. Let me take you away from this virus-nest, this depressing apartment, this mousehole, my sultana,' he'd said. 'The apartment building is quarantined, you say? No need to worry about that, my child. Just leave it to me.' So said he, touching her here and pressuring her there. She fell for his tricks and left. Women could never resist the promise of being spoiled. They went off, leaving the flat in a mess.

The dining-room table and chairs were piled with open books and bits of paper. I leafed through the notebooks beside her computer. She'd made notes in different-coloured pens, all of them concerning my book. It was obvious that the poor girl had been working furiously. And here I was, accusing her of running off to hotels with her old lover, searching for signs of a second person's presence. The butts of filter cigarettes? Two glasses? Leyla didn't drink. It seemed that after hearing that we'd surrendered to the construction mafia, she'd given up entirely on keeping her apartment clean. I hadn't seen her since Berin had played the piano for Edip's funeral ceremony on Saturday evening.

I returned to the dining room and looked through the pages of Leyla's notebooks. She had written down a quotation:

'Eventually, everyone comes up with a story that they think of as their life.'

Then a series of very brief notes: 'This chapter needs more explanation'; 'This scene should have more detail.' She had marked places where she'd found inconsistencies in what

I'd written. One note read: 'The brain corrects the past.' And another: 'There is no witness to test the truth of our remembrance.' And in capital letters: 'WHERE IS U?'

My dear Leyla was trying to weave a meaningful story out of my memories. I'd not yet told her that I'd given up on having the book published. What could I say? 'I am writing because the bridge between us is made up of letters, memories, sentences. I am writing because why else would you spend time with a seventy-five-year-old man if not for this goal that we share? I am writing because you're the kind of person who says "I'd go crazy if I didn't write", even if you've never actually said that. Even though your name has never appeared on the front cover of a book, my beautiful beloved, you are a writer. I offer you my memories so that you can continue to find pleasure in your creativity.'

Then, an idea came to me. Leyla should write my story as a novel! We'd just need to change the names of the people and the streets. (But then, who among those I'd named in my story was still alive? Nobody.)

At that thought, my eyes slid to the 'WHERE IS U?' written in capital letters. Ulker. Only Ulker was left from those days, and who knew where she was? If she read Leyla's novel and recognized herself as the heroine, then bravo.

Leyla's novel. Yes, from now on it would not be my book; it would be Leyla's novel. She could own it.

I went out to the corridor and into her bedroom. As I'd expected, that too was untidy. But there were no signs that a second person had slept in the bed. On the contrary, Leyla had used only the left-hand side of the double bed. There was evidence of only one head on the pillows. The bedspread hadn't even been turned down on the right side of the bed. The wardrobe doors were open. Among her hand-knitted sweaters and wool dresses, I saw summer dresses and green and blue blouses that I was not familiar with. When I caught sight of a beige flannel vest among the pile of sweatpants and sweaters thrown over the back of a chair, I looked away and left the room.

The room in the downstairs flat that was directly under my office was cold. Leyla had stored all the boxes that she'd not fully unpacked in there. Most of them had been opened and a book or a scarf taken out. When I noticed a notebook in one of them, I couldn't resist. It was now raining heavily outside and had turned dark, even though it was the middle of the day. I switched on the overhead light and beneath the yellowish glow of a Japanese lantern left from years ago, I leafed through the pages of the notebook. I was soon disappointed. They were notes she'd made for her father's book and a few scenes she'd jotted down.

My urge to know more about Leyla was overwhelming. My desire to capture her past, the inner world she'd kept hidden from me, was intense. Sitting down on the divan, I hurriedly emptied the box. Notebooks spilled out. A new notebook for every book she'd written for her father. I threw them aside. There had to be diaries somewhere, notes she made only for herself. I had to find them. I picked up a photograph of two young girls at the seaside. Despite the huge straw hat on her head, I recognized Leyla right away. There was a tanker in the background. It had to be the Bosphorus. I studied it carefully. The Anatolian side. A waterside mansion north of the second bridge. Leyla was wearing a black bikini top and cut-off denim shorts. She was pursing her lips. She must have been sixteen or seventeen. Beside her was a tall, thin girl with a troubled expression, maybe because the sun was in her eyes, maybe not. The girls were hugging each other. The tall one was hunched over to make herself the same height as Leyla.

I put the photo on the divan next to the notebooks. At the bottom of the box there was a big yellow envelope. I tipped it upside down and emptied it onto the divan. I assumed the photo had fallen out of the envelope and that there would be others in there too. But, no, it contained only letters; unopened envelopes, to be precise. The long, thin, white envelopes bore Leyla's name and address in Oregon, written out in graceful cursive handwriting.

I picked up the envelopes one by one and examined them in turn. There were at least twenty of them, maybe thirty. Not one had been opened. I held them up to the light, but all I could see of their insides was folded white paper. From the postage stamps I could tell that they'd been sent from Turkey, but there was no return address or name and I couldn't read the postmarks without my glasses.

I gathered up the letters and put them back in the big yellow envelope. I would take the letters upstairs, to my apartment, and I was going to read every single one. This idea excited me. I didn't feel at all guilty. Leyla hadn't even deigned to read those letters. When she was packing in America to come back to Turkey, she must have thrown the envelope into the box with the notebooks. They were not important to her, but they were important to me. I wondered who'd sent them. The ex-lover? The handwriting didn't look like a man's, but it wasn't feminine either. I threw the notebooks back into the box at random. Taking the envelope, I stood up. Leyla might come back any moment. I closed the door and went up to my apartment.

Stelio was sitting in the orange bergère armchair, looking at his phone. He raised his head when he saw me.

'Monsieur Pericles, do you think I can go out for a little walk? They took down my passport number, but do you think they'd check it?'

'I have no idea, Stelio. You're a young man. I can't think that they would stop you and ask for your passport. People your age are free to go out on weekdays, unlike children and the elderly. But please don't go into any enclosed spaces.'

'Of course not, Monsieur Pericles. I have my car, as you know, so maybe I'll just drive around and come back. I feel a bit depressed.'

Depressed! I hadn't been allowed to stick my nose outside for weeks. Without their usual daily walk, my legs had turned to jelly. Mumbling to myself, I went into my office, put on my glasses and opened the first of Leyla's letters that came to hand. Then the second and the third.

The many letters were from Leyla's mother. In them, she was trying to show Leyla a different side to their story. She apologized for not having been there for Leyla, for having been so preoccupied with her own problems that she'd not paid enough attention to her child's needs. 'I was afraid of you, Leyla,' she wrote. 'From a very young age you were always so sure of yourself. I saw something intimidating in the way you walked, the way you held your head, the way you so freely voiced your opinions. I didn't see that, like all of us, you needed to be loved. I'm not going to bring up my own youth and justify my mistakes. I can't undo the past, but my hope is that I might get you back. Your grandmother died a while ago. I sold the house in Osmanbey and am now living on Buyukada. I've opened a café, can you believe it! Business is good. Kamile Hanim is here with me. I would love it if one day you'd come to Istanbul and live here with us. You can cover your hair if you like, or wear a chador or become a nun in a nunnery – I accept you unconditionally, whatever your choice. You are my only child and my greatest dream is for us to be mother and daughter for the first time.'

I didn't open the other letters. I took the envelopes and went up to Berin's. My neighbour was as cool-headed as ever. 'I was aware that Leyla had at one time covered her head,' she said. 'She entered a dervish order as a novice. She has not hidden that. It is extremely shameful that you've opened and read her mother's letters. You must tell her what you have done.'

Yes, it was shameful. I had been been mad with jealousy, seeing her get into the black car and drive away, especially when the apartment building was under quarantine. Jealousy is a trait I inherited from my mother. I have very low self-esteem and am the worst coward. When a fit of jealousy takes hold of me, it's as if my blood has become infused with poison and I just can't stop myself.

I looked at the envelopes in my hands. I didn't know Leyla at all. But then I stopped myself. Why did I think a person was made up of their past? Why was it necessary for Leyla to record my memories so that she could know the real me? Why did I believe so strongly that the real Pericles was the young Pericles? Could our stories not begin with Leyla moving into The Circle, the here and now, our friendship, with no before and an unknown after?

I patted the envelopes.

'You're right, Berin,' I said. 'I did a shameful thing. Even though Leyla never read these letters, she brought them here from America. When she comes back, I'll confess and ask for forgiveness.'

'You never know, maybe you opening these letters will

make Leyla and her mother reconnect. Didn't you say that her mother seems very pleasant from the letters?'

I nodded. But I knew that I would keep the three letters that I'd read and would return the others to Leyla's box at an appropriate time. I would never mention it to Leyla.

# You Can't Stop a Person Who's Desperate to Die

The morning after our day on Kilyos Beach, I woke up with a headache. I didn't want to get out of bed. From my bedroom where I lay with the quilt drawn up, I heard the rustle of Aunt Ismene's slippers in the corridor. She was brewing herself some coffee in the kitchen and the smell was making my nostrils tingle. Markela was presumably still asleep. The old woman had spent the night on that uncomfortable divan because of me, and with only a thin blanket over her. Her back and neck would be aching. I got out of bed, dressed and went out into the corridor. Aunt Ismene was sitting at the dining-room table with a cup of coffee in front of her. When she saw me, she smiled wearily.

'*Kalimera*, son.'

I felt ashamed. She knew about my relationship with Ulker. She acted as nursemaid to my sick wife purely so that I could enjoy my romance. She was more of a mother to me than Mama. And she'd never once said 'I told you so', even though she'd warned me about Markela's illness, warned me that a towering wave would at some point come crashing down on me, a wave so vast and powerful that it couldn't be comprehended from a distance. She had said all that and I'd ignored her.

I sat beside her and took her hand. 'Thank you, Aunt Ismene.' I spoke quietly so as not to wake Markela. 'I came home very late last night. I apologize.'

She waved her free hand in the air. 'Don't worry about it, son. Markela and I watched *Falcon Crest*. I would have done the same thing if I'd been at my house, and at least I was able to be of some help to you.'

'These days... You know that I...'

She slipped her hand from under mine and placed it over my mouth. 'Shhh. I know, Pericles *mou*. You're working very hard these days. Of course you should go out with your friends in the evening. You're still young. If you only knew what sort of life Elena leads in Athens. As if she didn't have two little children, she is out every evening, at meetings, exhibitions, films. You have a right to enjoy yourself too.'

I hung my head.

Aunt Ismene patted my hand. 'Come now, get ready. I'll make you some breakfast.'

'No, Theia, don't bother about that. It doesn't matter if I don't go to the pharmacy today. I've got a headache. You go home and rest for a while. You've been here since yesterday morning. I will stay with Markela.'

She quietly placed her coffee cup onto the saucer. 'Markela is still asleep.'

While Aunt Ismene was putting on her overcoat and shoes, I stuck my head into Markela's room. In the dim light filtering through the wooden shutters of the window overlooking the courtyard I saw her hair fanned out over the bed. She was sleeping on her stomach. I needed to be on my own at home so I could think. With Aunt Ismene gone and

Markela asleep, I could relax and gather my thoughts for a couple of hours. I'd missed my home. In the months I'd spent with Ulker, this had become Markela and Aunt Ismene's home. Ulker's apartment belonged to her, of course, so I was homeless. It wasn't important, but on the eve of a serious decision I wanted my space back. I closed the door softly in order not to wake Markela, then accompanied Aunt Ismene to the lift. Before closing the door, I hugged her.

'Don't worry, Aunt Ismene, I won't be going out this evening. There's no need for you to come over. Stay in your own house and rest. Maybe you can go out with Madam Ani for a bit.'

'Where would we go, son?' she said, but her small eyes twinkled. She was going to go out all by herself and walk around aimlessly. I understood that, but said nothing.

Standing at the balcony window, I watched Aunt Ismene get in the taxi. I stayed in the living room until the taxi disappeared around the corner and out of sight. I couldn't get Ulker out of my head. There were pregnancy tests at the pharmacy. I could grab one and hurry over to her house and we'd know the result in five minutes. Our future would be laid out clearly in front of us. I would tell her how much I loved her, how well I was going to take care of our child. Again I felt a wave of joy swelling inside me, just as it had on the beach the day before. I was going to be a father! I would call Papa first. Perhaps the baby would help melt the frostiness between us. According to Mama, Papa was jealous of my staying in Istanbul, of my living the life he'd have wanted to live. Every time I heard that, I felt like laughing. But I also understood. A person's country is their memory. The Istanbul they had lived in didn't exist any longer, but the homesickness Papa suffered from was not based on geography. He missed a place he had lost at a certain point in time, missed the idea of it, what it represented, what it had promised.

I went into the corridor to make a phone call. I dialled Ulker's number. Best to be sure about the pregnancy before giving Papa the good news. Was she asleep, I wondered? She didn't have a phone beside her bed. I imagined her getting out of bed in her yellow nightdress, walking to the living room. Her short hair would be tousled, her nipples erect in the coolness of her apartment. I let the phone ring for a very long time. Then I remembered. On Friday mornings she had a postgraduate class, a three-hour seminar. The telephone jingled when I replaced it. I glanced in the direction of Markela's room. No movement.

Soon, a bulldozer started up, which meant I didn't need to worry about trying to stay quiet; the construction noise would wake Markela up anyway. Today they were knocking down buildings some distance from our apartment. The windowpanes weren't rattling as they had three days earlier, but, even so, the mechanical thuds reverberating around the living room penetrated my brain like hammer blows.

Markela had listened to Jacques Brel the previous night. The record cover was on the floor. I imagined her coming into the living room like a spirit just before dawn, a ghost wandering the apartment while Aunt Ismene slept in the office and I slept in our old marriage bed at the end of a long corridor, behind a closed door. Wrapped in her green cardigan, barefooted and with her hair hanging over her face, she'd walked to the record player, put on B-side and placed the needle on 'Jojo'. Then what? Then what did she do, my wife? Did she lean her head back on the sofa and think of the past? Did she wrap her thin arms around herself and dance? In the past, I'd twirled her around on that wooden floor, her hair flying. She didn't know how to dance. She had no sense of rhythm and would shake her long limbs awkwardly in my arms, smiling shyly.

Had Markela ever loved me? Had she ever really sincerely and passionately been in love with me? Did the mental illness that cut her off from the world and from herself also rob her of the ability to love; had my wife ever felt anything but numb? Her mind somehow never connected with her body or her heart, never registered sensations. Markela's sole reality was the world she created in her mind. She had never truly lived.

All that noise must surely have woken her up. I decided to go and talk to her. There was no reason to keep putting it off. I loved Ulker and I wanted to marry her, to raise a child with her. I was to become a father. This was what I wanted and I had never in my life been so certain about anything. There was not a shadow of a doubt inside me. After talking to Markela, I would go to the pharmacy, pick up a pregnancy test and go to Ulker's house. Her class would finish at two. I didn't even worry about who would stay with Markela when I went to Ulker's house. Everything was going to be fine. Life was beautiful. I was happy.

I finished my coffee. As I put the cup on the table, my attention was drawn to some small particles of white dust. There were some on the floor too. I picked a few up with the tip of my finger and touched them with my tongue. What was it? When my tongue reached the roof of my mouth, I sprang up. My subconscious understood what had happened way before my brain did, launching my body into action. It was pure heroin. I ran to Markela's room, flung the door wide open. She was still lying face down, as before, her hair fanned out on the bed, her legs under the quilt. I leapt onto the bed and turned her onto her back. Her head flopped to the side at a strange angle and her face was a purplish white, her eyes wide open. I recoiled involuntarily, stumbled backwards and gripped the door handle. My trembling hands found the light switch and turned it on.

The blood streaming out of Markela's nose had poured over her lips, her cheeks, the pillow. The foam spewing from her mouth had caked on her chin. Her enlarged pupils were staring at a spot on the ceiling. I understood from the stiffness and coldness of her body that she'd been dead for some time. Even so, I felt for her pulse. I ran to my room. Although I knew there was none in the apartment, I still searched for Naloxone among the heavy sedatives in the locked drawer that Markela didn't have access to. In vain. 'It's too late, Pericles. Too late,' a voice inside me kept saying. Her heart had stopped hours ago, before Aunt Ismene had left, before I'd woken up, maybe in the night. Markela had got up to listen to 'Jojo'. She'd put the needle on the record and snorted the heroin. The bleeding from the nose and foaming at the mouth both pointed to that.

I went back to her room and looked around it so as to be sure. There was no syringe, no cigarette lighter, no spoon. Rolling up the sleeves of her pyjamas, I checked her veins. It would have to have been very strong, very pure heroin, not mixed with anything. I didn't have to speculate where Markela could have got such pure heroin.

I remembered how preoccupied Nejat had seemed three days earlier. He must have already given Markela the heroin. He knew he'd given my wife incredibly pure stuff and when we'd met on Monday morning at the demolition site, he'd wanted to find out whether she'd used it or not. All those 'How is sister Markela? How's her health?' questions were intended to see what I knew.

I collapsed onto the bed next to Markela and took her hand in mine. A feeling was rising to my throat but got stuck there. My eyes filled, but not a single tear fell. I sat there for who knows how long, looking at the beautiful eyes that my unhappy wife had not been able to close in peace even as she was leaving this world.

It was evening by the time Nejat turned up. At least six hours had passed since I'd called Fortune Nightclub and asked Galip to find Nejat and send him to me very urgently.

There was alcohol on his breath, even though he didn't drink on Fridays because he attended prayers at the mosque. As soon as he arrived, swaying, it was obvious that he knew everything. Without saying anything, I held his arm and steered him to Markela's room. When he hesitated in the doorway, I pushed him in. *Go and confront what you've done!* Nejat limped two steps in. For a long, long time he looked at Markela's open eyes, at the dark crust of dried blood around her nose, the strange angle of her head, her stiff arms and legs. Then he fell to his knees beside my wife's single bed and did something I'd never seen him do before. He covered his face with his hands and began to cry. At that point his illness was developing, and he stuttered as he spoke; between that and the tears, it was impossible to understand what he was saying.

I wondered, then, if he'd had feelings for Markela. Had this hairy, blunt-fingered mafia godfather loved my wife? As soon as that thought occurred to me, what Nejat was stammering out suddenly began to make sense.

'I told her again and again, she could only take a tiny bit at a time. It made her feel good. I never left her with any. She never injected it, just took a tiny sniff up the nose. I always took it away when I left and I gave her just a teeny bit every time I came. But the last time she asked for more. It's that kind of stuff – don't I know it. "I cannot," I said. "If you only take it when I'm around, this will last you for years." She was fine, happy. When she laughed, her face was like—'

I pictured them sitting side by side in the living room, snorting their lines of heroin off the coffee table. Where did they send Aunt Ismene off to, I wondered? Markela would despatch her somewhere, away from the apartment. Then she'd call Nejat. Within a couple of minutes he'd come upstairs from his office at the back of Fortune Nightclub. All of this passed before my eyes like the frames of a film. I grabbed him by the collar and pulled him to his feet.

'What have you got to say for yourself, you bastard! You murdered the woman! Don't you see? You're a murderer. Turn around and look!'

I pushed his face nearer Markela's face, which had turned a deep purple, shoving him hard so that he'd fall on top of her. Then something else occurred to me.

'Did you sleep with her, you bastard? Did you take advantage of her illness, her frailty? Did you get her hooked and then fuck her?'

If he'd wanted to, Nejat could have knocked me down with a single punch. In spite of his illness and the limp, he was as strong as ever. But that day, although I yanked him up by his collar, shook him, kicked him and thumped him, he didn't say a word. When I'd used up all my strength, he picked himself up off the floor. His nose wasn't even bleeding. He was used to getting beaten up. He straightened the collar of his jacket and stood before me, trembling with nerves.

'I did not sleep with your wife,' he said. 'I swear on my mutha, I never touched Markela, never laid so much as a fingernail on her.'

'You killed her!' I shouted. My voice had cracked. 'What could be worse than that? You killed my wife.' Nejat bowed his head. I went on. 'You admit that you killed her!'

'The last time I came, she begged me to leave her a bit. I was goin' on a trip. I wouldn't be stoppin' by for a week. She promised me she'd use it careful. I trusted her. Ismene Hanim was always with her anyway. She was only gonna take enough so it wouldn't show.'

'Shut up, you bastard! You knew when you left that stuff with her. You knew how many anti-depressants she was taking. You knew mixing those medicines with heroin would kill her. You're a *murderer*.'

'Pericles, look, I'm gonna say somethin'.'

'Shut up! Don't say another word.'

'Listen to me a second. You know as good as what I do that Markela wanted to leave this world. If not like this, she'd have done it another way. You can't stop a person who's that desperate to die. My poor mutha—'

'Fuck you, Nejat! Don't make me say anything else. The police will come now, and you will confess. You'll rot in prison. They'll fuck you there. Woman-killer!'

Nejat looked at me sadly. He was standing right across from me. A chair had been kicked over during out fight and Markela's books and the red-topped cactus plants on the windowsill had also fallen over. Nejat picked up the chair and pushed it under the desk. He hung up her sweater and shawl, which had dropped off their hooks behind the door.

The police would not be coming, of course. Even if they did come, they would be Nejat's men. Who could I call? Nejat was part of a huge criminal network. No police officer would throw him in jail. And even if such an officer could be found, in the end it would be me that was implicated.

Nejat would save his ass and I would be left carrying the can. I would always be the suspect. I was an Istanbul Greek whose father had been exiled for treason. I was a pharmacist who had supplied the mafia with roofies, synthetic stimulants and diethyl ether for their drugs production. I was a silent partner in Fortune Nightclub, which laundered dirty money. Nejat followed the changing expressions on my face as reality slowly sank in. My hands were tied.

Together we closed Markela's eyelids. With a soapy cloth we wiped the blood from her lips and the dried foam from the corners of her mouth. We changed the pillowcase stained with her blood and saliva. We placed her head, which had flopped onto the edge of the bed, perfectly on the pillow. We lined up the cactus pots on the windowsill. From a drawer I kept locked we took a bottle of strong anti-depressants and left it emptied beside her head. We were setting the scene, even though there was no one we needed to convince. The forensic pathologist who came in response to a single call from Nejat confirmed suicide. The police officer and lawyer whom we called in were friends of Nejat's. Besides, we had documents proving that Markela had been in and out of hospital and had been diagnosed with a major depressive disorder. Dr Lefteris would have accepted this conclusion had we had phoned him, but there was no need for that. We got the death certificate that night. Markela's respiratory system had ceased to function after an overdose of tranquillizers, according to the report. My wife's corpse was taken to the morgue and from there to the church for her funeral.

Mama, who had refused to come to our wedding, flew from Athens to Istanbul for the first time in twenty-two years. As soon as she'd dropped her suitcase at home, she took Aunt Ismene's arm and off they went to the fish market as if she'd only been out of the city for a day. They needed to shop for the guests who would stop by to pay their condolences, something Mama had assumed, quite rightly, would not have occurred to me. She was going to stay with me for a while. We spoke briefly to Papa on the phone. It was a torturous conversation, full of long pauses, between two men who didn't know what to say to each other. Neither of us was interested in football and the moment we started to talk about politics, we argued. Not one of us could utter a sincere word.

Mama, not wanting to sleep in the room Markela had died in, moved into the apartment downstairs. In the six months she stayed there, she filled it with everything it had been missing. Who knows, maybe she dreamt of growing old with Aunt Ismene in Istanbul one day. She mentioned to me in passing that Papa had aged a great deal, far too early. It seemed to me that Mama had already accepted that Papa was dying and that, deep down, she was waiting for that. Life would begin after Papa had gone – in Istanbul, of course. Because of Mama's jealous nature, she had never left Papa by himself. She had built herself a prison and only once he was dead would she be able to leave. Because I was in mourning, she tried not to show how happy she was to be back in her home, but I could see it in her eyes. I felt sad for her. I hoped with all my heart that from then on she could come often to the apartment on the second floor which she had furnished so meticulously.

While Mama and Aunt Ismene were in the kitchen making wheat-berry *koliva* for the salvation of Markela's soul, I phoned Ulker many times. There was no answer. I was somehow unable to find the time to leave the house, walk to Tunel and ring her doorbell. As Mama had predicted, there was an endless stream of people coming to pay their respects.

More people came to the funeral at the church in Yenikoy than I expected. Dressed in black, our pale-faced community looked sadder than ever to me. The church was filled with friends of Markela's from Yenikoy and Buyukada whom I had never met, along with Dr Lefteris and the nurses from the hospital, Markela's sisters, their husbands and children and friends, and business acquaintances of my father-in-law's. Nejat, Galip and Zulfu stood at the back. They kissed the hands of Mama and Aunt Ismene and paid their respects as they were leaving. Aydin and his sweet-faced girlfriend, Mina, and Kemal and his friends sat with me. Once or twice I thought about asking Kemal about Ulker, then was ashamed of myself.

Markela's parents were sad but calm. They embraced Mama, whom they were meeting for the first time, like a very close friend. They didn't leave my side for one minute during the priest's prayers. From the corner of my eye I watched for any sign that they blamed me. No. On the contrary, it was as if they had known from the beginning that their daughter would leave this world by her own hand. Even in early adolescence Markela had twice attempted suicide. That was why she'd been hospitalized. Rather than blaming me, they told me how grateful they were. I had given Markela a life. I had taken care of her. I had admitted her to the hospital when she was having a nervous breakdown. I had put up with her capricious refusal to leave the apartment. If there was anyone who should feel guilty it was her parents. They repeated all this over and over to Mama, Aunt Ismene and my friends at the gathering of mourners who had come to the church, the graveside funeral and on to their beautiful apartment overlooking the Bosphorus in Yenikoy.

A week after the Friday morning when I'd found Markela

dead in her bed, I finally made up an excuse to leave the apartment and raced to Ulker's place. She'd not answered her phone once. She didn't open the door either. I used my key to get into the building and went upstairs. The flat was cold. I felt wind on my face. Immediately I knew. But I couldn't accept it. Ulker was not there. I ran down the corridor. In the bedroom her smell did not even hang in the air. I opened the wardrobe. Most of the hangers were empty. There was no sheet under the bedspread. I went into her office. The walnut desk left by her father was tidy. The papers, notebooks, stacks of books and electric typewriter that I was accustomed to seeing had all been taken away. Ulker had gone. Without even leaving a note or a letter for me, she had packed her bags and abandoned me once again.

I collapsed onto the springy chair in total despair. Taking my head in my hands, I lay my forehead on the desk and for the first time in years, I cried my heart out.

# A Person's Country
# Is Their Memory

'So where had Ulker gone?'

'I don't know. She might have gone back to Frankfurt, to her job at the university. She was also in touch with a university in America, so maybe there.'

'And you never saw her again after that day?'

'No.'

Without taking his eyes off the road, Stelio nodded. We were driving along the shores of the Golden Horn in his foreign-plated Volvo. Stelio hadn't had to persuade me to join him on his outing. He'd looked it up online and found that foreigners were exempt from the quarantine restrictions. For the first time in my life it wouldn't enrage me to be treated as a foreigner in my own city. It was still raining, but that was of no concern to me. I was smiling as heavy drops of rain fell onto the grey waters of the Golden Horn. As my mood lifted, I became talkative. Stelio was asking about the book and I told him about it. We crossed the bridge over the Golden Horn in the white sports Volvo and took the road towards Eyup.

'Then you don't know whether Ulker had a child or not.'

'I do not.'

If it had been Leyla, she would have bombarded me with questions. How come you don't know? Did you never search for her? Did you not ask the friends you had in common? Did you not hear any news at all? Why didn't you go to Frankfurt? Why didn't you chase after her? But Stelio stayed silent. He understood that Markela's death would have hung like a shadow between Ulker and me, would have followed us whichever way we turned. Ulker had left Istanbul not because I'd neglected her when she suspected she might be pregnant, but because she'd heard about Markela's suicide. Ours was a relationship that could not last. If she didn't leave me, one day I would leave her. She knew that. She did the right thing. Death had come between us.

After those painful days I stopped seeing Kemal and all my other friends. I sank into a deep depression. Mama cancelled her flight to Athens again and again. She couldn't bear to leave me by myself. I ate little, almost never spoke. I grew a beard, stopped getting my hair cut. I would go to the pharmacy without showering, leave Aydin to do all the work.

Tarlabasi was being demolished, leaving hundreds of people homeless overnight. The people building that gigantic boulevard didn't see the area's history, beauty or humanity. In the middle of January there was a heavy blizzard and the city remained snowbound for weeks. The schools were unable to open, but the demolitions and evacuations continued regardless. Our elderly neighbours were thrown out of their barely heated apartments, forced to live in the city's impoverished neighbourhoods on the few coins that were thrust into their hands. That was when Mama gave the apartment below us to two elderly Levantine sisters. She had known the retired teachers from the French school in her youth and was upset to see those once formidable individuals, famous disciplinarians, thrown onto the street. So as not to hurt their pride, she charged them very low rent. The women couldn't speak Turkish. They'd spent their entire lives in the apartment in Tarlabasi. They lived in The Circle's second-floor apartment until they died.

The French sisters sparked Stelio's interest.

'In the flat where Leyla lives now, you mean? How many years did they live there?'

'Quite a few. They died a couple of years before Mama.'

'It seems like nobody from that generation wanted to see the twenty-first century. The Levantine sisters, your mother, my *yaya*...'

'They weren't wrong. Look at the state of the world.'

When Stelio drove the car into Fener, I thought he was going to park in front of the Patriarchate and its Church of St George, but he turned right, then left, and came to a sharp incline. We wound around the Church of St Mary of the Mongols. Ours was the only car on the streets. Stelio knew that area very well; he'd done a lot of wandering around it on his previous visits. He was a confident driver and the Volvo was very comfortable. Even though it was low-slung, it didn't rattle on the cobbled streets and it climbed the steep hills easily. The neighbourhoods behind the Greek Orthodox College for Boys looked very poor to me. Starving dogs were rummaging through the rubbish on the street. I didn't ask where we were going. I didn't really care. I had missed going out so much that if Stelio had taken me to the ends of the earth, I would have happily gone with him.

We finally came to a halt on a street of wooden houses that leant into each other and had smoke spiralling out of their makeshift chimneys. I guessed we were somewhere near the old Byzantine Prison of Anemas. I got out of the car and followed Stelio. We hadn't brought an umbrella, but I was wearing a hat, as always, and Stelio pulled up his hood. We walked up a hill on a narrow road. There was no one around. The curtains in the windows of the ugly-faced apartment buildings were closed tight, the chairs in the coffeehouses were upturned, the doors locked. Life, stuffed into the houses, had faded and expired.

I soon got out of breath. Stelio slowed down to keep pace with me. I took off my mask, put it in my pocket and leant back against a stretch of the old city walls that extended either side of us. Stelio stopped too. The branches of a mulberry tree in the garden of a dervish lodge on the other side of the wall reached over into the street. The rain started up again. Turning, we gazed down at Istanbul through the ruins of houses canted against each other, electricity cables, lean-tos roofed with sheets of corrugated iron.

'I should have taken you to somewhere on the Bosphorus instead of here,' Stelio said. 'That would have been more cheerful.'

'No, Stelio, this is nice. Lovely. Like another city in a way, but also very familiar, somewhere I know like the inside of my palm.'

Magnolia trees were in bloom on the opposite shore of the Golden Horn and on the slopes of the hill on which we were standing. There would be yellow hyacinths on Buyukada and Judas trees along the Bosphorus. I didn't need to see them with my eyes; just the smell of rain brought all the colours of the flowers to mind. In spite of everything, little blue verbena were stubbornly coming out between the crooked stones.

Stelio pointed out a small mosque a little way off. 'That's an old Byzantine church.'

I looked at the quaint place of worship, standing neatly with its small dome.

'For some reason I keep imagining that one day my *yaya* will appear there. Don't laugh, but I think I've seen her in my dreams a few times. She was in that mosque. In my dreams it was still a Byzantine church, and when I woke up I even knew the name of the church. St John's. Whenever I heard the stories about her running away from home, it was always this place that I pictured.'

'Let's go in.'

'Do you think it will be open?'

'We can't know until we try. And anyway, we need somewhere to shelter from the rain.'

We couldn't get into the mosque, but the stone courtyard was open. We sat down beside the marble fountain, where at least our heads were in the dry, and listened to the raindrops falling on the roof of the fountain. There were two giant pine trees outside the courtyard, their slender crowns stretching into the sky. I stared wearily into space, feeling disconnected from time and place. Without time and place, who was I? Without memories, what meaning did the precious places, the buildings, the vast city itself hold? Beauty could be measured only in the feelings it evoked, and every feeling was a kind of remembrance. A person's country was their memory. Our past was our home.

'I've decided not to publish the book, Stelio.'

'*Yati*, Monsieur Pericles. Why?'

'It it is no longer my story.'

My young friend frowned. Since I had described the latest chapters of my book so enthusiastically while we were driving, my words must have been very confusing to him. The mask was misting his glasses up, so he took it off. In his brown eyes, which were now squinting doubtfully, I saw Aunt Ismene. At university we'd learnt that heredity is passed through the pupils of the eye. Was Aunt Ismene looking at me from the far end of the genetic corridor?

'I want Leyla to fictionalize the book. We'll change the names and Leyla can present it to the publishers as her own creation. She is such a good writer.'

Stelio's face relaxed. 'Like a biography? *Memoirs of an Istanbul Aristocrat*?'

'No, no. What a joke!'

He laughed and so did I.

'No, it would be a novel. A work of fiction by Leyla Duman. Maybe something like *The Story of the Last Apartment in Istanbul.*'

'Well, at the end of the day, it's your story.'

'Aren't you writing your grandmother's story? Isn't that why you came here?'

He nodded.

'Everyone eventually comes up with a story that they think of as their life,' I murmured.

'My story is also finished,' he said.

'Did your writer friend read it? Did she like it?'

Stelio bowed his head. Even in the rainy darkness, I could see that his cheeks had turned slightly red.

'Do you think it's possible to find true love at my age?'

I patted him on the back. Evening was descending and it had gotten cold. We stood up and walked down the hill to his car. On the way home I told Stelio about a social psychology experiment which Berin had read about online. A group of people who had suffered a lot in their lives for a variety of reasons were promised definite happiness. From then on they would never again feel the pain and trauma of their old wounds. There was one condition, however: their memories would be completely erased. They would not even remember their own names. They would start afresh, open a new, clean, carefree page in their lives.

'How many people do you think agreed to that, Stelio?'

He didn't answer. In the rain, you couldn't tell that it was evening by now. We slowly crossed the bridge over the Golden Horn. On our right was Maiden's Tower, and in the distance the Bosphorus, phantasmagoric in the murk.

'Zero! Not one person in the experiment agreed to give up their past. Every one of them decided to hold onto their memories, with all the pain they contained.'

Stelio accelerated. One or two cars and totally empty buses were travelling along the eight-lane Tarlabasi Boulevard. We swerved among them and went up to Taksim, then, driving through several unfamiliar tunnels, we returned to Kaymakcalan Street. Every floor of The Circle was shrouded in darkness – except Berin's.

# Little Victories Deserve
# Big Celebrations

I was walking around the living room with the envelope of letters from Leyla's mother in my hand. Stelio was taking a shower. There was no sound from the flat downstairs. Leyla had still not returned. The doorbell rang. I hurriedly hid the envelope on the bottom shelf of the coffee table. But it was only Tulin.

'What's up, Tulin? At this hour? Is Berin all right?'

That's the trouble with being our age: the possibility of sickness and death forever hangs over us.

'There's nothing wrong, don't worry. Berin Hanim would like you to come upstairs. She's been trying to get you on the phone all day, but you didn't pick up. We have news.'

'Okay, I'll be there shortly. You go on up.'

After sending the lift up, I took the yellow envelope of letters from Leyla's mother and went downstairs. The three letters I'd opened and read were also in the envelope. Before putting my key in the lock, I heeded the voice in my head and rang the doorbell. To no avail. Leyla had not returned. I felt crushed. Like a thief, I stole into the apartment that had formerly been Aunt Ismene's and then mine. I turned on the light in the corridor. The boxes in the office were as I had left them. I put the envelope in the box, switched off the light and left Leyla's apartment.

Berin was sitting in the living room in her customary armchair in front of the window that overlooked Temrin Hill Street. Tulin hurried to the kitchen to make my coffee.

'Don't make coffee, Tulin. If I drink it now, I won't be able to sleep.'

'What's happened, neighbour? You're frowning.'

I didn't answer, just sat down in my usual place, across from Berin.

'I tried to phone you several times today. Where were you?'

'I went out with Stelio in his car to get some air.'

Berin raised her pencilled eyebrows.

I didn't give her a chance to ask any questions. 'You have some news for me?'

'I do.'

Tulin came into the living room, glanced out of the window next to the piano, then left the room. Strange. She normally loved to sit with us. Perhaps she was still mourning Edip.

'Ferit telephoned today.'

'Yes? What did he say? Has he recovered?'

'He is better. Like you, he also went out. Apparently, no one but Tulin and me are adhering to the quarantine.'

'I was very depressed, Berin. I realized that when I went out for a short while today. Sitting at home suffocates me, sends me into a slump. Even if I don't meet up with anyone, I just need to get out of the apartment every day. For my mental health. Otherwise, I'm going to shrivel up and die.'

'Maybe that's what they want. I sometimes think that this virus was created to get rid of the ill and the elderly. We're a superfluous luxury on the world's back. As a cohort, we don't contribute, we're not part of the workforce, we get by on our pensions. If we were wiped out, the government's load would be much lighter.'

Berin was at it again with her conspiracy theories.

'What did Ferit say?' I changed the subject. They probably wanted us to vacate The Circle sooner than we'd expected. The government departments had begun working on it, albeit slowly. They might have already received the demolition permit from the municipality.

Berin smiled mysteriously. 'Guess what happened?'

Suddenly my heart began to race. That mysterious smile was hiding some news about Leyla.

'What's happened? Has something happened to Leyla? Is she moving out?'

Berin narrowed her eyes. 'Where did that come from? The girl just moved in; she's not going to move out that easily. Relax.'

'What do you mean then, Berin?'

'You look tense, neighbour. The outing with Stelio didn't do you as much good as you thought. You're in a bad mood.'

I took a deep breath and leant back. Berin called Tulin and told her to pour a glass of cognac for me and a sour-cherry liqueur for her. We clinked glasses – mine a fat one, hers a slender cut-crystal wine glass. I would be patient. I wished I had a cigarette. How quickly I'd picked up the habit again.

'Are we celebrating something?'

'Yes. We have something to celebrate – at least for the time being.'

I bowed my head. In the light of the lamp on the coffee table I tried to make out the expression on Berin's face. Shadow came in from the corridor, waving her tail in the air to greet me. She jumped onto Berin's lap. Stroking along the cat's spine, Berin said, 'Our building has been registered.'

'What does that mean? What register?'

'As a work of monumental art. By the Institute of Preservation.'

'A work of monumental art? Is that a good thing? Is that what we're celebrating?'

As far as I knew, all monuments were in trouble. If a building was classified as a work of monumental art, it couldn't be repaired or renovated. It was just left to rot until it fell down of its own accord. At least that was how it had been for the historical buildings that until recently had belonged to Istanbul's Greek citizens.

'The Circle is considered a historic building now. Do you know what that means? Even if a demolition permit were to be issued. It can't be pulled down.'

I couldn't quite fathom what she was saying. 'What do you mean... how could this have happened? I mean, we worked so hard for so long, getting reports from lawyers, architects, experts. And all along it was really this simple?'

Berin raised her crystal wine glass at me. 'It's thanks to the clever work of our young neighbour, Leyla. An old acquaintance owed her a favour. She asked him to sort out this business. That old friend didn't waste any time. In one day he obtained the ratification from the Institute of Preservation. The Circle is now a registered work of monumental art. Congratulations to us!'

I was stupefied. The official black car that had picked Leyla up came into my head.

Berin's eyes were shining. 'Hopefully, this news will put a smile on your face, neighbour – a little one, at least.'

I was gradually waking up to what had happened. The

Circle had been saved. We had survived. Perhaps Berin and I would live out the rest of our lives within these friendly old walls. With Leyla, of course. I couldn't help but smile.

'Yes, that's more like it,' Berin said, seeing my expression. Then she called out, 'Tulin, there should be some champagne in the fridge. Get it out and rinse the cut-glass flutes from the sideboard. But do please be careful and don't crush them in your hands this time. Then go down and call Leyla and Stelio. We have something to celebrate at last.'

I raised my hand to object. 'Leyla is not at home. She got into a car early this morning and left.'

'She went to sort out this business. Her old friend must have sent a car for her.'

'You knew about it then?'

'About what? I knew that she was trying to get in touch with the Institute of Preservation, but you were here when she told us that. She said there was an old acquaintance who might be able to help us.'

'Her former lover – that conservative scoundrel. The man who took Leyla as his second wife in a religious marriage ceremony.'

'Yes, that's the one. It seems he is not as uncultured as we thought. Even after so many years, he immediately did what Leyla asked him to.'

I grumbled in response.

Berin laughed. 'Your girl isn't some victim who was forced to cover her head. She did it willingly. She entered a dervish lodge. If there was a religious marriage, I bet it was Leyla who wanted it. She uncovered her head later, but don't be surprised if she fasts at Ramadan. Today's youth are not as black and white about religion and beliefs as we were.'

I downed my cognac in a single gulp.

'Is this registration as a work of monumental art for definite, Berin? Something won't go wrong further down the line? Will it get the construction mafia off our backs?'

'Leyla phoned this evening to share the good news. She called you too but couldn't reach you. She says it's definite. Her friend promised that we wouldn't be disturbed. We shall see, of course.'

The cognac had filled me with a sweet warmth. I stretched out in Berin's velvet armchair. In the distance I heard a ship's horn. Tankers, if only a few of them, were passing through the Bosphorus. I'd even missed their sounds.

Tulin came in, wiping her reddened hands on a kitchen towel.

'I washed the glasses, Berin Hanim. Nothing's broken. Has Leyla come back? Shall I go down?'

'Yes, go down. If she hasn't returned, she'll only be around the corner. Give Stelio the news and Leyla will be back by then.'

'All right, Berin Hanim. I'm going down right now.'

Tulin knew Berin well enough to understand that she wanted to be alone with me. She put a mask on, took the key and left.

Taking immediate advantage, I leant towards Berin and lowered my voice.

'Berin, you just said something about Leyla not moving out of here that easily. Did I hear you correctly?'

'You are a keen detective, Pericles.'

'And?'

Adapting her upright posture, Berin bent closer to me.

'Look, neighbour, I didn't hear this from Leyla's own mouth. I'm a little wary about telling you this, but whenever your name comes up, the girl's attitude and body language change. She asks a lot of questions about you. To make it clear that she has a special place in your life, she talks a lot about the time you spend together, the book you're writing together. It seems to me that she wouldn't easily give up on you. She obviously admires you greatly and feels close to you.'

As Berin spoke, my eyes filled with tears. It was ridiculous. I was hearing such beautiful things, such very beautiful things. I couldn't believe my ears. Was I a man who deserved such goodness, such luck? Could I repay Berin's friendship, Leyla's admiration, Stelio's trust? Could I find such wealth in my heart? It seemed that life had placed in front of me as much as it had taken away from me. I sniffled like a child. Looking up, I smiled at my friend. Just as a person's homeland was his memories, so it was also the people around him. Berin dipped her head in gracious acknowledgement.

The ceiling chandelier was suddenly illuminated, raining light across the lovely furniture and vast wooden floor. In the living-room doorway there stood Tulin, carrying a tray of champagne glasses, Stelio with a bottle of champagne in his hand, and further back Leyla, wearing her green woollen dress. Leyla had returned! All of my fears had been senseless and ridiculous. She had saved The Circle. She was our hero.

'Welcome!' said Berin.

Putting Shadow on the floor, she stood up and shook her guests' hands like a real lady. Stelio lifted Berin's hand to his lips. Leyla looked at me and giggled. Berin sat down at the piano and music began to flow. The champagne cork was popped and we raised a toast in Leyla's honour. Her face got very pink. We celebrated The Circle. We didn't know for how long this historic works register would protect us, but we needed big celebrations for small victories. Berin played a merry waltz. Stelio took hold of Tulin's thick waist and began to twirl her around the empty space to the left of the piano. He danced well, the rascal. Thanks to his expert steps, even clumsy Tulin kept time to the music. Well, he was my nephew, after all.

As Stelio whirled Tulin around the living-room floor, Leyla came over to me. Putting my champagne glass on the sideboard, I turned to her and extended my hand. Might I have the pleasure of this dance?

I woke up suddenly in the middle of the night. Birds had begun to twitter in the back courtyard. It must have been the darkest hour before dawn. A thin, silvery light was falling across the wooden floor from the window overlooking Temrin Hill Street. I must have forgotten to close the curtains before I went to bed. Inside the room, the furniture's shadows were shifting places. Silhouettes were passing across the mirror. Behind the tulle curtain of time I saw a woman lying with her back towards me. The quilt had slipped down and her bare back was so beautiful that I didn't dare touch it for fear of losing her. I felt a sweet shivering in my body. As I drifted back to sleep, I hoped that death would be like that: a deep darkness into which I would bow, even as my soul was still full to the brim with a great appetite for life.

# Glossary

| | | |
|---|---|---|
| *agapi mou* | *Gk* | my love |
| arcade | | historic Istanbul lane or passageway (*pasaji*) connecting two streets, often roofed over and busy with shops and cafés |
| Bey | *Tur.* | Mr |
| dolma | *Tur.* | roasted vegetables stuffed with rice or meat |
| Efendi | *Tur.* | term of address used when talking to male street vendors and tradespeople |
| *efharisto (poli)* | *Gk* | thank you (very much) |
| *ela* | *Gk* | come on |

| | | |
|---|---|---|
| *endaksi* | *Gk* | okay |
| *han* | *Tur.* | traditional courtyard inn (caravanserai) now housing shops and offices |
| **Hanim** | *Tur.* | Mrs |
| *kalimera* | *Gk* | good morning |
| **kurus** | *Tur.* | traditional monetary unit, now equal to one hundredth of a Turkish lira |
| **Kyra; Kyrie** | *Gk* | Ms or Mrs; Mr |
| *manoula* | *Gk* | mama |
| **Metaxa** | *Gk* | alcoholic drink made from a blend of spirits and Muscat wine |
| **mezze** | | Turkish or Greek hot and cold appetizers |
| *moro mou* | *Gk* | my baby |
| *mou* | *Gk* | my |
| **Panagia** | *Gk* | Mary, Mother of God |
| *papou* | *Gk* | grandfather |

| | | |
|---|---|---|
| **Poli/Politis/ Polites** | *Gk* | Istanbul/Istanbulite/s |
| **raki** | *Tur.* | sweetened alcoholic drink, often anise flavoured |
| *se parakalo* | *Gk* | please |
| **shared taxi** | | public minibus or car following a fixed route around the city |
| *signomi* | *Gk* | I'm sorry; excuse me |
| **simit** | *Tur.* | ring-shaped bread roll topped with sesame or poppy seeds |
| *theia* | *Gk* | aunt |
| *vre* | *Gk* | hey |
| *yavri mou* | *Gk* | my child |
| *yaya* | *Gk* | grandmother |

## About the Author

DEFNE SUMAN was born in Istanbul and grew up on Buyukada. She gained a master's in Sociology from the Bosphorus University, then worked as a teacher in Thailand and Laos, where she studied East Asian philosophy and mystic disciplines. She later continued her studies in Oregon, USA, and now lives in Athens with her husband. Her novels have been translated into more than 25 languages and many of her short stories have won international awards.

Find out more:
defnesuman.com
@defnesuman